JUNE FOSTER

Ryan's Father

By June Foster

Copyright © 2020 by June Foster
Published by Forget Me Not Romances

This book is a work of fiction. Names, characters, places, and incidents are the product of the author's imagination and are used fictitiously. Any resemblance to actual events, locales, or persons, living or dead, is coincidental.

All rights reserved including the right to reproduce this book or portions thereof in any form whatsoever – except short passages for reviews – without express permission.

All rights reserved.

ISBN: 979-8-8691-3808-8

Dedication

This book is dedicated to Fay Lamb who taught me so much about the craft of writing. Many times, I was afraid to allow Ryan to be the person he was at first.

Fay prodded, nudged, and coaxed me to permit my character to embrace his early thought processes. Then later she guided me through Ryan's difficult transformation.

For all this, I thank you, my friend.

For we know that our old self was crucified with him
so that the body of sin might be done away with,
that we should no longer be slaves to sin.
~ Romans 6:6

Chapter One

The walls at Starbucks groaned and crunched. The cardboard cup of steaming coffee flew from Ryan's hand and spilled onto the tile. He swayed as his foot slid out from under him on the undulating floor. He caught himself against a chair.

"What's happening?" A scream behind him split the air. "Help me."

He spun toward the woman's cries.

She tottered in the center of the room, eyes round and mouth wide. Her hands gripped her pale face.

Sympathy sifted through his own fear.

"Take cover, everybody," the barista yelled from the coffee bar. The strong smell of espresso filled the room.

"Quick. Under here." Ryan grabbed the panicked young woman's arm and pulled her beneath a wobbling table. "Hold on to the legs."

"Please don't let me die." The slender, dark-haired woman's face contorted as she sobbed beside him on the floor.

Ryan's normal sense of calm fled, and fear gripped him. He sucked in a breath. Would they survive or be crushed by the walls caving in upon them?

The shaking earth seemed relentless. A bag of coffee toppled from the counter and split, spraying brown beans across the quaking floor.

"God, please help me." Terror shrilled her piteous wails. She grabbed him, holding on tight.

"It'll be over in a minute." Ryan closed his eyes. Instinctively the prayer sprang from his spirit. "Lord, we need protection. Keep us safe." The words to God appeased his own fright, but most of all, he hoped they'd quiet the woman's fear.

The incessant rolling refused to let up. A display case toppled to the floor with a crash, and coffeemakers, mugs, and tins of tea flew in all directions. The woman tightened her clutch around his shoulders. The aroma of flowers wafted over him.

The room shook, and so did his thoughts. Most people would've chosen to hold on to a table leg, but she continued to cling to him. She sucked in air and exhaled in jagged spurts, no attempts at deep breathing. Terror possessed her.

How should he comfort her? His hand hovered over her shoulder then gave it a pat or two. "Don't worry, ma'am, God is in control. Try to breathe." Thank goodness, his voice didn't sound as shaky as his stomach felt.

Bottles of coffee flavors flew from a shelf behind the bar and landed with a thud. The sound of shattering glass made him jump. The syrupy aroma of vanilla and hazelnut blended with the dust in the air.

Warm breath fell on his neck. "How…how…much longer?" She tucked her face against his chest. Hot tears soaked his shirt.

Rising panic threatened to unravel his last fragment of control. Was it the quake or her death grip? "Dear God, see us through this."

He'd walked into Starbucks like any other day. Then the onslaught of the quake. Now an eternity elapsed since it began. *Lord, protect Uncle Frank and my students.*

The woman gripped him harder. Was she going to pass out? He forced a pat to her shoulder again. "Shh." What else could he say to reassure her?

Cracking and creaking and a crash sliced into his composure. He wanted to yell, but he had to keep his sanity—for the sake of the frightened person under the table with him.

What if this was the day the Lord called him home? Death didn't frighten him, but the process did.

A piece of drywall fell to the floor, exposing the building's frame. His ears rang from the woman's shriek. He hadn't planned to slip his arms around her when he jolted, yet the nearness brought a shred of comfort.

Almost as quickly as it started, the rocking and pitching ebbed and a semblance of normalcy returned to his world. Was it over? He remained under the table, forcing his heart to slow as his tablemate clung to him. He couldn't have endured the tremors much longer.

"Oh, thank God, it's stopped." A man's loud voice reverberated off the walls.

"We're okay." Ryan pried at her arms, trying to disentangle himself.

Tousled dark hair hung in her eyes. She pushed the strands from her face and attempted a weak smile.

Good. Maybe she'd get a grasp on her emotions now. "Are you okay?"

She nodded. "I...guess so."

"Let's get out from under here." Ryan grasped her arm as they inched out. Starbucks looked like a war zone—tables on edge, chairs broken, the front window shattered.

Water poured into the room through a broken pipe somewhere. Shattered dishes and pastries cluttered the floor. The odor of rotten eggs filled his nostrils—a gas leak.

He pulled the woman with him toward the door. "We need to go." He kept his voice quiet, hiding the undeniable fear inside. She was hysterical enough already.

A man in a business suit pushed in front of them. "Jack, wait for me," he called to someone ahead of them.

Another man pressed ahead of Ryan's tablemate, causing her to stumble. He grabbed her waist and righted her, then tightened his fingers around her hand as they shuffled through shards of glass and pottery littering the floor.

An employee elbowed his way out the front door. Ryan stumbled but hung on to the frightened woman as they followed the crowd. Polite notions of civility seemed to be secondary in a crisis.

He pulled the petite lady across the parking lot in front of Starbucks and stopped at the street to gulp a breath of clean, dust-free air.

On the sidewalk, a man checked his watch and another woman wiped her eyes. Clusters of people gathered in front of stores in the strip mall.

The woman beside him pinched her lips into a thin white line. "I'm...I'm Sandy Arrington. I'm sorry for my silly behavior."

He had to admit. For a while, he thought he might have to carry her out and take her to the hospital. "Ryan Reid." He gave her a quick smile. "It's okay. I can understand how you felt."

He knew fear when he saw it, had lived a childhood full of it. How many times as a boy had he been alone in the house? Every creak and bump sending a shiver down his spine.

A bird up in the poplar tree chirped, as if nothing had happened. Yet only moments ago, Ryan's world had tumbled upside down.

Sirens filled the air, and a few seconds later, a red and white truck with CEDAR FORK FIRE DEPARTMENT painted on the side screeched to a halt in front of them.

"There's a gas leak in Starbucks," Ryan yelled at the firemen scrambling out.

"Yeah, we got the report. Everyone needs to move away from this area. Now!" Two men in protective suits, oxygen tanks on their backs, pushed into the coffee shop.

Sandy looked at him with eyes the color of cinnamon and chewed her little finger. The remnant of a tear hung on her lash. "I know I've been enough trouble already but could I…impose on you to walk with me to my car? It's in front of Cramer's Drugs." She shielded her eyes with a cupped hand to her forehead and pointed toward the other end of the strip mall.

Was she in any condition to drive home? He'd better make sure before he said good-bye. At least she wasn't crying anymore. "Be happy to."

They trudged past broken store windows and downed tree branches.

Sandy's shoulders shook, but it probably wasn't due to the cool late-spring day in Western Washington. Fear was one thing. Terror another. She looked as if she were on the edge of a meltdown. Better keep her talking. "Do you have to go somewhere?"

She shook her head and blinked as if something important had occurred to her. "I…yeah. The hospital ER."

"What?" He looked her up and down. No signs of injury. "Are you hurt?"

She scanned the parking lot that now looked like a scene from a post-apocalyptic video game. Chunks of blacktop protruded up with rough edges.

If the quake could create the two-foot-wide chasm which ran the length of the sidewalk in front of the mall, what other damage occurred?

Emergency vehicle sirens wailed in the distance. "Sandy, are you hurt?" he repeated.

"No." She closed her eyes then opened them. "I'm a nurse. I work in the ER. I need to get to the hospital."

Ryan smothered a chuckle. An ER nurse who handled a natural disaster as badly as she did—what a contradiction. He cut his gaze to her. "See your car yet?"

A woman holding on to a baby whisked past them. She stared at her cell phone and threw it in the diaper bag.

Sandy's mouth fell open as her hand flew to her throat. She pointed toward the end of the mall and gasped. "My car. Oh, my car!" she cried. "It's crushed."

Ryan gaped at the luxury vehicle. A huge cedar had broken off mid-trunk, flattening the silver Mercedes parked in front of Cramer's Drugs. The top half of the tree lay crossways over the car's roof. Bits of glass reflecting the sun like a million diamonds decorated the parking lot around the damaged sedan. Sticks and leaves littered the pavement.

He examined the mess in front of them. Never had he seen such a look of shock on a woman's face. She gulped and raised wide eyes to him as if he had answers.

Not his problem, yet he couldn't allow her to drown in fear. "I hate to tell you, but it's probably totaled."

"Let me think." She rubbed her forehead. A search through her purse turned up a cell phone. "I'll call a friend for a ride." Her trembling hand punched a button, and she raised the phone to her ear.

Good. She appeared to have control now. He'd take off.

She grabbed a clump of hair and paced behind the useless Mercedes. "No cell service." She expelled a short breath. "I really hate to ask. Could you give me a ride to the hospital?"

What could he do? Leave her here alone when she couldn't find a ride? If he was stranded, he'd want someone to offer help. "Sure."

A Mercedes meant wealth, the finer things in life. His Corolla wouldn't impress her much, but then he lived by the Golden Rule.

Pink crept onto Sandy's cheeks. "I've never reacted to fear quite like that before. You'd think after all my years studying Kung Fu I'd have a little more courage. I'm braver when confronted by people than acts of God."

"Forget it." He slowed so she could keep up. "So, you're a martial arts fan?"

The beginnings of a smile crossed her lips. "Yep. Took lessons for years."

Kung Fu was the last activity he'd participate in. He didn't like contact sports. Jogging alone in the park appealed to him. Besides, his mother never encouraged him to take lessons of any kind. If she managed to feed him every couple of days, he'd counted himself lucky.

They wound around rocks, toppled trees, chunks of pavement, and scurrying people and neared Big Lots at the other end of the strip mall. The smell of burning wood stung his nostrils. A fire somewhere?

He spotted his Toyota parked next to the street. She'd see it now in all its glory. "Not even an earthquake could destroy a car like this." At least it was in better condition than her Mercedes. Something to be grateful for.

Once he opened the passenger door, she climbed in. He traced a line with his finger through the dust on the faded blue paint as he rounded the front of his vehicle. "We'll probably have to take some back roads to avoid traffic." The torn leather on the seat scratched his leg through his jeans.

Sandy smiled, seeming not to notice his fifteen-year-old car.

Ryan eased out of the parking spot. As they approached the exit, a lone figure drew his attention. Propped up with the heel of his old tennis shoe hiked on a tree trunk, a boy about fifteen gazed off toward the destruction. The kid's shaggy blond hair was a little too long, as if he'd missed a haircut or two. His tattered black T-shirt was dirty. Next to him, a rusted relic of a faded red bike lay on the ground. The look on his face tangled Ryan's heartstrings into knots. Not forlorn and lonely, but his face was hard, disheartened as he scowled at no one.

Ryan didn't know the teen, but the image clawed at his heart. He comprehended all too well the pain he saw on the kid's face. Not too many years ago, the boy could have been him.

Later, would the teen get on the broken-down bike and return to an empty house? Or maybe he'd try to ease his hurt with a substance some willing drug dealer might sell him. Or would he try to fill the gaping hole in his heart with love—love he never received from a mother and father?

Ryan's pulse pounded in his ears. More than anything, he wanted to help the boy. Help other boys like him. But what could he do?

Chapter Two

Sandy stole a look at the tall, dark-haired man. His hands gripped the steering wheel as he peered out the front window. What was he thinking?

His presence beside her brought peace, as if he could protect her from her fears. If nothing else, his prayer had calmed her. She didn't know any guys who considered it important to talk to God.

The familiar route to the hospital looked different with rubble in the road, trees lying prone here and there, and a few collapsed buildings. Almost as if she'd been transported to a parallel universe. She shuddered, trying to dismiss her bizarre thoughts.

What would she find at the hospital emergency room? Dozens of injured people? Ryan pulled into the circular drive in front of the ER. An orderly helped an EMS worker roll a patient on a gurney through the entrance.

"Can I let you off here?"

"Yes."

A man jumped out of a car in front of them, opened the passenger door, and lifted a woman into his arms, then made his way inside.

Sandy directed her attention to Ryan. "Thank you. Looks like the ER could be busy this afternoon."

Ryan stared at her with an expression she couldn't interpret. "If you'd like, I can check with you when my shift at work ends and see if you have a ride home."

"Thanks. I think I'll be okay. My parents are in Indianapolis at a conference, but I have a friend who could give me a ride." She took a scrap of paper out of her purse, scribbled, and held it out to him. "Here's my number in case cell-service is restored by then. Do you mind calling me when you get off?"

"Yeah, sure." Ryan sounded as if he were concerned she'd make it home tonight.

Sandy climbed out of his car and bent down to the window. "I appreciate this, Ryan."

He nodded. His eyes expressed kindness. A trait she found appealing in a guy.

~*~

Ryan trudged through the break room, rubbing his weary eyes, and punched in his employee's code at the backdoor. Though the part-time job exhausted him sometimes, at least the money helped pay off his college loans faster than his teacher salary alone.

He figured CF Hardware would be packed, but very few customers ventured in this evening. They'd likely start pouring in tomorrow for supplies to repair the earthquake's damages. Sales would probably soar in the next several weeks.

Ryan unlocked the car door and pulled out his cell. His muscles screamed at him after stacking lumber all afternoon.

His new acquaintance had probably gotten a ride home by now, but he'd call just in case. The scrap of paper was tucked in his shirt pocket. He pulled it out and pressed the numbers.

"Hello." A feminine voice mixed with other sounds met his ear.

"Sandy? This is Ryan."

"Oh, hi, Ryan. I'm so glad you called. The doctor in charge of the ER is sending all unscheduled staff home, and I don't have a ride. My friend can't take me. I hate to ask you, but could you give me one more ride?"

He rubbed his aching shoulder. "Sure, I'll be there shortly." He drove around the edge of the massive building to the front parking lot and the street.

How long would it take to drop her off? He hoped she lived somewhere close to the hospital. The thought of a hot shower and his bed beckoned.

An annoying headache spread across his forehead. The quake had stressed him out more than he'd first realized. After switching on a praise CD, he turned onto the street in front of the hospital.

Sandy waited at the entrance to the ER where he'd let her out. A man in a white jacket stood next to her, his arm draped over her shoulder. Her friend?

Ryan stopped on the curved drive, lowered the volume on his CD player, and leaned to roll down the passenger window.

She stepped toward his vehicle, followed by the man in medical garb.

He stared at Ryan's car and raised his eyebrows. "You think this wreck can get you home?"

She laughed. "Well, it got me here." She bent down and smiled. "Ryan, this is my friend Dr. Jason Jeffries. He's an intern here at the hospital."

Ryan nodded at the guy and looked at her. "So, he can't get off duty yet to take you home?"

"Oh, he got off when I did, but he's worn out and can't drive all the way to my house."

"Hey, sweetie. You don't expect me to go ten miles into the country tonight. I have to save my energy for tomorrow's shift." The doctor's voice held a note of sarcasm.

Ten miles to her house? He had plenty of gas. "I can take you. No problem."

~*~

Sandy peered out of the window of Ryan's car, catching a glimpse of the towering Douglas firs bordering either side of the two-lane highway. The road curved and climbed past fields of grass barely visible now in the darkened sky with only the slender moon to guide them.

She tapped a finger at the windshield. "The next mailbox. Turn right."

His headlights illuminated the paved path to the long circular drive. Her parents' wood and stone two-story estate with its glass windows and gables came into view.

"This is where you live?" Ryan's mouth dropped, then he shut it again. Same reaction she got from anyone who hadn't been here before.

The home of her parents, Dr. and Mrs. Philip Arrington. "Yes, since childhood." Sure, it was elegant and expensive, but it'd been all she'd ever known.

He stopped in front, coughed, and reached across her to open the passenger door. "I hope you're able to get another car pretty soon. Look, I need to get going. I'll wait until you're inside. Nice meeting you." He scratched his head.

Darkness shrouded the house, not a light shined. She hadn't expected to work today, or she'd have left them on. She had enough trouble walking into the dark place when her parents were home asleep. But they weren't due in until tomorrow. The familiar panic crept up her spine. She couldn't go in alone. What if there was damage, looters? Someone waiting inside. She shuddered.

He probably expected her to get out, but she was frozen. A deep breath didn't give her courage.

Ryan's stomach growled.

The way to a guy's heart was through his stomach. Wasn't that the old adage? Anything to get him to stay. "Hey, I bet you haven't eaten. Let me fix you something. You're probably starving."

"Another time. Really." He gripped the steering wheel, but she needed his presence a little longer.

She slipped a hand to her hip. "I'm not taking no for an answer." Piling out of the car, she dashed around the front and opened the driver's door. "It's the least I can do for a guy who drove me to work and home." A bold move, but she was desperate. "Now come on. Get out." She laughed. "I bet you've never been manhandled by a girl before."

"You got that right. Especially a Kung Fu expert." He stared up at her, closed his eyes for a moment, and opened them. "All right." He climbed out of the car.

Though he seemed to be digging his sneakers into the pavement, her grip impelled him along. She pulled her keychain out of her purse, unlocked the door, and with one more yank, drew him inside. With a flip of the switch, the entry lights came on. She took in a deep breath.

Ryan's mouth fell open as they stepped farther into the great hallway. He lifted his chin to look up at the ornate chandelier hanging from the ceiling and slowly gazed toward the circular staircase which led to the second floor. "This place is huge."

Sandy tensed every muscle. The large house was part of the problem. She'd probably feel safer in a smaller one, but she couldn't move out yet. She shivered. "Please, walk with me while I turn on all the lights and check the place." If he thought her an idiot, she didn't care. She couldn't do this alone.

He nodded and followed her around the lower floor from the formal living room to her mom's gourmet kitchen. She turned on light after light, sending the scary darkness to the corners where it belonged.

Despite the well-lit rooms, the thought of Ryan leaving her alone sent a chill down her spine. Could she get him to stay a little longer so the panic attack brewing beneath her sanity didn't blossom into a full-blown episode? She dashed into the kitchen.

Ryan paced in front of the mahogany stools separating the kitchen from the casual dining area. "To tell you the truth, I need to go. I've got to—"

"Let me fix you something to eat." In the stainless-steel refrigerator, she found a whole ham, a chunk of cheddar cheese, washed lettuce, and some sliced tomatoes.

Ryan twirled his car keys, shifting his weight from foot to foot. For the first time, she noticed. The guy was gorgeous. And single, she hoped.

He stuffed his hands in his pockets. "Look, I don't mean to be rude, but I've got to go now." He took a few steps toward the entry.

Sandy sucked in a long breath. The lights were all on. Ryan had seen her through fear of coming in alone. But there was another thing she needed from him. His connection with God which had been so evident this morning during the earthquake, something she never learned from her parents. "Do you go to church?"

Ryan raised his brows. "Church? Yeah, I do."

The words tumbled out Sandy's mouth before she thought. "Would you mind if I tagged along sometime?"

He swallowed hard, his hand on the door knob. "Uh, yeah. Sure. New Day Community of Faith on Olympic Way? Tomorrow at ten?"

"Can I meet you there?"

He nodded. "I'll wait for you in front."

Was she supposed to take anything or did it matter? "I don't have a Bible."

He slid his hand in his coat pocket and pulled out a small, black book. "Here. You can have this."

She stared at the little Bible with the black cover resting on her palm. She hadn't expected him to give her his. The guy probably didn't have a lot of material possessions, if his car and clothes were any indication.

He looked at her but not in the same way so many other young men stared at her, not the possessive way Jason's eyes roamed over her.

"Okay, see you tomorrow." Ryan backed out the front door, climbed into his car, and circled around the drive. The man was shy, guarded, even uncomfortable in her presence, yet at peace and relaxed with God. Not in a super-religious way, like the few church people she knew, but in a deep, personal way.

She waved a final good-bye, scurried inside, and locked and bolted the door. Ryan knew about God, but was his God powerful enough to change the results of the night so long ago?

Sandy leaned against the wall and peered through the foyer. Then with a deep breath, she pushed away. Walking through the hallway, she stared into the living room. Her mother's elegant draperies remained closed as they had since her parents' departure for Indianapolis.

She smiled in relief and made her way to the kitchen. Then she sensed movement to her left. A yelp gurgled in her throat. The blinds to the sliding glass doors on the deck were open.

She reached for the kitchen wall and braced herself. Had she imagined it, or was someone out there? To find out she'd have to walk through the breakfast room.

I can do this. She sucked in a breath, but it caught in her chest. She rushed to the door, tried the lock, and realized she hadn't exhaled. With a quick yank, the blinds on each side of the doors came together. She pulled the chain beside the cord, and they closed, blocking anyone's view. If there was someone outside, they couldn't get in now.

She peeked out. The deck and yard appeared deserted. With a flick of her hand, she flipped off the outside light and hurried to the window over the sink to close the mini-blinds.

Now no one could see her from the outside. She could clean up the kitchen and climb upstairs to her bedroom where she wouldn't feel so exposed.

Ryan's prayer during the earthquake brought reassurance and drew her. Something about him was different. Did it have anything to do with the God he prayed to? She determined to find out more. She needed a God who could erase this fear inside of her.

~*~

Ryan maneuvered his car around the drive, down the paved road, and onto the main route into town. His thoughts gave way to the youth at the strip mall's parking lot.

The sight of the boy had pricked a wound in his soul he'd tried to protect. The kid's scowl spoke to Ryan, saddening him. The aura of the young boy wrapped around him like moisture on a humid day. Did he have parents? No young man should have to grow up alone.

He slowed as he approached a winding curve in the road. What would Sandy say if she saw where he lived? The small apartment he shared with Uncle Frank was an outhouse compared to her mansion. He sure wasn't in the teaching profession for the pay.

After a while the city limits of Cedar Fork came into view as a thought nagged him. Her wealth clashed with his thrifty lifestyle.

When he finally pulled up in front of the apartment, he parked on the street. The creak of the car door reminded him of Sandy's Mercedes crushed by the fallen tree. Why did she live at home? To keep up her opulent lifestyle? She was a career woman. Registered nurses made good money in this town. But then, he never did understand women.

Chapter Three

A hand reached toward the boy and cuffed his wrists behind him. The youth's feeble attempts to squirm free were to no avail. The muscular cop towered over him as he jerked the kid and gave him a rough push. "Don't give me any trouble, you piece of scum." The officer opened the door of his police vehicle and shoved the boy inside.

Ryan bolted up in bed. Sweat dripped from his brow and down into his face. His hands balled into fists, first with emotion and then to rub his blurry eyes. He dragged his legs over the side of the bed and stood. His pounding heart echoed in his ears in the darkened bedroom.

Did the memory of the boy he saw yesterday after the earthquake provoke the dream? Sadness turned to pity, then to anger. In his dream, the kid was going to jail. Ryan tasted jail once and wouldn't wish it on any youth. In the real world beyond his dream, how long would it be before the teen or others like him landed in juvenile hall?

He couldn't ignore the nightmare. Maybe God Himself placed this burden on him. He wasn't sure. The boy and many like him suffered the same isolation and neglect he had as a teen before Jesus came into his life. If he didn't take a step, if he didn't act, who would?

He angled to his bed and dropped on his knees. "Lord what would you have me to do? I'm Yours. Send me." His breathing slowed. He waited.

~*~

Ryan stood on the church steps, his shoulders stiff. Tension knotted his back muscles. With another stretch and a scan of the road in front of the church, he twiddled his thumbs. Maybe Sandy was toying with him and wasn't actually interested in going to church. He folded his arms and propped his shoulder against the wall of the white brick structure. Its red roof towered overhead. Why was he standing in front of his church waiting for a woman who might never show up?

A horn honked, and a black BMW pulled to the curb. Sandy rolled down the window, leaned over the passenger seat, and smiled up at him. "Hey. Sorry I'm late."

His mouth fell open as he surveyed every inch of the sleek car when she pulled away to find a parking spot. Her parents probably made more money in a year than he'd make in his entire lifetime.

A herd of buffalos thundered through his stomach as he waited for her to park. The buzz of Sunday morning conversations on the front steps reminded him services were about to start.

From the parking lot, she floated toward him as if she weren't wearing those elevated heels which made her at least four inches taller. She stopped and stood beside him, too close for his comfort. A bright smile played at the corners of the perky young woman's lips. "I didn't exactly know what to wear. I hope this is okay." She did a spin in front of him.

The green dress, the color of rhododendron leaves in early spring, fit snuggly against her petite body. What did he know about women's clothing?

"You look fine." The collar of his Sunday-best white shirt made his neck itch.

"But it's not too much for church, is it?" She held out her arms.

The people in his congregation would welcome her, or anyone else, no matter what they wore. His gaze slipped down the dress. Maybe a little too tight. Could be too short. "You're fine." The flirty young woman, ready to walk into a strange church, should be ill at ease, but instead she exuded confidence.

She remained motionless, an expression he couldn't read flicked across her face. Then her smile challenged him. "Men. They're all clueless." She breezed past him toward the front doors. He stared after her then jogged to catch up.

She obviously placed him into a category of men in general and was teasing him. Without realizing it, she touched on a sore subject, one he smothered. He wasn't like most guys. Flirty women didn't faze him at all. In fact, they reminded him of his mother. He scratched behind his collar. "Where'd you get the Beemer?"

"Oh, it's my dad's spare. I borrowed it until he gets home tonight. He'll probably have my Mercedes hauled off." With a shrug of her shoulders, she moved toward him—too close again.

A spare luxury car? He took a step back and extended his hand for her to walk through the door first. "Well, let's go in."

In the middle of the sanctuary, he pointed to his usual pew.

After a quick glance at the seat and to him, she moved into the empty row. Not quite as confident as before. "To tell you the truth, I have no idea what to do or expect." She settled down on the maroon cushioned pew.

"No problem. Just follow along." Placing his Bible between them, he slid in beside her. Maybe God would touch her life through this ministry. After all, she must've wanted to know more since she'd asked to come with him.

He glanced around the sanctuary. Up front a few people from singles' Bible study sat together, including Greg. When the church counselor looked in his direction, Ryan raised his hand and waved.

The stained-glass window behind the altar reflected the sunlight. He'd always loved the scene of Jesus with a lamb on his shoulders. Praise God He led His people like a shepherd, something Ryan would be helpless without.

Ryan peeked at Sandy. She gazed around the room with wide eyes. The same flowery fragrance filled his nostrils.

After the worship, the ushers passed the collection plate. Ryan tried not to let his mouth fall open when Sandy tossed in a fifty.

He folded his check and thanked God he could give ten percent of his salary with enough left to live on.

Pastor Netherton stepped to the podium when the ushers finished. "Good morning and welcome. I'd like to start by saying we are all sinners in need of the salvation Jesus Christ can bring into our lives."

Good. A message about new birth. *Lord, help Sandy understand Your grace.*

Pastor had only spoken for a few minutes when she poked him, a wrinkle on her brow. "Isn't he talking about people who don't go to church?" she whispered.

Ryan leaned toward her. "I'll explain after the service." Such a common mistake about Christians, as if they attended church to work their way to God.

For the rest of the message, her eyes remained glued on the pastor. If the look on her face revealed anything, she'd absorbed every word.

At the end of the sermon, Pastor Netherton invited anyone who wanted to ask Jesus into their lives to come up front—like Ryan had done years ago at the youth meeting.

Sandy frowned and looked toward the altar. "Why did he ask people to come up there?"

Would God reveal to this rich girl the salvation which made an impact on his own life? "I'll explain later," he whispered. But he'd never be able to tell her the rest of the story.

As they stood when the service ended, people crowded the aisles. Laughs, coughs, and giggles filled the sanctuary. Before they could step out, Ryan spotted Greg threading his way toward them through the crowd.

"Hey, Ryan. How ya doing?" A strand of hair the color of a newborn fawn slipped down on his forehead above light brown eyes, and he pushed it back.

Ryan's heart rate quickened. Could Greg be the person who would work with him on a ministry to teens? "Sandy, my friend from our singles' Bible study, Greg Aldridge. Greg, this is Sandy Arrington. We met during the earthquake yesterday. Sandy's a nurse."

She drew her shoulders back, stuck out her hand, and smiled.

"Glad to meet you." Greg winked. "Hope to see you again." No doubt his friend felt confident around women, something Ryan lacked. If he were honest, something he didn't care to learn.

"Same here." She smiled a bright grin.

Since Ryan had Greg's attention, maybe this would be a good time to approach him. "Do you have a minute? I'd like to talk to you about an idea I have." Ryan couldn't do this alone. Too, he needed confirmation about this plan—and prayer. "Could we chat in one of the Sunday school rooms?"

Greg looked at his watch. "Sure, I've got time."

Ryan shifted his attention to Sandy. Though he'd rather spend the afternoon alone, she had questions, and he couldn't let her walk out of his life without answers. "You were wondering about a few things. Do you want to meet later?" Nothing could stand in the way of telling someone else about the Lord.

With a grin, she nodded. "I'd love to."

Guess he'd include her in his afternoon plans. "I was thinking of hiking up at Bear Mountain Park. You want to meet in a couple of hours?"

"I'll whip up a picnic lunch for us, since you didn't let me feed you anything last night." She turned on her high heels and bounced down the aisle toward the main door.

Greg chuckled. "So, you made a date with the pretty lady?"

Heat prickled the skin beneath his collar. "No, nothing like that. She's got questions about the service." If he left Greg with the impression he was interested in the woman, it'd be a lie.

~*~

Folding chairs encircled the multi-purpose rectangular table in the singles' Bible study room. On the wall behind Greg, a poster with an image of Jesus read: "Reckon yourselves to be dead indeed to sin, but alive in Jesus our Lord."

"What's on your mind, buddy?" Greg sank down into a chair.

Ryan edged into a seat across the table. His pulse pounded in his ears. No doubt enthusiasm for serving God brought the reaction. "I want to talk to you about something the Lord put on my heart—a possible ministry."

"From the look on your face, I can tell it's important to you." Greg folded his hands on the table and focused on him.

Ryan couldn't still the wild beating of his heart. A flame lit somewhere in the region of his stomach. Was he merely eager to get the project going, or did sitting here alone with Greg evoke the strong emotion?

With more passion than he anticipated, the story of the boy he saw in the park, the burden and his desire to be of some type of service, spilled out. "I was hoping we could brainstorm together and see what we could do for these kids." With his elbows resting on the table, he leaned toward Greg. "If we could only touch one boy or girl with the gospel, to lead them out of their dark existence into the light of Jesus, it would all be worth it."

Greg stared at the wall over Ryan's shoulder, motionless. He lowered his voice to almost a whisper. "I have a lot invested in this church, a lot of prayer, interest, and time. I'm even a member of staff, as you know."

"Yeah, I remember the Sunday you were commissioned as church counselor." Ryan's pulsed raced.

Greg kept steady eye contact, his pupils large. "I can't tell you what this means to me. I've had thoughts about the same kind of ministry. Thank you for asking me. It confirms the Lord is leading us in this."

Elation ran through Ryan's heart. He looked into Greg's honey-brown eyes, at the face of a man who loved God and put Him first. Thankfulness filled him. Greg had caught the vision of the ministry, but something else nagged him. He squirmed as a sensation stirred deep in his gut.

When the meaning slipped into his awareness, Ryan darted up. The discussion needed to be over now. He had to get away.

"Look. I'm going to try to arrange a meeting with the pastor and elders. But why don't we pray about it first? God will give us direction in His time. And don't forget we're on next Friday for a little one-on-one action on the court."

Fire flamed Ryan's face. Sweat broke out on his forehead. Feelings surfaced, feelings he thought long buried when he accepted Christ.

Greg believed this meeting, the fact they both carried the same burden for a teen ministry, meant God was in it. But was He? Now Ryan wondered. "Listen Greg, I gotta go."

"Shall we pray, brother?" Greg stood and his hand burned Ryan's shoulder. He fought from pulling away. Guilt swept through his stomach as the reality of his feelings washed over him.

"Lord, we commit our service to you. Please open the doors You want opened. Provide a way for Your will to be accomplished. Amen."

The sweat on Ryan's forehead trickled down his neck, and he wiped it away with the back of his hand. "Th–thank you, brother. See you next week." He paced out of the room, stumbled to his car, and pulled out of the church parking lot. Lofty firs cast shadows on the narrow road. An emerald green hill rose on the horizon.

The flood of Ryan's thoughts threatened to drown him. He was powerless, and they persisted in their pursuit of him. In high school, he never had an interest in girls. Then the incident before he got saved, the night with Allen, though it didn't go far. At the time he dismissed it as teenage foolishness.

After he became a Christian, he was sure things would change, but they didn't. Even in college, Ryan didn't date. He had a few women friends, but the attraction he heard the guys describe was absent.

Finally, he admitted the truth after he found himself snatching glances at guys in the locker room during a college soccer class.

No one knew. Humiliation and embarrassment inundated his heart so often when he first drew close to the Lord.

Awareness of other men always preyed on his emotions—the feelings existed, and no amount of grief changed anything, but never had they singled out one person.

Ryan was a Christian. He begged God for a different life, and he thought the Lord answered it by allowing him to bury the allure of other men. But was Ryan fooling himself?

The stirrings Greg evoked weren't pleasing to the Lord, but his friend enticed him, though Ryan never wanted to act on his feelings. The Word made it clear the behavior wasn't in God's will.

And now, Ryan's desire to serve God would have him work alongside Greg. Was this God's idea of punishment for living a lie, never telling anyone about his errant feelings? Or had Ryan allowed his wrong to jeopardize a ministry God called him to?

He pulled off to the side of the road. *Lord, help me. Help me get beyond this. To honor You.* Ryan leaned his head on his steering wheel. "I'm so sorry." He choked out the sob. "So sorry for bringing those feelings into Your house of worship."

Chapter Four

Sandy pulled up next to the wooden sign with *Bear Mountain State Park* carved on the front. The web site described it as *one of Washington's rich jewels bragging of old-growth forest, bubbling brooks, and glimpses of the Cascade Mountains.*

Cedar beams lay at right angles dividing the parking area from the entrance. The sixty-foot Douglas fir bordered the lot, and the sun bounced off tree leaves, reflecting sparkles of light.

No sign of Ryan's Toyota. Maybe he wouldn't show, though she hoped he would. Some confusion remained in her mind about the church service, but the feeling of peace when the pastor spoke touched her. Still, the answer to her fears seemed out of reach.

She jumped at the tap on the window.

"Sorry I'm late." Ryan's muffled voice sounded through the glass.

"I was thinking about church today." She hadn't seen him smile much, but the tight features on his face spoke volumes. Something was wrong. Maybe his meeting hadn't gone well.

She clicked the trunk open, hopped out, and walked around. "The cooler with our lunch is inside."

"Let me get that." He stepped in front of her, lifted the container out, and set it on the ground. A plastic bag swung on his arm. "I bought some cola and paper cups after I stopped at home to change."

He raised the tote bar on the cooler and rolled the heavy-duty box through the opening between the cedar beams leading into the forest. A deep groove crinkled his brow. He looked like someone on his way to a funeral instead of a picnic.

She yanked a canvas bag out of the trunk and followed him. A dark brown sweater fit his broad shoulders. The V-shaped curve of his masculine frame narrowed at jean-clad hips. Not a bad view.

A few quick steps took her to Ryan's side as the cooler bounced along the bumpy trail through the forest to the picnic area. "Are you okay with that?"

"What?" He glanced at her as if he'd forgotten she'd come along, too.

"The cooler. Are you okay?"

"Oh, yeah, sure." He gave her a half-smile. "Shouldn't be too much farther to the tables."

A jaybird flashed its royal-blue feathers and flitted from an oak tree to a cottonwood. Finally, after ten minutes or so, they stopped at the clearing with four wooden tables spaced throughout the area.

Sandy breathed in the delightful aroma of fresh cedar perfuming the air. The gentle breeze caressed her skin. She set the bag on the redwood table and pulled the plates, napkins, and silverware out. From the cooler next to the table she dug out sub sandwiches, potato salad, and oatmeal cookies.

Ryan eased onto the bench across from her. His wrinkled brow smoothed, and the stormy cast of his eyes lightened. "Do you mind if I say a blessing before we eat?"

It'd felt so good when he prayed out loud during the quake. "Please do."

He reached for her hand, and when their skin touched, her heart raced.

"Lord, thank you for the food Sandy brought and for the beautiful day You created. Amen." Was it this simple prayer or his touch that accelerated her pulse? She'd always thought prayers had to be long and drawn out.

What motivated him? Obviously not money. He seemed so unpretentious and exuded strength she lacked. Not at all like Jason Jeffries, so suave and sure of himself.

She'd known Jason forever, yet he couldn't be bothered to drive her home last night. A warm sensation curled around inside. Ryan had gone out of his way to make sure she was safe.

He lifted an eyebrow and held up a fork and knife she'd wrapped in cloth napkins.

"What?"

"Silverware and linens. Really?"

"That's all I could find." She giggled and handed him a sub.

After chewing a generous bite of roast beef and Monterrey Jack on whole wheat, he swallowed. "This is good. Not many women have slaved in the kitchen for me."

"You don't have a girlfriend?" She took a dainty bite of sandwich and hoped he didn't get the wrong idea. Like thinking she was interested in him. She swallowed. Well, maybe she was.

He flinched and looked over her shoulder toward the fir trees. "No, I'm too busy with my jobs."

"Jobs?"

"Yeah, I'm a first-grade teacher and work at CF Hardware after hours."

No girlfriend. Hard working. Goal oriented. How could she not be interest in Ryan? "You're a busy guy." Sandy jolted when a loud crunch sounded somewhere near the clearing.

A burly man in his late twenties with a brown bottle in his hand swaggered down the path from the woods. "Hey, look at this cozy little picnic." With a stumble, he tottered up to their table in his over-sized jeans that sagged low on his hips. A baseball cap turned backward covered his head.

A thin, blond woman trailing him slipped on a rock but caught herself. "Oh, how sweet. You two communing with Mother Nature?"

"Hey, Maybelle, maybe we should join their party." An alcoholic stench filled the clean air when he reeled toward them. "Whatcha got to eat?"

Ryan jumped to his feet. "You're not invited. Especially not in your condition. Why don't you move on?" His hands balled into fists.

A sliver of fear sliced through Sandy, but the drunk was no match for her skills. She paused while Ryan confronted the guy.

The intruder scowled. "Yeah? Try and make me."

Sandy's eyes widened, and she gulped a breath.

The obnoxious man lumbered toward Ryan, raised dirty hands, and shoved him over the bench.

Ryan flailed backwards, knocked against an exposed root, and moaned. Pushing up, he held one hand to his head.

Maybelle staggered toward the drunk. "Harry, stop it. Let's go."

"Shut up. We've got a couple of losers here." He balled his fists and swung toward Ryan.

The grimace on her friend's face told her he was likely dazed and in pain. Sandy stepped in front of Ryan facing the intruder, her fist in her open palm and her knees locked. "You need to leave. Come any closer and you're toast."

A brash laugh filled the clearing. "Ha. You think you're gonna fight me, little girl? Think again."

"I'm warning you." She inhaled a deep breath, allowing adrenaline to course through her veins.

The drunk turned to Maybelle. "This pea-sized girl thinks she's gonna beat me up. Funny, huh?" He spewed a toxic laugh and lurched forward.

Not again. She'd never let another man touch her like that again. The reason she'd trained. Sandy leaned away from his sloppy movement. "You asked for it. Yah." She threw a kick to the man's groin and a jab to the head.

"Hey, you little…" The drunken idiot dropped to his knees.

She brought a knife hand to the jugular.

The man fell forward on his face into a bush, arms spread out like a flying bird.

Sandy folded her hands on her chest. "I warned you."

"Harry." Maybelle stumbled to him, pulling him to his unsteady feet. She put her arm around his waist and tugged him toward the path.

Little cuts made by the evergreen shrub sent trickles of blood down Harry's face. He groaned and swiped at the gooey liquid. Loud coughs and a few expletives punctuated his exit.

Ryan sank to the table with a sideways grin. "Tell me I didn't see what I just saw." He gave a pained chuckle and rubbed his head. "You fought off a two-hundred-pound jerk, and you probably don't weigh a hundred yourself."

"I'm no weakling. I told you I know Kung Fu. I'm a black belt. Besides, he was drunk. Made it easy for me. I may be a chicken when it comes to earthquakes, but I can handle morons like him."

Ryan's eyes widened. "I believe you. Remind me to stay on your good side." He rubbed his head. "Sorry I didn't get to protect you. Instead you protected me."

"No problem. Let me take a look at your head. I'm a nurse, don't forget." She parted his hair. "Yep, you've got a knot all right. But I don't think it's anything serious."

"Thanks, Nurse Arrington. I…I owe you one." He squeezed his eyes shut and opened them again. "What a dork. I can't believe I didn't see that coming." He put his hand behind his neck, turning it one way and then the other. "I hate to say it, but I kind of lost my appetite."

"What if I send the rest home with you?"

"Sounds great, and I don't think I'm going to be much good on a hike today."

Sandy nodded. "You probably need to get home and apply some antiseptic. Besides, clouds are moving in."

"Guess we'd better head back." He turned a red face from her and stood, stuffing trash in an empty plastic sack.

Sandy stowed the leftovers in the canvas bag. The poor guy was embarrassed, but what was she supposed to do, let the drunken jerk beat them up? "Hey, Ryan, I have some questions about church today."

He cleared his throat and picked up a napkin off the ground. "You asked about attending. Whether you go or not doesn't affect your salvation. The important thing to know is everybody in the whole world does wrong. It's called sin, and it's part of the human condition. But God has a solution." Ryan tossed the sack of trash toward the metal can, and it fell short of the basket. "Oh, man." He blew out a stream of air, picked up the bag, and walked it over.

Sin. She couldn't disagree with him. What about the time she'd cheated on a final exam or another time when she'd lied to her mother about what time she came in from a date? They seemed like little white lies at the moment, but they kept adding up. "Why were those people going to the front at the end of church?"

He pulled the cooler along the dirt path and cleared his throat. "The pastor invited anyone who wanted the free gift of salvation, God's answer to our problem, to come to the front. See, even though we all sin, Jesus Christ came to earth to hang on a cross and take the punishment we deserve."

"Sounds too easy." She strolled alongside him. The moisture in the air brought a fresh, woody aroma to her nostrils.

"When we tell Him we want to receive His payment for our sins, He'll come into our lives and God will forgive us. We become a new person…acceptable to God." He stopped to take a deep breath then tottered along again. "Did that make any sense?"

She was like a dry sponge wanting to soak up more. "I think so. An amazing thought. Did you ask Jesus into your life?" Needing to hear an answer, she placed her hand on his arm to slow him a moment.

"Yes, when I was a senior in high school. Some guys I knew invited me to one of their youth group meetings. I prayed with the youth pastor." He stared off beyond her shoulder. "You see, I had..."

He flinched again and paused, as if weighing his next words. "I have a lot of sin in my life, Sandy."

"Does that mean you did and still do a lot of bad things and make mistakes you regret?"

He stared at the ground as he pulled the cooler over a bump on the path. "I work hard not to. I don't abuse God's grace by doing whatever I please, and then tell Him I'm sorry." His jaws clenched making his cheeks rise.

Ryan was the nicest guy she'd ever met. What could he do that was so terrible? "So even though God makes you a new person, you can't put sin behind you?"

He didn't speak, only nodded. The bar of the cooler slid out of his hand as he turned from her. The question must have struck a tender chord.

She always told herself God would accept her because the good she did outweighed the bad. After all, she helped people every day at the hospital. She hadn't murdered anyone. Or taken drugs.

"If I sin, Ryan, what's the good of God's gift?"

He turned to her. His eyes blazed with passion. "Don't you see?

Without the gift of Himself for our sins, we can't be close to God. If we can't be close to God, we have no hope…in this world or in the next. Yeah, we're going to make mistakes, but we have a safe haven in the Lord. He loves us despite our sin."

If God could come into her life like He did in Ryan's and give her half the fervor she saw in him now, she wanted the gift for herself.

He turned to face her. "Sandy, God doesn't play favorites. He loves you, too."

A sense of elation rose inside her. Joy, perhaps? She followed Ryan again as he picked up the tote bar and trekked down the trail to the parking lot. The *tap tap* of a woodpecker ornamented the sounds of the forest and the beating of her heart. Her keyless remote popped her trunk open.

Ryan hoisted the cooler into the deep storage area on her father's Beemer.

"Here's your doggy bag." She handed him the container full of uneaten sandwiches. Though unsuccessful, Ryan had tried to defend her out there in the forest. The thought flickered warmth to her heart. She barely knew the man, and yet she couldn't deny the growing attraction to him. She gazed at his face, but he rubbed his chin and averted his eyes.

"How's your vision? I'm pretty sure you don't have a concussion, but if you did, it would affect your sight."

"Other than a problem only an optometrist could solve, my vision is fine."

She laughed and gave him a playful tap. "You've given me a lot to think about today. I'd like to go to church again with you." A light drizzle fell, creating a gray veil of moisture. She blinked a drop of rain from her lashes.

"If you want, the singles are visiting the nursing home next Saturday. You're welcome to go. It's a ministry we do."

"Hmm. Let's see." She'd have to cancel her date with Jason for their outing to Leavenworth with all the German restaurants. "I'm off next Saturday. I'd love to go. Let's hope we don't have any more quakes. The hospital is cleaning up after the last one." Sandy giggled.

A slow smile broke out on his face. He cocked his head and peered at her. "You're probably much more capable of taking care of yourself than I am, but I'm going to see you get out of here safely."

She smiled, climbed in her car, and wiggled her fingers to him. A profound, spiritual person. Someone she'd like to know better. Someone she wanted in her life.

Chapter Five

"Almost finished with your homework, Bobby?" Ryan lifted his gaze from his lesson plan book to his student pushing a pencil around on a tablet of paper. Friday afternoon and for once he didn't have to take any work home. His tests were graded, and next week's lesson plans done.

Heat crept down his neck as he rubbed the still-sore wound on his head. Sandy probably thought him less of a man. Well, didn't he think of himself that way?

A weight heavier than Sandy's oversized cooler settled in his stomach. Where did the thought come from? The meeting with Greg disturbed him more than he'd realized.

Sure, he'd admitted to some troubling feelings, but doesn't everyone have an unguarded thought? *No, you're not like everyone else.* Why couldn't he accept it?

He never wanted to give in to the lifestyle, or allow the enemy to place him there. Yet the drama, the draining emotion of it all, he could do without. He drew his attention to his student.

The six-year-old sat at a rectangular wooden table. Two other identical tables, now empty, were staggered to the middle and side of the room.

"Bobby, how's it going, buddy?" he repeated.

"Two more problems on math." The curly-haired boy looked up from his notepad and chewed on his thick pencil.

"Good, because I think your mom's going to be here any minute. She said her visit with her grandma at the nursing home would take about an hour." He'd been more than happy to keep his student after school when Mrs. Isaac made the request. Bobby didn't have a father at home, and Ryan understood more than most the importance of a good role model.

A light knock sounded on the door then Mrs. Isaac peered inside. She crooked her finger at the boy. "Mr. Reid. Thank you. Come on, son."

Lifting his pencil with a flourish, Bobby continued writing.

"Tell Mr. Reid thank you, and let's go." With a glance at Bobby, she looked at Ryan and smiled.

Bobby was lucky to have a mother like her. No doubt she loved her son. Her sense of pride when she looked at her child or spoke of him at PTA meetings...so different from his own mother.

"I'm more than happy to help out. I know what it's like not to have a fath..." He coughed then reached down to pick up a piece of paper off the floor and pitched it into the garbage pail. "What's the name of the nursing home? I'm going to Woodbridge tomorrow with a group from church."

"That's the one. My grandmother lives there, Mary Mahaney." Her smile dimmed. "She moved in when both legs were amputated because of diabetes."

"Mrs. Mahaney? I know her. I've visited with her before." The lady was the epitome of a wonderful Christian woman, filled with the joy of the Lord despite her handicap. She always seemed to share the right Bible verse with him.

Bobby gathered up his papers and pencil, stuffed them in his backpack, and gave Ryan a high-five. "See you Monday, Mr. Reid." The child ambled down the hall next to his mom.

Ryan laced his fingers in front of his chest. A fatherless boy like Bobby would benefit from a ministry like the one he prayed about. Benefit from godly men—and women—who volunteered their time to give kids the attention they craved.

Now, if only Greg could convince the elders to meet with them.

~*~

Ryan pulled up to the curb at the southwest end of Rainier Park. Good thing Bobby's mother showed up when she did, or he might've had to call Greg and tell him he'd be late for their one-on-one game of basketball.

He strolled across the grass toward the concrete court. If Ryan could quell the anxious tension in his stomach, maybe he wouldn't look so unskilled when it came to playing the game.

At least he'd watched it on TV and shot a few hoops with the guys in the singles group at church. He stepped on the court and bent over in a leg stretch. He didn't stand a chance beating Greg.

Ryan prayed he and Greg would be able to arrive at some conclusion about the project and get the support of the elders.

But had he actually heard from the Lord? Doubts had flooded his heart since he talked to his friend last Sunday. He grasped his hands behind him and stretched.

"Hey, Ryan."

Ryan circled around at the deep voice he knew so well. "How ya doin', Greg."

His friend ambled toward him, a basketball in one hand.

"Are you going to give me a handicap?"

The corners of Greg's mouth turned up, and he chuckled. "That's in golf, dude. Don't start complaining. You can play this game as good as I can." He set his car keys and cell phone on the grass next to the metal pole attached to the backboard and glanced up at Ryan. "I've got an idea I want to share after I wipe the court with you."

Ryan nodded. "Yeah, sure."

Greg jogged onto the court dribbling the ball toward him. "You ready?"

Ryan nodded. "I'm dead already."

Greg laughed. "I was only joshing with you. I think you underestimate yourself, big guy." He tossed the ball to Ryan.

Ryan caught the basketball and dribbled, working his way around Greg's defense and toward the basket.

Greg kept up with him, his arms out wide in a block.

When Ryan jumped up for a shot at the basket, Greg blocked him with one hand, taking possession, and stood back, bouncing the ball.

"Oh, man." Ryan turned, keeping an eye on Greg's hand and his feet, trying to determine which direction he would dart around him.

Greg moved left, and Ryan stayed with him, countering his opponent's moves with an ease that surprised him.

Then Greg took a step to the left and back to the right. He shot past Ryan, and with a tilt of his hand, the ball was in the air. It bounced off the rim and toward Ryan.

Ryan jumped for it, grasping it in his hands.

Greg was there, on him like ink on paper.

Ryan pivoted around him, taking Greg by surprise. With Greg out of the way, Ryan dribbled one more time and went up for the shot. The ball swooshed into the net. "Yeah, that's what I'm talking about."

Greg retrieved the ball and tossed it to Ryan. "Now I really don't believe you don't know how to play."

Ryan shrugged and moved to the edge of the court, readying to throw the ball to his friend.

"Hey, guys, can we play?" A scraggly blond boy about fourteen approached alongside another dark-skinned boy with curly hair.

Greg glanced up at them. "Sure." He pointed to the dark-skinned boy. "You're on my team."

Ryan grinned and held out a hand to the blond kid. "I'm Ryan. He's Greg. Guess you drew the short straw, but it looks like you've seen a basketball court a few times." He tossed the ball to Greg's teammate.

The boy grasped his hand. "Charlie. He's my friend Jamal. Thanks for letting us play."

A chill ran down Ryan's spine. Charlie reminded him of the boy he'd seen the day of the earthquake, the kid he'd dreamt about. Could the Lord be communicating something to him?

Greg stuck his thumb out toward Ryan and turned to Jamal, who held the ball. "My friend thinks he's no good at this game, but don't let his talk fool you."

"Yeah, sure." Ryan laughed.

Jamal tossed the ball to Charlie, who rushed toward the basket, but not before Greg's partner darted in front of him. Charlie threw the ball to Ryan, and Ryan vaulted up, landing the ball in the basket.

The curly haired kid looked at Greg. "Okay, I see what you mean. Let's kill him."

Ryan shook his head and tossed the ball to his teammate. The kid threw it to his friend. Ryan rushed forward.

Jamal was quick. He leaned one way then skirted in the opposite direction. He raced to the goal and with a leap slammed the ball into the net.

Greg gave the kid a high five.

Ryan and the blond won the first of three games. Greg's team struggled, but came from behind to win the second game, and Ryan was winded as the third game came to a close. He gave Greg a smirk. "According to my records, Charlie and I are ahead." He blew on his fingers and rubbed them on his T-shirt.

Jamal looked at his buddy then to Greg. "Hey, man. I need to take off. See ya around, dude."

Greg gave a thumbs up. "Yeah, nice playing with you guys."

Charlie followed Jamal toward the evergreen trees lining the court, then turned, raising his hand in a wave.

Greg grasped his knees and whistled. "I guess I have to concede to you."

Ryan chuckled. "Didn't know my own skill." Then his pulse pounded. "You said you had something you wanted to discuss."

Greg spun the ball around on one finger. "Yes. I had a brief talk with the pastor yesterday. He reminded me of a topic the staff had discussed with the elders in recent meetings. The Barclays from church own the vacant land adjacent to the parking lot. They want to almost give it away to New Day, but Pastor Netherton doesn't want to buy it unless we can come up with a solid ministry utilizing the area." His strong fingers gripped the ball. "The elders have been praying about it and so far, they don't have any specific ideas. What do you think, Ryan? Can we think of some ministry that would be a blessing to the youth?"

Ryan swallowed his attraction he'd been able to avoid during the basketball game. A smile crossed his face. "Yeah, Greg, I think we can."

Greg laughed and slapped his hand on Ryan's shoulder. "Good, because I asked God to show me if I was on the right track. Those two boys who came up were as good as God whispering in my ear, 'Go for it.'"

Ryan's heart pounded. Was Greg's vision from the Lord? He had to believe the boys were confirmation as Greg had said. "We know we want to minister to teens, and you received assurance as I did the day after the earthquake. I think we have an answer, but where do we go from here?"

Greg cradled the basketball in his arm. "You want to pray again, brother?"

Ryan nodded and bowed his head.

"Lord, you know the call on our hearts. We need Your direction now. We want to quiet ourselves before you..."

Silence filled Ryan's ears except for the laughter of a couple of kids on the hiking trail beyond the court. He breathed deeply. The peace of the Lord wafted through him. He squeezed his eyes shut and in his mind's eye, he saw a large building. A facility where teens could come for basketball, Bible study, lessons in life skills. The large building loomed, but a second image arose in his mind. He saw a large caldron of boiling metal, perhaps silver. The scum rose to the top and flowed over the sides leaving bright, clear liquid.

Lord, what does it mean? A verse in Isaiah drifted through his mind. *I will thoroughly purge away your dross and remove all your impurities.* Ryan endured more discomfort now than any other time he could remember, knowing he'd face Greg and temptation day after day. But God had brought the temptation to the surface of his life so the Lord could purify him. God was using Greg to refine Ryan as gold.

Ryan lifted his head. "Brother, I'm wondering if the Lord's asking us to construct a building on the property."

"I think we're on the right track." Greg knuckled Ryan's shoulder.

"Now to convince the elders it's a worthy ministry."

"If the Lord's in it, we can do it." Greg bent down, retrieving his keys and cell. "Where are you going after this? If I were you, I'd call Sandy and see if she wants to go to dinner or something. She's a fine-looking woman."

Ryan shuddered. Greg thought he was interested in Sandy. "Nah, she's not my type."

"Look, buddy. I don't buy that. I don't think you could do much better than her. A nurse, is she?"

Ryan stared at the grass, heat rising from his ears to the top of his head. What would Greg say if he knew the truth? He had no interest in Sandy…or any woman, for that matter.

Chapter Six

"Hey, Greg." Ryan walked out his apartment and plastered the phone to his ear.

"Are you sitting down?"

Ryan chuckled. "No, I'm walking to my car. The singles outing is in a half hour."

"I know, buddy. I wanted to give you the good news first. Last night at the monthly elders meeting, I requested a day for them to hear our proposal. They've agreed."

Ryan caught his breath. "The first hurdle. Maybe this means we're on our way to building the rec facility."

"Yep. I hope so. Okay, I'll see you in a few."

After the ten-minute drive to church, Ryan pulled into a parking spot near the entrance. He looked toward the empty lot next to the church—the possible location. Now that they had a meeting with the elders, he needed to start putting together a presentation.

Since he had good internet at the apartment, he could do a search tonight. The differences between using an architect or a designer, construction companies in the Cedar Fork area, architectural styles similar to the existing church. *Whew.* His pulse picked up speed. How could they best sell their idea to Pastor Netherton and the elders?

Motion from the corner of his eye drew his attention to the right window.

From the driver's seat of a different Beemer, Sandy waved.

When had she pulled in next to his clunker? He stepped out onto the sidewalk.

She slid out of the luxury car and beamed. "Hey, Ryan."

"Hey. Got a new car?"

"Yeah. I decided to buy one like my dad's."

"Cool." Sandy—rich and self-confident. Her beautiful face cheered him, and her pleasant manner and sweet smile lifted his spirit. Yet their lives were so different. Though he'd never have the attraction toward a woman he'd heard guys talk about, nothing said they couldn't be friends.

A crowd gathered by the side of the church, around the corner from the main entrance.

She touched his arm. "Are they some of our group?"

"Yeah. Come on. I think it's Greg's turn to drive this month."

She reached into her Beemer to get her purse. "How was your week?"

"Oh, grading papers, teachers' meetings, and playground duty. Kept company with a lot of six-year-olds." Relieved she didn't mention the picnic, he relaxed the tense muscles in his neck.

"I hung out with a bunch of cranky doctors." She rolled her eyes.

He chuckled as they strolled from the parking lot.

Peals of laughter reached his ears. Suzie stood next to Greg giving him an easy jab on the shoulder. He threw his head back in a laugh.

Greg looked up and broke away from the conversation, dragging Suzie along with him. "Hey, Ryan, Sandy."

Ryan's heart beat a disturbing rhythm. *Ignore it, ignore it.* "Greg, can we catch a ride with you?"

"You bet. We'll make it a foursome." He winked at them.

Ryan's heart sank. Greg was jumping to false conclusions.

Sandy smiled at Greg. "Who's your friend?"

Nothing bashful about her.

Greg grinned. "This is my girlfriend, Suzie Stinson."

Suzie tossed long auburn hair to one side and slipped her arm through his. She gave a small wave. "Nice to meet you, Sandy."

Greg gazed at Suzie with a glance which fascinated Ryan. Was his expression typical of the way a man looked at the woman he loved? How did he get to that point?

Sandy grasped Suzie's long, slender fingers. "Glad to meet you, too." His new friend had a way of fitting in quickly.

Ryan had to admit she made him feel more sociable, different from his usual inclination to act like a hermit. It'd be great to feel comfortable in his own skin like he presumed Sandy did.

The breeze rustled the leaves of a cottonwood, like hands clapping in praise to the Lord. What better way to be free of his heavy spirit than to praise God? His burdens lifted a bit.

Suzie looked at Sandy. "You're going to love it at Woodbridge today."

Greg waved for them to follow him to his car. "Come on. I think the group is leaving."

Ryan held the backdoor of Greg's Jeep, and Sandy climbed in. When he ducked in beside her, she gave him a nervous glance. "I have experience with elderly patients, but I've never talked to them about religious matters. Any pointers?"

Ryan chuckled. "We don't usually talk about religion unless they show a desire to. I sit and listen to their stories. And they've got plenty to tell."

Suzie curved around from the front seat and grinned at Sandy. "I'm so blessed by the wisdom they've gained over the years. And they love to share it."

Greg drew her hand to his lips and kissed it, then started the motor.

Suzie communicated something to him with her look as if they had their own secret language.

Would Ryan ever be able to feel the same about a woman, to touch her, and to feel the love Greg expressed with his eyes?

Greg peered at him from the rearview mirror and winked again.

Ryan's heart lurched. His face flamed from shame welling inside, and he looked down at the floorboard.

Sandy's hand brushed his. "Are you okay?"

He allowed the warmth of her fingers for only a brief moment before looking up with a forced smile. "Just tired." He pulled from her caress, her touch doing nothing for him—not like the single glance thrown his way by his friend.

~*~

Sandy glanced from one wall to the other as she tucked a strand of hair behind her ear. Seniors sat at tables, in wheelchairs, and a few were restrained in their seats. Some mumbled to the air, their gazes fixed on a distant time or location and not on anything in the room.

A nurse pushed an elderly lady in a wheelchair through the lobby. The occupant of the chair murmured something about her baby. Dementia of some sort.

The familiar odor of disinfectant filled the corridor. Sandy relaxed. It smelled like the hospital.

What did Ryan say? Encourage them to talk and listen to their stories.

She glanced over her shoulder.

Ryan shook hands with a man on a walker then looked up to her. "Sandy, I have an idea. The great-grandmother of one of my students is here, Mary Mahaney. I talk to her all the time. Let me introduce you."

Ryan led Sandy past a nurse rolling an elderly man down the hall in a wheelchair and another administering medication, something she did every day.

Wheelchairs and tables became obstacles in their path as she followed

Ryan toward an old woman with white hair pulled into a bun.

The lady raised her hand to Ryan. "Hello, dear. Who's the lovely young lady with you?" Her face glowed with an emotion Sandy couldn't define.

Ryan grasped her hand with both of his. "Mrs. Mahaney, this is Sandy Arrington. She's new to our group. I thought you might like to visit with her today."

"Yes, sit down, Sandy. It's so nice to know you." Her blue eyes twinkled as if she knew a secret.

Sandy slid a chair beside the woman's wheelchair. A blanket covered her lap, and the lack of legs became obvious. At her advanced age, diabetes could be the culprit of the woman's double amputation.

Ryan waved to her as he sat beside a white-haired man in a wheelchair near the window.

Mary stared out into the room. "Sometimes it can be a depressing place. All my life I took care of my family. Now I'm dependent on others."

"I can understand what you're saying."

"I'm sorry, young lady. I don't mean to complain, not when the Lord has given me so much. Tell me about yourself." She placed a wrinkled hand on Sandy's.

"I'm a nurse at Cedar Fork General. I work in the ER." Her heart swelled with pride. "I like being able to make a sick person a little more comfortable."

"When I was there, they had some mighty good nurses." Mary touched her upper legs. "They couldn't get my sugar levels down. Diabetes, you know." She stroked the blanket framing her two stubs. "I may have lost a part of my body, but I have something no one can take from me." A dreamy expression fell across her lined face, and her eyes shone.

How could she possibly be so happy in her situation? "Tell me more."

The woman's face radiated with a look of peace. "Christ." Her smile stretched wider. "A long time ago, I made a commitment to God. I asked His son, Jesus, into my life and thanked Him for dying for my sins. He changed my life and my attitude." Mary patted Sandy's hand. "This life is temporary. Where I will spend eternity is most important now. The older I get, the more I'm aware of this truth."

Tears welled in Sandy's eyes. Mrs. Mahaney lived in a nursing home, helpless with no legs. Yet she glowed with something not dependent on circumstances. What was the source of her confidence? Asking Christ into her life? "Ryan told me the same thing about how God changed his life." She reached over to give Mrs. Mahaney a hug. "I came here today to cheer someone. But I'm the one who's benefitted."

"He's a fine young man." She peered over her glasses. "Is he your boyfriend?"

Her boyfriend? "No. My boyfriend's an intern at the hospital. At least my dad thinks he should be my boyfriend. But there is something about Ryan. He seems to understand God in a special way." Sandy laughed. "I don't know why I'm telling you this. I'm just figuring things out right now."

Mrs. Mahaney's aged blue eyes held hers. "Be patient with him. He's a wounded young man. I pray for him frequently, but I'll tell you the truth. Someday he'll make a loving husband and father. I'm sure of it."

Ryan, a husband and a father? Her husband? Father to their children? "Wow, Mrs. Mahaney. I hadn't thought that far ahead." A nervous laugh escaped.

"I know, dear, but at some time you may have feelings for him." Mrs. Mahaney winked as she fingered the lace handkerchief in her lap. "Don't let him get away."

The old woman possessed the benefit of many years of experience. Could she possibly be right about him? "You've given me a lot to think about."

"I'm sorry. I hadn't intended to say this. Somehow, I felt led. But then maybe it's only the musing of an old woman."

Sandy's gaze found Ryan across the room in front of the elderly man in the wheelchair. Both men bowed their heads, their eyes closed. Ryan's lips moved and the other man nodded. Ryan, a man of faith. Could a relationship with him be in her future?

After listening to several of Mrs. Mahaney's compelling stories of her childhood, Sandy checked her watch. She'd talked to the delightful lady for an hour.

Greg and Suzie's laughter caught Sandy's attention. They shook hands with someone who looked like a staff member and headed toward the door.

"I won't forget what you said. Or you." A longing welled up within Sandy, a hunger for the peace Mrs. Mahaney possessed.

"I'll keep you in prayer, young lady."

"Thank you, ma'am." Sandy caught Ryan's eye when he looked up from his discussion with another man.

"You ready?" He mouthed the words.

Sandy stood and squeezed Mrs. Mahaney's hand. "The things you've shared with me today may change my life. Thank you." Sandy followed the group out the door.

Ryan waited for her beside Greg's Jeep. "How was your visit?"

"Mary is the most interesting lady."

"I figured you'd like her."

Ryan held the car door for her then crawled in. When Greg reached his arm around Suzie and patted her shoulders, Ryan leaned toward them, a hand on his knee. What was his expression? Longing?

He cleared his throat. "Greg. We need to get together before the meeting with the elders."

"I know. How about tomorrow after church?" Greg's grin spread over his whole face.

"That's great. I'll bring everything I find on line—and my ideas of how we'll utilize the building including a gym."

Another look crossed Ryan's face she didn't understand. This meeting must mean a lot to him.

As if he heard her unspoken thoughts, he turned to her. "A project we're praying about. To serve needy teens."

Greg dropped them off in the church parking lot in front of their cars parked side by side. She unlocked the door of her new Beemer and leaned against it. The warm metal of the car door felt good against her back.

She needed to know more, why they sang those songs and why people placed so much value on the words in their book, the Bible. The little copy Ryan gave her left her confused.

"Are you coming to church again?" He shifted his weight from one foot to the other.

"Wouldn't miss it." Her faced warmed. Part of the reason was to see Ryan again. She climbed into the driver's seat.

"Okay, then I'll see you tomorrow." He smiled and tapped the roof of her car.

Sandy punched the button on her MP3 player and paused to take in the sounds of smooth jazz. A sideways glance toward the Toyota caught her by surprise.

Ryan leaned on the steering wheel as if in pain. The trees beyond the parking lot appeared to be the object of his focus when he raised his head. A frown creased his brow.

He said he was happy about meeting with the pastor concerning the project. Now he was clearly troubled about something. Sandy put the car in reverse. The longing look on Ryan's face. Was he in love with Suzie? Had Greg stolen her from him? Surely not.

Chapter Seven

Ryan quickened his gait as he walked through the foyer of the church with Greg and exited into the sunshine. The brilliant blue sky allowed a rare view of snow-topped Mt. Rainier peeking up on the horizon.

"Praise the Lord, that went well." Ryan's excitement spilled over into his voice.

"You know, brother, I think we're off to a running start." The upbeat tone of Greg's words echoed Ryan's. "Amazing. We actually got permission to present the project to the congregation."

They strolled the length of the sidewalk to the grassy landing next to the front parking spaces. Ryan dropped on to the white wrought-iron bench, Greg plopping down beside him.

Ryan swiveled toward his friend. "Guess we make a good team; you in charge of construction details and me heading up finances. I pray the congregation will catch our vision."

Greg gazed at him. "We both feel this call. I don't think God would've put it on our hearts without reason." He smiled then crossed his ankle over his knee.

Ryan's heart pulsed in his chest as he glanced into the eyes of the man next to him, his partner in the project. He couldn't deny the churning in his stomach.

He pulled in a deep breath and cut his gaze to the rhododendron bushes near the side parking lot in a lame attempt to rid himself of the unwelcome emotion making an effort to surface. "The bottom line is to serve the Lord by helping kids who need an adult who's willing to offer companionship and teach them about the Lord. I wish I'd had the opportunity growing up." The second the words came out of his mouth, he wanted to call them back. He'd revealed too much.

"Did you have a difficult home life?" Greg focused his gaze on Ryan.

He's a counselor. Of course, he's going to ask the question. Ryan didn't trust his voice, only shrugged. A searing pain burned his belly. He could never tell Greg about his life.

Greg slapped a hand on his shoulder. "Look, buddy. I'm a good listener if you ever need an ear."

The contact burned. Ryan fought the crazy notion to embrace him, to give into his attraction and know what it felt like. Greg cared about him, but it wasn't the same. Greg's affections were godly, a Christian man who appreciated his brother in Christ.

Greg stood as if to leave. "Hey, VBS is coming up after school lets out. The first-grade teachers voted to take the kids on a field trip at the end of the week to Northwest Trek. Suppose you could come along?"

With all the willpower Ryan could muster, he forced his feelings inside. "Sure, count me in."

Greg laughed. "I'll keep on praying about our presentation. Could be a month or so until Pastor can schedule us."

Ryan cleared his throat as his jangled nerves quivered. "The time will give me opportunity to build up my courage. Are you sure you want me to go first? You're used to talking in front of the congregation."

"You can do it. Concentrate on the message."

Ryan stood and stretched his legs. "You're right."

Greg's face lit up. "I need to leave. Suzie's waiting for me to pick her up. She wants to go to dinner and a walk in Rainier Park."

Ryan's gaze followed him into the parking lot. Greg had his thinking straight. Would Ryan ever get there?

~*~

Ryan swallowed the lump in his throat. New Day Church's sanctuary seemed extra crowded today. His stomach churned. More people to hear his and Greg's presentation to the congregation. At least he'd had over three weeks to think about it.

Sandy patted his arm. "You'll do fine."

Did he look nervous? He nodded. "Well, here goes."

Ryan coughed, summoned his bravery, and stepped up to the podium. Several hundred pairs of eyes fixed on him. "Good morning. Pastor Netherton and the elders have granted me and Greg Aldridge permission to bring before you a project which the Lord has placed on our hearts."

Ryan's knees wobbled, but he managed to keep his voice steady. "As you know, New Day is located in the midst of a poverty-fraught area of Cedar Fork with needy families surrounding our church. Greg and I have a vision—building an annex to the church to minister to many of those children and teens." He cast a glance toward Greg in the front row. Though Ryan's palms were wet, his hands didn't shake.

"The building would be available to church members and their families as well. We've envisioned the annex to be staffed by volunteers and opened to neighborhood kids." Ryan gripped the podium. "Our purpose today is to ask you to pray about the idea. I've worked up a budget which you will receive along with the response cards." He nodded to the teens he and Greg enlisted to pass out the information. "Please pray about what role if any you feel led to accept. God bless you." Ryan took a couple of steps away from the podium.

Greg smiled and rose from his seat, stepping up to the microphone. "Ladies and gentlemen, I am happy to co-chair this project with Ryan Reid. I wouldn't endorse a project unless I believed in it. I'd be in charge of overseeing the construction phase." Greg smiled and turned toward the pastor.

Pastor Netherton joined him. "I encourage you to express your opinion. The elders and I have deemed this a worthy cause."

Ryan walked from the stage and slid in beside Sandy.

"Good job," she whispered and patted his arm.

"Thanks." He settled in the pew. The presentation was over. He could relax and listen to Pastor's message.

But thoughts of Sandy drifted into his mind instead. She was beautiful and so filled with cheer. Nurturing, friendly, and compassionate. Of all the women he knew, she'd be one he could trust—more than he ever could his own mother.

Sandy. Where was she spiritually? She'd heard Pastor's message about God's salvation now for over a month. He praised the Lord she wanted to attend church.

Finally, Ryan redirected his focus to the front. For thirty minutes, he allowed the message to soak into his heart.

Pastor Netherton's eyes shone. "I want to conclude by saying man deserves nothing, yet God gave us eternal life through His son, by His grace. If there's anyone here today who'd like to avail themselves of this unmerited favor and receive eternal life, I invite you to kneel at the altar."

Sandy looked at him, her eyes glistening with tears. "I want what you have, what Mary has."

His heart rate quickened. Sandy desired to receive the Lord in her life, the best choice she could ever make. "All you have to do is ask Him."

"Come with me?" A tear trailed down her cheek.

He took her hand and smiled. They stepped into the aisle, and his heart threatened to pound out of his chest. The sight of her kneeling at the altar sent a ripple of joy through him. He sank to his knees by her side. *Thank you, Lord, for this opportunity to walk with Sandy as she enters into Your Kingdom.*

Pastor approached and Ryan caught his eye over Sandy's head. The preacher smiled then nodded for Ryan to proceed.

"What do I do?" With large shining eyes, she lifted her gaze to him.

"Would you like to repeat a prayer after me?" He squeezed her hand.

She nodded and closed her eyes.

The sound of her feminine voice echoing his words touched a place in his heart he didn't know existed. She finished her prayer and raised tear-filled eyes toward the cross on the wall under the stained-glass window.

He slid his arm around her shoulders and raised the other in praise for a child who'd been born again. The terror-struck woman he'd met in the earthquake had given her life to the Lord.

Sandy possessed everything money could buy. Today she received something neither silver nor gold could purchase—a new life. For a time, he pushed away thoughts of himself, the annex, and his unwanted inclinations.

He slipped his hand around her waist when they returned to the pew.

A woman in the row behind them wiped away a tear and smiled.

Sandy eased into the pew beside him. A look of wonder filled her eyes, then she closed them and folded her hands in her lap.

He bowed his head as he caught his breath. *Lord, thank you for my new Christian sister.*

Christian sister. He wished she could be more, but it would never happen.

~*~

Sandy floated out of the church, wandering toward the parking lot. Everything seemed more beautiful now. The rhododendron bushes set her heart on fire with their blaze of color. A robin's trill sounded more melodic and sweeter than ever before.

She scrunched her nose. What would her parents think of her new relationship with Christ? And Ryan? Her father came from a wealthy family, her grandfather a doctor as well. Money and position meant everything to Daddy. *You need to marry a doctor or a lawyer*. His edict rang in her mind.

Ryan's touch had sent a warm tingle down her spine when they returned to the pew, though his hands were by his side now as they shuffled along the walkway to her car. She reached toward a bush and stroked a dark green leathery leaf, admiring the flowers aflame with the hues of fuchsia, red, purple, and pink. "I'm not sure about everything that happened today, but I think my life has changed." She ran a finger under her eye to capture the threatening tear.

Ryan picked up a blossom which had fallen to the ground and passed it to her then clasped his hands behind his back. "I can't tell you how joyful I feel right now. Heaven's celebrating. The angels have a party when someone gets saved."

"You know, my visit with Mary last month at the nursing home spoke volumes, her peace undeniable. I can describe you in the same way." She ran her finger down his bare arm. Her heart tripped with her churning emotions.

Ryan's shoulders tensed at her touch, as if she'd startled him. He jerked his head away from her, gazing off toward the parking lot.

She moved the fragrant petal across her cheek, hiding her warm face. "Mary said this life lasts only for a short time, and eternity is what matters." She glanced down at her feet. "She knows where she's going. I didn't until today. Pastor Netherton's sermons—and you made the answers clear." Tears trickled down her face. She touched a giant lavender-pink bloom on the rhododendron bush and moved closer to Ryan.

He turned to her and studied her with dark, narrowed eyes. What was he telling her by his look?

Ignoring all restraint, she slipped her arms around his neck and whispered in his ear. "Thank you for leading me in the right direction. You're the best friend I could ever have." But her feelings told her more than friendship dwelled in her heart. She cared about him in a way she never had about a guy before. Was this what it felt like to fall in love?

He remained in the embrace for a moment then raised his hands to her arms and gently pushed her from him. His full lips stretched into a tight smile, and he took two steps backwards. "I'm glad you've found the Lord. I prayed you would." His gaze focused on something beyond her shoulder.

An icy wind of doubt blew through her. She'd expressed more than gratitude with her hug. He must've figured it out. Though kind, he nudged her away. It was obvious he didn't think the same way. Maybe she'd been right—he had feelings for Suzie.

~*~

Ah, Sunday. Dr. Phillip Arrington's favorite day of the week. A day all to himself. Maybe he wouldn't get any calls from the hospital. He didn't feel like seeing patients.

He kicked his feet up on the reclining lawn chair and gazed at the splendid view of Mt. Rainier. Sometimes it amazed him to look at the looming mountain and think of the forces in the earth necessary to propel it upward. The millions of years it must have taken for this beauty to unfold before him. He closed his eyes and basked in the sun, the aroma of the cedars on his property wafting toward him. Life couldn't get much better. A gorgeous wife in the kitchen preparing a gourmet lunch and a moment to relax. The sliding door from the kitchen opened and shut.

"Hi, Daddy. Getting some sun?"

He sat up on his deck chair and threw his shoulders back. His daughter, a true beauty. Philip was a lucky man.

"Hello, Sandy. Where'd you go this morning?" He'd never seen her face glow before. "I noticed your car missing from the driveway."

"Oh, I went to church with a friend." She pulled up a chair beside him.

The hair on Phillip's neck bristled. Surely his daughter didn't buy into any of that religious nonsense. He'd taught her to approach the world logically—what would she need with a bunch of stories that amounted to little more than myths? "Church? Since when have you been going to church?"

She put her hands behind her head and looked toward the sky, her face shining in the sun's rays. "About a month, with a guy I met."

Hmm. She obviously didn't mean the intern. The Jefferies were friends of the family for years, and in all the time, he'd never known them to go to church. "Jason?"

"No. Another guy. The one I met during the earthquake. His name's Ryan." The breeze whipped a strand of hair into her eyes, and she brushed it away.

"Oh, is he the spiritual type?" Phillip crossed his arms over his chest. He didn't like the sound of this.

"Well, I don't really know. He doesn't seem fake or anything about his beliefs." A fanciful, faraway look fell over her face.

"Sandy, be careful about this man and his church." If some religious nut tried to turn her into a judgmental fanatic, he'd be sorry. Philip didn't mind stepping in and taking matters in his own hands.

"Oh, Daddy. Don't be silly. What harm could come from it?" She settled into the chair, her attention captured by something in the distance.

Phillip slowly lifted his fingers to his temple and rubbed. The radiant glow of her face made him wonder? Had the church put it there—or Ryan?

Chapter Eight

"Please, Mr. Reid. Teach second grade next year." The chubby six-year-old raised her chin and stuck out her lower lip. "You're my favorite teacher."

The bare classroom, stripped of its colorful bulletin boards, watercolor paintings, and the pet hamster, Pinky, looked different without his busy first graders. The kids' tables were shoved along the walls against the windows. The teacher aid had cleaned the whiteboards and piled the children's books on a shelf toward the back of the room. A much different sight than a week ago.

Judy tugged on his shirt sleeve. "Pleeeassse."

"Give some of the second-grade teachers a chance to enjoy teaching you like I did." He patted the little girl's shoulder. "Now go and have fun. You've got almost three months until you're in second grade."

"Okay." She grabbed him around the waist, looked up with a smile, then sailed out the classroom door.

No more lesson plans or papers to grade all summer. A twinge of nostalgia drifted over him. Teaching had become second nature. His career was his identity. The reward didn't come monetarily, but he gave kids what he'd never had, someone who cared.

Strains of "Amazing Grace" filled the empty classroom. He stuffed his hand in his pocket and pulled out his cell. "Hey, Greg." His pounding heart brought heat to his neck. He walked to his desk and sank into the chair.

"Can you talk?" Greg's bass voice sounded serious.

"Sure. The last child darted out of the classroom giving me three months of fabulous freedom." With his elbows on his desk, he held the phone to his ear, closed his eyes, and rubbed his forehead.

"I can remember those days." Greg gave a soft chuckle. "I hate to be the bearer of bad news, but the responses to the building were sparse with almost no pledges." His tone became a bit more chipper. "But then, it's only been a week. Let's pray things will pick up."

Disappointment threatened Ryan's optimistic attitude. But Greg was right. They'd only begun work on the project. "Tell you the truth, I don't know when I've felt more inspired about something." Ryan considered his next step. "When I get off, I'm going to work up a flyer we can pass out after services. Maybe spark some interest."

"I'm trying to get some bids from a couple of construction companies. Including Dad's. And we might want to think about a fundraiser. Suzie suggested a bazaar which would get some of the ladies involved."

"Sounds good. Well, I guess I'll see you Sunday. Anything else?"

"Nope. That's it for now."

"Okay. Later, Greg." Ryan clicked off his cell and stuffed it in his pocket. He pulled a manila folder from his file cabinet labeled "Tommy Friedman." In the pile of papers on his desk, he found the remainder of what he needed for the meeting with Mr. Clark and Tommy's mother. He had a few minutes to spare.

With his back against the swivel chair, he stretched his legs. Memories of last Sunday's church service thrilled him—Sandy's salvation. She was his new sister in the Lord. But a suspicion lurked in the corner of his mind. Their embrace outside the church lasted longer than a friendly hug. He feared she felt something he didn't—attraction.

Her large cinnamon brown eyes and petite nose complemented her full lips, and her slender body was eye-catching. Any guy would be happy to hug her. Any guy but him.

He ground his molars. Was there a way to let her down in a gentle manner if he needed to?

Time for his last duty of the school year. With the folder and the documents in hand, he trudged down the hall and knocked on the principal's door. The frosted glass window on the top veiled the occupants.

"Come in, please," Mr. Clark called.

Ryan twisted the doorknob and walked into the compact office. The principal's desk faced the door, its back to a wide window with the horizontal blinds closed. Ryan smiled and dropped into the chair next to Mrs. Friedman.

Mr. Clark cleared his throat and thumbed through the contents of a manila folder. He picked up a paper, turned it over for a quick glance, and laid it down. Then his gaze turned to Ryan and Mrs. Friedman. The attractive woman with long blond hair folded her arms across her chest, a frown tugging the corners of her mouth down. No doubt she had an inkling of what Mr. Clark would say.

"Mrs. Friedman, as you know from our previous meeting, we discussed how it's in Tommy's best interests to repeat first grade. He's younger than his peers, and the fact he failed the math and reading portions of the state standardized test impacted our decision. In addition, his performance this last year has not been satisfactory." He thumbed through two papers and picked up a document underneath.

She pointed at Ryan. "Well, what do you expect? A teacher like this."

Why was she attacking him? He'd done everything he could to help Tommy.

"Mrs. Friedman, I assure you, Mr. Reid is highly qualified. He came to us from the university with a 3.9 grade point average, and he's scored at the top of the scale on his teacher assessments each year."

Ryan blew out a breath. The principal's support boosted his outlook.

"I don't think Tommy could relate to him. I probably should have requested a woman teacher." She rolled her eyes. "Besides, Mr. Reid gave them too much homework. It wasn't fair to Tommy." She jiggled her foot in the air. "I'm a single mother. My new job at CF Hardware requires me to work odd hours. I can't always help him when I'd like." She scowled at Ryan and peered at Mr. Clark.

Ryan froze as his pulsed raced. An employee at CF Hardware? Since when? Working with an unhappy parent might make for a long summer.

"If he wasn't able to finish his homework this year, it's all the more reason for him to catch up next year." Mr. Clark tapped the eraser of his pencil on the desk and shuffled more papers in the file.

To know Tommy had no father at home saddened Ryan. "Mrs. Friedman, let me assure you, it gives me no joy to see a student repeat a grade. I worked hard with Tommy, but developmentally, he's not ready for second grade. Don't you think it'd be better to start out next year with material he's comfortable doing rather than placing him in a class he's not ready for?" Surely, she saw the logic.

Mrs. Friedman glared at him and pushed up from the chair, pinching her lips in a straight line. "Well, I'm going to have to think about this. I may insist you send him on to the second grade. And in the meantime, I'm going to tell every parent I know to keep their kid out of Mr. Reid's classroom." She turned and jerked the door open, allowing it to bang into the table before she stormed out of the office.

The school secretary stuck her nose around the door. "Everything all right?"

"Oh, yes. A disgruntled parent. Thanks." Mr. Clark ran a hand through his hair. "I hope you have a great summer. Don't let her bother you. You can't reason with some people. I'll see you at church."

Ryan wanted to discuss the annex but guessed he'd better not talk church business now, even if Mr. Clark was an elder. Instead, he stood and shook his principal's hand. "Thank you, sir, and you too. See you Sunday."

Ryan swiveled around and trudged out of his office. An ache began in his stomach and intensified with every breath. It wasn't for himself but for Tommy Friedman. Like Ryan as a child, the boy didn't have a father in his home. Probably no one to fulfill the need for a father's love.

~*~

Ryan's eyes blinked open. His watch on the bedside table told him he had an hour to get to work. Guess he'd be seeing a lot of CF Hardware this summer. Like a cup of extra strong coffee, the thought sent a wave of encouragement. With the extra money, his student loans would be paid off in December.

Sunlight squeezed through the closed vinyl blinds into his room. He plodded over and rolled the plastic rod to the right. The glare made him squint as he peered out at the Douglas firs which dotted the length of the street. A man pedaled a bike and passed an Asian woman jogging down the sidewalk, her dark ponytail swaying with every step.

He rubbed his eyes then strolled to the bathroom, showered, and wrapped a towel around his hips.

"What are you up to today?" Uncle Frank knocked on the door.

Ryan opened it and lathered shaving cream over his face. "Probably mixing paint or restocking or throwing boxes around in the warehouse. I've done about every job in the store." He moved the razor along his chin in short swipes.

"Say, I've been so busy I haven't had time to ask. I've noticed you with a girl several times at church. You went forward with her at the end of the service last Sunday. Any reason you didn't introduce me?"

"Oh, yeah. Sandy. She's a friend." He put the razor down on the sink and curved his head toward Uncle Frank. "I had the privilege of praying with her. She asked the Lord into her life."

"Amazing. Maybe she's your one and only?" Frank winked and moved in the direction of the kitchen.

"Nah. I don't have a girlfriend." Ryan called after him, staring at himself in the mirror. He poked a contact lens in his eye. With improved vision he could see the face of a phony looking at him. He lowered his head. How much longer could he pretend to be normal?

"Well, if you ever do get one, she looks like she'd be a good candidate." Frank banged something in the kitchen.

"I'll keep it in mind." He closed his eyes so his mirror image couldn't condemn him. Instead, his heart betrayed him. She was only a friend. He had no romantic feelings for her. And he didn't think he ever would.

"Have you heard from your mother lately?" Frank ran water in the kitchen sink.

"No." He didn't like to talk about his mother. It reminded him of all he lacked growing up, a good home and a parent's care.

Frank appeared at the bathroom door again, a frown on his face. "I'm sorry, buddy, but I can't give up on her. I wonder what she's up to."

Ryan furrowed his brow. "Last I heard she was living in Puhoma." *Could we get off this subject?*

Middle age had caught up with Ryan's uncle, leaving a spare tire around his stomach. "Ryan, I—"

"Forget it. There's no point in discussing it." Ryan ambled to his bedroom and tugged on his jeans.

"You're right, sorry."

Ryan swallowed the lump in his throat. "No, I'm sorry, Uncle Frank." Ryan lifted his voice to the paper-thin walls. He shouldn't have been so curt. She was Frank's sister, and he suffered from her actions, too.

Ryan buttoned his shirt and straightened the collar. "You know Mom's a touchy subject with me." He moved to the kitchen and checked his pockets for his keys. "Do you work today?"

"Yeah. I think they're sending me out to a new construction site on the northeast side of town." His uncle measured the fragrant coffee into the wire basket and plugged the pot into the wall. "Not a highfalutin' college-educated job like yours."

"It came with a price, the loans I have to repay." Ryan moved near the door and reached down to tie his tennis shoes. He threw his CF Hardware vest over his shirt.

"Ryan, one of these days..." Sadness blanketed Frank's features. "You know, I pray all the time for Thelma. If she could come to the Lord as I had the chance to do...." Frank looked around the room. "I'd like to move out of this place someday. Think we could afford something a little better?"

"Maybe. As soon as I get my loans paid off. But as we well know, the Pacific Northwest isn't the cheapest part of the country to live in. See you tonight." Ryan shut the door behind him. Why did Uncle Frank have to mention his mother? Nothing changed with her. The sound of her name always cast a dark cloud about him. He jangled his keys in his hand and remembered another mother who reminded him of his. Would he see Tommy's mom today and, if so, would she be civil to him?

~*~

"How ya doing, Ryan?" Larry, his boss, pushed a wheelbarrow laden with backyard tools and set it down in front of him.

"Morning, Larry." The checkout lines were short for a Saturday. The odor of insecticides wafted through the air to sting Ryan's nostrils. Another clerk stocked the pest control aisle, pulling bottles and boxes of merchandise out of a cart. He clicked his scanner as he placed each item on the storage racks.

"Could you shelve these tools in the garden department then work in building supplies today? I need you to stock insulation on aisle fifteen." Larry snatched a clipboard off the wheelbarrow and reached for the pen behind his ear to scribble on a notepad.

"Sure." Ryan grabbed his apron at the information desk then pushed the wheelbarrow to the garden center on the side of the main building. He liked working for Larry. The big guy was always fair with him in his six years at CF Hardware.

Stocking supplies in the garden section took an hour—longer than he thought. He placed the last spade on the top metal shelf next to the pruners. A piece of dust invaded his eye, and he blinked. The only option was to take off his contact and rinse it. Good thing he always brought his solution. He felt around in his vest pocket. Yeah, there it was.

The employee lounge was at the back of the store. This wouldn't take long, then he'd get to work in building supplies.

Ryan plodded down aisle seven neatly arranged with light switches, light bulbs, light dimmers, adapters, and extension cords.

He popped into the men's room near the lounge and washed his contact. He glimpsed his watch. Oh, yeah. Time for his break. Caffeine could jolt his mood. From the restroom, a hall led to the employees' lounge. He paused to check the bulletin board next to the entrance.

"Tommy's teacher, Ryan Reid, is holding him back another year." Mrs. Friedman's voice startled him. "The idiot didn't teach him a thing."

"You're kidding? You know he works here, don't you?" Another feminine voice—Dana Feldner?

He stuffed his fingers in his pocket. Dana was the tall blonde who ignored him most of the time. He'd go in there and get his cola, but his feet adhered to the spot.

"You mean I have to look at his ugly face all summer?"

"Well, let me tell you something else." Dana lowered her voice. "I've known him for six years. A religious nut. Acts like he's so righteous. He's worked here since he was in college, and he's never mentioned a girlfriend, never brought a girl to one of the company parties. He either doesn't like girls because he's some kind of a zealot or he might be, you know, gay."

His heart dropped into his shoes. Did he exude the impression?

"He's not a normal guy, you know. I can sniff out those types." Dana giggled. "He doesn't flirt with any of the girls here or even look at them like a regular man would."

"Wonder what Principal Clark would say if he knew the guy teaching boys in the classroom is attracted to them."

Ryan clamped a hand over his mouth, smothering the gasp. The ugliness of her words tore at his stomach. How could she make the leap from gay to child molester? Mrs. Friedman's allegations were untrue, and they could ruin his reputation and his career.

"Nah, these days, school districts don't care, as long as the teachers keep their hands to themselves," Dana said.

Gall rose in his throat. He'd never acted on his attraction to men, and he'd never looked at a child. Sucking in a breath, he marched into the lounge.

Dana looked up. "Hey, Ryan. Have you met the new employee, Maggie Friedman?"

He took a soda from the machine and slowly circled around. "Hello, Mrs. Friedman."

"You can call me Maggie. It's funny. Dana and I were talking about you, wondering if you had a girlfriend." She popped a potato chip in her mouth.

"Yeah, you never mention anything about women. Seems strange for a healthy young man like yourself not to date," Dana chimed in.

He popped the top on the soda. "I always make it a point not to bring my personal life with me to work for people to gossip about." What were they trying to pull on him?

"I guess you don't go out too much. You must spend all your time thinking up assignments for those poor first graders." Maggie shot a glance at Dana and rolled her eyes.

"Look, Mrs. Friedman...Maggie, we shouldn't discuss school business at CF Hardware."

He downed the cola and tossed the can in the recycle bin. Their senseless teasing mutilated his calm. "Excuse me. I've got to get to work." He turned toward the door and paced out of the lounge. Their mocking laughter followed him as he trudged to the warehouse to pick up his stock. He balled his fists and breathed hard.

The cumbersome bundles of pink insulation wrapped in plastic lay on the flatbed cart as he found aisle fifteen. After he dragged the stocking ladder to the shelf, he slung a package over his shoulder and climbed to the top. The product wasn't heavy, only bulky.

For the next fifteen minutes he tried to force the hurtful conversation out of his mind and concentrate on what he was doing. From his perch on the top shelf, he glanced down at the flatbed. He'd only shelved about half of the product.

Maggie rounded the corner from aisle fourteen. Brushing by the ladder, she stumbled against it, causing it to wobble. He lost his balance, and a bundle of insulation plummeted to the concrete floor.

She gasped and fell on her backside. "You threw that at me."

He gulped a breath of air and scrambled down. "No, you're mistaken." She had knocked the ladder. He didn't throw anything.

She remained on the floor, her legs sprawled out in front of her.

He held out his hand. "Let me help you up."

She scowled up at him. "Leave me alone, you…"

He drew his hand away. They were alone. No witnesses. It was his word against hers. Was she trying to get revenge because of Tommy?

Dana materialized at the end of the aisle.

"Call Larry. This guy allowed insulation to fall on me and knock me down." She folded her arms around her chest and made no attempt to get up.

Dana gaped at Ryan. "You idiot, what have you done to her?" She stomped off toward the front of the store.

Maggie peered at him with hatred in her eyes. She wasn't hurt at all, only angry.

Dana's blond ponytail bounced as she rushed toward them, Larry on her heels. She glared at Ryan and kneeled down near Maggie.

"What's going on here?" Larry joined the group of employees and customers gathering at the scene.

"Ryan hit me with the insulation, Larry." She slowly got to her feet with Dana's help.

"I saw it all. She's telling the truth," Dana said. A gleeful expression crossed her face.

"Ryan, what happened?" Larry said. His eyes bore into him.

"Unfortunately, Maggie bumped against the ladder, and I lost my grip on the insulation. The bundle tumbled down on her, but I certainly didn't throw it."

Larry's chest rose and fell. "Really ladies, why would Ryan do it on purpose?" Larry turned toward Dana.

"Ask him. He was her son's teacher this year. Maggie complained about him to the principal, and he's getting revenge." Dana's frown delivered an icy bite.

"Let's talk about this in my office, Ryan. Dana, finish stocking the insulation."

Larry's lofty frame led the way to his cubbyhole near the information booth. He inched behind his small desk in the unpretentious room and peered at Ryan with a wrinkled brow. "What happened?"

Ryan met his boss's gaze. "It's like I told you. And Dana's right. We did have some issues at the end of the school year. I regret she's brought them into this work environment." He took a deep breath trying to still his pounding heart.

"She's saying you attacked her with CF Hardware merchandise. Pretty serious business."

Ryan shook his head. Sweat poured off his brow. "Look, Larry. My conscious is clear. I've told you the truth about what happened."

"All right. You've been at CF Hardware six years. You're a good employee, and I believe you. Get to work, and I'll try to get to the bottom of this when I look at the camera footage." With heavy steps, Larry marched out the door.

Ryan made his way to the warehouse for more insulation. Dana and Maggie disliked him, like his mother. And probably most women.

How did he get to this place in life? So often he felt rejection from others, especially females, pointing to the fact he wasn't good enough. Sometimes he wondered how God could love him.

How would God allow someone like him to be a part of the construction project? Ryan would never be worthy enough. And what about the bazaar Greg wanted to hold as a fund raiser? He'd mentioned Suzie being involved. Would Sandy like to help?

Ryan thought of how Greg touched Suzie's arm the day when they went to the nursing home and of Sandy's hug after church. What would it be like to truly welcome a woman's caress?

He shook his head. No. Dana and Maggie were closer to the truth than they knew.

He stopped and rubbed his forehead. He had to get these thoughts out of his mind. "I can do all things through Christ which strengthens me."

A snicker behind him drew his attention.

Ryan ignored Dana and grasped a package of insulation off the shelf.

JUNE FOSTER

Chapter Nine

Ryan bounced his knee when Greg stood to speak to the congregation. Would they like their idea of a bazaar? "Ryan and I have an idea. The funds would help in getting construction of the gym underway. Again, we're passing out cards. We'd like your opinions and if you'd like to participate. We're asking for volunteers to serve as coordinators, some to man booths, others to run the food station, and lots of other jobs. Please pray about your role in getting this venture off the ground." Greg smiled at the congregation and sat down in the front row.

A bazaar didn't seem like it would bring in enough money to be worth the effort. But he'd support Greg anyway.

"I think the appeal went well," Ryan whispered to Sandy next to him in their favorite row, the third from the front. At least Sandy seemed to like the row.

She nodded and turned to him with a sweet smile, rubbed his hand, and looked at the pastor.

The desire to see the construction of the annex break ground felt more important to Ryan than anything else. In his mind's eye, needy teens paused at the front doors. How long would they wait for a listening ear, a healthy snack after school, a midnight game of basketball?

Ryan's gaze fell on Pastor Netherton towering behind the pulpit after he finished his message then to the altar rail extending the length of the front of the church. The prayer warriors stepped forward and perched on a ledge behind the railing.

"If the message has touched you today, allow someone to join you in prayer. God said to cast all your burdens on Him."

Ryan leaned toward the pew in front of him, his head in his hands. The enormity of his burden squeezed him, not only the annex but the heaviness in his heart, his desire to overcome his unwelcome inclinations.

He closed his eyes. *God, a war is going on inside me. I need your peace.* The incident yesterday at CF Hardware bothered him, but more, he needed to be free to behave like a man, the way God designed men in the first place. He lifted his head to gaze at the pastor again. The sun cast green, blue, and yellow rays of light through the stained-glass window behind him.

Sandy's soft touch fell on his arm.

Though he was suspicious of women like Dana and Maggie, maybe Sandy was different. Or would she eventually humiliate him like the others? He pushed from the pew.

She tightened her hold, and he turned to her.

"Do you want me to go with you?" The look in her radiant eyes seemed sincere, but even if she was, he couldn't reveal his heart to her.

He shook his head and crept out toward the altar rail and kneeled, his eyes on the carpet. Maybe here he could find healing and change. He raised his chin to the prayer warrior waiting to pray with him.

Greg.

His pulse pounding in his throat strangled him. He couldn't reveal anything to Greg, not when he provoked those feelings.

Ryan started up.

Greg's hand landed on his shoulder. "How can I pray for you, brother?" His voice was soft, almost like a loving father's.

He turned to him, feeling the heat rise from his neck onto his face. Greg's light brown eyes offered him concern.

He took a deep breath and steadied himself. Greg's touch blazed.

"What do we need to take to the Lord, Ryan? Besides the annex." Greg gave him a soft chuckle.

How could he tell him about the uncontrollable thoughts, uncomfortable visions? "I…I had some problems at work yesterday. I need insight and God's…uh, direction, His healing." He willed his nerves to calm.

His heart dissolved at Greg's smile, and his knees weakened as his hand remained on his shoulder. Greg closed his eyes and lowered his head.

"Lord, I lift up to You my brother, Ryan. He loves You. I've watched this man daily try to live for You, Father. Please provide direction and wisdom in his life, and Lord, for those of us who love him as You do, please give us the insight to offer him guidance."

Ryan staggered to his feet. "Thank you, brother." He couldn't allow Greg to see his tangled emotions.

"I've told you before if you ever want to talk, I'm here for you." Greg's eyes glimmered with compassion, and he reached up to pat Ryan's arm.

Ryan nodded. Greg loved him as a brother in Christ, but his prayer offered no comfort. Of all people, he couldn't accept God's love from Greg.

He made his way to the pew to gather his Bible.

"Everything okay?" Sandy offered him an engaging smile, eyes filled with empathy. She'd waited for him, though most of the congregation exited the church.

What did she see in him? Her thoughts were written all over her face, the turn of her lips, the sparkle in her eyes. He was afraid she wanted more than he could ever give.

He diverted his attention toward the altar. Greg, too, offered him a smile, one which warmed him more than hers ever could. He pushed his soaring desires down and swallowed the truth. "I'm fine."

She picked up her purse and handed him his heavy black Bible. He took it and gave his arms a stretch. They sauntered into the foyer and out the main door.

Sunny weather abounded during the summer months in western Washington. Maybe a day outdoors would lighten his mood. Sandy seemed to relish the forests and lakes the way he did. Would she get the wrong idea if he asked her to share it with him?

He'd sensed her attraction to him. There were a lot of reasons he shouldn't ask her, but…he needed a friend. A safe one.

"You want to go to Lake Quitama and take a hike? We better enjoy this weather while we have it." He stopped to pick up *The Daily Bread* from the table near the long glass windows at the front of the church.

Sandy's face lit. "Great idea." She gave him a sideways glance. "You want me to drive?"

Maybe she didn't trust his old Toyota. He chuckled under his breath. "Might as well. It'll be a new experience, riding in a BMW." He raised his arm to wave at Greg and Suzie as he and Sandy strolled into the glorious light of the day and the cool, fragrant air. The alders and elms in full bloom in the front landscaping lifted his mood.

She clicked the locks on the Beemer, and he edged into the passenger side of the luxurious car.

"I've got some tennis shoes in the trunk. Good thing I wore jeans to church." She took the main road out of town.

Ryan glanced down at his old pants. "Yeah, I'm fine, too."

"Let's stop and grab a deli lunch. I'm starved." She patted her stomach.

"Great. I'm buying since you're driving." He fingered his wallet. Yeah, he had enough cash. He offered her a smile he didn't feel. He was an expert at disguising the real Ryan Reid. He could do it again today.

~*~

Sandy glanced over at Ryan. He stared out the window, his jaws rose and fell with the clenching of his teeth, and she wondered if he even noticed the passing scenery, the emerald green fields. Hungry cows grazed on clumps of green grass, dry stems protruding from their mouths. Farmhouses dotted the landscape. The elevation rose as their route transported them eastward toward Mt. Rainier.

His invitation to go hiking today surprised her though she'd been overjoyed. An intuition, maybe even a feeling about him told her he hid something. What was he afraid to reveal? His life reflected his deep love for Jesus, something he could never hide.

The sign for Lake Quitama State Park came up on the right past a narrow wetland. She pulled into a parking space at the entrance.

The trail to the hiking area took them across a suspension bridge over Quitama Creek. A chipmunk scampered across the path near a clump of yellow wildflowers.

"Let's hope we don't run into any uninvited guests today." She chuckled.

"Yeah." A grin spread over his face, and it was a joy to hear his rare laugh. He grabbed a sturdy branch on the ground. "Hiking stick." He pointed at the pole and smiled.

Good, he didn't take her comment about uninvited guests the wrong way. She could relax. With Jason, she felt the need to pretend. He wanted her to be witty, a modern woman in today's world. She could be the Christian woman God wanted her to be around Ryan.

The trail which led to the source of Quitama Creek, Lake Quitama, became no more than four feet wide and wound around the side of a steep hill. Alder and fir trees grew on the edge of the trail, a barrier from the drop below. The crystal blue lake, the shape of an oval, appeared at the next turn, the perimeter embellished with evergreens.

Her breath caught. "Spectacular."

He pointed toward the lake. "Wanna sit?" A boulder rested about ten feet from the water in front of a Douglas fir. He propped the hiking pole on the tree and pushed himself up on the rock.

She scooted next to him, leaning against the fir. "How does it feel to be out of school?"

He squinted toward the clear sky. "Okay, but I miss my first graders. Teaching is a lot better job than my summer one."

"How much longer will you keep working at CF Hardware?"

He looked away, his voice gruff, even curt. "I don't know, Sandy. I guess until my student loans are paid off."

She jerked her head toward him and stared. He'd never spoken harshly before. Why would he be so emotional about paying off his student loans?

She slid from the rock and brushed off her jeans. "I didn't mean to pry."

He held his folded hands under his chin. "Sorry. Sensitive subject. I had some problems yesterday. I overheard something. Two employees talking about me. I...uh, didn't handle myself very well."

So, it was about CF Hardware and not the student loans. "What did they say?" Would he growl at her again?

He cut his gaze toward her. "Can we drop it?"

His tone slashed at her heart. Okay, she needed to back off. Ryan was visibly upset about something.

She stared out at the water and crossed her arms over her chest. To shut out the stab of pain from his words, she closed her eyes and drank in a deep breath of fresh mountain air. What had he overheard to cause such anxiety?

~*~

He'd been obnoxious. Hurt her. He saw it in the way she flinched from him. The Lord convicted him of his wrong immediately, but he found no words for her. The incident... Still, he shouldn't have taken it out on her.

"I think we should go." Her whispered words said so much.

Regret pierced his heart. "Forgive me, Sandy. I didn't mean to sound rude." He reached toward her and rubbed her shoulder a couple of times as if the touch would make up for his words.

Her red face stared at the carpeted forest floor. "Maybe I shouldn't have gone on about it. I thought it'd be easier for you if you had somebody to talk to. A buddy?" She picked a wildflower and stuck it behind her ear.

An ache coursed through his heart. He couldn't tell any of the guys from church about his problems.

Sandy was his sister in the Lord now. How much did he trust her with the facts of his life? A squirrel scampered up the fir tree near the lake like the anxiety scuttling through his stomach. "Can I talk to you?"

"You know you can. I'm a good listener."

"Then, I'll start with my mom. She lives in Puhoma...with her boyfriend." His halting words sputtered from his mouth. "If you want to know the truth, I've basically lived on my own since I was a freshman in high school. The school district never found out." Speaking the words made the reality more painful.

"How did you do it?" Did he see concern on her face...or pity?

"I stumbled a lot. It was hard and lonely. But the Lord...and God's people..." He gazed out at the lake. The light breeze sent blue ripples along the surface. A cardinal flew from the fir near their rock.

"She's an alcoholic, Sandy," he blurted. The statement came out of nowhere.

"I'm sorry." Her fingers on his arm brought an ounce of comfort.

He turned away, his back to her. "I can't believe I told you. I don't like to talk about it."

She grasped his hand in hers. "You don't deserve that. You have such a good heart in here." She touched his chest.

For a moment her touch soothed him, but then annoyance stirred in his gut. He bolted and paced in the direction of the lake. How did she disarm him, pull out his vulnerabilities? "You want to know what else? Huh? You want to know something else?" His voice rose to a crescendo, and he was out of control. "I never knew my father. I was conceived during a one-night stand. My mother never bothered to learn his name." He spat the words out in an angry torrent.

He stared off in the distance, looking at the beauty around him but only seeing the ugliness of his beginnings and his past. Her embrace brought warmth to his back as her arms tightened around his waist and her head rested on his shoulder.

He basked in her caress for a split second. A woman's touch. A woman's concern.

"Oh, Ryan," she whispered against him. "You're the sweetest man I know. I think…"

He turned to her, and she fell into his arms. Her uneven breath tickled his neck. He closed his eyes and held her a moment then a wave of tension crossed his chest, and he pulled from her grasp. "Please. Leave me alone."

"I'm…I'm sorry. I didn't mean…" Tears filled her eyes and when she blinked, they ran down her face. She didn't deserve to live in his torment, yet he'd brought her here.

He stepped toward her.

She stepped away.

"Sandy, listen, I'm really sorry, but I'll keep hurting you." How could he ever respond to her touch, to hold her in his arms? He had no desire for her, and it was all too obvious she wanted him.

"Please don't tell me to get out of your life." Her eyes glistened with pain. "I didn't want to tell you, but I can't hold this any longer. It's been building in me. I think I'm falling in love with you, Ryan."

He stumbled backward at the force of her declaration. Love? Why did the thought of it both repel him and fill him with exhilaration?

She stood as if waiting for an answer.

What could he say to her?

Her gaze examined him as he said nothing in response. She looked away beyond the trees and turned to walk up the trail. She ran her hand through her hair and increased the speed of her steps.

The walk to the car was uncomfortable, and the long, silent drive home did nothing to soothe his rattled nerves. He jumped when her phone rang.

She fumbled in her purse, jerking her head toward it, and at the road. "Ryan, can you reach in the little pocket on the side of my purse? I can't seem to get my phone out."

The third ring irritated him. First time he'd ever fished in a woman's purse. He pulled the cell out and handed it to her.

"Hello. Oh, hi, Jason."

He looked at her face expecting to see a big smile, yet her expression was solemn.

The thought of listening to her personal conversation with the guy made him cringe. Wasn't he offering what she wanted from Ryan?

"Yeah, I'll be home in about thirty minutes." She paused. "Tonight? Yes, I'd love to."

When she pulled alongside his car, he stepped out of her BMW without saying good-bye. What could he tell her? If he told her the truth, she'd never want to see him again. But isn't it what he wanted? Now he wasn't so sure.

The intern asked her out. She'd probably forget about being in love with him after a few more dates with the doctor.

He ducked into his Toyota and watched her from his rearview mirror as she pulled from the parking lot and drove away. Finally, her Beemer disappeared in the next block beyond the church. He clutched his steering wheel and bowed his head. Then he lifted his gaze to the church's steeple. With a quick glance around, he found no cars in sight, no one to witness his display of grief and confusion.

Ryan shut his eyes and saw Sandy's radiant face. Jason was claiming the woman who'd declared her love for him. Now he wasn't a hundred percent positive he was fine with it. His chest tightened. A tiny spark ignited in him. Was it enough to be fanned into flame?

Chapter Ten

Sandy glanced in her rearview mirror as she pulled onto the main road in front of the church. Ryan sat motionless in the driver's seat of his car. What was the guy thinking?

Heat filled her face, and her stomach roiled. Now she regretted the words she blurted to him. She'd bared her heart, held nothing back, and he wasn't in love with her. She'd made a fool of herself right there beside the lake. He didn't even have the decency to let her down gently—only ignored her.

The traffic through town was heavy, slowing her progress. She came to a stop when the light turned red. How could she love Ryan with no encouragement except being nice to her in church and asking her to go hiking today? When she glimpsed the traffic light's green glow, she scrunched her nose and accelerated.

She needed to walk away from him. Yet her heart told her the opposite. He was responsible, unpretentious, and genuine. She was attracted to him, but he'd also led her to the One who'd filled her hungry spirit. She sensed a strong bond, a connection with him.

Had she misinterpreted gratitude for love? Unless her feelings were lying, she'd fallen for him. Every time she thought of Ryan, her pulse raced. She pictured him—long lashes above wide brown eyes, a long nose curved at the end—and pouting lips. She'd wanted to run her hand down his cheek with the light layer of whiskers?

She followed the familiar route out of town. After the ten-mile drive, she turned at the mailbox. Ryan couldn't have wounded her more if he'd slapped her face. When Jason called, she wanted to hurt Ryan, to show him another guy found her attractive. Maybe even make him jealous, but it hadn't seemed to work. Now she had a date with Jason tonight for dinner.

She parked in her usual spot in front and rushed to her room to change. When she descended the stairs again, she pulled her sweater out of the hall coat closet and set it on the entry table, then lowered herself into the armchair in the sitting room.

When the bell rang, she darted up, grabbed her sweater, and walked through the entry. She leaned against the unopened door for a moment, wishing she'd see Ryan on the other side. She gave herself a mental shake and opened the door.

"Hello, Miss Gorgeous. How's the most alluring girl in Cedar Fork?" Jason slid his hand over her shoulder as they strolled around the circular drive to his Lexus. He clicked the door open and held it with a flourish. She crawled in, and then he grabbed her hand to kiss it. "My lady." He raced around to the other side and climbed in, tossing her a wide grin.

She enjoyed Jason's attention, but he didn't make her knees weak like Ryan. "Were you on call today?" She smoothed the hem on her azure blue V-neck silk dress.

"Don't you think about anything besides work?" He blew her a kiss. "No, I lay around the pool at my apartment. Why don't you come over after dinner and let me show you how inviting it looks?"

"I don't know, Jason." She glanced out the window at the evergreens zooming by at top speed.

"Okay." He drew out the syllables. "How was your day?"

She gulped a breath. "I went to church and Lake Quitama with a friend."

"Church? What's up with that? As many years as I've known you, you've never gone to church." His sideways smirk stirred discomfort inside.

She cleared her throat. "I...uh, I've been going lately."

"Humph."

She didn't expect Jason to understand and wouldn't try to explain. The rest of the quiet drive into town made her uncomfortable.

Jason turned the corner onto Highland. A strand of straight blond hair fell on his forehead above bright blue eyes. Any woman would consider him handsome.

Finally, he broke the silence, probably uncomfortable as well. "Look, Sandy. I hope you don't get all religious on me." He slowed when the route took them through town.

Since they were kids, both sets of parents had make it clear they expected Jason and Sandy to end up together. He probably wouldn't understand the change in her life and certainly wouldn't want a *religious* wife. "I..."

"Hey, let's forget about it." He stopped at a light. "How about dining at The Falls tonight? We can walk down by the Tenochee River to see the fish ladders afterwards."

Whew. The tension eased a little. "I haven't been there for a while."

The brakes screeched when the car came to a stop. He pulled into the last parking place in front of The Falls, opened her door, and offered his hand. One thing about Jason, he was a gentleman.

She sailed in front of him when he held the restaurant door.

"Yes, sir." A college-age hostess grinned at him.

"A table for two by the window, please." He gave the girl a wink.

They followed her down the stairs. The entire wall was comprised of glass with a view of the river and falls beyond. The buzz of conversation and piped-in classical jazz set the mood.

Jason pulled out her chair, and when Sandy slid into it, his hand lingered on her shoulder before he took his seat. Not long ago, she would've liked the feel of his fingers on her, but now she could only think of Ryan. Why didn't he ever touch her?

"I don't know of anywhere on the earth you can look out the window of a restaurant and watch salmon jump. Of course, they're not coming upstream now. Probably in August or September." He reached across the small table to hold her hand.

The server arrived with a wine menu.

Jason's baritone crooned. "Glass of wine, Sandy?"

"No, iced tea will be fine."

"You used to drink it. What happened? Your religion getting to you?" He shook his head at the server and returned the menu.

"No, Jason, I've got to go to work tomorrow, and I don't want to feel woozy." His remarks began to irritate her. "What rotation are you on now?"

"Pediatrics. Those brats are driving me crazy." He sat back in his chair and took a sip of water.

"Have you decided on your specialization yet?" She laced her fingers under her chin then turned to watch the falls send sparkles of water sailing down to the stream below.

"Yeah, cardiology, like your dad."

The server brought the menus.

Sandy held up a hand. "I don't need to look at it. My favorite is charbroiled shrimp, the specialty of the house."

"I'm going for the lobster. Can't pass up drawn butter, rice, and broccoli spears." He handed the menus to the waiter. "And cherry cheesecake for dessert. How about you, Sandy?"

She nodded and smiled as she wondered how she'd eat it all. Then she remembered the simple meal she had with Ryan at lunch. If he ever took her to dinner, they'd probably never go to a place like this.

After fifteen minutes, the server brought the steaming plates of seafood garnished with drawn butter and sprigs of parsley. She shut her eyes a moment to give thanks for her meal, as she and Ryan had done earlier. No way she'd ask Jason to pray with her.

She cut a small piece of shrimp and took a bite. Though Jason sat across the table from her, she'd left her heart with Ryan this afternoon. Then, she remembered, he'd flung it back at her. A small tear betrayed her.

Jason leaned across the table. "Do you have something in your eye? You seem so far away. Is everything okay?"

His voice soothed her. He cared about her, maybe even loved her. Yet she'd have to get Ryan out of her heart first to make room for him. "Yes. I'm tired. I hiked a long time today." She stabbed a piece of broccoli.

"Who'd you go with?" He reached for her hand again.

"Uh…a teacher I met. A guy named Ryan."

He straightened and searched her face. Then his hand rested on hers. "You should've seen your eyes light up when you said his name. Are you falling for him? Tell me he's not my rival." He raked his hand through his hair.

"No, of course not. He's a friend. You remember, the guy who gave me a ride to the hospital the day of the earthquake." Did her voice sound convincing? "We were both in Starbucks at the time of the earthquake."

A sparkler sizzled on top of a mound of ice cream and meringue as a server passed by their table with a baked Alaska.

"The dude with the broken-down car. Now I know you wouldn't be interested in somebody like him." He smiled and raised her fingers to his lips.

When he released her hand, Sandy managed to eat the rest of the entre.

Later the server set the bill on a tray, and Jason slapped his credit card on top. "Okay, since we've both got to get up early tomorrow, you can wait for another time to see my pool. We've got all summer." He threw his napkin on the table.

The server returned with the receipt. After signing it, Jason stood as if he intended to cut off any further conversation. He'd been possessive of her in the past. He probably didn't care for her going hiking with another guy.

When they walked out of the restaurant and to the parking lot, he opened the door, and she slid in his car.

Sandy held her breath as he whipped around corners and turned on Highland again. The guy was taking his feelings out on the road. Not a good idea.

The ride became smoother on the country highway, and she gazed out the window. A full moon blinked beams of light. Did Ryan see them, too?

"Sandy, I've called your name three times. Are you there? I don't know where you were tonight, but it wasn't with me." His voice reflected his frustration as he pulled into the circular drive. Had she dreamed about Ryan during the entire drive home?

"I'm sorry, Jason. I enjoyed the meal. I do appreciate you." She patted his arm.

He moved the gear shift into park and stared out the front windshield. With two fists, he tapped the steering wheel, shoved his door open, and crawled out. There was no flourish this time, no offered hand to help her. His blue eyes flashed with obvious annoyance.

She followed a step behind on the pebble walkway to the front porch. The house was so dark. Her parents must've gone out. Would Jason see her inside?

He turned to peer at her. "Sandy, you know how I feel about you. I've always cared. I don't want to lose you to my competition. Can you understand that?" He pulled her roughly to him and took possession of her lips.

Her first reaction was to pull away, but she remained in the embrace. She needed to give this every chance. They'd been friends for so long. But she felt nothing toward him—not even the slightest bit of attraction. Was this how Ryan felt toward her?

She couldn't invite him in, no matter how scary the dark house looked. She rummaged quickly for her keys.

What was she thinking? She couldn't step inside alone. "Jason, would you mind coming in for a minute? The house is dark."

"Don't tell me you're still afraid of the dark. Come on, Sandy. You treat me the way you did, and you want me to peek around corners for you. Not going to happen."

Sandy swallowed hard. Ryan had sacrificed his time. Yes, he didn't know about her fear, but he'd been there for her. Jason claimed he cared, but he couldn't give her five minutes. "Good night, Jason."

The porch light glared above the ornate door she opened with her key. She gave it a little push and shuffled in. The door shut, and she took a ragged breath. "Mom, Dad, are you home?"

No answer.

She flipped on the light quickly, closed her eyes, and opened them.

"Hey, honey." Her father, in his pajamas, came from nowhere.

Sandy's scream split the air, and she wrapped her arms around him. "Daddy, you scared me." She sobbed against him.

Afraid of her own father's voice? Preposterous. Would she ever conquer the irrational fears and make a life on her own away from this house?

~*~

A week now since Ryan had seen Sandy, and they'd parted on less than favorable terms—thanks to him. His Bible lay on the old bookcase by the wall next to Uncle Frank's bedroom. He looked around the living room for his keys, then his pocket buzzed. A glance at the screen said *Greg*.

"Hey, Greg. I'm on my way now. No announcements today?"

"No. I wanted to warn you before you heard it from anybody else. The bazaar's been cancelled. Not enough interest." His usual enthusiastic tone disappeared.

Ryan's heart plummeted into his stomach. "Do the elders have any idea about the lack of concern?"

"I think the problem is most people are so busy, they don't have time to participate, but response cards indicated they're still behind the project."

Ryan released his frustration with an exhaled breath. "I hope the congregation will eventually catch the vision and be willing to contribute time or money."

"Mr. Clark mentioned an elder's meeting. They're going to call you in because you're involved with finances."

"Well, one possibility is starting construction without all the funds. We could finance a portion of the cost and continue to ask for pledges and gifts."

"Yeah, that's an option. In the end, the elders will have the final say, though." Greg paused. "Dad got the bid. It's a good thing now because nobody else would start the job with a smaller initial payment, which we may have to offer. His designer will be drawing up the plans."

"Okay. I'll keep thinking of more alternatives until we meet with the elders. See you at church."

"Bye, dude."

Lord, please open up the doors and provide a way. This was tearing him apart. The annex had to see the light of day. Ryan fired up his clunker and pulled out of his parking space.

Maybe he could start a savings account and try to build up additional funds besides his pledge. At the light, he came to a stop. What if he skimped on groceries and gas? Even worked more hours at CF Hardware.

CF Hardware. His thoughts shot to Larry's words the day after the incident. "Look Ryan." He'd peered down at him when Ryan sank into the chair next to his desk. "I think we'll let the incident drop with Maggie Friedman. Unfortunately, the camera jammed on the footage. I know Dana confirmed her story, but another employee saw everything from his vantage point. He said she didn't come out of the lounge until after Maggie fell. I think her version was less than truthful, but again I can't prove it without concrete evidence."

The light turned green, and Ryan stepped on the accelerator. He worried about the situation at work, but at least it'd been resolved.

After the ten-minute drive to church, he pulled in, slammed the door shut, and locked it with his key. The blooms on the rhodie bushes along the sidewalk were beginning to fade. He couldn't help but remember two weeks ago when Sandy hugged him here.

Sandy. He prayed she would continue to come to church after their conversation at Lake Quitama. He'd shut her out of his life. But even now he sensed tugging in his heart. Warmth traveled from his head all the way to his toes. Nothing romantic, nothing like the pull he felt toward Greg. He merely enjoyed her company, especially since she was his sister in the Lord.

He made up his mind. If she'd have him after his behavior last week, he'd ask her if she wanted to be friends. Unless she chose to spend all her time with the intern.

But was it fair to her knowing how she felt? He'd never be able to love her in the way she wanted? For now, he'd ask her, then tell her the truth one day. He didn't need to worry. In time, the doctor would win her heart anyway.

~*~

After the service, Ryan looked out over the sanctuary. Relief coursed through him when he spotted Sandy making her way down the far aisle. He sidestepped through a couple of pews and followed her out into the foyer. "Can I talk to you?"

She raised her eyebrows. "Okay, I guess." With a shrug, she headed out the main entrance.

He caught the door as she allowed it to swing shut. "Let's go for coffee. Come on. Ride with me."

Sandy stopped and looked up at him with a frown. "If you want." She followed him to his car.

He held the door and looked down at her solemn face, attempting a smile.

She stepped forward to get into his car then paused, gazing at him. "Ryan, I think... "

"Yeah?"

"Nothing, forget it." She sat in the seat and placed her Bible on her lap.

"Okay." What was she going to tell him?

A few minutes later, he held the door as she marched into the Starbucks near church, different from the one where he'd first met her.

"Sit over there, if you'd like, and I'll get the drinks." He pointed to a table for two near a display case.

When he returned with the coffees, he searched her eyes, praying she'd understand his words. "Sandy, I'm sorry about my attitude." He sipped his Americano. "It's hard for me to face the facts about my mother. And I'm stressed about the annex project. I know there's no excuse to treat you the way I did. Can you forgive me?" *Tell her the truth.* Was now the time? His hands turned to ice. He'd wait.

She looked up at him then studied her latte as she whispered the words. "Maybe I shouldn't have expressed my feelings knowing you don't feel the same about me."

"No, Sandy. It's not that at all." It was his problem, not hers. His shaking hand spilled a few drops of coffee on the table. "I guess I'm not ready for a relationship with a girl right now." *Will I ever be?* "But my feelings don't have to stop us from being friends. Is it okay?"

"What?"

"To be friends even though your feelings are deeper than mine."

Her eyes were bright with tears and pain. "I don't know, Ryan. I'll try." She dabbed at her face with a tissue.

"I'd understand if you never wanted to see me again." He knew what it was like to love someone who didn't return his affection.

She shook her head then lifted her gaze. "Things aren't looking too good on the recreation project?"

"Yeah, Greg called me this morning to say the last fundraiser was cancelled." He rested his head in his hands. "I don't know. I was so sure it was what the Lord wanted me to do." He looked up at her and shook his head.

"I guess I didn't realize how strongly you felt about this project. I've never spoken to the Lord out loud before. May I pray for you?" She placed her hand on his.

Ryan's eyes grew wide. Her simple question touched him. "Yes, thank you."

She bowed her head. "Lord, I ask You to open up the doors for this project to go forward. Please bless my Christian brother Ryan and bring him wisdom as he serves You. Thank you. Amen."

Ryan raised his head. Her cinnamon brown eyes flashed sparkles of light.

He wasn't attracted to Sandy like Jason probably was. But whether he could ever change his feelings toward her or not, he knew one thing—he didn't want to choose the alternative, to openly live the gay lifestyle. He had free will. He wanted to live life God's way, whatever it meant. He shivered. But how long could he hold out?

"I don't know if you would want to come, but my folks are having a birthday party for me next week." She raised the paper cup with the familiar mermaid logo to her lips.

He downed the remainder of his coffee. The thought of being in her large home with her parents made him queasy. On the other hand, friendship sometimes called for sacrifices. He swallowed his apprehension and forced a smile. "I'd like to come."

"I'm glad. Don't be surprised by my mom's elaborate preparations. She goes all out when she entertains."

Ryan chuckled. "So, you're warning me to expect caviar and champagne."

Sandy's face lit up with her smile. "Something like that."

He pictured Sandy in the large entry of her parents' home the night he took her there. "Say, Sandy. Do you ever think about moving into your own place some day?"

She shivered. "Uh, ya...yeah, just saving up some money. One of these days." She squirmed in her seat. Sandy was keeping secrets, too.

Chapter Eleven

Darkness shrouded the hallway. Ryan tried to block out the sounds coming from his mother's room. She moaned, the sound frightening him. He pushed open the door and peeked in her bedroom. Mom was with a man.

"Leave her alone. Get away from my mother."

"Ryan, snap to, boy. Wake up. You're having a bad dream." Uncle Frank shook Ryan's shoulders.

He shot up, his tee shirt bathed in sweat, and covered his face with his hands. A dream. When he lowered his hands, he could see Uncle Frank bending over him, concern etched on his face.

"Must have been a doozey of a nightmare. You were hollering something about your mother. Heard you from the other room." Frank straightened and rubbed his eyes.

Ryan heaved a deep sigh. "Sorry to disturb you."

"Look, if there's anything you want to talk about..."

"No. Must have been the pepperoni pizza last night." How could Ryan describe the dream about his mother? The thought sickened him. Frank was a Christian man. They attended services together. He didn't want to clog his mind with garbage. A long, deep breath filled his lungs. He exhaled the air in a steady stream.

"Okay, then. Watch the spicy food." He scratched his head and tousled his thinning brown hair as he made his way out the door.

Ryan swung his legs over the side of his twin bed. His gaze settled on the night stand, but its chipped veneer offered him no answers. No light made it through the vinyl blinds over his single window.

The shadows of the nightmare hovered in his mind. He stretched, trying to alleviate the fatigue washing over him. Why did he dream about his mother? Could it be because he was ashamed knowing she lived with a man who wasn't her husband?

The dream wasn't merely a fabrication of his unconscious mind. He remembered the night...the night he'd discovered her with some man. The animal-like noises emanating from her room. He shuddered. The act seemed disgusting. He cringed and paced to the window and returned. Had to rid himself of the memory.

He stumbled out the bedroom to the kitchen. A twist of the tap brought a flow of water to soothe his dry mouth. He shut off the faucet and trudged past the dining table to the orange-flowered couch. The decrepit thing sagged under the weight of his tired body. He closed his eyes. The harsh beating of his heart quieted some.

He was doomed to emotional failure as the project was doomed. With a push off the couch, Ryan bolted to his feet, his eyes wide. Where did these thoughts come from? He needed to be free of this crippling guilt.

If only he could make the congregation catch his vision for this youth center. Why couldn't they see how important it was, how it had the potential to change people's lives?

If he could influence one struggling young person, maybe he'd be free of the shame haunting his life. The finished annex would stand as a monument to God's power to transform lives, including his.

He trudged across the floor and returned. If he could do it alone, he would. But it was too big, too overwhelming. He needed help. Maybe he could get someone from the singles' group to organize a phone campaign to remind church members to make pledges. He couldn't sit back and allow failure to conquer him.

~*~

Ryan veered off on Route 32 toward the Cascades after he left the construction site. His heart pounded hard. When Greg called him this morning and said construction had started on the gym, he had to see it for himself. The sight of two cement trucks, excavated soil, and ground stakes protruding out of the dirt had thrilled him. The gym. A reality. He hadn't expected it to be this soon, but Greg's dad hadn't wasted any time. Good thing Ryan and Greg had convinced the elders to move forward with the possibility of financing the rest of the funds.

Exhilaration swirled through him, as if his problems had lifted from his shoulders. Praise God. The first step in accomplishing their goal had happened.

A purple bag rested on the seat beside him. He'd figured out exactly what he wanted to get Sandy, a daily devotional book and a pink bear with a little white bow around her neck.

The day he brought Sandy home, there was an earthquake. Now another quake erupted in his heart as the Toyota rounded the circular drive.

He parallel parked on the circle a few cars from the entrance. A Cadillac, a Porsche, and a sea of other luxury vehicles filled the spaces in front and at the side of the house. His car was a stepchild among the expensive vehicles.

His hand trembled as he removed the key from the ignition and inhaled a deep breath. Maybe he should go home.

Ridiculous. *Think of Sandy, somebody besides yourself.* He raked his hand through his hair.

Seconds after he poked the antique bronze doorbell, Sandy peeked out.

"Hi, Ryan." Her smile lifted the heaviness. "Please come in."

He gulped and followed her through the door into the entry. "You look pretty, Sandy. This is for you." He held the package out to her. "Happy birthday."

"Can I open it now?" She gave the impression of a child when she held the gift to her chest.

"Sure."

She glided through the entry into the sitting room and perched on the couch. With a pat on the cushion beside her, she smiled.

First the tissue paper flew out, then the devotional. She pulled out the bear and held it to her heart. "Thank you, Ryan. This means a lot to me. I plan on reading the little book when I first get up every morning."

He nodded and grinned at her.

She leaned nearer to him on the couch and raised an arm for a hug then moved away. "I'm glad you came. Let me introduce you to everyone." She hopped up and led him through the living room and den to the deck. "Come meet my parents."

A crowd milled around a cloth-covered serving table near the back wall of the house. A large variety of hors d'oeuvres filled the table, stuffed shrimp, a cheese tray with crackers, little sandwiches, pastry balls stuffed with some kind of seafood, thin slices of ham with melon and figs, and chocolate-dipped strawberries. Over it, colorful balloons hung from a banner which read: HAPPY BIRTHDAY, SANDY. A bar stood on the opposite side of the wooden structure nearer the trees.

She led him to the edge of the deck to an attractive woman in her late-forties standing next to a tall, dark-haired man. Ryan lifted his gaze above the towering fir trees to the magnificent sight of Mount Rainier.

"Mom, Dad, this is Ryan Reid. He's the guy who rescued me from the earthquake."

He saw the resemblance when Mrs. Arrington held out her hand to him with a warm smile of greeting. "It's so nice to meet you, Ryan. Thanks for coming to Sandy's aid."

If this woman was as gracious as Sandy, he figured he would like her. "My pleasure."

"Ryan, this is my dad." She turned to the towering man with piercing dark eyes standing beside her mother.

"How do you do, sir?" Ryan stuck out his hand hoping he didn't present a wet and clammy grip.

"Hello, Ryan. Sandy tells me you're a teacher." Her father gave him a weak shake.

"Yes, sir." His voice wobbled. How could he make a good impression on a man like this? The doctor probably perceived him as dirt under his feet, his position so much higher than Ryan's. "I teach first grade with the school district." The annoying habit of biting the inside of his cheek reminded him of his nerves. He braced for the man's comments.

Dr. Arrington stared at him, his brow furrowed. "I've never understood why a man would want to teach primary school. Though I suppose it's less demanding than the higher grades."

Ryan's pulse raced. The doctor's scrutiny wore on him. "First grade is probably the most significant year for a child, the foundation for the entire educational process. In particular, laying the initial groundwork for the development of the skill of reading." He hoped he sounded intelligent enough for this man.

"How valuable for small children to have a male figure to relate to," Mrs. Arrington said.

"I guess if you want to play nursemaid to a bunch of kids..." Dr. Arrington looked over his shoulder at the intern who strolled toward them. "Ah, Jason. Welcome. Ryan, Sandy's gentleman friend, Jason Jeffries. He's a doctor at the hospital."

"How's your car running, Ryan?" Jason turned to give Dr. Arrington a vigorous hand-shake.

Ryan determined to ignore the remark. It wasn't hard to recognize a dig when he heard it.

Jason stood by Sandy's side and put his arm around her waist, pulling her closer to him. "Happy birthday to the most beautiful woman in the world. Not going to tell your age, I presume."

She didn't comment, only smiled up at Jason.

Ryan comprehended more clearly now the difference between him and Sandy. They originated from two different worlds. This was her domain, and he didn't belong here. Her father made it clear he didn't respect his profession. The collar of Ryan's dress shirt itched.

"Ryan, why don't you have a drink? We've got beer, wine, mixed drinks." Mrs. Arrington gave him a friendly smile. "Here, I'll walk with you." She slipped her arm in his and led him to the bar at the opposite side of the deck. "What would you like?" She smiled up at him.

"Thank you, ma'am. I'll have a cola, please."

"Oh, don't you want a drink?"

"I don't drink alcohol. But thanks all the same." His mother was an alcoholic with an addictive personality. He could fall into the trap along with her.

"With ice, sir?" The bartender in a white shirt and black pants set a glass on the bar.

He nodded and pushed his glasses up.

"Hey, man. So, you're the guy from the earthquake." Jason approached him at the bar, his hand around Sandy. "Scotch and water, please."

"Yeah." He gaped at Jason's fingers moving on her waist. She was merely Ryan's friend. It shouldn't matter what the guy did. Ryan had no designs on her. So, what was with the twinge loping through his stomach? Probably because he didn't want to give up Sandy's friendship, and if Jason stole her away, he'd lose her.

Jason twirled her around to face him. "Hey, sweetheart, time for your birthday kiss." He moved his head down to her and held her in a kiss for longer than seemed comfortable. Ryan glanced up to discover Dr. Arrington scrutinizing the scene from across the deck, a smile on his face as he observed the intern holding his daughter in an embrace. When his gaze slid to Ryan, the smile became a smirk.

The doctor probably saw him as some kind of threat to Jason's relationship with Sandy. From the look on Dr. Arrington's face, he must be confident Jason won the battle. Ryan didn't want any part of this war. His jangled nerves imprisoned him, and he needed to escape.

Sandy seemed to tolerate the kiss and attention from Jason without much objection. If she loved Ryan, did Jason's affection mean anything to her? Maybe she was trying to make him jealous. In his case it wouldn't work.

The intern finally let her go but held on to her hand and retrieved his drink from the bar. Ryan caught the vengeful glance Jason cast his way as Sandy took a few steps back, pushing a strand of hair out of her eyes.

Dr. Arrington moved toward Ryan and looked at his wife. "Victoria, don't you think you better take care of some of your other guests?"

"Excuse me." With a half-smile, Mrs. Arrington headed toward the hors d' oeuvres table.

Drink in hand, Jason ambled over to Ryan, pulling Sandy along. "I hear you're a teacher. Don't think a real man would want to spend much time with those little monsters." He glared at Ryan.

Sandy pulled her hand away from Jason and gave him an angry stare.

"Jason, how could you say something like that?"

"Aw, Ryan's a good sport. He knows I'm kidding, right?" Jason downed the rest of the scotch and water.

The intern had it in for him. The guy was half-drunk and acting like a jerk. How ironic, though. He unknowingly touched on a secret no one knew, a secret he couldn't tell even Sandy. Was he like other men?

Dana Feldner thought he looked different. *Okay, say it. Gay.* Did this guy see the same thing in him? The thought heaved discomfort on his shoulders, becoming heavier by the moment. His only option was to leave.

"Uh, Sandy. I need to go. Sorry I can't stay longer, but I've got plans with my uncle."

Jason shrugged and walked to the bar.

Sandy pulled at a strand of hair as she blew out a breath. With a furrowed brow, she looked up at him. "Ryan, I am so sorry—"

"It's okay." He paced toward Mrs. Arrington at the food table. "Thank you so much for having me."

Mrs. Arrington caught his arm. "I wish you wouldn't run off."

"If the man needs to go, let him go, Victoria." Dr. Arrington's voice boomed.

Ryan trudged down the wooden steps of the deck into the side yard and toward the front of the house. None too soon, he spotted his car and increased his pace.

"Ryan."

He spun around at Sandy's breathy voice.

She picked up her step as she neared, her boyfriend nowhere in sight. "Please wait. I'm so sorry. They were horrid. I don't know what got into them, especially Jason."

"Forget it." He arrived at his car and opened the door. A quick brush of his hand over his hair didn't alleviate his frustration. He stared at the grass and in slow motion turned to face her. "I don't belong in your world. Don't you see that?"

"Ryan, you led me to the world where I belong, one where God resides."

"What do your parents think?"

"About my becoming a Christian?"

"Yes."

She ran her hand over her forehead and stared at the ground. "They don't know. I told them I went to church, that's all. I'm not sure if they'd understand." She twisted her fingers into knots.

"I never told my mother either when I connected with God. But she figured it out." He turned his face toward the trees.

"What led you to the decision?" Her eyes widened. "I've wanted to ask you for a while."

She already knew so much about him. Could he trust her knowing the events which led to his salvation? Yet, he could never tell her about the encounter with Allen. He looked down at his shoes and up again. "I was a senior in high school and lived alone."

"Where did you live?"

He reeled, knowing he'd reveal his humble beginnings to her. "In a government housing project." Doubt inundated him. Maybe he shouldn't have begun the story. His gaze fell on the pink and orange blooms of the azalea bushes near the walkway.

A deep breath spurred him on. "I had a friend from school, Allen Cantereni." He cringed at the sound of his name. "We were stupid eighteen-year-olds who didn't have two nickels to rub together. Every young man needs wheels, right? We decided to steal a car." He dared a quick glance at her. "A stupid decision."

"You were young."

"We hotwired a Ford Explorer in the parking lot of Albertson's. Allen got scared, so I took off for Seattle alone." He wiped perspiration off his forehead with the back of his hand.

She ran her fingers along his shoulder, her voice husky. "It's okay, Ryan."

"It didn't take long for the owner to report the car stolen. The cops stopped me, and I was arrested." He paced beside his car. "I guess God was looking out for me even then because I only spent one night in jail." He kicked at a rock on the driveway. "My case was assigned to an accountability board, and they sentenced me to community service. Thank God the offense didn't go on my record. I wouldn't have a teaching certificate today."

"God cared a lot about you."

He gave her a half smile. "I used to go to Rainier Park three or four times a week to pick up trash and pull weeds after school. New Day is across the street, as you know. Bill Bauer, the youth pastor, visited me while I worked. And once he brought some of the guys in the youth group to help me. He invited me for a meal at the church almost every week. Finally, the guys started picking me up at my apartment for youth meetings. I gave my life to the Lord one night at a service. Everything changed then." *Almost everything.*

"Oh, Ryan." Sandy kept her gaze on him, even as tears trailed down her cheeks. "To see how God worked in your life..." She covered her face.

Ryan lifted her hands and squeezed them. "Thank you for believing in me. I don't deserve it."

"I don't know how you can say that." She reclaimed a hand and wiped at the tears.

Ryan brushed the remaining moisture away. "Sandy, I..." Something inside of him flamed. Had his pulse quickened? He lowered his hand, and the feeling died.

"What separates us? I'd never betray you. Your darkest secrets would stay right here." She touched a palm over her heart.

How could he tell her? He had faith in her friendship, but what would she think of him if she knew? Not yet—he couldn't tell her yet.

"Ryan." Her eyes pleaded with him. "Please trust me with whatever it is."

He cast his gaze to the heavens. Was God trying to push him into making a decision? To tell her? "There's so much more to me, things you'll never understand. I don't understand them myself."

"Is it money? I don't care about that."

He looked into her dark eyes. "Even if I came from wealth, if I earned the money your father makes, I couldn't give you what you need."

"If you'd tell me, maybe we could work it out together."

He shook his head. "I care about you, Sandy. I really do, but I can't talk about it." He needed her, even loved her as a friend. But how would he know if he'd ever have romantic feelings for her?

Tears filled her eyes again, and he turned to get into his car.

"Ryan..." Her breathless call caused him to look up.

"I need to go." He closed his door and drove past her around the circular drive. A glance in his rearview mirror revealed her running toward the house.

Jason met her halfway and opened his arms.

She fell into his embrace and reached for his neck.

Jason looked up with a smug smile on his face.

Chapter Twelve

Ryan threw on jeans and a dark brown tee shirt. He glanced out the window of his bedroom. Not a cloud in the sky. Perfect day for the Vacation Bible School trip to Northwest Trek. He grabbed a bowl of cereal then wandered down the hall and the three flights of stairs to the front entrance of the apartment.

If he had time afterward, he'd go by church again and check on the construction. He'd probably see workers laying the cement foundation at this early point. But it was a start.

The woody scent of Washington air filled his lungs. A day off from CF Hardware brought relief. He got into his car. *Good, plenty of gas.*

He regretted he'd left Sandy in tears at her party two weeks ago. Now he began to understand. She needed to be held, to be kissed. But not by that jerk, the intern. Yet Ryan couldn't give her the attention. Did he dare admit it? The doctor could make her happier than Ryan ever could.

When he arrived at church, an orange school bus waited on the blacktop in front. Mrs. Sizemore stood out front with a group of noisy first graders, some hopping and dancing around.

"Okay, kids, get on the bus and fill up the seats in the back first," she said.

Ryan chuckled as he walked up. Mrs. Sizemore was a brave woman.

"Hi, Ryan. Thanks for volunteering to help out today. We studied the story of Noah's Ark this week in VBS and thought a field trip would be a valuable culmination." She smiled and motioned at a little girl. "It seems I'm always prodding Amy to keep up. She's last in line every time."

"I see you survived the week. Do I need my lasso for any who might attempt to escape?" He surveyed the group of children, an enormous smile on his face. Kids, now he was in his realm.

"These are good children." The teacher positioned her hand at the side of her mouth as she laughed. "Between you and me, we better keep an eye on Charles and Tommy. They're two rambunctious boys." She pointed at the last two boys in line in front of Amy.

"Right. Those two won't leave my sight. I'll put them in the seat by me." Ryan stared at the youngsters. "Is that Tommy Friedman with Charles?"

"Yes, do you know him?"

Ryan tensed. He cared for little Tommy, but what would Maggie say if she knew he accompanied her son on a field trip? "He was one of my students last year."

"Oh, okay. Then you're already acquainted with him. Well, all the kids have nametags with a picture of an animal. You've got one too." She handed Ryan a plastic covered card with his name and a lion on it.

"Does that mean I'm king of the jungle now?" He smiled as he pinned it to his shirt.

"Well, of course. We have two more helpers. Greg Aldridge, the bus driver, and Sandy Arrington."

He straightened his spine. Sandy. Would she even speak to him?

The sound of children's laughter met his ears when he climbed the stairs at the front of the bus. To snake through the aisles edging past joyful kids was a familiar challenge, one he relished. Finally, a seat in the middle of the bus. He glanced up and caught his breath. Sandy sat in the seat across the aisle with two little girls. He shifted toward her. "Hey."

"Hello, Ryan." She paused to take a breath. "These are my two new friends, Anita and Stephanie." The girls smiled up at her. "I didn't know you'd volunteered today."

"Hello girls. Yeah, Greg asked me a couple of months ago." He pulled his knees against the seat in front of him. Would Mrs. Sizemore pick up on the tension between them?

Charles and Tommy pushed their way down the aisle as they shoved to the back of the bus.

"Hey, guys, come over here and sit by me." He patted the empty seat.

Charles scowled as he moved from the last seat to sit with Ryan.

"How ya doing, Tommy? Enjoying your summer?"

His former student gave him a wary look and scooted down beside Charles.

The bus wrenched and made a slow exit from the church parking lot. The kids' voices added to the clamor of the engine. Two boys in front scooted across the aisle to sit in an empty seat.

Greg turned the steering wheel to the right and glanced up in his rearview mirror. "You kids sit down unless you want me to stop the bus and speak to you."

Ryan snickered to himself. Somebody besides himself disciplining kids.

The bus weaved along the winding country road past lofty Douglas firs and dozens of farms. After the twenty-mile drive, they pulled in next to the wooden framed structure at the entrance of the park with the name "Northwest Trek" carved into the wood near the roof.

Mrs. Sizemore stood and faced the wiggling kids. "Our group is first to take the tram around the park to view the animals. Stay with your assigned leader—me, Ryan, Greg, or Sandy." She smiled and turned to exit the bus. The kids followed her off with a minimum of pushing.

Charles, in Ryan's group, made a valiant attempt to run in the direction of a wooden moose next to the entrance sign. "Hey, hey, Charles. You need to stay with me." Ryan grabbed his hand.

Four groups of first graders galloped under the timbered arches painted with images of bear, elk, buffalo, antelope, and peacocks and paraded down the path to the tram and through the turnstiles.

A tram with Plexiglas windows waited. The driver smiled and waved to the kids.

Sandy's group climbed on first. She moved her four children toward the rear of the vehicle, seating one child with her and the other three together in the seat behind.

Ryan herded his bunch, Charles and Tommy and two more boys, on the other side of the aisle. "Hey Sandy, what a concept. The kids are behind bars and the animals roam free," he laughed.

She gave him a weak smile and turned around to the girls behind her. "Now don't get up."

After the other two groups boarded, the guide flipped a switch on his microphone. "Okay, children. The tram follows the road through the various habitats. Watch closely because you may see bison, deer, wolves, and possibly a bear. Or even rabbits, goats, and antelope. Keep your eyes open. Let's see who can find the newborn babies."

He repositioned his cap on his head. "Now listen up. I don't want to see anyone standing at any time. That's for your safety. On occasion, animals get curious about the tram, but there's no danger. The windows are down so you can see better but do not stand or put your arms outside the car. Enjoy your ride."

The tram lurched forward down the winding road. An elk lay in the open grassy space bordered by a stand of evergreens. The environment evolved into a forest of Douglas fir with ferns growing between the trees. About a hundred yards away, a black bear rested under the wide trunk of an evergreen.

"Wow, look at the bear." Charles tripped over Ryan's feet as he shoved toward the window.

"I see it. Charles and Tommy, you boys trade places with me and sit by the window so you can see better. Let's spot some more animals." Ryan scooted toward the aisle.

"Anita, sit down." Sandy echoed his orders. "I don't want anyone falling."

"I want to pet the bison." Tommy poked at Ryan.

"When the tram stops, we can get a closer look, but you can't pet them. They're dangerous. Sit down now, Tommy."

The tram came to a halt at the bison habitat. Two furry creatures lay sunning in the grassy open field. "The bison is an animal native to the United States. Look carefully and you'll see a couple of reddish-brown calves." The guide raised the volume on his PA system. "They can weigh over two thousand pounds and have a long dark shaggy coat in—"

A scream sliced through the air. "Oh, Amy, no, no." Mrs. Sizemore shrieked as she pointed to Amy Sanchez behind the tram walking on the grass.

A thousand-pound bison snorted and plodded toward her as if sensing a threat.

The hair on Ryan's neck stood up. How had the little girl gotten out of the tram? If he didn't do something, Amy could be crushed to death.

Ryan jumped out of his seat and ran to the back of the tram. His heart sank into his shoes. Windows were open wide enough for her to crawl out.

He didn't have time to go up front and out the door. If he lowered the window all the way down, he could crawl through.

Ryan jumped down on the dirt road and inched toward the child. "Amy, this way!" he hissed. "Turn around and run toward me." Bison were easily spooked.

"Careful, Ryan." Greg was behind him.

Ryan's gaze focused on the sharp horns on either side of the bison's massive head. The animal, confused by the action, became agitated and bellowed, his enormous nostrils expelling air.

Amy stood between the beast and Ryan and Greg. The bison began at a trot, gaining speed, running in their direction. Ryan ran forward, scooped the child into his arms then jogged backwards, his eyes on the creature. He felt strong arms go around him and pull him farther toward the tram. He slipped and landed on his backside, cradling Amy. The bison moved closer but came to a stop.

His heart pounded as he caught a frantic glance towards Greg, who struggled to his feet and yanked him and Amy along while the bison thundered toward them again. Ryan recovered his footing, and he and Greg scrambled to the tram.

"Ryan, pass her to me," Sandy hollered and extended her arms out the lowered window.

He shoved the child into Sandy's arms.

"Go. Go. Go!" Greg shouted to the tram's driver. The bus lurched forward.

Ryan hiked his foot up on the bus under the window and dove through. He turned and offered a hand to Greg, who grasped hold. Ryan pulled hard as Greg climbed through.

The bison charged the back of the tram, giving it a jolt.

Ryan held to Greg as the animal stopped in the road.

Greg clasped him in a fierce hug. "Thank you, brother."

Ryan clung to him, his eyes closed, his feelings out of control.

"Hey, it's okay." Greg pulled free. "She's safe. We're all safe."

Ryan swallowed and nodded.

Sandy held Amy in her arms. "Ryan Reid, you're the bravest man I know."

"Thank you, Lord. Thank you." Mrs. Sizemore folded her hands as the tears rolled down her face.

For a moment Ryan couldn't speak. His emotions were out of kilter. Amy's soft cries brought him from his thoughts.

"Amy, what were you thinking?" He demanded an answer from the little girl now sitting on Sandy's lap.

"I'm sorry. I wanted to see the bison better." She sobbed as Sandy hugged the child.

"Okay, okay. You're fine now." Sandy comforted the girl and stroked her dark hair. With a tissue, she mopped the tears streaming down her cheeks.

"How did you get off the bus?" Ryan asked.

She pointed to the back of the tram. "I'm sorry." She buried her face in Sandy's chest.

Ryan fell into his seat and bowed his head. *Thank you, Lord, for averting disaster.*

Greg slapped him on the shoulder. "You're my hero."

Guilt thundered down upon Ryan like the charging bison. Greg's embrace prompted an unholy desire in him. Ryan gave a shaky laugh. "Not exactly my favorite pastime, hanging out with hairy bison." He mopped the sweat off his brow then buried his shameful secret in a lonely place in his soul. Now if he could make peace with Sandy.

~*~

Sandy quivered when the bus pulled into the church parking lot.

"Thanks so much for your help." Mrs. Sizemore patted her shoulder. "VBS fieldtrips aren't supposed to be this eventful. Were you able to find out anything from Amy?"

"Yes. I put her with two other girls in the seat behind me. Amy was on the aisle and the two others were plastered against the window trying to look at the bison. Amy figured she could see better by crawling out. I can't imagine why she didn't think about the danger. I feel horrible we didn't see her."

"We can thank the Lord she's okay. I'll have to write up a report about the incident and notify the parents, but it's only for church records. The next time I take first graders on a trip, I'm going to have one escort per child." Mrs. Sizemore offered a feeble smile. "Thank goodness for Ryan and Greg."

"Those are two courageous men." Sandy never prayed so hard as when she witnessed them rescuing Amy. Her heart swelled with pride at Ryan's heroic act. "Well, see you Sunday. Try to go home and get some rest." She waved at the exhausted woman.

The last child disappeared into his parent's car at the front of the church.

Sandy strolled to the parking lot, staring at the cement walkway. The Rhodie bushes had lost their blooms, leaving a dried, colorless mass of pedals.

The vision of Ryan rescuing Amy flashed in her head. He was kind and gentle with children, his life's work to teach and nurture them. *Why does he continue to endear himself to me?*

He'd faced grave danger, a daring man yet held in an emotional stronghold by his past. She glanced up. One puffy white cloud floated close to the horizon, alone in the atmosphere. Was it as forlorn as she? Her heart longed for his touch, to hear him whisper a tender word in her ear.

"Sandy." His soft, baritone voice called behind her as she sauntered to her car. "Got a minute?"

She spun around. Her heart skipped a beat as she saw him, his deep brown eyes gazing at her as he neared.

"Thanks for helping today. I know Mrs. Sizemore appreciated it," he said.

"You're welcome." What else was she supposed to say? She turned again, making her way toward her car. To her surprise, she heard his footsteps as he followed her.

"I've missed talking to you. I'm sorry. I know I probably confuse you. I confuse myself. Can we talk?"

She faced him again. "Do we have anything to talk about?"

"Maybe not." He stopped and stared at the ground before walking away.

Tears welled in her eyes. *Why does he make it so hard, Lord?* She ambled toward her car and clicked the lock open a the hand touched her shoulder.

He was behind her again. "Yes, we do have something to talk about."

She swung around and her heart melted at the look in his eyes.

"I care about you and need you. But I know it's not all about me. I'm not much of a friend to you, Sandy." The expression of pain tore at her emotions. He brought his hand to her shoulder again and pulled her near. His arms slipped around her. "I'm sorry." He whispered in her ear.

"I don't know what to say." She closed her eyes, and her fingers followed the curve of his neck.

He stiffened and moved away from her. With a hand through his hair, he paced. "I'm trying…as hard as I know how…to fight against my past." His tone wavered, expressing his anguish and frustration. "Sandy, I don't like this thing between us..." He lowered his head and rubbed his forehead.

Whatever it was, he felt it deep inside. "I'll wait until you're ready." Ready for what? Her? She surprised herself with her words. Could she really wait until he decided to love her?

Chapter Thirteen

Ryan squinted against the sunlight when he ambled out of the hardware store. Good. He had a few daylight hours left after his shift. For once, he wasn't exhausted. He spotted his car in the next row when his pocket vibrated with a call. "Hello, Mr. Clark."

"Ryan, I'm in the pastor's office. Do you suppose you could drop by later this afternoon?" Was it Ryan's imagination or did he hear an edge of tension in his voice?

"Yeah, I'm leaving work right now. I can be there shortly."

"Fine. See you then." *In Pastor's office.* What did they want to discuss? Probably something about construction of the annex.

Ryan got in the car. With closed eyes, he rubbed his forehead. A picture of Sandy when they talked in the church parking lot flashed through his mind. Feelings for her had deepened, as a friend. When he'd held her in his arms after the fieldtrip, she yielded to him, her warm breath falling on his neck. But he couldn't deny the uncomfortable sensation. Yet, this time her embrace hadn't felt as awkward.

After he moved from her, he knew she wanted him to stay close. She felt desire he didn't and maybe never would. His secret had almost escaped his lips then.

The drive from CF Hardware to church was short, less than ten minutes. After his visit in Pastor's office he'd drop by the construction site again. Viewing the progress excited him and brought him hope. His and Greg's vision was now a reality.

Ryan strolled toward the front entrance of the church. No greeters in the foyer today. The door to the pastor's office stood ajar. Ryan tapped a couple of times and poked his head in. Mr. Clark sat in a chair in front of the wide desk opposite Pastor.

His principal stood and shifted toward him. "Hello, Ryan. Come in." With a warm smile, he pointed to the chair beside his. "Thanks for stopping by. I know you just got off work."

"No problem. I was planning on visiting the construction site anyway.

I assume that's what we're talking about." He smiled at Pastor Netherton and slipped into the seat.

Mr. Clark nodded and sat down beside Ryan. "Good news. We've received a few substantial donations, and interest in the project has increased. Thank the Lord. But that's not what we wanted to talk about." Mr. Clark glanced at Pastor Netherton and at him.

Pastor smiled and focused on Ryan. "We wanted to thank you for your brave rescue of Amy Sanchez on the VBS trip. You and Greg literally saved her life." He appeared to search Ryan's face as if he attempted to discover something.

"I did what any other man would've done. I praise God she's safe." He looked from Mr. Clark to Pastor.

"Unfortunately, there's another problem." Pastor stroked his chin as he cast his gaze on Ryan.

"What do you mean?" Ryan said.

Mr. Clark turned in his chair to face Ryan. "I told Pastor about how we had to keep Tommy Friedman in first grade again." The man rested an ankle over his knee. "That has no bearing on church business except Mrs. Friedman came to me with an ugly accusation, really a rumor I think she wants to spread. I'm sure she'd disappointed her son failed first grade."

Ryan furrowed his brow and stared at his principal. Would his suspicions about what she said be confirmed, the words he'd overheard in the lounge at CF Hardware?

"Ryan, Mrs. Friedman said she objected to you working in a church setting with her son because you're…uh…gay."

Blood buzzed in Ryan's ears. It was happening. Really happening.

Mr. Clark continued. "Now, we're not buying her accusation, of course. And even if it were the case, I set her straight about our church. We hate the sin but love the sinner. I explained that all of us have done wrong and fallen short of God's standards, whether we've lied, stolen something, committed sexual sin, or murdered."

Pastor folded his hands in front of him. "Sinners of all kinds are welcome here though we don't condone or excuse wrong behavior. In fact, we offer help and healing. If a gay person who's seeking restoration and change wants to worship with us, he or she is more than welcome."

Mr. Clark patted Ryan's shoulder. "As your principal, I understand why Tommy's mother might say this. She's probably trying to blame you for her son's failure."

Pastor scrunched his eyebrows. "Ryan, you need to know what she's alleging, to guard against any other repercussions of her lies." His eyes glistened with compassion. "Jesus said to be as shrewd as snakes and as innocent as doves. What she's claiming is merely gossip. But stories can get out of control."

A sick knot formed in Ryan's stomach. Gossip destroyed people's reputations. And this time, there was a shred of truth.

"Pastor Netherton and I want you to be aware of it." Mr. Clark tapped his fingers on the edge of the desk.

Ryan's minister rose from his chair. "I'm your pastor. You love the Lord, and I've always known you to be a solid Christian man. Jack and I support you and are here for you. I'm sorry we had to discuss this garbage. We both love you." He reached out his hand to shake Ryan's.

Ryan's heart turned to ice. Dana passed on information to Maggie, and now she was spreading the rumor even farther, to his church. *Lord, how is this happening?* "I...I don't know what to say." He heaved himself to his feet.

"Look, Ryan, let's pray about this." Mr. Clark bowed his head. "Lord, we know You don't allow us to suffer more than we're able to bear. Please bring wisdom to my brother Ryan in dealing with this lie. Protect us from the evil one. In Jesus name. Amen."

Ryan did need shelter from evil, but had Maggie really lied? Was he gay? "Thank you. I guess I'll make a visit to the site now. If there's nothing else."

"No. We'll meet soon concerning the annex. Thanks for coming in." Mr. Clark shook Ryan's hand.

He stumbled out of Pastor's office and trudged through the front entrance. Around the side of the building and one hundred yards beyond, the construction site appeared. He gulped a breath of clean air. If one could drown in humiliation, he'd be dead. Did Mr. Clark and Pastor believe the rumor?

But what about himself? Did he believe it? *Lord I'm powerless over this. You know I don't want to walk in this lifestyle. But for someone else to associate me with it...*

The cloak of dark, cloying fear wrapped around him. Even if Pastor and Mr. Clark didn't believe it was true, the rumor was close enough to a personal truth he'd do anything to keep hidden forever.

As if his shoes had brakes, he came to a halt. Though he wanted with all his heart to obey God, would temptation overtake him someday? Would he commit the sinful act despite his determination not to?

The building site was deserted now—workers gone home. Not too much progress. Two-by-fours created empty frames waiting for concrete to be poured. Exposed nails lay scattered on the ground. A crane remained parked to the side of the church next to a pile of I-beams. No buzzing of saws and men in hard hats right now. A generator sat useless near the crane.

The annex lay unfinished, barely even started. Doubt began to niggle him. What if the gym never got finished after all? All kinds of problems could crop up. Future lack of funds. Objections by disgruntled congregation members. Though he'd been hopeful before, his heart broke, and he sank to his knees on the soft dirt. He couldn't fight the growing feeling of defeat. This project would be a failure, like his life.

~*~

Phillip Arrington leaned back in his black leather chair and propped his feet on top of his elegant mahogany desk. The poster on his wall, a color representation of the human heart, captured his attention. His gaze traveled from the Aortic to the Pulmonary Valve. The heart—such a marvel, but the heart could steer people in the wrong direction too. Like with Sandy.

An impression annoyed him. His beautiful, intelligent daughter showed more interest in that nuisance Ryan Reid than he'd first realized. Here every other word lately was about Ryan—how he saved a little girl on a church outing or how he was involved in some building project. If she mentioned Jason half as much as she did the jerk, he'd be happy. He buzzed his office manager. "Susan, when's my next patient?"

"Looks like your next one is…in fifteen minutes."

"Thank you, Susan. Hold my calls." He might cook up something to discourage the creep. But he had another idea, too. He reached down and opened the bottom drawer on the left side of his desk, feeling the contents. Not there. He dug deeper. His hand made contact with a thick paperback book and retrieved the phone directory for Cedar Fork and surrounding area. Flipping through, he found the yellow pages.

He'd learned to go after what he wanted. To live up to his wealthy father's expectations had been imperative. It was the only way he could earn his love and respect. Performance was key.

Phillip rubbed his forehead. A day years ago pressed on his mind. He'd asked his friend to come home with him after school to play, a buddy from class. Maybe his clothes weren't as nice, but what did he care? Jamie could pitch and catch a ball, and he wanted to practice with Phillip. More than Phillip's own father ever did.

He'd never forget the lecture from his dad, heard the words even now. "The kid's father is a janitor. My son doesn't associate with those kinds of people. Now go to your room and think about it."

Lady luck and hard work had been good to him overall. A beautiful home, a gorgeous wife and daughter. He wanted other children, but Victoria's endometriosis put an end to their dream. One thing he couldn't control.

He'd achieved the status and the material things which made his father proud. Now, he wanted the same for Sandy, the delight of his life.

She was a delicate flower. He celebrated the day she graduated as a registered nurse, but he wanted her to go on to medical school. There was still the possibility. If he could eliminate any entanglements in her life, get rid of obstructions in her way.

That schoolteacher, Reid, he was such a distraction. A waste of his daughter's valuable time.

If he could pick a husband for her, Jason Jeffries would be the man. Hadn't he and Victoria been friends with Jason's parents since Sandy and Jason were in elementary school? The family had money, Mr. Jefferies a prominent banker. Jason was on his way to success with a first-class career in medicine. If Sandy chose not to go to med school and decided to marry Jason, she wouldn't have to keep working. If she married the loser, she'd be forced to slave the rest of her life as a lowly nurse.

He found the page he searched for and ran his finger down the length of it. Toward the bottom, he tapped on an entry. Bradley Truelock, Private Detective. There had to be something he could dig up on the creep, Ryan Reid.

Sandy might say the teacher was a mere friend, but a father's intuition told him differently.

He sat up straight in his chair. The corners of his mouth turned up. Sandy had said he worked at CF Hardware during the summer. The information and his name would provide all he needed to get the good-for-nothing out of her life. Everyone had a little dirt on their hands. He'd pay the detective to dig deep for it.

He picked up the phone and punched in the numbers. "Hello. Yes. Mr. Truelock. This is Dr. Phillip Arrington."

Chapter Fourteen

"How ya doing, Larry?" Ryan filed past the main checkout area to pick up flyers from the information desk to deliver to aisle twenty.

Larry nodded and crooked his finger. "Can I see you a minute in my office?"

Ryan didn't like his tone. The situation with Maggie was resolved. Surely, she wasn't trying to resurrect it. His chest tightened as he followed the burly man. He waved at a cashier waiting for the next customer.

Larry shut the door and motioned for him to sit down, then cleared his throat. "I don't want to meddle in people's personal lives, but I think you need to know about the rumor going around." He rested his weight on the side of his desk.

Ryan cringed. Not again. He knew what Larry was going to tell him. His knuckles turned white with his grip on the arms of the chair.

"I wouldn't ordinarily mention something like this, but because of the occurrence with Maggie, I feel it's better to tell you. The rumor has it, you have a proclivity for…uh, the same sex, if you get what I'm saying. Now, I couldn't care less either way. Wanted to let you know. You tend to keep your personal life to yourself. Good. You don't want to give those two women any ammunition."

Should he deny it? Maybe the less said the better. His stomach was an acrobat inside his body. "Uh, I want you to know I intend to do my job at CF Hardware and mind my own business." Ryan stood to leave. Maybe he should confront Maggie and Dana, tell them to back off.

"Go ahead and give Louise a break in the garden section." Larry turned around to his desk and picked up a pile of papers.

His heart pounded with Larry's warning. Did he do the right thing in keeping his mouth shut? Since he didn't refute what Larry said, his boss probably thought it was true.

Ryan stared at the concrete floor as he left Larry's office and plodded in the direction of the outdoor center. He righted a toppled Boxwood bush and approached Louise at the cash register.

"Isn't it about time for your break?" He pointed to the employees' room.

Louise straightened the apron which barely reached around her middle and gave him a warm, matronly smile. She had been quick to accept him, to mother him when he started working here. How different would his life have been if his own mother had acted like Louise. She even patted his arm as she passed him. "Sure thing, sweetie. Back in twenty."

He sorted through a pile of receipts and glimpsed the list of trees on new inventory.

"Hello, Ryan." A deep voice yanked him from his work.

He glanced up. Dr. Arrington. How had the man remembered his name, much less recognized him?

"Hello, sir. Good to see you again." What was the man doing here? He was the last person he would expect to shop at CF Hardware, especially in the garden center. Didn't he have a gardener to pick out his plants?

"I need some pampas grass for the corner near my rock planters in the backyard. Could you help me?" Dr. Arrington avoided eye-contact. Instead his gaze darted around the area.

"Well, sure." Ryan stroked his chin. "You made a good choice. Pampas grass is a hardy addition to a yard and is outstanding as an accent plant. We carry white or pink."

Was this man for real? Ryan couldn't imagine he actually came to pick up a plant for his yard. *I know why he's here.* Ryan caught his breath. More than likely, the doctor wanted to check him out. Dr. Arrington hadn't appeared to be any too fond of Ryan.

"White would work best." The doctor blinked when his eye twitched.

Ryan's lips puckered to the side as he chewed his cheek. "This way."

He led the doctor past patio furniture and stopped at the pampas grass, their large stalks covered by thick plumes.

"I'll take three." Now Dr. Arrington directed his gaze to Ryan.

Ryan positioned the plants on a flatbed cart and pushed them to the cash register. "You've got a deal today. These are three for ten-ninety-nine." As if a man like Sandy's father needed a deal. "I'll ring you up."

Dr. Arrington pulled out a twenty and set it on the counter.

"Need any help to your car?" Ryan's voice squeaked, and he cleared his throat as he counted out the change.

"Yes, please." Dr. Arrington folded his arms in front of his chest and marched out into the sunshine. *He assumes I'm following him. Not even looking back.*

Ryan pulled the cart into the parking lot. If Sandy drove a Beemer, what did her father use?

"Here it is." The doctor stopped at a late model, orange Hummer.

Ryan swallowed hard as Dr. Arrington raised the trunk of the cargo compartment. Ryan slid the plants in. "These should be okay until you get them home."

"All right. Thank you." He slammed the cargo door shut and twisted to Ryan with folded arms. "You say you're a teacher?"

Here it came, the fifth degree. "Yes, sir. I work at CF Hardware during the summer and at night."

"Two jobs, huh?"

"Yeah, I'm paying off some college loans."

"You know, Ryan. I have a feeling my daughter's quite taken with you. Tell me more about yourself."

He gulped, his heart racing. "Uh, what do you want to know?" *Look, Dr. Arrington, I know what you're thinking, but your daughter is safer with me than a lot of other guys. We don't need to have this talk. Save it for Jason.*

"Oh, I guess...what are your future plans?"

Did the man think Ryan a prospective son-in-law? Why did this feel like a job interview? He cracked his knuckles. With a gulp, he opened his mouth. "Not much to tell. I'm going to the university at night this fall to get a Masters in Administration. I applied for a scholarship and received it." Is that what the man wanted to hear? Ryan scratched his head.

Dr. Arrington moved around to the passenger door and leaned against it, his arms folded on his chest. "Sandy mentioned she went to church with you. Are you a religious man?"

Ryan wilted under the obvious cross-examination as the perspiration formed on his forehead. He was a caged animal. But the man asked a question, and his conscience demanded he answer. "I'm a believer in Jesus, the Messiah. I've been a Christian for eight years." Saying the words brought courage.

"Well, I certainly hope you're not filling my daughter with those fairytales. I'm warning you..." The man glared at him.

"I'd never force any beliefs on her, but I think Sandy's old enough to make her own decisions." Ryan looked at his watch. "I've got to get to work, sir. Maybe we can continue this another time."

Dr. Arrington leaned closer with narrowed eyes, his daunting gaze issuing a threat. "I'm advising you, Reid. You better not feed my daughter any of your malarkey or I'll..." He turned around, got in his car, and slammed the door. The motor revved, and the orange box raced out of the parking lot.

The doctor may have assumed he won this round, but if the man thought Ryan would back away when it concerned Sandy's relationship with God, he was in for a surprise.

~*~

Sandy strolled into the sunroom overlooking the backyard. A rare day. Mom was home. "Hi. What's up?" She plopped into the wicker chair across from her mother and drew her knees to her chest.

"I've got a garden club meeting in a little while. Guess I better ask some questions about Pampas Grass bushes. Your father called and said he bought three of them. I can't understand what possessed him. What are your plans today, sweetie?" Mom brushed a hand over her jeans and straightened her silk blouse.

"I work tonight. Maybe I'll go to the gym in a while." Or maybe she'd find Ryan. What were the chances?

"You okay, honey?" Mom reached over and patted Sandy's hand. "I'm a little concerned about you. You don't seem like your usual perky self."

"Thinking about a guy." She pushed a smile in place.

"I've noticed you haven't been out with Jason lately." Mom folded her hands over her waist.

"We're both busy at the hospital." What a lie. She turned him down twice in the last week, giving him the excuse, she was tired. In her daydreams every moment was spent with Ryan Reid.

"Don't you want to invite Jason for dinner one of these nights?" Mom pulled a leaf from the English Ivy hanging in a pot next to the window.

"Let me think about it." She had no desire to spend time with Jason. They'd end up talking about medicine.

"What about the good-looking guy with the gorgeous brown eyes? The one you invited to your birthday party. What was his name? Ryan?"

Her heart stopped. How could she explain to her mother he introduced her to a new way of life, in Christ? Dad was so anti-Christian, and Mom never voiced an opinion.

"He's a friend." She gazed out the window at the brick walkways sculpted in and out of the Hybrid Fescue. The English primrose on the side of the house was in full bloom.

"I know a thing or two about love, sweetheart. Your father and I had strong feelings…once. I saw how you looked at him. If it wasn't love, I don't know what it was."

Sandy jerked her gaze to her mother. "I guess you know me pretty well, but the truth is, he's not interested in me, not like that."

Her mother laughed. "What? Is he gay? How could any man not fall for a beautiful young lady like you?"

"Ryan's complex, Mom. I can't begin to tell you how he thinks. Please don't tell Dad about this." She searched her mother's eyes.

"Of course, not, honey. This is between you and me." Mom cleared her throat. "But I think your dad believes you have feelings for him. He's probably going to discourage you from a relationship because he's not impressed by his career." Mom glanced at her watch.

"Well, I don't think Dad has anything to worry about." She swiped at her eyes, her back to her mother.

"In any case, I need to leave. If you ever want to talk, I'm here." She blew her a kiss. "See you tonight, honey. I love you." Mom headed off in the direction of the garage.

Sandy ascended the circular staircase to her room. After donning her gym clothes, she trudged to her car. How had life become so complex after the earthquake—the day she met Ryan Reid?

Chapter Fifteen

Tap, tap.
Ryan rolled onto his back. Did he hear a sound or was he dreaming?
Knock, knock.
There it was again. He turned on his side, pushed up on one elbow, and squinted at the clock. Seven in the morning.
Bang, bang.
Who would knock on the door at this hour on Sunday morning? He swiveled his legs around the side of the bed and sat up. His running shorts dangled from the arm of the plastic chair beside his bed. He stepped into them, rubbed his eyes, and stumbled into the living room.
Bang, bang, bang.
The sounds vibrated through his befuddled brain. The chain lock remained attached, and he opened the door a couple of inches to peer out and discover the identity of the early morning visitor.

He let his hands drop and leaned against the doorframe as he stared at the pathetic, emaciated woman in the hall. "Mom, what are you doing here?"

A painful mix of emotions knifed through his stomach. Grief to see the disheveled woman, pity for who she'd become, regret things weren't different, and apprehension about her visit.

He unchained the bolt. His mother looked tired, older than her forty-seven years, her dark brown hair a tangled mess. Black circles marred her once pretty eyes.

"Ryan, honey, I've come for a visit. I got on a bus in Puhoma and rode all the way here. Only thing, I used my last buck." She stumbled through the door, her eyes darting from one side of the room to the other. The smell of alcohol and stale cigarette smoke hung like a cloud over her.

"How are things in Puhoma?" He opened his eyes wide and plodded into the living area.

"Oh, you know, the same. Pete kind of kicked me out and told me not to come back without some dough. I think I'm going to stay in Cedar Fork for a while and look for work." She pulled out a cigarette from her worn cloth purse.

He furrowed his brow. "Mom, not in here. I'm allergic to the smoke."

"Oh, all right." Her polka dot skirt clung to her legs as she staggered into the living area. "Your Uncle Frank here?" She wandered over to the old bookcase, drawing her fingers along the edge.

"Yeah. In his bedroom asleep. Mom, I got a scholarship to get my masters." He blurted out his news like a little kid. What was wrong with him?

"Well, Ryan, that's mighty nice. I'm proud of you, son." The words departed from her tongue as if it was a great burden to articulate them. "You look so much like your father. He was a cowboy, you know." She smiled, pulling at the neck of her thin brown shirt, and plopped on the couch. It gave a groan and a squeak. Her eyes drooped as she laid her head on the couch cushion.

"You never told me much about him." Ryan wanted to know more, yet fear of what he'd hear disturbed him.

"Oh, honey. People make mistakes. I guess I never should've gone to the bar that night, but he was such a handsome man with his winking belt buckle and sleek cowboy hat. Sometimes I can't get him out of my mind."

Now the subject of how he was conceived made his stomach turn. He had to change the topic. "Why are you here so early?" He dropped down next to her on the couch.

She raised her voice. "Now why shouldn't I be?" She glared at him and rolled her head to stare straight ahead. "Thought I might stay a while."

Mom living here would be a disaster. "I don't know." He blew out a long stream of air. She was a different person every time he saw her. He didn't know how to read her or what to expect. Maybe the booze did that to her.

"Can't a woman come to visit her own son when she wants to?" His mother barked at him.

"Yeah, Mom, but..."

"Look, I've been having a few financial problems. I need a little money until I can get a job. Could you help me out?" She closed her eyes.

He wanted to lend her a hand, but his resources were limited. He saved every spare dime for the annex. Yet, if she was desperate, he should help her. Didn't the Bible instruct him to care for his family? But on the other hand, the Lord wanted him to use his money wisely.

The squeak of Frank's bedroom door caught his attention.

"Thelma, I thought I heard your voice." Frank emerged in a pair of jean shorts, his dark hair scruffy. "What are you doing here?"

"Don't you start with me. I need a little cash until I can get myself situated. Is it too much to ask?" She opened her eyes and rolled her head toward him.

"Hey, Thelma. Back off. Ryan and I work like dogs and don't have a spare penny. We wouldn't give it to you anyway. You'd buy booze and cigarettes with it." He put his hands on his hips as he raised his eyebrows.

"Is that the way a brother should talk to his sister?" Her eyes drooped closed, then she opened them with great effort. She coughed a heavy, wet cough, and seemed to lose even more energy.

"Thelma, you appall me, showing up here drunk and asking for money." Frank folded his arms on his chest and scowled at her.

Uncle Frank was right. She'd only spend it on liquor. He trusted his uncle. He'd known her a lot longer than Ryan had.

"Don't lecture me. I don't want to hear your preaching. You have no right. You're the one who taught me how to drink. What about all those nights I saw you drunk on your backside, couldn't even make it off the floor. You stupid hypocrite, you have no room to talk."

"Shut up and listen. I quit and I'm a better man for it."

"So…got religion, too, like Ryan?" Her eyes were wide now and her voice harsh.

Frank opened his mouth then closed it as he balled his hands into fists. "Thelma, Thelma." He shut his eyes and lowered his head then let out a long breath.

Ryan plodded into his bedroom and threw on his clothes. His frayed nerves couldn't take much more. His emotions played tug-a-war. He wanted his mother to embrace him and treat him like a son, yet he felt repulsion toward the woman she'd become.

What else could he do but slip down beside his bed? *Lord, how could I go on without You?* Thank God, he'd never have to face a life without Him.

The muted sounds of argument continued, along with Mom's coughing. Then the debate quieted. Ryan wasn't sure how long he'd remained in prayer. When he rose, he thought about the church service. Praise and worship, the Word, and the pastor's message would be cool water in the desert of his life.

He circled toward the knock on his door.

"Ready anytime you are." Though the arguing had quieted, Uncle Frank's voice held tension.

The loud snoring coming from the couch was hard to ignore. Ryan picked up his Bible.

"I'll drive my truck today," Frank said.

Ryan nodded and wiped his face with his handkerchief as he walked out the front of the apartment building with his uncle, crawling into the old truck.

Frank shook his head as he scooted in. "She was the last person I expected to show up on the doorstep today. The minute I saw her, I knew what she wanted. Money." He rubbed his chin. "I'm not so sure it's a good idea to leave her in there alone, but I can't see waking her now. She doesn't look well, Ryan. Not at all, and I'm sure she wouldn't want to go to church."

"Yeah, let her stay awhile, I guess." Ryan squeezed his eyes closed trying to get past the pain of seeing his mother like that.

"Sorry you had to hear all the shouting." Frank turned the key in the ignition. "There was a time when my behavior was no better. The Lord always seems to convict me of a judgmental attitude. We both need to learn to forgive her."

"I don't know, Frank. Maybe if I could get her to church..."

"Maybe. All things are possible with God." His uncle veered onto the street in front of the apartment building.

Without notice, a volcano erupted in Ryan. He banged his fist on the dash of the truck. "If things were only different with her."

"I know, buddy. All we can do is pray." Frank's soft voice brought his outburst to a steady simmer.

~*~

Ryan sneaked into the sanctuary and slipped into the last row. Seeing Sandy today would be too tough. So many tense issues at once. He stuck his nose in his Bible, slumping down on the padding of the maroon upholstery. Frank eased into the pew beside him. The soft notes of the organ soothed his anger. He put his hand on his forehead and closed his eyes.

A long breath filled his lungs as he glanced up at the stained-glass window of Jesus with the lamb on his shoulder. "Lord, my mother is a stray lamb. Please leave the ninety-nine and go get her." He ignored the remorse threatening his emotions and tried to figure out what he should do about her.

His voice joined the congregation in singing "Father I Adore You." He lifted his arm in praise and surrender to God's mighty power, his only hope. God knew he needed to hear the last song the worship team sang—" God Will Make a Way."

Pastor Netherton began in Colossians. "Bear with each other and forgive whatever grievances you may have against one another. Forgive as the Lord forgave you. And over all these virtues put on love, which binds them all together in perfect unity.

"Forgiveness is a choice. We don't do it because we feel like it, but because God's Word commands it. It's not easy, but I always think about how much God forgave when he saved me. It helps in forgiving others."

Ryan's anger and frustration seemed to melt with Pastor's words. *Lord, why does it seem like Pastor Netherton spied on me during the week? He always speaks to the issues in my life. I choose to forgive my mother.*

~*~

Frank pulled up in front of the apartment. "Your mother will probably be snoring away."

"Yeah. I wonder how long she's gonna stay." Ryan climbed the stairwell and trudged down the lengthy hall past his neighbors' doors. The key turned in the lock, and he thrust the door open. No one on the couch. "Mom, you here?"

No answer. He circled around the apartment, checking the bedrooms and bathroom. The apartment was empty.

"It's for the best." Uncle Frank set his keys on the coffee table.

"Maybe she stepped out to go for a walk." He put his hand on his forehead and paced a few steps to the kitchen and returned. The odor of cigarette smoke hung in the air.

"I'm not counting on it." Frank strolled into his bedroom.

The tension he thought he'd released at church built again in Ryan's gut. A run through Rainier Park would do him good.

The chest in his bedroom held shorts and old tee shirts. He opened the drawer and noticed the contents more rumpled than usual. An appalling thought hit him, and he dug furiously through all his clothes. The envelope with the money he'd been saving for the project should be in the bottom drawer. He'd given up buying new tires last month to save the funds. He kicked himself for forgetting to take it to church today.

After more digging, he emptied the contents of the entire dresser. His grandmother's engagement ring in the black velvet bag was there, but the money was gone. His heart sank with the realization. Then he noticed an empty, flattened envelope in the corner of the room on the other side of the bed. She must've tossed it there after taking the money.

Uncle Frank ambled into his bedroom. "I hate to tell you this, but your mother was busy while we were in church." He balled a fist and drove it into his palm. "Like an idiot, I left my wallet in the closet. You guessed it. The money's gone. I probably had two hundred dollars." Frank stared at him and shook his head.

Exasperation backfired in Ryan, seeping from his throat down to his stomach. He kicked the wall when he could no longer control himself. An obscenity came to mind, but he squelched it. "I thought I'd forgiven her this morning. And now this. What is God asking of me?"

"God will never ask more of you than you can handle. Come on. Sit on the couch with me. We're going to pray, buddy," Frank said.

Ryan could barely concentrate on his uncle's prayer, the brutal storm inside raging. The money he'd worked so hard to save would go to an alcoholic woman. Not to the project dear to his heart. How much more could Ryan take before he said to heck with everything? He had little power left with which to fight.

Chapter Sixteen

"Greg." The word resounded in the silent bedroom. The image of his soft brown eyes, the curve of his muscles, his flat stomach...Ryan shot up and closed his eyes against the powerful dream sending his emotions reeling.

"Stop." He cried out, but only he and God heard his words. He fell to his knees beside the bed. "Lord, I don't want this craving, this feeling inside. I don't know how much longer I can hold on. You didn't make me this way. Help me." With a push he stood.

He lumbered into the kitchen and glimpsed at Uncle Frank's empty bedroom.

The clock on the bookcase said nine o'clock. How had he slept so late? He shook his disheveled hair trying to rid himself of the uncomfortable haze gripping him with icy claws. Had his mother's difficult visit yesterday somehow prompted the dream?

He rummaged in the cabinet for the coffee canister. Nothing like the dark brew's earthy, smoky aroma to perk him up.

After he put on a pot, he trudged to the bedroom. A search of his closet turned up old jeans and a blue polo. No sense in dressing up on a Monday off.

Tap, tap.

Ryan tensed his shoulders. Not his mother again. Here for more money? He didn't have any left to give her.

Tap, tap, tap.

He unlocked the door then took a step back, his mouth open. Sandy.

"Hey." He smiled and unhooked the chain lock. "For some reason, you're the last person I expected."

"Hi, Ryan. I...I took a chance you'd be here."

He ran a hand through his hair. "Yeah. The store changes my schedule from week to week. I never know when I'm going to work. Come in."

"Well, I'm on my way to Kalaloch, you know, near the Hoh Rain

Forest up on the peninsula."

When she walked in from the shoddy hallway, he saw his small apartment as if for the first time and cringed. His humble surroundings paled in comparison to her elegant home. Yet as he stood to the side and Sandy wandered into the living room, no disdain touched her face. Only a bashful grin and her usual warm acceptance.

"My aunt, Mom's sister, is at her beach house for a month or so. I'd like to visit her. Would you drive with me? I don't want to make the trip alone."

He'd witnessed Sandy's fear once before during the earthquake. Did her alarm extend to a fear of driving out of town alone?

His plans for the day were nothing more than hanging out here. Why not take a drive to the beach? "Yeah, sure. Sit down." He motioned toward the decrepit couch. "I've got coffee perking. Want some?"

"Oh, no thanks." She crossed her legs, a sandaled foot bobbing in the air, a fresh sight in her jeans and soft white blouse.

He plopped down at the other end of the couch and shifted to face her.

Sandy slid her fingers through long strands of hair. "My aunt lives in Chicago. Her husband didn't come with her because his law practice keeps him busy. I haven't seen her in months." She uncrossed her legs and locked her ankles. "The drive's not too bad, about three hours up and back. I want to go out on the beaches to see the sea stacks and shallow tide pools."

"I'm glad you thought about me. Would your aunt like some fresh fruit? I went to the Farmer's Market." The idea of sailing off with Sandy to the peninsula sounded more appealing each moment.

"She'd love it." Sandy offered a smile then lowered her lashes.

"Let me grab them, and I'll be ready to go." He rose from the couch and took the bag of fresh marionberries, raspberries, and peaches out of the fridge. After pouring his coffee into a travel mug, he darted into the bathroom and picked up his bottle of aftershave, splashed some on his neck then joined her in the living room. "All set?"

With a stretch of her arms, she rose from the couch then leaned toward him and sniffed. "Mm. You smell good, reminds me of the rainforest."

Her beautiful face so near him, a feeling stirred within then faded. "My new aftershave."

He hooked the bag of fruit on his arm, coffee in hand, then Sandy followed him down the stairwell and out the door of the apartment building to the Beemer. A robin's song in the boxwood hedge lifted his heart and almost erased the memory of yesterday.

RYAN'S FATHER

~*~

His spirits soared along with the sleek BMW as they zipped through the rare country roads found only in Washington State, winding through lush hills ornamented with meadows of wildflowers and patches of evergreens. Manicured lawns embellished farmhouses, which dotted the countryside as they glided toward the coast.

Closer to Kalaloch, the Douglas fir became a lofty partition on either side of the narrow highway, obscuring the woods beyond. The trees broke, and a sparkling stream rippled over rocks and small boulders.

They rode in comfortable silence awhile. Sandy seemed quieter today than usual.

Ryan snatched a glance at her. "How is everything?"

"I started working out at the gym. The ER requires physical strength." She turned on her blinkers and passed a car. "You know, the most vital thing is to remain calm and use my head. What do you think? Am I'm capable of remaining calm?" She winked and turned to the road again.

"I'm sure you're quite capable as a nurse, but if there's an earthquake, watch out, ER." He gave her a playful poke.

His relationship with Sandy was a cozy fire on a cold, misty day in Cedar Fork. With the aroma of toasted marshmallows thrown in. Her angelic face brought him hope. She was his best friend. It'd become safe to share anything with her.

Almost anything.

In a field near the road, a mare stood nursing her foal. "I've never known anyone like you before. Sandy, I'm probably hard to get along with, but I wanted to tell you, I appreciate your friendship and you." Warmth traveled from his neck to his cheeks. He could do no better in showing her what was in his heart.

"I can say I've never had a friend quite like you." She tossed a strand of hair out of her face.

"Hey, was that a wisecrack?" He chuckled.

She lowered her voice. "I've never had such a lopsided relationship before. My feelings being so different than yours." Her cheeks shone a dark pink.

How easy it was to forget she had feelings, too. She loved him in a much different way than his regard for her, and he didn't return her affection. A wave of regret shifted from his stomach up to his heart. If he really cared about her, why couldn't he give her what she needed?

She veered off the highway onto a paved road bordered by elm and birch trees. The route snaked around to a cottage with green siding, white steps, and a railing. A striking woman wearing dark blue slacks and a red blouse reclined in a lawn chair on a wrap-around porch. Sandy parked in front.

"Aunt Molly." Sandy bounded out of the car and raced up the stairs to embrace the middle-aged woman.

He trailed her, the sack of fruit in one hand.

"Oh, Aunt Molly." She curved around to him. "This is my friend, Ryan Reid."

"Hello, Ryan. I'm so glad Sandy brought you with her." She pushed her dark, shoulder-length hair off her face.

Sandy slipped her arm around Molly's waist.

"It's very nice to meet you." He grinned and held out his hand to her.

"It's obvious what Sandy sees in you. She chose a very handsome boyfriend." She smiled and winked at her niece.

"Oh, Aunt Molly. Ryan's a friend, silly." Her face flushed.

"Well, then, he should be your boyfriend."

Guess it looked like it to Sandy's aunt. He had her fooled.

"But enough of my teasing. You two are in time for lunch—chicken Caesar salad, hot sourdough rolls, and cold iced tea."

"And Ryan brought some fresh fruit, mostly berries."

"Marionberries?"

"Yep." He nudged the bag toward her.

"I'll make a pie." She motioned for them to follow her into the cottage. Was Aunt Molly as kind and gracious as Sandy's mother?

"Sounds wonderful. I love homemade pie. Get 'um at the church socials sometimes," he said.

"Right this way. Lunch is already on the table." Aunt Molly grinned.

They followed her past a cozy sitting area with a loveseat and easy chair. A ceiling-high shelf was filled with books behind sliding glass doors.

Sandy fingered the elegant dinnerware on the cozy table set in the kitchen. "Blue Willow?"

"Yes, dear. My favorite. I've been collecting the stoneware for years. Sit down, you two."

He held the chairs for Aunt Molly then Sandy and sat in a seat across from them. He looked between the two with lifted brows. "Do you mind if I say grace?"

The answer came when Sandy smiled and nodded.

"Thank you, Lord, for this meal and bless it to our nourishment. Thank you for the hospitality. Amen." He looked up as he finished the prayer and grinned at the two women.

"Thank you, Ryan." Sandy's aunt searched his face.

"Please pass the bread, Aunt Molly. I'm starved." Sandy removed the cloth covering the brown wicker basket and helped herself. The hot roll she spread with a generous layer of butter made his mouth water.

Aunt Molly took a bite of the chicken salad then swallowed. "How are your mom and dad?" She smiled, dabbing her face with her linen napkin.

"Oh, you know. Mom's always at her club meetings and Dad, well, he keeps his office hours and tries to make his hospital visits in between." She stabbed a bite of salad.

He flinched. Only a few days ago, Dr. Arrington wasn't at the hospital or his office. Ryan tried to disguise his shudder as he remembered the man's scrutiny at CF Hardware.

"How's Cousin Linda doing?" Sandy lifted an expensive looking goblet to her lips and took a sip of tea.

"Oh, you know my dear daughter. I can't keep up with her. She travels all over the world with her job."

"She's a flight attendant, Ryan. Linda and I used to be playmates when we were younger. Spent lots of summers together."

"How's your job at the hospital?" From a cruet, Aunt Molly splashed more Caesar dressing on her salad.

"I love being a nurse. Dad's pushing me to go to medical school, but I'm happy where I am." She lavished another piece of bread with butter.

"Oh, Phillip. He has his notions. How about you, Ryan? What do you do?" She gave him a pleasant smile.

"I'm an elementary teacher." He tensed, waiting for the usual negative comment.

"Wonderful. I was a teacher until I married. We need more men in the profession." Her bright smile cheered him.

He breathed deeply. "I feel the same. Teachers certainly don't get rich, but it's a gratifying profession." He liked this woman. Not at all ostentatious like her brother-in-law.

"Well, I wish you the best." She smiled at him and reached to squeeze Sandy's hand.

He chewed a few bites of salad and exhaled a deep breath. A good meal and good company. When had he relaxed like this in the last year? He needed more of these days.

After they'd finished the meal, Aunt Molly patted Sandy's hand. "Dear, why don't you take Ryan to the beaches? Spectacular views of the ocean are only minutes north of here, as you know. Simply breathtaking. I'll make the pie while you're gone." She grasped a handful of dishes and placed them in the sink.

"Good idea. It's been years." Sandy directed her gaze to him. "Have you seen the area, Ryan?"

"Once. I went to a church camp at Terry Park south of here, and we visited several of the beaches one afternoon." He pushed back his chair and picked up the glasses, placing them alongside the other items in the sink.

"Sandy, take my camera, if you will. I would love some pictures of the tidal pools and any wildlife you spot." Aunt Molly opened the sack with the berries.

"Sure. You ready, Ryan?" They descended the steps of the porch. When they neared her car, Sandy gave him a crooked grin. "Hey. Wanna drive?"

"You mean you actually trust me?" He beamed, then his heart beat faster at the thought of driving a luxury car.

With a shake of her head, she rolled her eyes and crawled in the passenger seat. "Come on, Ryan. Let's go."

He eased into the driver's seat, pushed a button to move the seat back, and adjusted the mirror.

"Take a left at the main road." She pointed to the hydrangea bushes at the end of Molly's drive. "It's about another mile. Then turn at the sign with an arrow pointing to Indian Head Beach."

The parking lot, bathrooms, and informational signs emerged as they rounded the next curve onto the gravel side road.

She pointed to the wooden sign marking the entrance. "There's the trailhead to the beach."

The narrow path zigzagged through a growth of evergreen trees. At the end, the trees broke, revealing a breathtaking scene before them. Sea stacks, large rocks with gentle slopes, rose out of the sea. A mist formed, casting a soft blue hue on the ocean and the rocks beyond.

"Ryan," she gasped. "Look, a rainbow over the last rock in the distance." Her hand flew to her chest.

"It's outstanding." The most spectacular sight he'd ever seen lay before him. The smooth rocks of the sea stacks blending into the ocean and meeting the sky in a blue haze, like shades of watercolors melding into one hue. How could anyone miss God's hand in the creation of the earth after observing a sight like this?

The knowledge of God's greatness and power slapped against him with the force of a tsunami. God's purity and His plan for mankind would prevail despite the dismal circumstances humans created for themselves. God could mold Ryan's feelings and emotions. He could change him as surely as He changed the shape of the rocks over time. The ideas showered down on Ryan like fresh rain.

If he could have feelings toward a woman like God ordained, he would choose Sandy as his wife. He'd thought about every alternative, even considered going through with a marriage to her though the desire wasn't there. But what about their wedding night? He couldn't do that to her.

What if he acted like a man with romance on his mind—would it change his feelings, his inclination?

With the brilliant ocean as background, he turned from its beauty to face the delicate, lovely woman in front of him. In slow motion, he grasped her hand and pulled her to him. *I can do this.* Her radiant brown eyes gazed at him as he touched her cheek. *The desires will come. Make it happen.* Love, after all, was a verb, action. He yielded his lips to hers, his hand on her arm. She moved into his embrace, sliding her arms around his waist.

Please God. He held to her for a brief second then turned from the kiss and pulled away, his eyes cast down to the mossy forest floor. She was beautiful. She was his for the asking, but he was wired differently. Maybe God meant for him to stay alone.

When he looked up, she stared at him, her eyes full of wonder. He drew her to him. Holding her against him, his shoulders shook.

When he pulled away, she reached to his face, moving her finger down his cheek and gazed into his eyes. "Ryan, what happened? I need for you to tell me." Her tone pleaded with him.

"Sandy, I...I...it's too complicated. Please don't ask me to talk about it." He brushed at the tears on his face. "It's not you. It's me. I...I'm different." How could he tell her? He was appalled at what he perceived and couldn't even face it himself.

"You can tell me anything. Why won't you trust me?" Her eyes were wide as she studied his face.

"I don't understand it. I think it has to do with my mother. My feelings for her are so messed up." The words spilled out, spinning in circles. She deserved to know the truth, yet he couldn't bring himself to tell her about his unnatural feelings toward men, one man. Finally, the conclusion came to him—he had to tell her. In a day or two. Not now. Not after he'd given her this false hope. He'd lose his best friend soon enough, but he needed her today.

"Then tell me about your mother."

He grasped her arm and turned her down the path toward the car. "She showed up at the apartment yesterday. She'd been drinking. I could smell the liquor on her breath. She stole money from Uncle Frank and me while we were at church. The money she took from me was to go toward the annex." His voice wobbled, his emotions in high gear.

She saw another vulnerable side of him, and he didn't care now. He trusted her, loved her, but he couldn't muster the romantic feelings he'd hoped would emerge.

"I'm so sorry. I know things must be horrendous for you." She stopped to face him, sliding her fingers down his arm. Her touch brought comfort but nothing more. He captured her hand in his but allowed it to drop.

"I promise you. I'll tell you soon about what's going on with me. I'm sorry this was so confusing today. I..." He poured all the earnestness he felt into his words. "I wouldn't hurt you for anything in the world." She passed him a tissue, and he wiped his eyes.

"I'm a patient person. If there's ever a chance you could feel about me the way I do about you, then it will be worth the wait." She glanced down at her shoes and up at him, her eyes bright. "No matter what's keeping us apart."

His heart sank. She had the impression he was getting his thoughts straight and one day he would profess his love for her. If he had more tears, he'd cry, unashamed in front of her.

Sandy loved and respected him, but he didn't deserve it. He disgusted himself. When he'd kissed Sandy, he'd fought against the image of Greg in his arms.

~*~

Sandy drove the route home in the darkness and in silence. Ryan remained wordless as he stared out the window. He said he'd never had a friend like her, and he appreciated her. What did he mean? Probably what he said. He appreciated her for her friendship, nothing more. Why hadn't their relationship gone any further? There must be a reason. She'd find out the answer one way or the other. Life couldn't go on like this.

Yes, she wanted Ryan as a friend, but she needed him to hold her in his arms, to tell her he loved her, to caress her. The feel of his lips on hers...she needed so much more from him. And he seemed unwilling to give it to her.

An odd sensation crept along her spine. Her mother's offhanded joke replayed in her mind. The indications seemed to be there. She didn't attract him, yet he said he cared for her. He didn't have a girlfriend, didn't date as far as she knew.

Before she got saved, she believed gay people were born that way—a different kind of sexuality governed their lives. No big deal. Gays were gay and straights were straight—like her and Jason.

But after she began going to church and reading her Bible, she discovered God had another opinion. He forbade homosexuality. He called it an abomination.

What if Ryan was gay? Such a godly man. How could it be?

How would it affect her feelings for him if he was? No matter what, she'd always love him. Aching began in her heart and moved up her throat, sending hot tears to her eyes. They'd never be able to become husband and wife. Never be able to have a family together.

Her mouth went dry. Surely, he didn't have a gay relationship now. She tightened her grip on the steering wheel. She could never see him again if he did. Of course, even if he didn't, it would break her heart to continue in their friendship if Ryan couldn't be the man she needed.

A long breath escaped her lips. The gorgeous guy stared out the side window. She didn't know for sure if Ryan was gay. Maybe he wasn't.

But what if he was? She couldn't have fallen in love with a gay man. Surely not.

Chapter Seventeen

August would be here in another week. Only a little over a month before school started. Ryan parked on the side of the apartment building and switched off his headlights. With aching arms and legs, he dragged himself out of his car and trudged up the sidewalk. Ten o'clock, the latest he'd worked in a while.

Stacking boxes in the warehouse and piling lumber in the building materials department wasn't his favorite job. All he wanted was a relaxing shower and his bed.

He shooed away thoughts of Sandy at Kalaloch, how he wanted to find romantic feelings. *God, sometimes I wonder if You still care about me.* An uncomfortable distance separated him from his Savior.

He staggered down the sidewalk staring at the grass, his ability to focus vanished. The shortcut by the evergreen boxwood hedges on the side of the building offered quicker access to the entrance.

"Hello, Ryan." A smooth deep voice murmured behind him. He recognized the source and wrenched around to see the muscular man in jeans and a black tee shirt, his dark, curly hair longer than before.

"Allen, what are you doing here?" His heart pounded with the revulsion of seeing him again.

Allen took a few steps toward him. "I came to see how you're doing. It's been forever since I've seen you." His breathless voice transformed Ryan's mood from tired to agitated.

"I'm exhausted. I busted my tailbone today at CF Hardware." He squared his jaw and gritted his teeth. Allen's presence delivered a stab of unease…yet at the same time exhilaration.

"Need some company?" Allen's gaze traveled down Ryan's body.

Company. Such an innocent, friendly word. How many times did he settle in for a quiet evening and want someone to talk to? Frank had filled the void. His uncle was the father he never had. He was there when Ryan needed to talk.

But Uncle Frank was out of town, and only silence waited for him in their worn-down apartment. What if...what if he did invite Allen up?

But he knew what—and it was nothing good. "Look. I got into a lot of trouble once because of you. And my own foolishness. My life is different now." He fiddled with his keys. Knowing the truth, knowing the words...why, then, did they not sink all the way down?

"Yeah, and I'm sorry. I am." Allen held out his hand. "I've changed too, Ryan. Can't we talk? We've got a lot to catch up on."

Had Allen struggled as he had all these years? Did he fight the same temptation...did he feel it now? The pull started in his gut, and his feet had a mind of their own. They wanted to propel him toward Allen when he needed to run in the opposite direction. *Please, God, help me.* He took a step backward on the grass. "I don't think we do."

Allen's face twisted in the moonlight, pain—and something darker—in his eyes. "The night, the night before we stole the car. I remember...those feelings...I can't stop thinking about you. I've wanted to tell you for the longest time. I couldn't work up the nerve." He reached for him with both hands.

Ryan gave a rapid glance over his shoulder and swallowed hard. "That part of my life's dead and gone. I'm not the same person anymore." His hands trembled.

"But I need you. Can't you understand?" He licked his full lips. "All we've been through together...we're friends, right? Shouldn't friends be there for each other?"

Something within Ryan beckoned, drew him. Maybe Allen was right. Maybe it was a matter of need, of sticking with those like him. Maybe...maybe if he got it out of his system, he'd be able to go on with his life. Maybe then he'd forget about Greg, maybe Allen could be a substitute

The thought pierced his gut like a dagger. Gasping, he shook his head. How could he have entertained the idea? He fought the anguish. *God, forgive me.*

He'd never actually committed the act—the one God condemned in the first chapter of Romans. If he gave in to his lust now, it would only make things worse. He fought the yearning. *Lord, God. I need you now more than ever.* A gentle breeze on his cheek quieted him.

"I can see you have feelings, too, Ryan. Give me a chance." Allen grabbed his hand, held it tight.

The Lord's strength, not his own, surged. Part of him wanted to give in. The pull was strong, almost magnetic. Something in his mind whispered, *it's okay.* He'd been born with these feelings and was powerless to them. They were accepted these days, fashionable even. Nothing to be ashamed of.

With a shake of his head, he expunged the veil of deception in his soul. The Word of God told him differently. He spoke under his breath. "In Jesus name, I resist you." The statement wasn't addressed to Allen, but to one unseen.

Ryan took another, decisive step backward. "I am a changed man. God has come into my life, and things are different with me, very different. If you ever need spiritual guidance, I can be found at New Day Community of Faith Church on any given Sunday—but don't show up at my home again. I'm not a homosexual, Allen. It's an ungodly lifestyle, and I choose not to be a part of it. Do you understand?" The elation of standing up for truth bubbled inside.

Allen made no move to leave. He shook his head, stared hard at Ryan. "I don't believe you. I think you still have something for me."

"I'm giving you five seconds to back off, or you're going home with a broken nose." He squeezed his hand into a fist.

Allen scowled and turned down the street. After the man stuck his key in the door of his late-model Chevy, he drove away, his taillights disappearing into the night.

Ryan lumbered on to his apartment, unlocked the front door, and staggered into the living room. He dropped to his knees next to the couch and folded his hands. "Lord, thank you for helping me resist temptation. The fact that it was temptation in the first place repulses me. I've done everything I know to do. Your word says when I'm weak, You are strong. I confess to you I am weak. God, if I never change, I'll serve and love you. I want freedom. In Jesus name I pray. Amen."

The realization came to him of how close he'd stood to the edge—the fall into temptation. One more little push from Allen and he might have given in. He stumbled into the bathroom, collapsed on his knees in front of the toilet, and vomited.

~*~

Ryan parked his car behind CF Hardware. A little distance between the ugly encounter with Allen improved his disposition. What had it been? Two days ago. He'd prayed until midnight. The part of the Lord's Prayer, *deliver us from evil*, meant more to him now. He didn't classify Allen in the evil category, but there had been other powers at work—the powers and dominions the Lord spoke about in the Word, those humans wrestle against.

He grabbed his apron at the information desk and checked his assignment. The garden department. At least he didn't have to lift boxes in the warehouse.

Someone caught his attention on aisle three as he passed by. Dana set a handheld device on the shelf and stepped out in front of him, something she didn't usually do.

"Well, hello there, Ryan. Met a friend of yours last night." She raised her chin as her lower lip pushed up to give him a glare.

At CF Hardware? What could she possibly be talking about? "Who?"

"Allen. He and I had a revealing talk about you and him." She threw her head back in a sardonic laugh.

Allen conversed with Dana? She hated him, and he had an ax to grind. Must've been a cozy little conversation.

Ryan's breath caught as his hands turned to ice cubes. "I don't know what you're trying to prove, but Allen is not a friend of mine." Ryan adjusted the tie on his apron.

"Well, maybe not anymore. That's the whole problem. You dumped him for somebody else. How could you, you cad?" She waved her hand in a mocking gesture.

Now morbid curiosity clothed him like a death sentence. "I have no idea what you're talking about." He stared at her cold, blue eyes.

She shook her head. "Ryan, don't play dumb with me. Allen said you two were together for three years, and you up and left."

"That is a nasty lie." Ryan moved to one side. He needed to leave. This conversation was going nowhere.

Dana matched his step and stood in front of him again. "You know what bothers me the most? You're one of those holier-than-thou types who says being gay is wrong. But you're a hypocrite because you're gay yourself. Why don't you admit it?" She raised her voice a notch. "Gay people don't deserve to be ignored the way you're ignoring Allen." Her stance was rigid. She was so tall he could almost look directly into her eyes.

"Dana, look, you couldn't be more wrong. I don't know what he said to you, but I've never had any kind of…relationship with him, not that it's any of your business. Now if you'll move out of my way—"

"Allen gave me his phone number in case I find out who your new boyfriend is. Why don't you make it easy and tell me now so I can help the poor man?" She didn't move out of his way.

Ryan's breath came faster now as he restrained the urge to shove her. She deserved it, but he'd never harm a woman. "I've got one question for you. Why do you hate me so much?"

He suspected he knew the answer. He'd seen her glaring at him in the lunchroom when he bowed his head to say grace.

She narrowed her eyes again now. "You know, my mother used to make me go to church with my grandmother. I saw what a bunch of frauds those church people were. You're one of them." She placed her hands on her waist.

"Yes, I go to church. But the Christian people I know aren't hypocrites. And the Christians I know would be happy to welcome any sinner into church, including a homosexual. In fact, my church is full of sinners, saved by grace, and I'm sorry you feel that way about us. Why don't you come along with me sometime and see for yourself?" There. He'd challenged her.

"Are you kidding? I wouldn't be caught dead in church."

Ryan eyed her carefully and weighed his next words. "The irony in your statement is most people who feel that way wind up lying in a coffin in the front of a church they never would've entered during their lifetime. I'd rather a group of caring, loving friends say their final good-byes to me, wouldn't you?" He turned away from her then spun around again. "And Dana..."

She stared after him. "What?"

"I'd appreciate you not spreading untrue rumors about me."

"Don't give me that. You're gay, and I know it. Nothing could convince me otherwise. Not even if I saw you out with a woman."

Chapter Eighteen

Sandy tried not to stare at Ryan, but he had to be bothered about something. He clinched his jaws as he ran his fingers along the steering wheel.

He gave her a quick glance and peered at the road. As if feeling soothed, his face softened, and his lips curved into a smile. What was he thinking? Would he explain why he'd cried in her arms at Kalaloch? And would she find answers to questions she held about him?

He made the turn off the main highway onto a hard-packed dirt road which wound through a forest of Douglas firs. "Tell you the truth, I can think of other places I'd rather be on a Friday afternoon." He stretched his arms as he held the steering wheel. "The annual CF Hardware picnic is not my favorite event, even if they did close down the whole store at noon. The only bright spot is having you with me."

Sandy's heart fluttered. "That's sweet of you to say, but why don't you enjoy it? We couldn't ask for a more beautiful July day."

Ryan cleared his throat. "Let's say I'm not on the best of terms with some of the employees." He fiddled with a piece of torn upholstery. "In a way, I feel selfish about asking you to come."

She wrinkled her nose. "Selfish? I don't understand."

"I can't think of any other way to say this. You're my friend, and I want to be with you. But I had other motives, too."

"Now I'm stumped." Why did this feel like a confession?

"Having you by my side... well, I'm hoping certain people will leave me alone today."

"Those employees you were talking about when we hiked up to Lake Quitama?"

"Yes." He wrinkled his forehead. "I guess I'd better come right out and say it. A couple of women have been spreading rumors about me. One of them is an unhappy parent of a student from my class last year. Since I haven't brought a date to this before, I hope they don't start in on you."

"What kind of rumors? I don't understand why they would want to bother me, too?"

Ryan tightened his fingers on the steering wheel until they turned white. "If you don't mind, we'll talk about it later."

Hmm. Touchy subject. "You're a nice guy, Ryan. It's too bad people have to behave like that. The parent is probably being vindictive." She patted his arm. "I'm happy to see you through the afternoon. It couldn't be too bad."

He gave her a smile and veered off at a sign for Canyon Lake Park. The gravel road jostled and bumped the car until he pulled into a dirt parking lot. "Thank you for being you. You're already lifting my grouchy mood."

They left the car and strolled toward a crowd milling around a barbecue grill. The picnic area was set up with long, cloth-covered tables. People in lawn chairs lounged near an economy-sized cooler.

A huge hulk of a man stood at the grill blinking smoke out of his eyes. When he glimpsed up, he gave Ryan a friendly wave.

"Hey, Ryan." He smiled then turned to the grate to retrieve a blackened meat patty from the coals.

"Sandy, this is my boss, Larry."

Larry twisted around from the grill, balancing a spatula in one hand and a long-handled brush in the other. His eyes widened as he appeared to push a smile to his face. What did he mean by the look? Almost as if he were surprised to see Ryan with her. Maybe because he hadn't brought a girl before.

He shifted the spatula to his left hand with the brush and extended his other to her. "Nice to meet you, Sandy."

"You must know your way around a grill," she laughed.

"I don't know about that." He grinned and revolved to the grill again, chasing another charred chunk of meat.

"Well, see you later, Larry." Ryan nudged her elbow as he curved in the direction of the picnic tables toward the lake. They meandered around groups of adults and kids—probably families, sitting in clusters. Some of the children plopped down in miniature lawn chairs and a few ran around on the grass.

The long tables with dishes of potato salad, hamburger trimmings, and fruit sat on a grassy spot near a sprawling willow that looked like a gigantic umbrella. Sandy's stomach growled when she caught the aroma of Larry's barbequed hamburgers.

Behind them, skirting around the families, three women advanced in their direction. At first, they seemed involved in animated conversation. Were they the women Ryan spoke about? He'd only mentioned two.

Ryan gave them a quick glance and grasped her hand, steering her downhill toward the lake. Obviously, they were *the* people he was avoiding.

"Hey, Ryan."

Sandy peeked over her shoulder. The tallest of the three, her hair up in a blond ponytail, waved at him. "Aren't you going to introduce us to your girlfriend?"

His hand gripped hers harder as a shadow fell over his face. From the scoffing tone of her voice, the woman probably wasn't trying to be friendly.

Ryan's lips hardened into a straight line as the three quickened their paces and marched up in front of them. A nice looking blonde with long flowing hair and a curvy woman with red curls sidled up alongside her.

Ryan lifted his eyes to the tall blonde, his body rigid. "Sandy, this is Dana, Maggie, and Becky."

Sandy smiled. "Nice to meet you, ladies." What should she say to them? Ryan obviously didn't want to stay and chat. She'd follow his lead.

Dana eyed her. "We're glad to meet you, too. Ryan never brought a date to the company parties before." She looked down her long nose at him and to Sandy.

"Sandy, let's go for a walk down by the lake. Excuse us." Ryan wiped his brow, grasped Sandy's hand again, and nudged her along towards the water.

She allowed Ryan to tug her down a grassy hill toward Canyon Lake but had to increase her pace to keep up with his long strides. "They're the troublemakers?"

"Yeah. Dana and Maggie. I don't know Becky very well."

The trail forked, one section curving toward the evergreens and the other down to the water. Ryan took the path heading through the forested stand of Douglas fir. "Thanks, Sandy. Couldn't take anymore of Dana today."

The narrow dirt pathway meandered around an abundance of fern and clumps of wildflowers. Sandy's nose tickled, and she sneezed. "Must be a lot of moss around here. I'm allergic to it." Her eyes itched and watered.

"Should we find the others?" He brought his gaze to her, his face filled with concern.

"I guess so. I need to get some tissues out of my purse in the trunk."

"Sure. I think it's almost time to eat anyway."

"Good, because I'm hungry."

The grassy path led to the picnic area and the cars. When they arrived at the Toyota, Ryan stuck the curved key in the lock and opened the trunk.

She bent her head inside, reaching down toward her purse. A

thorough search revealed no tissues. "I can't believe this. I always have Kleenex in my purse."

"Sorry, I don't even have a handkerchief. What about some toilet tissue?" He pointed to a wooden building at the end of the parking lot. "I can run over to the men's room."

"No, it's okay. I need to use the facilities anyway." Sandy walked to the bathroom and into the ladies' room.

She halted as if her shoes were stuck. Two of Ryan's adversaries huddled in the corner and giggled. The third, Becky, gazed in the mirror combing her hair.

Meeting up with them in the restroom. An uncomfortable coincidence. "Hello again." Sucking in a deep breath, she walked toward a stall.

Dana sauntered toward her, blocking her way. "Well, fancy meeting you here."

Here it came. The confrontation Ryan warned about. Curiosity overcame good sense and told her to leave these women alone.

"It's really nice to meet Ryan's girlfriend. How did you two meet?"

Sandy peered at the blonde who'd given Ryan such a hard time. "During the earthquake in April. The brave guy saw me through a pretty scary time."

Dana shrugged as Maggie walked toward them.

Becky continued to focus on her image in the mirror.

The tall woman tightened her ponytail. "Well, if you don't mind me saying, I'm surprised to see you today. Ryan never brings a girl to any of these events."

Maggie lifted a cheerless face. "Yeah, he's kind of a loner. Not really the best of teachers either. My son had a hard time in his class last year."

Sandy froze. Ryan was an excellent teacher. She'd seen his eyes light up when he talked about his students. Knew better than to believe the dissatisfied parent. "I'm sorry to hear your son had problems, but I have no doubt Ryan's a good teacher."

Dana stepped nearer Sandy. The tall woman held her hand on the side of her mouth and lowered her voice. "Look, Sandy. I don't think you know Ryan very well. We'd better clue you in."

Here came the attack. Dana had a bomb ready to explode in front of her. "I don't care to hear any rumors. Ryan's my friend."

"Maybe so, but you really need the truth about him." Dana obviously couldn't wait to spew her piece of juicy gossip. "I had a long talk with Ryan's…how would you say it politely…ex-boyfriend." A devilish smile slid into place. "Honey, Ryan's gay."

Sandy gasped. She didn't want to believe Dana's words, but a tiny seed of doubt gnawed at her and morbid curiosity impelled her to listen.

Becky turned from the mirror. "Yeah. For three years I've had a crush on him. I've tried everything to get him to notice me."

Sandy lifted her chin. Becky was in love with Ryan and saw Sandy as competition. That's what this was all about. The redhead was jealous, and these women were helping her, trying to make Sandy think Ryan was gay so she'd have doubts about him. "Look, Ryan Reid is a good teacher. He's the bravest man I know. Whatever he is or isn't, I love him. If you have nothing else to do but spread gossip, then you have my pity." She stormed into the stall and slammed the door.

~*~

"You haven't said two words since you went to the restroom. You were so quiet during the meal." Ryan steered his car onto the main road as they left Canyon Lake. "Are you feeling okay?" Her allergies might've caused her to dab her eyes and blow her nose, but allergies didn't make her sigh.

"Wow, I'm not taking you to the forest anymore. It's odd you didn't have a reaction like this the other times we went."

"I'm just tired."

Ryan had zero experience in figuring out women's moods. Unless she told him what was going on, he wouldn't have a clue. Such a sudden change in her. "Sandy, what's wrong?"

"Nothing, really. Maybe a little hormonal."

He shrugged his shoulders. Her face held a glassy stare he couldn't understand.

After the fifteen-minute drive, the lights of Cedar Falls came into view. He turned onto Highway 32 and drove the ten miles to Sandy's. The mailbox marking the house appeared, and he curved up the circular drive.

What was he supposed to do now? He stopped in front.

She stared straight ahead, making no move to get out.

He lumbered around to the passenger side of the car and opened the door.

She stepped out, then gaped at him, the same glassy expression over her face. "Can we talk?" She folded her arms over her chest.

"Are you kidding? That's what I've been trying to get you to do for the last two hours." Now maybe he could understand. She was clearly upset.

She gulped, and a hiccup escaped her throat. "When I went into the restroom, I ran into those women."

Ryan groaned. "I was afraid of something like that." Wasn't hard to figure out what they said. He'd have to deny everything. "Will you tell me about it?"

Her lips trembled. "They…they told me I should know…you were…gay."

His nostrils flared. Big mistake bringing Sandy. Then his chest ached. His dear friend stood before him in tears, and he'd done this to her. The spunky young woman he'd grown to care for had a broken heart. The other day at Kalaloch, he'd decided he'd tell her the very words Dana spoke. Now he saw the effect the message had. Her tears disturbed him more than he could say.

How could he have considered telling her the truth? There was only one way to refute Dana's words. Lie.

Sandy blinked a tear away. "I think Dana had another reason for cornering me."

Another reason? But now Sandy surely had an inkling of the truth. "What do you mean?"

"Ryan, did you know Becky is in love with you?"

Ryan threw his hands into the air. Sandy, and now Becky? Some guys would kill to have these two good looking women running after them. But him? *Lord what's going on. You know if I could get my head on straight, Sandy would be the only woman for me.* "No, Sandy. I had no idea."

"I think Dana and Maggie were trying to scare me off so Becky would be free to pursue you."

He chuckled at Sandy's analysis. She didn't believe them, thank goodness. But he needed to keep it that way. He put his hand on her chin and gently lifted it. "Will you let me prove to you they're wrong?" Now there was no turning back from his plan.

She blinked up at him with fresh tears rimming her eyes. "How?"

An owl called as if in warning not to continue his charade.

"Like this." He put his hand on her neck and trailed his thumb down her cheek. He'd seen Jason do it at Sandy's birthday party. Ryan would perform even better. His lips parted before they met hers. He wrapped his arms around her, pulling her to him. In his embrace, Sandy trembled. Jason's lengthy kiss came to mind. Ryan would make his longer. The kiss deepened, and he moved his hands to her back then through her long strands of hair. With a slow motion, he pulled away from her and gazed into her brown eyes. Tears trailed down her face.

"Ryan, I believe you." She swiped at her cheeks. "Forgive me for doubting you for a moment."

He saw desire in her eyes. A stab of guilt cut a cavern out of his gut. *God, forgive me.* He kissed her for his own selfish purposes. So, he could keep her as a friend and make her think those women weren't telling the truth. When his heart rebuked him, shame tortured him. Hollywood should hand him an Academy Award. He made her think he was feeling passion, when in fact he felt nothing at all.

Chapter Nineteen

Sunlight streamed past the blinds when Ryan dragged himself out of bed. Wrestling with his sheets all night had worn him out—worse than having a nightmare. Sleep had alluded him again. Three nights and no sleep. Something had to change.

Ryan's stomach churned. Even clapping his hands over his ears didn't silence the sound of Sandy's voice asking for forgiveness. Forgive her? She'd done nothing wrong.

He'd found the strength to resist temptation with Allen. Yet when he needed to preserve his reputation, he slipped easily into sin—lying to the person he called his best friend. The harassing guilt clenched his heart.

Sometimes he thought about the oblivion alcohol might bring. Anything to make him sleep. Yet the problem would be there when he sobered.

He stumbled into the bathroom and threw cold water on his face, glad he had another Monday off. Friday afternoon at the picnic, Dana and Maggie had mocked him by confronting Sandy. They had their reasons. Dana hated him because he was a Christian, and Maggie resented him because of her son. But Becky, in love with him? He'd never have guessed. She did act flirty at work, but he hadn't thought much about it. In any case, he resented Dana and Maggie. No way could he turn the other cheek like the Bible said.

The cold water ran down his face before he toweled it off. Now a mental splash smacked him. They'd only told Sandy the truth, and he'd deceived her.

Sure, he had his job and served God by teaching children. But what good would it be if he didn't have someone to share his life with? Once Sandy found out what he was and how he'd lied, she'd never consider it, even if God did give him freedom.

He pulled on old jeans and a tee shirt, shaved, and brushed his teeth. Several days had passed since he visited the annex construction site. He jogged downstairs and jumped into his car. *Better call Greg.* He had the most up-to-date information on the work.

Ryan keyed in Greg's number on his cell and started the ignition. "Yeah, Greg. I'm coming over there. What's the latest?"

"Seems like I've always got bad news." Then his tone brightened. "But the good news is we've received more pledges and even got another sizeable contribution. The bad news is one of Dad's subcontractors has a few problems."

Ryan turned the corner onto the main road toward church. "What happened?"

"His men are on strike, something about a wage dispute. As you know, the concrete is laid. But now, until we get the framers out there, construction has halted." Greg's deep sigh hinted at his frustration.

"At every turn, there's been a roadblock. What's the Lord doing?" Ryan gripped the steering wheel until his fingers ached.

"Ryan, it's not the Lord. We need to pray against the obstacles in our way. I know it's frustrating. I feel the same way."

"You're right. I guess it's easy for me to get discouraged." He pulled up into the church parking lot and raced around the main building. With every step, anxiety scudded through his stomach.

Would this project see completion? He hiked the hundred yards to the site.

Now a long rectangular concrete slab sprawled before him, almost filling the lot beside the main church. Lumber, stacked near the foundation, was covered with a large plastic sheet. A small area was framed with no more than ten vertical studs attached to the base plates.

Ryan gawked at the few pieces of wood in place. The recreational annex had a long way to go to completion. He prayed one day he wouldn't have to bury his hopes for the project in the dirt where this unfinished building stood.

A nail gun hung on a sawhorse near the pile of lumber. Hard to believe one of the framers would go off and leave the expensive equipment. *Well, fine. I've watched plenty of demonstrations on YouTube about how to use these. Looked easy.*

Obsession replaced commonsense. He turned on the compressor and grabbed the nail gun with his dominate left hand. Since the gun had a one hundred ten nail capacity, it'd keep him busy for a while. *If those guys can do it, so can I.*

A near-completed section of framing the workers had begun to assemble lay on the ground. It only needed two more studs. He hoisted a pre-cut piece of lumber and placed it in line with the last one. With the nail gun firmly in his hand, he aimed at the plank and fired nails to attach the stud. He could do this. He set the next piece of wood in line and pulled the trigger again. This time, the gun slipped in his hand, and he missed his aim.

For a moment his mind went blank, and he shook his head. But he peered down at the plank again. Surprisingly there was no pain. Then the excruciating hurt began. He swayed with the dizzy wave of nausea and tried to stand. Blood oozed slowly around the long, narrow nail puncturing his right hand, entering near his thumb and exiting on the other side at his palm.

He dropped the gun and grasped the wrist of his injured hand, staggering around the main building and through the front door. "Greg." He didn't dare pull the nail out.

As he neared the church office, he yelled again. "Greg!" The door was open. He staggered up to Rosie's desk.

"Hi, Ryan. How are…" She looked at the nail sticking through his hand and toward Greg's open door. "Greg. Come out here now." She grabbed a handful of paper towels on a table behind her desk. "Here, Ryan, let's wrap these on your hand to contain some of the blood." She started around the counter toward him.

With wide eyes, Greg rushed out of his office. "Yeah, Rosie?" He glimpsed at Ryan. "What…what happened?"

"I…I need to get to the emergency room. Can…can you drive me?"

Greg paced toward him and wrapped the paper towels around Ryan's wrist and thumb, avoiding the nail. Part of the towels turned red, absorbing the blood. "Let's go, buddy. I'll find out the details later."

Greg held the front door of the church as Ryan stumbled through.

What an idiot. How could I have pulled a stupid stunt like this?

Greg raced around the passenger side of his Jeep and opened the door. "Get in. Don't worry. You're going to be okay."

Ryan crawled in holding on to the paper towels. He rested his head against the seat as he tried to disregard the pain.

Greg revved his car, and his tires squealed as he turned the corner onto the main road toward the hospital.

A tangle of ugly words shoved through Ryan's mind. "Like a fool I tried to help the framers out there." He closed his eyes humiliated by his dimwitted actions. "It was idiotic. I was careless."

"Don't think about it now. Let me pray for you." Greg blew out a breath. "Lord, please give the doctor wisdom as he brings medical treatment to my friend. Heal him. I pray in Jesus' name."

Ryan had never experienced pain like that before. His hand ached, stung, and throbbed all at the same time. Greg couldn't get to the ER soon enough. A moan slipped from his throat.

What about Sandy? Was she on duty? He needed her—her gentleness always calmed him.

Greg turned into the circular drive.

The sign with the words *Emergency* towered in front of Ryan. He'd been here recently—after the earthquake.

"Go on in. I'll catch up with you after I park the Jeep."

Ryan nodded. He staggered through the sliding glass doors and up to the front desk, unwrapping the paper towels.

A woman stared at him as if she were bored. Her eyes widened when she saw the nail. She picked up the phone. "Assistance needed at the front desk."

A guy in scrubs rolled a wheelchair toward the front.

"Take him to exam room eight," she said.

"Sir, sit down, please." The orderly pushed the chair closer to Ryan.

"I don't need help." He wasn't an invalid. Frustration built in his gut.

"All right, then. Come this way."

Greg jogged up beside Ryan, and they followed the hospital worker down a short corridor.

"Wait in here."

Ryan eased down into a hardback chair next to an exam table.

Lord, please let them hurry. Ryan propped his elbow on the table next to him. When he glanced up, a familiar face strolled by and glanced in, then stopped at the door. "Ryan. What happened?" Sandy rushed in, her hand to her mouth.

"He had a little accident at the construction site," Greg said.

Sandy placed a pillow under his arm and examined the nail through Ryan's hand. "It passed between the first and second metacarpal. You're a lucky man. The nail barely missed your bones. I'll get Dr. Cohen."

She sped out the room and whispered something to another orderly standing in the hall outside the door. Not more than five minutes later, she raced into the room accompanied by a staff person in a white lab jacket.

"I'm Dr. Cohen. A friend of Nurse Arrington, I understand. How did you do this, young man?"

For an instant, Ryan could see the humor in the situation. "I tried to use a nail gun. I suppose I better stick with teaching and not bother going into the construction business."

"I'd have to agree with you." Dr. Cohen rinsed the area around the nail using a gauze pad and antiseptic. "I'm giving you a pain blocker for this removal procedure. The nail has penetrated soft tissue, but I don't believe we'll have a need for stitches."

Ryan gritted his teeth as Dr. Cohen injected the needle near the entry site.

The doctor rummaged in the cabinets on the opposite wall then shifted toward him after five minutes. "I think the shot had enough time for the numbing process. Now, I'd advise you to look the other way."

Sandy stepped to his left side. "Look at me, Ryan." She smiled at him and held his uninjured hand.

Greg stood behind her and gave him a wide-eyed half-grin.

Ryan kept his eyes on Sandy's face as he felt the sensation of the nail sliding out of his hand. He squeezed hers harder and gulped for air.

She smiled and rubbed his good hand again, her beautiful face lifting his unease.

"Sandy, will you get me a butterfly bandage and a tube of antibiotic cream?" the doctor said.

She released her hold and moved toward the cabinet to pull out the supplies.

If he could, he'd hold on to her the rest of the day. Her touch reassured him.

"Get him set up for imaging and administer a tetanus shot, please." Dr. Cohen peered at Ryan then wrote out a prescription. "Take this for pain. I'd suggest you stay away from nail guns in the future." He smiled and gave him a soft pat on his shoulder. "Come back if you experience any complications."

"Yes sir. I'll be happy to take your advice."

"A few papers to fill out." Sandy held a clipboard in her hand.

"Give those to me," Greg said. He sat down again in his chair.

Feeling relief, Ryan lifted his gaze to Sandy. "You must've used your influence in getting the doctor in here so fast. Thank you."

She grinned at him. "Always helps to know people. I hope this doesn't hurt." She pushed up the sleeve of his tee shirt and rubbed his arm with alcohol. "This time, you better not look at me." She laughed and stuck the needle in his arm.

Ryan circled away from her but angled his head as she placed a bandage over the area. "Thank you for being there for me during the procedure."

Sandy smiled, placed the needle and bloody gauze in the garbage can, and put the tube of antibiotic back in the cabinet. "I'm glad I was on duty. You're going to be fine, Ryan." She touched his shoulder and paused, giving him a look he couldn't interpret. When she left the examining room, she wasn't smiling any longer.

"You can go to imaging now." The orderly popped his head in the door.

Ryan stood, and Greg pulled out his cell phone. "I'll wait for you in the entry."

When Ryan returned to the waiting room, Greg was sprawled out in a chair with a magazine. He jumped to his feet when he saw Ryan. "Ready?"

The double doors to the entrance swung open. Greg was a guy Ryan could depend on, showing him the love of Christ. Maybe even a friend who wouldn't judge him. "Thanks for bringing me today and filling out the paperwork. I appreciate you."

Greg pulled out of the hospital parking lot and stopped at a red light. "You look like you could use some lunch. Then if you're up to it, I want to have a serious discussion—about you."

Chapter Twenty

The hamburger and French fries chased away the empty, gnawing sensation in Ryan's stomach. It wasn't easy to sit at the fast food restaurant and eat with one hand.

Ryan glanced across the table at Greg sipping a soda. When was he going to instigate the serious discussion he mentioned? And what topic of conversation did he have in mind? Surely his friend didn't have any suspicions about the issue Ryan wanted to bury. He hunched down in his chair.

Greg finished chewing the last of his hamburger. "Do you mind stopping in at the church when I take you to your car?"

"Sure." The words sounded more willing than he intended. "You said you wanted to talk about me. But it seems like we've got a lot better things to discuss, like the annex." Knots formed in Ryan's stomach, threatening to do battle with the hamburger.

Greg smiled. "If you're ready, I'd like to continue this in the privacy of my office."

Uh, oh. Ryan closed his eyes. Greg was the church counselor. He counseled people in his office. Had Greg heard the rumors and wanted to counsel him? Ryan thought this living nightmare couldn't get any worse, but it had. He slowly pulled his legs out from under the table and stood. He was in no hurry to get back and face whatever Greg wanted to discuss. "Thank you for lunch."

"You're welcome, buddy."

Ryan crouched down in the seat on the silent ride. He gazed at Greg when he pulled next to Ryan's car in the church parking lot then trailed him through the foyer. Still no clue.

If Ryan wanted to get out of this, his hand might be an excuse, but it was numb from the shot. He turned away from the church office and retreated toward the sanctuary. If he walked into Greg's small room, the walls would close in on him.

"Where ya going, Ryan?"

"I...uh don't know." He staggered toward the pulpit. Ryan did know where he was going, anywhere besides Greg's office. The glass window with Jesus and the lamb on his shoulders reflected the sun. He slumped into the first pew, and Greg slipped down beside him.

"Don't you want to go in my office?"

"No."

"Ryan, I need for you to place a little confidence in me. I love you in the Lord, and I'm your brother. Can you trust me?"

Can I really trust Greg not to judge me? "I...of course I trust you. You and your father have been so instrumental—"

"I'm not talking about the annex. I mean me personally. As a counselor, as a friend. Can you trust me with things going on inside of you?"

"How do you know about what's going on inside of me?" He sat up straighter. *Greg's on to me. He's figured it out.*

"I don't know exactly. I'm not a mind reader, but there's something holding you captive." His gaze bore into him.

Ryan shifted away. This was too uncomfortable. If he told him anything, he'd lose his friendship.

"Look. I don't usually solicit clients, but I want to help you."

Ryan's heart pounded. Could he really tell him the truth?

Greg was right. Ryan's past held him captive. He wanted—no needed—to be free. If there was some way Greg could help... Maybe, just maybe. But Ryan could never tell Greg his feelings about him. He raised his eyes to the man sitting next to him on the pew. They were godly, kind eyes, full of the Lord.

If he could trust any man in this world, it had to be Greg. He took a deep breath. "I'm willing to try."

~*~

Sandy sank into the lawn chair, allowing the sun to warm her face. The glass of ginger peach iced tea refreshed her. The deck was a good place to think after her long day in the ER. The scene with Dana Friday at the picnic bothered her, and then seeing Ryan today in the ER.

The dahlias next to the house were the size of saucers. Their pedals folded in upon each other, the multitude of colors exquisite. A dove's call didn't do much to soothe her aching heart—to relieve the pain of the decision she'd made.

The sight of Ryan with the nail in his hand this morning prompted her sympathy. The poor guy was so tense about the building project.

He'd kissed her Friday night, but... Why would those women tell her he was gay if he wasn't? Was it really about Becky? Or was Ryan interested in Suzie as she'd thought? Suspicions swirled in her mind making her dizzy.

For days now she'd pondered her relationship with Ryan. In the past, guys had found her attractive. Jason, for one. With Ryan, something was missing. Her woman's intuition told her he never treated her like a typical man would.

A tear rolled down her cheek. Ryan had become a dear friend. She loved to worship with him, to go hiking together, to have a cup of coffee, and chat. But telling him she couldn't see him anymore was the only answer. She loved him despite his sexual preference—if he were gay. But she couldn't abide the pain any longer. She needed to move on.

Sandy closed her eyes and pictured Jesus on the cross. He'd died for her. And for Ryan. "Lord, I don't understand where Ryan's at, but I beg You, if You can help him, please heal his life."

~*~

"All right. Can you come into my office now?" Greg got to his feet and waited.

Ryan nodded, his nerves on high alert.

Greg rose from the pew, and they stepped out of the sanctuary and down the hall to the church office.

"Rosie, hold my calls."

She nodded. "Ryan, how's your hand?"

"Okay, thanks." He liked Ms. Calderon. Every time he'd ever come into the church office, she'd offered him a smile.

Greg motioned him in and closed the door. "Go ahead and sit there." He pointed to a couch upholstered with floral fabric of greens and blues.

The picture window to Ryan's right afforded a view of a greenbelt of Douglas fir and fern, a bird fountain next to an outdoor bench in the foreground. A painting of Jesus with his disciples in the boat calming the wind and the waves hung beside the door.

Ryan squirmed on the comfortable couch. He wanted to walk out the door and never return. If he revealed anything, it'd be more painful than the nail penetrating his hand.

Greg leaned forward. "I can promise you, whatever you say today will go no further. You can trust me. I'll think no less of you, regardless of what you reveal." He picked up his Bible from a small table beside his chair.

The words assured Ryan, but he tried not to think about it. This guy, the very one with whom he'd discuss his feelings, was the man he found attractive.

"Let me start by praying." Greg bowed his head. "Father, give us the courage to reach out to You for healing and truth. Bless my brother Ryan and bring him freedom."

The prayer made a vital statement. Their session didn't depend on worldly counsel but wholly on the power of God.

Greg lifted his gaze to Ryan. "Now, you need to know you are no different from anyone." Greg flipped some pages in his Bible. "Jeremiah tells us the heart is deceitful and desperately sick. Not only you, buddy. We're all sinners."

Ryan crossed his ankle over his knee and uncrossed it again. At least he wasn't alone under the curse of sin.

"Where should we start?"

"I...I don't know." Ryan gulped.

"How about with this morning? Something caused you to become careless at the construction site."

"You're right. I'm stressed to the max." Ryan rubbed the bridge of his nose and looked at Greg. "Friday, I went to the annual CF Hardware picnic with Sandy." He swallowed the dread in his throat. "Three women employees who don't like me cornered her." He bolted up and faced the picture window staring at the greenbelt then at Greg.

"What happened then?" Greg folded his hands on his lap.

"They told her I...she needed to know..." He made a circle around Greg's office.

"Needed to know what, Ryan?"

Ryan couldn't control the volume of his voice. "She needed to know I'm gay."

The expression on Greg's face never changed. "And how did you react?"

"When she told me, I tried to prove to her it wasn't true by kissing her and making her think I had feelings for her." He covered his eyes with his hands. Reliving what he'd done was tearing him apart.

"Do you agree with the women's assessment of you?"

Ryan's throat tightened as he yelled the words. "Yes. I'm gay." Did anyone outside the office hear?

Greg looked down at his Bible. He lifted his head and a stoic expression fell over his face. "How has this knowledge impacted you?"

Ryan's shoulders shook. "I don't want to be gay. Sandy's in love with me. I want to love her back. And what's worse, I lied to her and denied what the women said." He paced away from Greg and back again. "I've done everything, Greg. The problem is I don't have romantic feelings for her, but I love her all the same. It's not a physical love." He plopped down on the couch, his head in his hands. "I hate to tell you this, but I have feelings for men. I fight it night and day." Ryan huffed. "I'm exhausted, and I don't know how much longer I can do this."

What was he saying? His feelings were for Greg. *God, I can't go there. I could never plant those ugly seeds and live with myself.*

"I know this could lead me to a lifestyle that's not pleasing to the Lord." He lifted open palms. "I love Him, you know, with all my heart."

"It's okay, buddy. I'm telling you, your God is bigger than this. We're going to work through it." Greg stood and placed his arm on his shoulder.

It was tough telling him, but he continued with his story, about his mother, his father, how he stole the car, and how he was arrested. In fact, it was the hardest thing he'd ever done. It had been easier to tell Sandy about his parents and his life of crime. But when he finished, some of the weight lifted.

Greg's eyes didn't leave his face through the whole ugly story, and his expression remained calm, even compassionate.

Ryan blinked and gazed at Greg. "Is it hopeless?"

Greg grinned and shook his head. "I want to start by telling you who you are." Greg's face lit up.

"What do you mean?" He knew who he was—a nobody.

"First of all, when you received Christ, you became a new creature. The old Ryan died. The Bible tells us you are holy, blameless, and covered with God's love. If you were the only person in the world, Jesus would have come to earth to die for you. You are complete in Christ, like God wants you to be. Can you see how important you are?"

"I don't know. All I see is a messed-up moron." He raised his eyebrows and stared at him. "Maybe I was born like this."

Greg reached for his Bible and held it up. "Ryan, do you believe the words in this book?"

"You know I do."

"I'm only telling you what's in God's word. Now listen carefully to me. This is important. Why would God make you into something He's forbidden? The book of Leviticus says committing sexual acts with another man is an abomination to Him. God is not in favor of homosexuality, and he certainly didn't wire you to be *gay*. To think He did is a lie." Greg wiped his brow. "We live in a fallen world, and your life circumstances have given you the emotional thought processes and feelings you now experience." He raised the Bible again. "But your emotions are not indicative of truth, this book is."

"But why am I like this?"

Greg folded his hands around the Bible in his lap. "Maybe you were born with a predisposition to it. Like I was born with a predisposition to alcoholism. My father is a recovering alcoholic. But does it mean I have to be an alcoholic?"

Ryan soaked in the words and shook his head.

"Some people are born predisposed to bad temper—does it mean they have to be a murderer? As I said, we're all born sinners, but are we helpless to sin? Not at all. Christ has brought us victory over sin through His death on the cross."

Ryan's mouth fell open. He'd never thought of the concept. Yet frustration built. He frowned. "I *have* chosen to obey God. I've never…never committed this sin with another—only in my mind. The feelings are there. How am I supposed to get rid of them?"

"Look, Ryan. The enemy has said you're gay—it's the way you are and you can't change. Your feelings confirm it as well. But that's not what God says. God has a different opinion and a different plan for you. You have a choice." Greg thumbed through the pages of the Bible. He squeezed his eyes closed and took a deep breath. "You used to be dead in your sins and your sinful nature, but Jesus died on a cross to set you free of those sins. When you received Christ as your savior, God forgave all your wrongs. You were raised from your old life like Christ was raised from the dead. Now you can live filled with the power of God because of your faith in Him. God has removed all the control of the enemy, but the devil doesn't want you to know. You can walk as a free man. It will take time, months or even years of work, but it can happen. The sin of homosexuality doesn't have to hold you."

Ryan grasped at the hope Greg's words held, but could he believe them for his own life? "Is being gay a sin if I don't act upon it?"

"Is it a sin for a married man to look at another woman?"

"If lust isn't involved, no." Ryan shook his head.

"But what if lust is involved?"

"Yes, it's a sin." Ryan waited, not understanding where Greg was going with his questioning.

"When you say you're gay, what does it tell me? Think carefully, because you've already told me the answer to your question."

Ryan turned toward the window trying to recall his words. When the truth hit him, he swallowed hard. Greg had left him no argument to broach.

"You understand where I'm going, don't you?" Greg said.

Ryan nodded but didn't turn to look at his friend. He understood all too well.

"Say it, Ryan. You need to tell yourself the truth. It starts with you admitting it. Only then can you turn it over to God."

But he didn't want to admit it.

"Come on, buddy. It's you and me and God here. He's always known the truth and now I do, too."

But Greg didn't know the entire story. If he did...Ryan spun toward his friend. "When I admitted I'm gay, I told you I have feelings for men." The words screamed from him. "I lust after...after men. And that's a sin."

Greg nodded. "Like lusting after a woman who's not your wife, lusting after a man is a sin. You have to decide homosexuality is wrong. You can choose not to participate in it."

Ryan raised his hands and let them fall in defeat. "But I have those desires." If Greg only knew how much...

"Those desires have been with you for a long number of years. It'll take a while to see the results of any decisions you make." Greg stretched his legs out and crossed them at the ankles. "We can compare our feelings to a train. The engine is like your mind where you make your choices. It's in your hands, and you're in control. The caboose represents your feelings. The decision comes first, then the feelings."

Ryan studied Greg. The truth of God's word began to seep into his spirit.

Greg continued. "You believed a lie. God didn't make you this way. Circumstances planted the thoughts in your head. God can uproot those desires. The Bible says if God is for us, who could be against us? Stand up for yourself."

The words pounded against Ryan's heart. Did he dare think he could change? Or better yet, could God give him the freedom he desired?

"Remember how much God loves you. I'm proud of you for opening up to me today. I'd like for us to pray, but I believe you need to lead the prayer. First, I want to hear you say you don't have to allow lust or sinful desires to control you. Say it, Ryan."

God's strength coursed through his heart. "By the grace of God, I don't have to let ungodly passion sweep over me." The declaration brought exhilaration surging through his soul.

"Okay, now see if you can pray and choose righteousness."

Ryan regarded Greg with new eyes. More as a counselor than an object of lust—though Ryan knew the battle for freedom had only begun. Behind his friend, the picture of Jesus calming the storm brought Ryan peace. He wanted to make a declaration of independence from his old life. He knelt down by his chair, and Greg slipped down beside him, his hand on his shoulder.

"Lord, thank you for showing me who I really am. I never understood before. I make this choice today in front of You and my friend, Greg. He is witness to this. I ask You by Your grace to allow the feelings to follow one day. But if they never do, I want to stand in my confession. In Jesus name." He turned to Greg. To his amazement, his eyes glistened with moisture.

They rose from the floor. "God has heard your prayer and will give you the strength and wisdom to live your life according to His will. Things are not going to be different overnight. You've made a courageous start today. I love you, my brother." Greg slapped him on the shoulder. "We need more sessions like this. I'd like for you to commit to weekly meetings."

"Me, too. Thank you, Greg." Ryan floated out the door of Greg's office lighter somehow, a weight he'd been carrying lifted by the mere act of sharing his burden. He nodded and smiled at Rosie.

"Hey, Ryan."

He turned toward the voice.

Greg stood in the doorway, a finger to his temple. "Had a thought. Suzie and I are going to Pikes' Place Market in Seattle soon. Come go with us and bring Sandy if you'd like."

Chapter Twenty-one

Sandy rose from her lawn chair and slid the glass door open into the kitchen. Her pocket buzzed. She set her tea glass on the counter and pulled her phone out. Hmm. Ryan Reid. Her pulse raced. She hadn't talked to him for over a week.

Maybe she should ignore the call. But then, she had to get this over sooner or later. She could tell him good-bye on the phone. "Hello, Ryan."

"Hi, Sandy." His smooth, quiet voice brought a lump to her throat. "Would you, I mean, if you're free, do you want to go to Seattle tomorrow afternoon after church with Greg and Suzie?"

"Greg and Suzie? What about you?"

He laughed. "Yeah, me too."

The sound of his pleasant chuckle chipped away at the decision she'd made. "How's your hand?"

"It's going to be fine. Thank you for being there for me."

"And your arm where I gave you the shot?" Hopefully he wouldn't complain about her nursing skills.

"Had a knot, but I'm good now." He laughed. "I'll try to remember my manners when you have a needle in your hand."

Her heart implored her to go on an outing with him, but she wouldn't, she couldn't turn back on her decision. She'd tell him she didn't want to see him anymore at the end of the evening. It'd be the last time she'd go anywhere with Ryan Reid.

~*~

Ryan couldn't figure out why Sandy wouldn't let him pick her up—wanted to meet him at church. He pulled up in front and parked in a slot—the lot now deserted after Sunday morning services.

He turned off the ignition and rubbed his forehead. The time he'd spent with Greg was pivotal. Sunlight seemed to sparkle brighter on the leaves of the trees in front of the building. He'd made a choice and was determined to honor it, but he didn't fool himself into thinking he'd find freedom after the first counseling session. He'd merely made a start and didn't feel any different, even after the second one.

Sandy inched her black sedan in a few spaces away.

He hopped out to open her door, but his smile dimmed when she offered him nothing but a cold stare. She slipped her fingers away from his when he tried to catch her hand.

"Sandy?" She'd been so kind to him at the hospital. Clearly something had changed. Would the day ever come when he'd understand her?

"Hello, Ryan."

Greg pulled up in front of the church and honked. With a wide arc, he circled his arm out the window of his Jeep Cherokee. "Hey, you guys. Ride with me."

With his good hand, Ryan opened the backdoor for Sandy then marched around to the other side. She scooted toward the window when he crawled into the backseat.

Greg rotated in his seat to face them. "Hi Sandy, Ryan."

Suzie swiveled around and offered a friendly grin. "Glad you could join us." Turning back again, she gazed at Greg. Her eyes glistened as she focused on him.

Ryan forced his thoughts to the outing and ignored the nagging feelings of jealousy.

Greg grinned at Sandy. "Last time I saw you, Ryan was tangling with buffalos at Northwest Trek." He gave a loud guffaw.

"Yeah, I remember the day." A flicker of some emotion akin to regret crossed her face.

Suzie glanced to them again. "You guys been dating long?"

Greg's shoulders tensed as he pulled out of the parking lot and onto the main road. The remark probably made him as uneasy as it did Ryan.

"Oh, we're not dating. We're only friends," Sandy said. She glared out the window.

He'd never heard a sarcastic word from her before today. "Yeah, we're good friends. In fact, she's my best friend."

Greg slowed as the lanes of cars came to a standstill on the freeway. "Traffic seems worse today than usual." He drummed his fingers on the steering wheel.

Ryan twisted in his seat. The tension between him and Sandy formed an impenetrable wall he didn't know how to break through. Whatever the issue, he accepted responsibility.

After thirty minutes, Greg pulled into a parking place about five blocks from the market. They trekked through a shopping district and entered from the street. A long narrow set of stairs led to the upper level and the front entrance.

"Pike's Place Market is the oldest operating farmer's market in the USA. You ladies have your choice of about anything you want, from fresh flowers to vegetables, crafts and art work, clothing, Native American artifacts, you name it," Greg said.

"Hey Greg, if you ever decide to take up a new profession, you could be a tour guide," Ryan said.

"Right." He focused on Ryan and laughed. "Did you guys know one of the restaurants in the market is where a scene from *Sleepless in Seattle* was filmed?"

"Didn't see it. I think it was before my time." When did he ever have time to go to the movies?

"It was popular back in the day," Suzie said. "You've seen it, Sandy?"

"Yeah. On TV."

Ryan took a deep breath. Greg and Suzie were bound to notice her bad mood.

"There's nowhere else I'd rather be in the summer than Seattle and Elliott Bay." Suzie slid her arm through Greg's as they pressed their way through the crowd, passing booth after booth of homemade jellies, handmade jewelry, lavender products, fresh bakery items, crystals, room sprays created from pine needles, and woven baskets.

"Look at the guy at the fish market." Suzie pointed to the display case where dozens of salmon were arranged on ice. "The clerk weighed a fish on the digital scale and threw it to another guy at the end of the counter waiting on a customer."

"Yeah, the place is called the flying fish market. I get a big laugh out of watching them." Greg slipped his arm around Suzie's waist. "Even the original Starbucks is across the street." He pointed to a small building with the mermaid logo. "Where it all began."

Greg glanced down the aisle at a booth. "I've got an idea. Be right back. Come on, Ryan."

Greg marched farther down the row of booths. He stopped at a stall with dozens of bouquets of fresh local flowers, some in glass vases. "Let's get the ladies some flowers."

Greg surveyed the bundles of blooms, each in a small vial of cool water. Colorful bouquets of dahlias, roses, sunflowers, geraniums, and baby's breath filled the booth. "I'll take two."

He paid for the flowers, and the girl behind the counter wrapped the bundles in wax paper and handed them to Greg. "Now, come on." He passed one to him. "We're going to surprise Sandy and Suzie."

Ryan reached in his wallet, pulled out a ten-dollar bill, and passed it to Greg. Would the flowers help tear down the barricade between him and Sandy? "Thanks. I don't think Sandy's too happy with me right now. I hope this is going to smooth things over a little."

"I noticed. How are you doing so far?"

"I'm holding on to my faith in God." If only normal masculine feelings of friendship could replace his old longings.

The women browsed a jewelry booth when he and Greg returned.

"These are for you, Sandy." Ryan cast a cautious eye to her as he placed the flowers in her arms.

Her face lit up, a smile dawning, the first she'd given him today.

"They're beautiful." She held the flowers near, cradling them to her chest. For an instant, he saw a glimmer of expectation in her eyes, but then it faded.

"How about Don's Boathouse for dinner? I hear their crab cakes are the best." Greg pointed to the row of piers jutting out into Elliot Bay. They followed Greg and Suzie, strolling hand in hand down the promenade linking the piers.

Ryan breathed deeply, pulling in the aroma of fish and saltwater.

Greg angled toward the next pier to the right and indicated the front door. "Don's Boathouse." The restaurant was in a three-story building, the exterior painted a brick red. Picture windows on the first floor afforded a view of the bay. Must have been an old warehouse.

"You'll never find a more spectacular view of Elliott Bay. Come on, you guys. I'm starved," Greg said.

~*~

The silent ride to the church made Ryan uneasy. The dinner was probably as uncomfortable for Greg and Suzie as it was for him. Sandy hadn't said anything other than brief answers to someone's question. Maybe Ryan should throw up his hands and sail off on one of those sailboats in Elliot Bay if his life didn't straighten out.

He tried to hold her hand again, once during dinner and again on the ride home. She drew away both times. Well, did he blame her? He only did it to act like a guy on a date.

Finally, Greg pulled into the church parking lot. "Well, here we are, people. Hope to see you guys at church next week."

"Thanks for driving, Greg. We both enjoyed the afternoon and the evening." Ryan didn't know what Sandy would do or say next, so he figured he'd speak for her as well. He guessed women could be temperamental creatures, but he'd only seen her like this one other time, the evening of the picnic.

"I'm sure I'll see you around." Sandy got out and paced to her car.

Ryan twisted toward Greg and shrugged, his palms up.

"I'm going to take Suzie home, so I'll say good night." Greg raised an eyebrow, waved, and drove on to the main road.

Ryan jogged to catch up with Sandy. She neared her car and whirled to face him, the flowers clutched to her chest.

"Ryan, can we talk for a minute before you go?" The words plummeted from her lips in a monotone.

"Sure." He looked down into her eyes. Maybe she'd finally tell him what was going on.

Though the air was pleasant, she shivered.

"Do you need a jacket?" he said.

"No." She paused to take a deep breath. "I've come to a decision about us." She gave a scornful laugh. "In actuality, there is no *us*. I've been thinking for days. I guess I'm not what you're looking for in a woman."

"Sandy, wait—"

"No, let me finish. Maybe I'm not pretty enough for you or maybe it's because you want to date another teacher." Her voice broke. "Or maybe Dana and Maggie were right."

A painful thought flooded his mind. The night of the picnic his deceptive kiss hadn't convinced her. He didn't dare try to kiss her again. God already convicted him for misleading her.

"I've decided I can't see you anymore. I'm only dating Jason. I can't go on like this, waiting for you to make up your mind if you love me." She brushed away a tear and clung to the flowers like a shield. "I need for you to hold me in your arms." She amplified the volume of her voice. "I need for you to say you have romantic feelings for me. But I know you don't." Now she shouted. "I don't attract you, and I'm afraid I know why. I hurt so badly because I melt in your presence. You make me feel like a woman, and I want you to feel passionate about me, too." Her tears streamed down her face. "I've got to go. Thank you for dinner and the flowers." She ducked into the Beemer and slammed the driver's door.

Was there nothing he could say to make her stay? The taillights of her car disappeared around the corner. He couldn't ask her to remain in a relationship with him when all he could give her was friendship. *Lord, after some of the worst and the best few days of my life, my closest friend walked out on me.*

Ryan maneuvered his car toward the apartment. Since the earthquake, the petite woman with the beautiful face and angelic voice had been his friend. Now, she was gone from him, like a dear companion who moved away to a distant city. He wanted to fall in bed, to forget what happened.

Ryan took the stairs with a slow gait. He opened the door to the sound of a praise and worship CD and Uncle Frank on the couch, his hand on his chin. He looked as if he were galaxies away.

"Hey, Uncle Frank. What're you doing? You look like you're in dreamland."

"Sit down, Ryan. I've got something to tell you."

Chapter Twenty-two

"What's up?" Ryan made an attempt to keep his tone upbeat. He couldn't allow Uncle Frank to see the ache inside. He dropped onto the couch.

"There's been a change—in my life. I've been putting off telling you because I wanted to make sure." Frank peered at him as if wanting to see Ryan's response.

"I'm listening." Ryan tensed. Was it something positive? From the look on Frank's face, it was.

"I'm in love with a woman in my singles' group." His eyes sparkled. "Her name's Lynn Bradley. I don't think you know her."

"Wow. I've noticed you've been gone a lot. But you could've fooled me. I haven't seen you with her at church or anything." He smiled and scratched his head. Instead of bad news, for once something positive happened.

"No, we've mainly come to know each other at Bible study. We met at Beth and Orville Simpson's home. They have a ministry to older singles and host our group. Lynn and I've gone out for coffee quite a few times."

"Great." Frank needed someone in his life, someone to share his days with.

"Here's how it affects you. We're planning to get married fairly soon, so I'll be moving out."

Optimism, an emotion he hadn't experienced much, helped to ease some of his heavy load. Joy for his uncle's future. "Have you set the date?"

"Yes, we've planned on August thirtieth. But I figure you'll probably be getting a new apartment anyway. I've seen you with the pretty lady at church. Sandy? Maybe one of these days, you'll be hearing wedding bells, too."

"I'm happy for you, Uncle Frank. I'm anxious to meet Lynn. But as for me, don't count on a wedding. There's something about me I think you need to know." As much as he hated to dirty Frank's mind with the truth, it was time to tell him. "I haven't said anything to you before. Probably because I was ashamed."

"What are you talking about?" Frank furrowed his brow.

"I've had a problem for a long time—given it to the Lord. By faith, I'm trusting Him for freedom." Ryan brushed a strand of hair off his forehead.

Frank blinked and peered at him. "Ryan, what are you telling me?"

"I don't have romantic feelings for Sandy. I'm fighting against homosexual thoughts. I've started counseling." He raked a hand through his hair, waiting for Frank's rebuke.

Frank peered at him. "I'm sorry. I don't know what to say."

"I've talked to Greg Aldridge a couple of times and plan on weekly sessions. My life isn't going to change overnight." Telling Uncle Frank peeled off another layer of the weight he carried.

"What about the way Sandy's big brown eyes look at you? She must be in love with you." Frank bit his lip as his brow formed a frown.

"She is, or was. Tonight, she told me she never wanted to see me again." He cleared his throat. "Frank, I need to make something plain. The attention of a pretty girl doesn't change a man steeped in ungodly thoughts about another man. It's like taking an anorexic to a banquet. The abundance of food doesn't make them want to eat."

Frank gazed at him a few minutes as if taking in Ryan's words. "Does Sandy know about your feelings?" Frank leaned toward Ryan.

"Someone from my work told her. It's tearing me apart."

Frank closed his eyes as he pinched the bridge of his nose. "I'm sorry, buddy. You haven't..."

"Acted on my feelings? No, thank God. And I don't want to. But lately...it's been hard." He sat against the couch, a lumpy pillow poking him. "If I never find freedom, I'm determined to live a life of celibacy and walk by faith. I love the Lord too much to ever go into the lifestyle." Ryan shook his head. "I pray I can maintain those standards."

Frank pounded his fist into his hand. "I know this has all come about because you were virtually abandoned by your mother and never had a father to show you attention and love." The volume of his voice grew loud, and his words quivered. "I'd give anything now if I could've been there for you when you were younger." Frank gulped and looked toward his lap. Finally, he looked up. "Let me pray for you." He grasped Ryan's shoulder. "Lord, I lift up my nephew to You. I ask for Your power in his life to carry out Your purpose for him. For whatever road he must travel, go with him and cover him with your Holy Spirit. Be Ryan's Father."

Ryan's Father. He liked the ring of it. Indeed, God was the father he'd never had. A perfect Father. "Congratulations on your upcoming marriage.

We'll think about vacating this place soon." He stood and dragged into his room, staring at the floor. His uncle found the love of his life. Would he ever be free to love a woman? If it happened, would it be too late for him and Sandy?

~*~

Ryan lumbered out the employee's door at the rear of the building. He'd lifted boxes from trucks at the loading dock all morning, though he made sure to wear the brace on his injured hand. The hard work-out helped. So much easier to fall asleep at night when exhausted.

Frank's move-out date loomed. He hated to admit it, but he didn't look forward to his uncle's departure. Frank had been Ryan's roommate since college. Yet the other man's happiness was more important.

Ryan opened the driver's door on his car, slid in, and gripped the steering wheel. At least there hadn't been much time to think about Frank leaving since Greg changed Ryan's counseling schedule to twice weekly—every Tuesday and Thursday.

He closed his eyes and remembered the quiet office he'd feared at first and the counseling sessions. Each time they started with a prayer. Then Greg encouraged him to talk about his childhood. As a child, he didn't know his life was any different than others. But now, in retrospect, he understood how many events became instrumental in shaping his outlook. For one, how all he wanted as a small boy was a father's touch and attention. In his teens, the unfulfilled desire turned sensual.

Ryan relaxed his fingers and stuck the key in the ignition. He took a cleansing breath. Greg had made an important point. He couldn't be attracted to Sandy until his own broken image of himself changed. Though it would take work, Greg wanted him to become more aware of his own masculinity, to think of himself in those terms.

Because Ryan was a Christian didn't mean he would automatically find his way out of homosexuality. He'd proven it to himself since college. He had to strengthen his relationship with Christ, the living Son of God so he could better understand how to die to sins and live for righteousness. He thought his convictions were strong, but Greg helped him learn how to walk by faith every day.

He glanced at his watch—off work early for once. He'd drive to the construction site, though he promised himself he wouldn't pick up a nail gun. Since Mr. Aldridge announced last Sunday the framers' dispute had been settled, would he see a difference in the progress? He turned on the street in front of CF Hardware and headed toward church.

Without Sandy in his life he had more time to work on the project between his counseling sessions and CF Hardware, though he missed her friendship every day. He'd been pleased when the phone volunteers from singles had reported they'd spoken with each member of New Day and more people pledged support. Even Mr. Aldridge accepted Ryan's revised, streamlined budget. Though some of the people in his singles' group worked at the site every Saturday, he decided not to risk it.

He pulled up into the church parking lot near the new building. He held his breath. The framing was finished with Tyvec covering the OSB board. More of the interior framing was up now.

He stepped into the hull of a building. The largest area in the center was the basketball court. Did he dare dream the annex would be a reality? The thoughts overwhelmed him. If only his best friend were here to share this moment.

Images of Sandy, tears streaming down her face, wrenched his heart. How would he feel if the situation were reversed? Conviction swept over him.

She was adamant. Never wanted to see him again—ever. An idea formed in his mind. It wouldn't hurt anything if he caught a glimpse of his friend in her nurse's uniform, maybe in the cafeteria or outside the ER. She didn't have to know he was there. He wanted to see her.

He left the newly framed building and returned to his car. Before he thought, he'd veered off on Highland toward downtown.

Parking places at the hospital were tough to find, but finally a spot in front of the main building turned up.

Memories of the last time he'd come to the ER washed over him. He shuddered. *I'm grateful to be here for a different reason this time.*

Apprehension slapped him in the face. *Maybe I shouldn't have come.* Yet he pushed through the double doors. If he could go unnoticed, he'd be happy. The same grim-faced woman at the front desk glanced up.

"Can I help you, sir?" Good. She didn't remember him.

"Uh, is Sandy Arrington on duty?" If she wasn't at work today, he'd leave.

"Yes, I believe she is. Excuse me." The woman turned her attention to the ringing phone.

His courage waned. With a twist, he started to the door. *No.* He needed to see her sweet face.

A long corridor veered to his left on the opposite side from the exam room where Dr. Cohen removed the nail. A glass window stretched along the length of the hall. A door toward the center led outside. The hospital gardens. He stepped out into the warm sunshine.

A flagstone pathway wound around angular planter boxes filled with evergreen trees, cypress bushes, a hemlock hedge, and mountain laurel. A reflecting pool split the path. He dropped onto the metal bench on one side gazing at the fountain in the center of the pool sending splashes of water into the air.

Since the night Sandy left him at church, longing for her companionship grew. How different was it than feeling romantic about a woman? He bolted from the seat. To be in love was about as foreign as a relationship with a human father.

The Bible said love was patient, kind, not proud, or rude. It always protects. Ryan would give his life to protect Sandy from harm. But the scripture passage spoke of *agape* love.

He continued down the path until it converged again with the other. Narrow steps led to a terrace paved with bricks. Sitka spruce grew in wide dirt circles cut into the bricks. The area seemed more secluded, private, a place for patients to be alone.

He stopped at the entrance behind a lilac bush and noticed a familiar woman in scrubs. Her short stature brought the top of her head to the chin of the man in the white coat. Jason bent his head to her lips then pulled her into an embrace. The kiss enduring longer than the last one at her birthday party, longer than the one Ryan gave her. Sandy slipped her arms around his waist. When the kiss ended, she rested her head on his chest.

The sight twisted his stomach. His friend was in the arms of another man. Moving in a slow circle, he turned toward the building.

He had feelings for her, though he couldn't define them—a longing he hadn't felt before. Was this what a man felt the first time a woman stole his heart? Or did he merely want something he couldn't have?

He returned to his car, a scalpel wedged in his heart. Had Jason won his friend's love?

~*~

Ryan grappled with the haze of drowsiness then shook his head. Another restless night. He'd dreamed of Sandy. He saw her face clearly and reached out for her. As a cloud dissipates when a gust of wind pushes through the atmosphere, her image faded and disappeared.

Sandy, don't leave me. I lo... What had he said to her?

He flipped onto his stomach and pulled the pillow over his head. Seeing Jason and Sandy kissing yesterday had impacted him more than he first believed. Jealousy grabbed his belly and spun it around. What was he thinking? Yes, he was jealous. Tossing onto his back, he pulled the pillow under his head.

I will never leave you nor forsake you. His God was faithful. *Seek first the kingdom of God and all these other things will be added to you.*

Ryan heaved himself up and climbed out of bed. Though his appointment with Greg wasn't until 10:00, and Ryan didn't have to go to at work until 1:00, maybe Greg would see him early. He needed to talk to his friend and counselor.

He put on jeans and a tee shirt with the message *God doesn't believe in atheists* on the back.

Instead of driving, he'd jog. Needed the exercise.

Ryan locked the apartment door and raced down the stairs into the bright sun. It only took twenty minutes to run to church. When he got there, he burst through the front door and into the church office.

"Oh, hello, Ryan. How's your hand?" Rosie looked away from her computer to give him a grin.

"Almost healed. I'm not going to get stupid again anytime soon." Ryan grinned at her.

The corners of her lips turned up. "Be careful, my friend."

"I'm early. Could Greg see me now?"

"Let me holler at him. He doesn't have anyone else." She knocked quietly on his door.

Greg poked a smiling face out.

"Ryan's early. Is it okay?"

"Sure. Send him in."

"Thanks for seeing me now." Ryan lowered himself onto the familiar couch.

"How's it going, buddy?" Greg broke the ice as Ryan settled into his chair.

He didn't wait for formalities but blurted out his feelings. "I saw Sandy yesterday, kissing a guy at the hospital gardens. Greg, I think I'm jealous."

Greg peered at Ryan as he talked about his trip to the hospital. "I wanted to punch Jason out when I saw him with his arms around Sandy."

"Is it a new reaction, jealousy because of another guy's attention to her?" Greg scratched his head.

"Yeah. I mean, I'm not glad I wanted to hit Jason, but yes, I never felt like this before concerning Sandy."

"I think what's happening here is you're in the process of moving toward heterosexual attraction. You've stated you love Sandy as a friend. Your feelings about her are evolving into something more. Though jealousy is not a godly virtue, it's an indication of a change in your emotions and your thinking."

"Since we've been examining my life, I sometimes marvel at how far off the path of God's truth I wandered." The strangled note in his own voice punctuated his statement.

Greg grasped his Bible from the side table. "Remember what we talked about. Your old feelings resulted from a sinful response to your difficult circumstances."

"I know, but why couldn't I overcome those feelings?" The frustration of his past struggles continued to weigh on him.

Greg sat, his head bowed.

Ryan rose from the couch to stare out the window, his breath deep and heavy. He gazed at the beauty of the trees outside, waiting.

His counselor cleared his throat and thumbed through his Bible. "Psalm sixty-five. Let's read it. I think God has a message there for you. We're going to ask Him to clear your mind of these sinful thoughts, to ask Him to allow you to love the woman He's brought into your life. This might not happen today or tomorrow, or even this year. It'll happen in God's own perfect timing. You've felt a change, but be patient. This is a start."

"Is it possible it won't ever happen."

Greg nodded. "Yes, it's possible, but we're going to trust the Lord for His will to be done."

Ryan took a deep breath and exhaled slowly, dropping onto the cushion of the floral couch. He raised his eyes to Greg.

"Here, follow along with me." Greg passed him a spare Bible. "Psalm sixty-five is about God hearing David's prayer when he says he was overwhelmed by his sins. David learns God forgave him his transgressions, but more, he was blessed because God chose him to dwell with Him. God reminded David He's so powerful, He controls all of nature. The psalm says He's the hope of all the earth. Now, He's the God whom you love and serve. Don't you think He can grant you full release from your sin one day?"

With misty eyes, he looked at Greg, a true friend and messenger of the Word of God. Sandy's image danced before him and knocked at the door of his heart. He rose and slapped Greg on the shoulder. "I'm going to try to get her to give me another chance to be her friend and, God willing, more. We parted in anger before. I'd like to ask her forgiveness and at least part friends next time."

"What do you have in mind?"

"Maybe I'll ask her to go hiking with me on Mt. Rainier while the weather is still nice. She loves the outdoors, and I always feel so close to the Lord up there. At the end of the day, I'll explain everything."

"God bless you, buddy." Greg stood to meet him at eye level.

"Greg?" Ryan stuck out his hand to shake his. "You're about the best friend a guy could have." His heart leapt with joy when he recognized his old feelings for Greg were gone. In fact—Ryan smiled—he couldn't even remember what he saw in the guy.

~*~

"Morning, Mom." Sandy sauntered into the gourmet kitchen where her mother sat on a bar stool, writing. She'd been drained of emotion after telling Ryan good-bye. Of all the things she'd said to him, she hated telling him of her suspicions.

"Honey, you look a little down today. Have you been getting enough sleep? I see circles under your eyes." Mom set her pen on the counter and closed her notebook with its cover of blue and purple geometric patterns.

"Oh, some guy problems. Wanted to let you know, I'm dating Jason. And Dad will be happy. I'm not seeing Ryan anymore."

"Are you okay with that?"

"Yeah, sure." Though she missed Ryan with all her heart, if she spent time with Jason, maybe feelings for him would evolve.

"Well don't forget, your father and I are leaving for Chicago tonight and will return next Tuesday. He has a conference, and then we're staying a few more days to visit with your Aunt Molly and Uncle Ted."

Sandy swallowed. "I'll be here alone?" She shook off the fear and planted a smile on her face. "I'll be fine." Her cell vibrated in her pocket. "Okay, Mom. See you later." She moseyed out onto the deck to take the call. *Ryan.* Her heart pounded. Why was he calling her? "Hello."

"Sandy, don't hang up."

He merely perpetuated her pain. "What do you want?" She strolled to the edge of the deck.

"Hear me out. Would you go hiking with me to Mt. Rainier Sunday afternoon?"

"Why?"

"I need one more chance. I promise I'll explain about myself. Afterward, if you want, you can say good-bye again—forever."

"What kind of a chance do you need?" She twisted a strand of hair around her finger, pacing the wooden deck.

"I want to see you again, even if it might be for the last time. Maybe God…oh, I don't know. Please, Sandy."

His earnestness won her over. "Okay." She stared at her feet, a tear on her eyelash.

"Meet me at church first. Come a little early. I want you to see the construction site then sit with me in the service."

"I'll see you Sunday." What was he up to? It was over with him.

Well, one more time with this perplexing young man on Mt. Rainier. *Lord, please give me the strength.*

Chapter Twenty-three

Before the service started, Ryan stepped into the foyer for a glimpse of Sandy. On the other end, he spotted her.

She drifted toward him. Her long brown hair swung against her shoulders, and her filmy dress hugged her body.

Time was his enemy. He was up against the clock. If he didn't get his thinking straight soon, he'd lose her forever—to Jason. Greg told him to be patient. How could he with the doctor's determined pursuit of her?

She stepped toward him but stopped a few feet away.

If he were to guess, she approached with caution. He could hardly blame her.

"Hello, Ryan. I left my hiking stuff in the car in case you still wanted to go."

"What do you mean, in case? Yes, I do. I made us lunch." He blinked, looking down at her, searching her face. Did she think he'd change his mind?

A slow grin crept to her lips. "You, Ryan? I didn't know you knew how to cook."

"Well, I wouldn't say I know how to cook. I made some turkey sandwiches and brought some fruit from the Farmer's Market." He gave her a half-smile. His pulse kicked up a notch, but it was probably because he stood face to face gazing at his friend.

The thought of what the day could bring weighed on him. "Wanna go out to the site first then into the sanctuary? We've got plenty of time."

"Sure. This project is important to you."

"More than you know." They walked around the building, and Ryan caught his breath. The roof had gone up, and electrical wiring and plumbing started.

Sandy clapped her hands and held them to her chest. "I can't believe the progress. Unbelievable. You were so instrumental in this."

Finally seeing the annex with a completed roof brought a sense of pride. Not a self-centered pride, but satisfaction in what God could do. He didn't trust his voice. With a smile down at Sandy, he touched her waist and nudged her toward the main church building.

Before they reached the front door, he stopped. "May I say a prayer for us?"

She gazed at him with wide eyes and nodded.

He thought about taking her hand but didn't. "Lord, I accept whatever plan you have for me and Sandy. Please bless our time together."

By His grace, God had brought Sandy to worship with him one last time. Something he feared would never happen again considering her absences from services in the last several weeks. Would the Lord complete his life as well with the freedom he sought?

~*~

"I'm going to put on my jeans in the ladies' restroom." Sandy headed outside to get her clothes from the trunk of her Beemer. The message on Romans 6, dead to sin and alive in Christ, lifted her like no other she'd heard Pastor preach.

"Okay, I'll meet you in the foyer. Did you bring your backpack? How about an extra sweater? It gets chilly at Paradise."

"Got both. Back in a while." His interest in her welfare amused her.

She switched her dress for jeans and a red tee-shirt, tied her jacket around her waist, and found Ryan, arms folded over his chest, staring toward the parking lot.

"If you don't mind, let's take the Beemer up to Paradise." The road through Mt. Rainier National Park was steep and winding, and she wasn't sure if she trusted his car.

"Okay. Let me get the lunch." He rummaged in his backseat and pulled out his backpack, a large shopping bag with handles, and his jacket. "Okay, all set." He carried his load with both hands and strolled toward her car.

Something had changed—the way he held his chin a little higher. A chuckle found its way from her throat to her lips.

His prayer this morning before church blessed her—God's plan for them. Did he mean them individually or together? She stiffened. *Don't get your hopes up for a relationship with him. It's not going to happen.*

She couldn't make herself vulnerable to him again. Still, she wasn't sorry she'd agreed to go hiking.

~*~

Sandy breathed in the fresh mountain air. The Beemer wound its way through the countryside to the entrance of Mt. Rainier National Park. The road curved around the side of the mountain, the drop off steep. The Nisqually River flowed past them for part of the journey to the visitor's center, its waters gushing over rocks, the sprays resembling smoke. On the banks of the river, clumps of pink and purple wildflowers grew out of mossy rocks. A stand of ash shared the earth with Bear Grass bushes.

"Looks like we picked a good day to hike. No rain and no clouds." Ryan rolled down the window on the passenger side.

This Ryan was different than the man who rode with her to Lake Quitama at the beginning of summer.

The mountain air refreshed her. "I'm in another world. As if this amazing scenery erases the demands of our lives in Cedar Fork. The waterfalls, the little springs gurgling out of the earth, the deep canyons covered by wildflowers. Nothing else seems important now." She exhaled a long breath.

At the next curve, a vast cone-shaped peak sprinkled with snow at the top came into view. Old growth forest encircled its base, probably western hemlock, Douglas fir and red cedar. One more curve then they pulled into the parking lot at the Jackson Visitor's Center. Paradise Lodge soared to their right.

"Hungry?" Ryan piled out of the passenger seat.

"Starved. The high altitude's giving me an appetite."

He pulled the shopping bag out of the backseat. "There's a picnic area on the other side of the visitor's center. Let's grab our stuff and go over there."

It wasn't hard to sense her Savior's presence as she studied the magnificent landscape. She turned her face to the man who led her to Him, the man—if she were honest—she loved.

Her parents wanted her to marry Jason. She'd known him since he was a little blond headed boy who used to fall down and scrape his knee every other day. But because they grew up together, was it a basis for marriage?

Jason didn't know the Lord like she did. Wasn't she first attracted to Ryan because of his love for God?

Her thinking had changed. A husband's relationship with the Lord would have a bearing on her own life.

"What did your parents think of you coming up to Mt. Rainier with me today?" Ryan pointed to an open table.

"Mom and Dad aren't home this weekend. They went to a medical conference in Chicago. They left me like an orphan." She chuckled. "I'm an adult now. So, it doesn't really matter. In fact, I was thinking about getting an apartment on my own pretty soon, as soon as…"

"As soon as what?"

"Oh, nothing." Sandy sighed a heavy breath. The reasons she lived at home pressed her. Would she ever be free of her debilitating fears?

Ryan held the truth about his life from her. But she did the same. Would she…did she feel free to tell him? She trusted him. Maybe he could even pray for her.

"I may start looking for a new apartment around the first of the school year. Uncle Frank is getting married and moving out pretty soon." He opened up the brown paper bag containing the lunch.

"Cool. Who is the lucky lady?" If Sandy allowed herself to dream, she'd look for a new apartment with Ryan and move in with him—as man and wife.

"A lady he met at church."

She took a bite of turkey sandwich. "Hmm. This is good. You may not be able to cook, but you can make a mean sandwich." She laughed for the first time in a week. The breathtaking beauty of their surroundings lent her peace.

Before she took the next bite, her throat tightened. A new doubt assailed her, clouding her joy and igniting her nerves. Why had Ryan brought her here? What would he tell her?

Fear frayed the peace she'd enjoyed. He was preparing her for the painful truth—he's gay, shattering any chance of a future together. An ache zigzagged to her toes. He'd probably shred her heart to ribbons. But for now, she had to live in the moment and bask in God's beauty.

"I picked out a trail for us. See what you think." He showed her a brochure with descriptions of hikes and maps. "Look, on this one we pass two lakes. The trail is a succession of gradual ups and downs crossing low ridges on the mountain. We're getting a late start, but we've got plenty of daylight hours. We'll be up the trail and back by about seven. You'll be home by eight, well before dark."

Dark. Her mind filled with a formless fear. What if something happened, and they didn't get down the mountain before nightfall? She'd have to return home in the inky darkness to an empty house again.

~*~

Ryan owed Sandy the truth, if for no other reason so she'd understand the issue between them had nothing to do with her. Yet, he wanted more than anything to have a God-pleasing relationship with her, to experience the feelings a man has for a woman. She said she wanted to appreciate the day. He'd tell her later—didn't want to spoil it now.

The view from the trail took his breath away—a meadow of purple wildflowers and the mountain towering in the distance.

"Is the backpack too heavy?" He shouldered his with the bottles of water and the emergency supplies.

"Ryan Reid. Don't tell me chivalry is alive and well. Yes, it's fine. Thanks."

He didn't want the day to end and was afraid to look at his watch. Yet they'd been on the trail for quite a while. A glance at his watch startled him. "It doesn't seem like we've been hiking for over two hours. Maybe we should consider turning back. What do you think?"

He looked over his shoulder at Sandy following him.

She took a step forward. Her right shoe wobbled on a flat granite rock, which turned upward with the weight of her foot. She fell forward and hit her head on a tree stump and landed with a thud on the grass.

He rushed to her. "Sandy, are you okay?"

She pushed up on her elbow and touched her hair on the side of her head. With a start, she stared at her red fingers. "My head's bleeding." Her nurse's training must've kicked in, as she sounded calmer than he would have.

He grabbed his first-aid kit from his backpack and hurried to mop up the blood on her forehead with a sterile wipe. He parted her hair, like she'd done with his once. The wound was superficial, not nearly as bad as he'd thought. He dabbed around the area. "Okay, I put some antiseptic on it. I don't think it's too serious. Grab my hand. I'll help you up."

She held out her hand and jumped up. "Ow. My ankle's killing me." She hopped on her left leg and attempted to put her right shoe down. "I've got to sit down."

He kneeled to inspect her ankle. Swelling had already begun. "I think you sprained it or something."

She grimaced. "I need an icepack to keep the swelling down, but I'm afraid we don't have one."

"Wait, I see a spring on the other side of that spruce tree—see where that group of rocks is?" He took a kerchief from his backpack, hurried over to the spring, and doused the cloth in the water. "Here you go. An icepack."

He wrapped the icy wet cloth around her ankle, gently lifted her leg, and placed a flat rock under her foot.

"Who's supposed to be the nurse around here? Maybe you should've gone into medicine instead of education." She laughed and then winced. "Ow, Ryan. This is painful."

"Just rest." For a makeshift pillow, he placed his backpack behind her. She leaned into it and closed her eyes.

While Sandy rested, he doused the cloth a couple more times and wrapped her foot. *Lord, please ease her pain.*

Was it his imagination or had the shadows cast by the evergreens grown longer? "We need to think about getting down this mountain. I can't believe it's already 5:30."

Her mouth fell open. "Maybe I can hop if you can support me."

"Let me try something. I'm going to squat down in front of you. Keep your backpack on your shoulders and try to carry mine. I'm going to give you a piggyback ride." If they didn't start now, they'd be going down the trail at twilight or, worse, stuck up here all night—something he didn't relish for himself but more for Sandy's sake.

"Ryan, you're crazy."

"You don't weigh more than a hundred pounds. It'll be easy." He tied the wet cloth around her ankle and backed up to her. She grabbed hold of his shoulders and hugged his waist with her legs as they started down the mountain trail.

Ryan kept up a good clip for twenty minutes or so. He stopped when he heard her swift intake of breath. He must have bounced too much.

When he started again, his pace slowed. The extra weight of Sandy and the backpacks took more strength than he thought. After another twenty minutes, he needed a break. Now the sun had dropped farther in the western sky.

He eased Sandy down near a tree trunk so she could lean against it.

"How far…do you think we've gone?" The rising tone of her voice held a degree of panic.

He was afraid to look at his watch again. "Do you remember this area, how long it took us to get up this far when we started?"

"I hate to say it, but I remember the little meadow, especially those purple wildflowers when we hiked up. We'd been on the trail for at least an hour and a half. I'm starting to get worried."

He figured the temperature had dropped ten degrees. At least the wind wasn't blowing. He couldn't avoid the truth any longer. The light from the sun grew dimmer as he backed her onto the trail and squatted down to face her. He kept his words gentle, quiet so as not to panic her. "If I didn't have to carry you, I could get down the mountain quickly and go for help. You wouldn't have to wait long."

"No." Her eyes held a frantic sheen. "Don't leave me." She reached out and grasped his arm. "There's something you don't know about me."

Chapter Twenty-four

Ryan fought the urge to laugh. Something he didn't know about her? Her secret couldn't be as flagrant as his.

"I never told you because I'm ashamed." She trained her gaze on something over his shoulder then pulled her focus to him. "I've been afraid of the dark since I was a child—the reason why I live at home." She sucked in a quick breath. "I sleep with a night light in my room."

He hated the frightened wide eyes and the frown on her face, but from what he could tell, she had to be serious. Why would she think it such a terrible secret? Ryan furrowed his brow. "What do you mean, fear of the dark?"

She lowered her chin and closed her eyes. "It's so hard to talk about."

Tightness in his chest told him the question sounded harsh and insensitive. Greg had maintained neutrality though Ryan revealed sordid details about his life. A standard Ryan hadn't lived up to.

He held his hand out to her.

She grasped it, hopped to a flat boulder, and eased down.

Counseling told him his problems were dictated by the past. Had something earlier in Sandy's life made her fearful?

It became obvious now. Since daylight faded quickly in the densely forested area, they needed to wait until dawn to continue. But could he tell Sandy yet? "I'm sorry for my unkind tone of voice. Would you tell me what makes you so afraid?"

She looked past him, avoiding eye contact.

"Hey." He lifted her chin. If she felt even half as shy about confessing failure as he did with Greg, he felt for her.

She opened her beautiful cinnamon eyes.

"I really want to know," he whispered. His sessions with Greg began to teach him to think of others instead of self all the time as he tended to do in the past.

"When I was a kid, I—I..." She swallowed hard, and her hands began to tremble. "I played in the family room in the evening. Dad and Mom were usually in the kitchen or living room." She reached for his hand and squeezed.

Ryan smiled. He'd held her hand like this the day the doctor removed the nail. "Go on."

"Don't laugh at me or make fun of me. I couldn't take it if you did."

He shook his head. "Something that scares you this badly isn't a laughing matter."

"I was little, so I don't remember how many times it happened, but sometimes I'd played alone, and I'd look up. I'd see a face peering at me from the sliding glass doors. I'd scream, and Mom and Dad would come running. They never found anyone. At first, they thought I was making it up, scaring myself. Then the nightmares started."

He touched her with his free hand and fought against a wince as she held to his other hand more tightly.

Sometimes as a child alone, he'd imagined noises, and he'd hidden under the covers waiting for his mother to return. Most times she stayed out all night, but the morning light would chase away his fears. When she did come home, she was never in a mood for his little-boy worries. Ryan didn't think Sandy's were caused by her own imagination. "But you didn't make it up, did you?"

She shook her head. "Nooo." The sound came from deep inside her. "Ryan, it's getting dark. I'm afraid."

"I'm with you," he said as calmly as possible. He couldn't leave her now, and she couldn't make her way down the trail. He was all she had. "So, when did your parents come to realize the truth?"

"You—you really want to know?"

"All about it." He'd never suspected Sandy suffered this kind of trauma as a child. "Tell me, please."

In the fading light, her gaze connected with his, and he saw her horror there. He lifted his arm and drew her to his chest, wondering for the first time if she belonged there.

"One night I was playing. I remember trying to concentrate on my dolls and not look at the glass doors. I sensed him there. His eyes were on me, but I wouldn't look. Even when I felt the cool air from outside hit my back, I closed my eyes tight and told myself it was my imagination."

Ryan stopped breathing.

"When he grabbed me from behind, I screamed, and I fought him. He held me tight, but I struggled. He kept saying something, and I couldn't understand the words." She wrapped her arms around him. For several seconds, she sobbed against him, and he remained silent, telling himself to breathe.

When the silence stretched out for too long, Ryan became worried. "Sandy, tell me he didn't force himself on you. Did your dad get there in time?"

She nodded against him. "Daddy wrenched me from his hold. I ran to Mom, and when I looked up, Daddy pounded him, knocking him down, and shouted to Mom to call the police."

"What...what happened?"

"When the police arrived, they took the man into custody."

"Oh, Sandy, I'm so sorry it happened."

"It turned out he was the son of our gardener, his mentally disturbed thirty-year-old son." Sandy heaved a sigh. "The man knew his way around the outside of our house because he'd come to work with his father sometimes."

"Did the gardener's son stay in jail?"

"No, even now it bothers me. Dad decided not to press charges, and he didn't fire the gardener. Only forbade him to bring his son with him anymore."

If Ryan could express his opinion to the doctor, he'd tell him what a jerk he was for not pursuing legal activity. To at least give his daughter the security of knowing the man was locked up.

"I can't shake the fear, Ryan. I can't."

Ryan rested his head on top of Sandy's. "Do you trust me? Despite everything I've allowed to come between us, do you think I'd let something or someone harm you if I could help it? Any more than you would've let the bully in the park beat me up?"

She smiled through her tears. "I trust you, Ryan."

"Then I think I should tell you, we're stuck up here for the night."

~*~

The last shreds of light faded fast. Sandy tensed as she realized she'd be in total darkness soon.

Ryan wrapped her ankle in the wet, cool cloth, and she covered her arms with her sweater. The old fear gripped her as terror crept down her spine. The only thing standing between her and sheer alarm was Ryan. He lowered himself beside her and leaned back. A patient smile filled his handsome face. She moved closer to him. Her attempts to breathe deeply did little good.

"Come here." He held out his arm.

She settled into his embrace and buried her face against his chest.

"How's your head?" he asked.

"A little sore."

"And your ankle?"

"Hurting, too."

"Sandy, I'm so sorry."

"Let me feel safe in your arms."

"So long as you do."

She lifted her face to his. "Do what?"

"Feel safe. That's all I care about."

She pushed upward and kissed his cheek. "Seems you're always protecting me from my fears, Mr. Reid, and I love you for it."

In the darkness, Ryan remained silent. Sandy clung to him, and he held to her even more tightly. In the stillness, she could have sworn the courageous man was crying.

~*~

Ryan held Sandy with her head on his chest and his arm around her as they rested on the trail in darkness. Once he'd asked her why she chose to live at home, and she gave him some evasive answer. Now his skepticism changed to empathy.

He hadn't dreamed, but awoke with a start when he heard a snap. Something or someone stepped on a branch as it made its way through the trees. He reached over Sandy, resting on his shoulder, and punched the glow-light on his watch. Four o'clock. It'd be light soon. Sunrise came early in the summer months. What kind of creature would be so near he could hear the sound of its movement?

Sandy's quiet, even breath told him she was asleep, so he supposed he could move away from her a moment. He needed to divert the creature if there was any possibility it would travel in her direction. A few paces toward the trees should allow him to investigate the source of the sound, though it'd be hard in the pitch-black night. Why hadn't he brought a flashlight? He pulled away from her, allowing her head to ease onto the backpack.

He took careful strides toward the dark shadows, the trees, about fifty yards away. His foot tangled in something, maybe a root, and he stumbled. The sharp prickles of a bush caught his fall. He twisted off a branch to use as a weapon, though he wasn't sure what good it would do if he was attacked by an animal. *Lord, we need Your protection.*

Whatever was out there, he had to sneak up and scare it off. Maybe it was an elk, a deer, or even a cougar. He neared the trees and took careful steps through the darkness. A scream jolted him nearly out of his own skin.

"Ryan." Sandy's voice was eerie, bloodcurdling.

The hair on his neck stood up.

"Ryan, where are you? Please, please come back."

He raced toward the sound of her cries, stumbling again on the rocks and high grass in the dark. *Lord, please don't let the animal follow me.* He knelt down in front of her as she sat up on the path and wrapped his arms around her shoulders.

"Ryan, I woke up, and I was all alone. All alone on this mountain." The words tumbled out like an avalanche. "You were gone. But you're here now. I'm not completely alone now. You're here…with me." Each word was punctuated with a gasp. "Don't leave me. Please don't leave me."

"It's okay. I'm sorry. I had to figure out what made the sound." He hoped he didn't scare her even more. "You're okay." He eased her from him to move a strand of hair out of her face. The sound of her terror chilled him. He was supposed to stay with her. He'd promised. *Why did I leave her?*

Her body shook, and he enveloped her in his arms again.

Her cries wracked her limbs, and her breath came in uneven puffs.

He rubbed her back with a gentle touch and stroked her arms. "Shh," he whispered in her ear. "Lord, please calm Sandy. Comfort her. Bring Your peace upon her and wash over her by your Holy presence."

As he spoke the prayer, his hand caressed the length of her long silky hair. He opened his eyes to see a ray of light glinting through the trees, the first light of dawn on Mt. Rainier.

He closed his eyes again and nuzzled her hair. Her body was warm against his. With all his heart he desired to protect her.

She relaxed against him.

He thought about the sin which formed a barrier between them. God designed humans in His own wisdom. A male and a female. God created families and children, His plan for mankind. Ryan traveled down a crooked road in his heart, not a straight and narrow path.

But his lack of romantic feelings. How could he deny them? His problem resulted from circumstances which weren't his fault. Yet, he was an adult. Time he took responsibility for his life. The realization hit him squarely in his spirit.

Ryan was a Christian. Jesus himself bore his sins in His body for him so he could die to sin and live for righteousness. He had a choice, and he wanted to do it God's way. All the principles Greg had stressed flooded his mind and made perfect sense.

Love. What about love? Sandy loved him. Her love was patient and kind and not self-seeking. He didn't deserve her love. But when she'd been hurting, needing him, his heart had warmed at her need. Her touch no longer repelled him. A vision of Greg no longer stood like an unnatural specter between them.

God had begun His work. Ryan was sure.

He'd been crucified with Christ and his old self no longer lived, but Christ lived in him. Through Christ living in him, he could return her love, because God was love.

The insight penetrated his soul. He knew then he loved her. Did he love her like a sister or was it romantic love or both? Now he had a chance to protect her from danger on the mountain and comfort her in her fear.

She moved from his arms and blinked at him in the early morning light. "I'm sorry I acted like a child...again. Thank you for your strength. What kind of sound did you hear?"

"I heard something snap. Please, don't let it scare you. I didn't find anything out there when I went to investigate, but I guess we better make our way down the mountain in a few more minutes, as soon as it's light enough."

"You went out into the dark to fight off a vicious animal for me?" The mountain ranges through a break in the trees were a dark silhouette in front of a soft orange glow. Above the light, the sky turned from black to navy.

He smiled at her. "Yeah. I did. I'd do anything to protect you."

"Oh, Ryan." She peered into his face for several moments. "I don't think we'll see each other again after today. I need to say good-bye." She put her hand on his face. Her kiss was tender and sweet. "I don't like to admit it, but I'm going to miss having you in my life."

He breathed deeply. The awareness of Sandy and her lips on his filled his mind.

"Please don't give up on us." He picked up her hand and lifted it to his heart.

"*Us* is about friendship. I've told you a hundred times. I've moved on, and I can't wait any longer for you to say—"

"I love you?" He searched her eyes.

Desire flowed through him. He slid his hand on her neck, her soft hair falling through his fingers. His lips brushed over hers, and he feasted his eyes on her. He studied her and examined his own feelings deep inside.

She gazed at him as if surprised.

He scrutinized the depths of his soul. There was tenderness there, softness toward her. It wasn't strong or passionate, but the desire was quiet and warm. He couldn't live without her, one way or the other. But if he didn't love her like a husband, passionately...then he could never ask her to hold on.

In slow motion he moved a strand of hair off her face then covered her mouth with his. His lips moved more deeply over hers, and he wrapped his arms around her, lost in her femininity. He didn't pretend this time.

She slipped her arms around his neck, and he knew nothing but the nearness of her.

He closed his eyes as he lifted his lips toward her ear and whispered. "I love you, Sandy."

He knew the truth now. God's plan was for a man to love a woman. The enemy of his soul almost stole her from him. He'd believed a lie and had been so entrenched in it, he thought there was no escape. But Christ set him free. The temptation to sin would always be there, but nothing said he had to give in. God offered him the power to live according to His will. His desire for Sandy was a gift from God. He raised his hand in praise to his Lord and Savior.

"Are you telling me because you want to keep me as a friend?"

He knelt in front of her. "Sandy, look at me. I love you with all my heart. As a friend, yes, but more, much more. I love you as a desirable woman too."

"I don't understand. You are the most perplexing man I know." But she smiled up at him, hope in her eyes. "Miss Mary knew what she was talking about after all. I doubted her for a while."

"What? Who?"

"Oh, never mind."

He looked once more at the sunrise in the east. A scripture from Proverbs came to him: *The path of the righteous is like the first gleam of dawn, shining ever brighter till the full light of day.* They were God's righteous people. Their path was illuminated by His light.

But they needed to go. "Okay, Miss Arrington, we're playing piggyback again." A doe with her fawn scampered across the trail. "Look. The creature I heard," he laughed.

"Weren't you going to tell me something about yourself?"

Blood drained from his face. If Sandy never wanted to see him again after she learned the truth, he'd have to take the risk. Couldn't put it off anymore. He opened his mouth. "I...I, you see, Sandy, God has done something in my—"

"Ryan, it doesn't matter anymore. If you love me, it's all I need to know."

"I do." Sandy seemed content with his words. Maybe it was best. "But right now, we've got to get you down the mountain for medical help."

Chapter Twenty-five

Ryan's calves complained as he plodded down the mountain trail—Sandy holding onto his back. Her grip around his shoulders tightened when the terrain became steep but loosened moments later. A mist settled over them. The towering firs and hemlocks were a blur, the trek down the path obscured. Hiking was easier now. He carried precious cargo. He'd do anything to get her help.

The visitor's center came into view. "Wait here, and I'll see if I can find the closest clinic."

She slid off his back and hobbled to the picnic table resting her leg on the bench. "It's only seven. I can't believe we made it so fast."

He gave her a smile and pulled on the door. Locked. A map of Washington was posted on a bulletin board outside the building under the overhang. As he thought, Cedar Fork was the nearest town of any size.

"Are you exhausted—carrying me all the whole way?"

"I could have carried you down ten mountains if I had to. But right now, we've got to get you to urgent care. Cedar Fork seems to be it."

"The best place is the emergency room at the hospital. What a laugh! I'm showing up as a patient where I work." She grimaced as she slid her foot forward on the bench.

"Come on, Miss Arrington. I can't stand to see you suffer anymore." He swept her up and headed toward the car. "Hope you trust me to drive the Beemer down the mountain," he laughed.

"Here's the key." Sandy pulled her keychain out of her backpack.

Ryan slipped her into the passenger seat, threw the backpacks in the trunk, and raced around to the driver's side.

The clouds hadn't pursued them down the mountain. Rays of sunlight bounced off the roofs of cars in the visitor's center, overnight hikers on the trails.

"It almost seems like a dream—our time up there. Except for my ankle and panic attack, this morning was amazing."

He put the key in the ignition and craned his head toward the back window pulling out of the parking space. "I've prayed for changes in my life, for the Lord to make me into the man He wants me to be."

He glanced toward her as he pulled onto the main road to the park's exit. "I need to ask you to hold on. Give me a chance to show you how I feel. Unless the intern's stolen you away from me."

She chuckled. "How could he? You already owned my heart. What I said about us never seeing each other again, I didn't mean it."

"Then how come I saw that jerk kissing you the other day in the hospital gardens?"

"What? What were you doing there?"

The evergreens beside the road were dark except for a bright strip illuminated by a shaft of sunlight. "I was lonely. I wanted to catch a glimpse of you. I caught a glimpse all right."

"I was trying to convince myself I loved him. I thought you were out of my life forever. But you know what? My heart was smarter than I gave it credit for. It didn't buy the story that I didn't love you."

"I want to start over and try this romance thing again. I can't let you walk out of my life." The leaves of the darkened trees became more visible.

She leaned her head on his shoulder and closed her eyes. "Umm."

"Don't worry. I'm going to get you help soon. Are you okay for now?" He didn't get an answer. She must have been exhausted.

He rubbed his temple with two fingers. How bad was her injury? Would not getting to a doctor right away delay healing? His responsibility weighed on him more than he'd first believed, yet transporting her to the hospital was a task he welcomed. He wanted Sandy to be a part of his life always.

~*~

"Ready to get your splint?" Sandy's co-worker zipped into Dr. Cohen's office and gawked at Sandy's ankle. "What in the world happened to you?" Jane handed her an 800-milligram dose of ibuprofen and a paper cup filled with water.

"Nurse Foreman, don't you dare make fun of me." Sandy grinned and reached for the pill and water. "I went hiking with my boyfriend and stepped in a hole. Now, no more comments." She flashed Jane a smile. *My boyfriend. I love the sound.* "Dr. Cohen ordered imaging and found partial tearing of the ligament, so I'll have to immobilize my ankle for about four weeks. Hopefully I can go to part-time duty before then."

"With all the first aid instruction we studied during our four years of nurses' training together, I'd think you'd be more cautious." Jane laughed as she put her hands on her waist. "So, you and Jason went hiking?"

"No, Ryan and I."

Jane threw her hands into the air. "I can't keep up with all your boyfriends." She picked up Sandy's chart from Dr. Cohen's desk and scribbled something.

"He's the guy I met during the earthquake."

"So, he rippled his way into your life after the quake." She snickered. "Guess that wasn't too funny. Uh oh, there's my page. See you later." She rushed out of the office into the hall.

Sandy smiled and relaxed into the chair, her foot elevated on a stool while she waited for the doctor.

She couldn't help the smile on her face. Ryan couldn't be gay. Not after the way he kissed her. The memory of his lips on hers lingered. She'd felt dizzy and out of breath when he released her. He'd spoken the words she waited so long to hear. Finally got his thinking straight. What more did she need?

Then apprehension grabbed her stomach. What would Jason say when she told him she was in love with Ryan? Worse yet, what would her father say?

~*~

Ryan paced the waiting room, pulled his cell out of his pocket, and punched his uncle's speed dial. Frank could be worried. Too, Ryan didn't want to wait another minute to share the news about his freedom and ask Frank to pray for Sandy.

"Ryan, tell me you're okay. I was a little concerned. I didn't see you at home last night."

"I spent the night with Sandy," Ryan teased.

"What?" His voice held an incredulous note.

"Gotta josh you, Uncle Frank. Actually, it's more serious. Sandy had an accident when we went hiking yesterday, but she's getting help now in the ER."

"I'm sorry, buddy."

"There's something else. I think I'm in love." Ryan heard only silence. "The Lord, He's doing a work in my life. Frank, I'm finding the freedom we've prayed for."

That was the good news. The bad news was Ryan felt guilty now about not telling Sandy the truth. Sure, he'd tried, and she said it didn't matter. But above all, he had to tell her, even if the truth destroyed their romantic relationship.

~*~

Remorse rammed through Ryan when Sandy hobbled out the clinic on crutches with an air splint on her ankle. Was there anything he could have done to keep this from happening? Maybe if he'd hiked by her side instead of in front or chosen a different path.

"Wait here. I'll bring the car to the door." He drove the Beemer up the circular drive. Grasping his hand, Sandy inched into the front seat then lifted her leg in. He tossed her crutches in the backseat behind her.

"Your Toyota is at church." Sandy ran her hand along the top of the splint.

"I'll call Greg to come pick me up at your house. I want to get you settled first. When do your parents come home?" A glance at her told him she looked comfortable.

"I think tomorrow evening."

She laid her head on his shoulder and dozed again on the drive through town and out to the house.

He turned in at the mailbox and cut the motor. "We're here." The least he could do was get her settled and fix something to eat.

Sandy sat up and rubbed her eyes.

"I'd do anything if I could change what happened. I'm really sorry. I feel terrible." He raced around and held his hand out to her after he passed her the crutches.

"It wasn't your fault. Besides, it brought us closer. If for no other reason, it was worth it."

The brilliant blossoms were gone, and only the rounded, vibrant green leaves remained on the azalea bushes. A hopeful butterfly flitted around the plant.

"Are you okay here alone? I could stay with you, but your parents might get the wrong idea when they return home."

She cast a nervous glance toward the front door. "I'll be fine in my own room. I've got my pink bear to keep me company, remember?" Her frown turned into a smile.

When he opened the door, Sandy hobbled through the entry and eased onto the black and white floral couch next to the massive stone fireplace in the living room.

He set her backpack on the stairs. "If you'll risk letting me loose in the kitchen, I'll try to see what I can find for you to eat." Who'd believe he'd make a meal in the Arrington's house?

"Things may never be the same in there again. Do you suppose you could concoct a couple of sandwiches and heat up some soup?" She stretched her leg out on the couch.

"I'll see what I can do." He relaxed in her company. His friend…and now the woman he loved.

Canned goods sat on every shelf of the pantry. He found a loaf of bread and pulled a jar of mayo from the fridge. The electric can opener buzzed as he pried the tops off the tuna and soup. Finally, he set a tray on the coffee table with four tuna sandwiches and two bowls of steaming tomato soup. "Gotta start working on this cooking thing."

She laughed and pointed at the tray. "I'm not going to eat that much. Have some."

He picked up a sandwich and munched. When he finished the food, he dragged out his cell again. "Guess I better call Greg for a ride."

He answered on the second ring. "Greg Aldridge."

"Greg? Ryan. I've got a huge favor to ask you. Can you come get me at Sandy's? I'll explain on the way to town."

"Sure. I noticed your car at church. It hadn't moved since yesterday after services. Is everything okay?"

"Pray for Sandy. She sprained her ankle."

"Sandy? I guess you were successful in getting her to see you again."

"Yeah." He couldn't say anymore in front of her. "Look. I really appreciate this." He gave Greg directions and stuck his cell in his pocket. "He'll be here shortly."

Ryan walked toward the sunroom. "Let me check all the doors and windows so you can rest comfortably. If you're scared for even one moment after I leave, call me. I'll come back. I don't care what time it is."

He made his way around the downstairs. He'd never ask, but he wondered if the man who'd attacked her was still in the area.

Finished with his task, Ryan dropped down beside her on the couch.

"Thank you." She crooked her finger. When he moved closer, she kissed his cheek. "I love you," she whispered.

His skin tingled. "I need to tell you…I've got uh…feelings for you which I wasn't aware of before. I don't know how to explain it."

"I've had feelings for you for months." She played with the collar on his shirt.

"I'm talking about things like—"

"What, silly?"

"Like…I guess how a husband desires his wife." The revelations came to him at the same time he informed her.

"Well, I'm glad, but why did it take so long?"

He shook his head. "You're an amazingly beautiful woman. I was an idiot."

"I've been in love with you for a long time and attracted to you since the day you brought me home. I've longed for you. Dreaming of the day we…"

He looked deep into her eyes and saw the woman he wanted to spend the rest of his life with. Tomorrow, he'd talk to her about their future. And tell her the truth. But he couldn't do it now. Couldn't spoil this moment.

Careful not to disturb her ankle, he scooted nearer and took her in his arms. He wasn't sure how long they clung to each other. Her nearness seemed so right. Finally, his lips brushed her ear, and he moved away to gaze at her, his heart hammering in his chest. "How could I have been so blind before? I'm so in love with you, Sandy." Frustration flayed his emotions when the doorbell rang. His ride was here.

He pulled away and ambled to the door. "Hi, Greg. Come in and see the poor crippled woman in here."

Greg's eyes were wide as he made his way through the massive entry into the living room. "Sandy, what happened?"

"Don't even ask. Ryan won't let me live this down."

Ryan never saw her look so pretty. His heart swelled with pride imagining she might be his one day.

Greg sat in the light beige chair across from the couch and listened to Ryan's story about how Sandy fell, the first aid, and the trek down the mountain.

He purposely didn't tell Greg anything else, yet. There'd be time later. After thirty minutes or so, he figured they'd better go, but he worried about her staying alone tonight. He stood. "Are you sure you'll be okay, Sandy?"

She nodded. "I've got all this food when I get hungry." Reaching for his hand, she smiled. "And you made sure I'm locked safely inside."

He bent down and placed his lips on hers. "No matter what, don't forget. I love you," he whispered.

"Bye, Sandy. I'm praying for you." Greg called as they walked out the entrance.

Ryan stepped in again. "See you tomorrow. Be sure to turn the bolt lock before you go upstairs."

Ryan piled in the Jeep, and Greg drove out of the driveway onto the main road. "I owe you one," Ryan said.

"She has a gorgeous house. I'm impressed."

"Yeah, her dad's a doctor. But you'd never know she comes from wealth. She's the humblest woman I know." His heart beat faster thinking of her.

"Ryan, you don't know too many women."

"Okay, you're right." He laughed.

"Hope you don't mind me asking, but did I see you kiss her, buddy? What gives?"

"Are you ready for a long story?" Ryan rested his hands behind his head.

"I've got plenty of time."

The memories of Sandy, their night on the trail, her fear, their kiss, and the freedom he'd found gushed over his emotions as he told Greg the story. "Please keep the part about her fear to yourself." Though he didn't want to betray her, her panic attack was a part of the story. Greg would hold it in confidence.

"Of course, Ryan. That goes without saying. So, what are your next steps?"

"I'm in love with her, and I want to marry her." Ryan caught his breath. "I don't think this would've happened if you hadn't approached me the day I shot the nail in my hand. Your patience with me and your knowledge as a counselor was a God-send. Literally."

"Whew. You don't know how that blesses me. To see fruit from my efforts. As I've told you all along, I care for you as my Christian brother."

Joy bolted through Ryan's heart. "I'm not discontinuing our sessions, though. I know I've got a long way to go."

Greg glanced at him as the Jeep sailed down the tree-lined road. "I'm happy for you, but take it slow. Make sure of your feelings before it goes too far. You've hurt Sandy once or twice. If you hurt her again, you may never win her back." Greg smiled. "I know I'm talking to a brick wall right now. You can't even hear me over your thoughts of her."

Ryan lowered his head and studied a hole in his jeans. "I did hear you. There's an something I have to deal with. She asked me about the rumor Dana and Maggie repeated to her. I led her to believe I'd never had a problem."

Greg lowered his voice. "If nothing else, you've got to tell her the truth."

"I know. Guilt hounds me constantly." Ryan had gotten so used to telling Greg his every thought, the words flowed. "Honestly, I'm procrastinating. I had a chance this morning, and started to, but Sandy interrupted, and I didn't. I'm afraid of what might happen."

"Like what?"

"She may not want to marry me if she knew."

"Yeah, but it's something you've got to do. Sandy deserves the truth. She'll find out eventually anyway."

The lights of Cedar Fork appeared on the horizon. After ten minutes, Greg pulled up in the church parking lot. He shut his door and got out. "As soon as you can, tell her."

"I know." Ryan paced a few steps to his car and curved around to face Greg. "How do I start?"

Greg held out his palm. "Look, when you come in for your next session, I can help you figure out the right words."

"Thanks." A twinge of relief coursed through Ryan. "I will, and thanks for being my friend." The old, dead feelings he used to have faded into the past—like a forgotten nightmare. Vanished in the wake of Ryan's new freedom. God had a plan, and Ryan intended to walk in it.

"Have you looked at the annex lately? I'm encouraged with the progress."

Ryan forced away tears of gladness that threatened. The Lord did a mighty work. By the fall, maybe he'd be organizing the schedule for volunteers to man the various activities. He'd be the first person on the list for midnight basketball—especially since he'd learned he could actually play.

He started his car and drove onto Olympic Way. What would it be like married to Sandy? Mrs. Sandy Reid. Could she really be his? What would her parents say? Would Dr. Arrington give his permission? What if Sandy told her father the truth after Ryan revealed it to her?

A shudder of fear ran down his spine. Most likely, Sandy's father would do everything he could to prevent his daughter from marrying Ryan.

Chapter Twenty-six

Ryan pressed the ornate doorbell. His heart pounded when the door swung open. A beautiful woman with a crutch under each arm stood before him. For a moment he paused, astounded by his new perception of Sandy—a desirable woman as well as a comfortable friend. He loved her now more than ever.

"Good morning. Come in." Her smile sent him to the moon.

"How'd it go last night?" He strolled into the hallway, resisting the urge to take her in his arms. For the first time, a woman tugged at his heart strings, but he was an awkward kid in the game of romance. Could a person like Sandy really love him?

"I left the light on. I did okay. Let me fix you breakfast." The arm pads on her crutches rested under the sleeves of her pink short-sleeve top. Her air splint met her leg mid-calf under her jean shorts.

"No, you won't. I'll fix you something. A bowl of cereal?" He chuckled at the thought of working in her kitchen again.

Sandy hobbled to the bar, her progress slowed by the cumbersome crutches. "How about a bacon and veggie omelet?" She slid onto a bar stool and propped the crutches against the counter.

"Are you kidding? I can do scrambled eggs, but I'm not sure about omelets, especially with all those ingredients."

"I'll guide you through it."

He amazed himself as much as he probably did Sandy when after thirty minutes, he placed the tempting meal on the bar in front of her. Walking around, he sat beside her, grasping her hand. "Lord, I praise you today and ask for Your healing power upon Sandy. Bless this food to our nourishment."

As they devoured the breakfast of fresh cantaloupe and tasty omelets, he had to admit his cooking wasn't too bad. After taking the last bite on his plate, he wiped his mouth with the cloth napkin. "Don't think I'll give Wolfgang Puck competition, but I can't complain about the food."

"Umm. I'm impressed." Sandy finished the last of her omelet. "Do you want to go to the sunroom? I'm trying and stay off my foot. Dr. Cohen recommended I don't go to work for a couple of weeks."

"I'm sure this isn't the kind of vacation you'd envisioned." He picked up their dishes. "I'm on the evening shift at the hardware store, but I've got time now." Ryan arranged the plates in the dishwasher and wiped off the counter. There was something pleasant about sharing a meal and daily chores with Sandy…something he hoped they'd do for a long time in the future.

Sandy shuffled to the sunroom. The rays of the sun bounced off the ivy leaves on the hanging plant near the wicker loveseat. He dropped down beside her.

Would he be rushing things if he asked her to marry him now? Should he hold off for further confirmation? For months, he'd thought about how if he ever loved a woman, it'd be Sandy. Why should he wait to think about marriage? They both had careers, were in their late twenties. With his student loans paid off soon, he could take care of her. Of course, anything he provided would be far less than she had now. Would it matter?

He couldn't afford a ring. Especially the kind he'd like to give her. But he had the little velvet bag in his drawer with his grandmother's diamond, the one thing his mother had given him when Grandma died. The ring was exquisite, a white gold solitaire with a double row of diamonds on the band. Nearly one carat.

As lightning strikes a tree, a thought jolted him. The ring would remain in the drawer forever if Sandy didn't understand about his past struggles. Hadn't Greg, his confidant and counselor emphasized he *had* to tell her? It was time. He breathed hard as his heart drummed. "Sandy, there's something I need to…" An iron clamp on his mouth cut off the words. *Dear Lord, I can't do it. Not yet.* Perspiration ran down his back.

He'd put it off—for now. Wait and talk to Greg like he suggested, to help him come up with the right words.

From the side yard, the pampas grass swayed with a calm breeze. Sandy gazed up at him with a dreamy look. "What did you say?"

If Sandy loved him enough to accept a proposal of marriage, she'd forgive and accept him, despite his past. It didn't really matter what came first—the confession or the proposal.

He covered her hand. "Uh…I think now is a good time to talk." He swallowed hard. "Have you given much thought to your future? I mean, where you're going? I guess I'm trying to say, do you see a wedding and a husband in your life someday?" He stammered. The subject of marriage wasn't exactly his area of expertise.

"Ryan Reid. Are you trying to talk to me about getting married?" Her eyes danced with joy. "I'm interested in marriage only if it's to you."

The words he wanted to hear. "I think I'm old fashioned. My grandma told me Grandpa got down on his knee with a ring when he asked her to marry him. I want to, also. Just checking, though. To hedge against humiliation, do you think your answer would be yes?"

She lowered her eyes. "I'd be happy to say yes, if you ask me."

He squeezed her hand. "I feel right about God's timing. In fact, I don't even think we need a long engagement." He laughed. "For the moment, will you be my girlfriend?" He was in junior high school, experiencing things never opened to him before.

Sandy studied their joined hands. "Yes." She smiled and traced his chin with her finger. "What changed in you?"

"I've loved you for a long time. It's been a slow, gradual emotion. After our night on Mt. Rainier, God's given me the ability to show you how much." He turned his gaze to the landscaped backyard. A blue jay flitted from one tree to another. "Before, I didn't know how to accept your love and didn't feel worthy of you." Though he spoke the truth, it wasn't the whole truth. An ounce of remorse chipped away at his conscience.

"I'm sorry, Ryan." Her touch on his arm was tender and her look sweet.

Now guilt hung on like a plague, stabbing at his stomach. *Face it.* He'd lied to Sandy and hadn't confessed the truth yet. He made a mental note to call Greg when he got home. He couldn't procrastinate any longer. He needed his friend's help.

~*~

Sandy relaxed on the sunroom couch. Their joined hands sent contented waves of warmth inside. Her heart melted with the thought. He wanted to propose. After a quiet time of prayer last night, she'd become more convinced. She wanted to be married to Ryan.

Yet doubt crept into her mind. Maybe she'd acted in haste. Ryan had put her off for so long, and now the minute he wanted to be more than friends, she fell into his arms.

But she wasn't interested in playing games. Ryan was sincere. Somehow, he felt freer to love her now. She only wanted honesty. If Ryan had those inclinations in the past, and if God changed him, she would understand, but he hadn't said anything.

Sandy lifted her hand and ran her finger down his rough cheek. "There was a time when you pushed away when I touched you."

He caught her finger. "Please, Sandy. Don't talk about it."

"I'm sorry."

"No, I'm sorry. It was my problem, not yours." He touched her neck and brought his lips to hers. Her pulse raced when he slipped his arms around her. His lips were on hers when she heard voices.

"Hello. Anyone home?"

They pulled away from the kiss. "It's Mom and Dad," she whispered. "Yes, here in the sunroom."

Banging of suitcases echoed in the entry, followed by footsteps through the den.

"Hi Sandy." Mom strolled into the sunroom. "Oh, hello, Ryan."

He stood. "Hello, Mrs. Arrington. How was your trip to Chicago?"

"Other than the traffic, it was great. Aunt Molly said hello." Mom's eyes widened. "Honey, what happened?"

"What in the world happened to you? And why is he here?" Dad's voice boomed behind Mom.

~*~

Ryan cringed when Dr. Arrington stomped into the sunroom, though he anticipated facing the man eventually. Once again, the question disturbed him. Would it be possible he'd accept their marriage? A cold shiver careened down his spine. "We went hiking on Mt. Rainier Sunday. Unfortunately, Sandy fell. She saw a doctor in the ER and should be out of her air splint in four weeks." He dreaded the man's reaction.

"You went to the ER Sunday night?" Dr. Arrington knelt down in front of her, examining the splint.

"Uh, no. Monday. We had to spend the night on the trail. It was too dark to hike down."

Dr. Arrington stood to his feet and twisted toward Ryan. "You mean first you took my daughter on some hike, and she injured herself, then you couldn't even see she got down the mountain? She spent a whole night on Mt. Rainier?" He yelled. "I can't trust you to take care of her."

"Daddy, Ryan carried me down the mountain. It wasn't his fault."

Can't trust me to take care of his daughter. He'd never agree to their marriage. Ryan pressed his lips in a straight line. "Look, I'm terribly sorry about what happened to Sandy. I care about your daughter, more than I can say, and I'd never purposely allow anything to happen to her. Sandy, I'll let you catch up with your parents, now." He trudged toward the entry.

Mrs. Arrington followed him to the door. "Ryan, I'm sorry he was so hard on you. I'm sure it wasn't anyone's fault. I appreciate you getting Sandy off the mountain."

"Thank you, ma'am. Please tell Sandy I'll call her later." Why couldn't the doctor be half as nice as his wife?

She lowered her voice. "I thought Sandy said she wasn't seeing you anymore. I can't keep her friends straight."

He raised his eyebrows. Was she trying to tell him Jason played a part in Sandy's life? "Yes, ma'am. But a lot has changed in the last week. I'll leave it for her to tell." He gave her a smile and paced out the ornate door to his car. Securing Dr. Arrington's approval could prove to be the most difficult thing he'd ever done, even more demanding than seeking God for healing.

Then again, who was Dr. Arrington to talk about keeping Sandy safe? He'd allowed Sandy's attacker to walk free when he should have been locked up for a long time.

~*~

Sandy laid the crutches on the chair by her bed and crawled up on the down comforter, allowing the praise and worship CD to quiet her. Though Mom had offered to bring Sandy a supper tray, she couldn't eat anything. The image of Ryan's wide eyes this afternoon after Dad's outburst wore on her.

The white lace pillow with the lattice quilting pattern cradled her head. She closed her eyes, picturing Ryan standing in front of her.

Even after her version of the story, Daddy hadn't changed his attitude. Sandy tried to make it clear Ryan did everything humanly possible to get her off the mountain. He even suggested he go for help, and she stopped him because of her fear.

It wasn't his fault. She'd been a klutz and fell. Daddy wasn't impressed when she told him how Ryan went out into the dark to scare off a wild animal. But his reaction to Ryan's likely proposal could be even worse. Maybe she wouldn't tell him. Only wait and show him the ring. She'd elope if it came to it. Ryan was the love of her life, and she didn't intend to allow her father to prevent her marriage to him.

When her cell chirped, she reached toward her nightstand.

"Hi, Sandy. How's your ankle?" The quiet voice she'd grown to love brought a smile unbidden to her lips.

"Probably a lot better than my disposition. I'm frustrated with Daddy for giving you such a hard time. I'm so sorry, Ryan. You didn't deserve the way he spoke to you." She pulled a strand of hair through her fingers.

"It's okay. I'm learning a lot about forgiveness lately—including forgiving myself. Anyway, he wants the best for his daughter. I guess he thinks Jason is the better option."

"How could he think a person I don't love a better choice for me? I love you, not him." She ran her finger across the speaker.

"You can't know how much it means to hear you say it. I don't think I could love you more." He gave a soft chuckle. "If I come to get you tomorrow night, do you suppose you could go to dinner?"

"My dad's leaving again in the morning for Boston, so the coast is clear. Since I'm off from work a couple of weeks, I've got nothing but time."

"How does your mom feel about me?"

"I get the impression she thinks I should marry the man I love." She reached for her cup of hot mint tea on the night table and took a sip.

"I guess that's me."

"You know it is." Breath caught in her chest.

"Seems like all my dreams are coming true. I've got you, and we're even seeing progress on the annex." His pleasant laugh rang in her ears.

"It was your vision. So many lives are going to change because of it."

"Thanks for your confidence. Pick you up at six?"

"Can't wait." Her heart beat triple time. She knew what he had in mind for tomorrow night. A proposal.

Chapter Twenty-seven

Ryan stepped out of the shower, wrapped a towel around his waist, and hummed "Amazing Grace" as he shaved. What did a guy wear when he proposed?

He drifted into his bedroom and poked his nose in his closet. The pair of light beige pants with his charcoal gray shirt and the pink and gray tie should do. Frank tied the knot in it, so all he had to do was slip it over his head.

Once at the PTA meeting when he wore the same clothes, a student's grandmother raved about how handsome he looked, embarrassing him at the time. But tonight, he'd accept her opinion.

He looked at his watch. Plenty of time. He hoped Sandy would like The Falls where he'd made reservations.

The black felt box sat on his dresser. Gibson's made Grandmother's ring look brand new. The diamonds sparkled and winked at him. Soon Sandy would be wearing it on her left hand. He slipped the box into his pocket and tried to still his racing heart.

~*~

Ryan was a child awaiting Christmas morning. He turned in at the mailbox. Once again, he pressed the ornate doorbell and held his breath.

"Come in, Ryan." Mrs. Arrington opened the door and smiled." You look very handsome this evening."

"Thanks." Words failed him from the excitement bubbling inside. He'd stammer if he said anything more. Maybe his wide grin would suffice.

"Sandy's in the den. I'll call her."

He followed her from the entryway into the living room but stopped. Tapping his foot, he waited.

Sandy, in a fitted print dress, hobbled toward him, Mrs. Arrington behind her.

Even on crutches, Sandy looked stunning. She gave him a grin that said more than hello. Maybe echoing her words from last night, *I love you.*

Mrs. Arrington held the front door as Sandy tottered out. "Have fun, you two."

Ryan's pulse pounded. The occasion seemed surreal. "Thank you, ma'am." He grasped Sandy's hand to ease her down into the front seat of his car.

She slowly dragged her right foot up and buckled the seatbelt.

When he sat in the driver's seat, he couldn't wait a moment longer to kiss her. "Sandy, you look ravishing." With his hand on her chin, he brought his lips to hers. He forced himself to take his eyes off her and fire up the ignition. When they were married, he'd hold her in his arms all night. He stole one more glance when he pulled onto the road, amazed at the radical change in his thinking.

She touched her finger to her lips and placed it on his cheek. "Would you mind stopping by Cramer's drugs before we go to the restaurant? I need to pick up another bottle of ibuprofen."

~*~

Ryan followed Sandy as she shuffled down the hair products aisle.

She hobbled to the next row with multiple bottles of pain meds and slowed to peruse the shelf stocked with the pain killers, nasal sprays, stomach remedies, and allergy pills.

A name-brand bottle of ibuprofen sat on the shelf. "I hope this is the last time I'll need these."

Though they were in a drug store, Ryan couldn't resist brushing her cheek with a kiss.

From the corner of his eye, a person in a black tee shirt at the pharmacy counter caught his attention. Allen. The blood pounded in his temple. He was the last person Ryan wanted to meet up with.

Ryan turned around staring at the bottles with Sandy. If he kept his back to Allen, maybe he could avoid eye-contact. Of all the nights he didn't want to spoil by talking to Allen…

"Hello, Ryan."

Ryan's heart fell when he heard the voice at his ear.

Sandy rotated toward him and stared at his ex-friend.

Ryan didn't want to introduce them, but Sandy would wonder if he didn't. "This is Allen." The look in Allen's eyes twisted his stomach. He was up to something. Probably like the night he went to CF Hardware to cause trouble.

"Hello, Allen." Sandy lifted her eyebrow and grasped a bottle of pills.

"I'm ready if you are."

Allen stepped in the middle of the aisle, blocking their way to the register. "Looks like you and Sandy must be good friends."

Ryan thrust his chest out as heat rose on his neck. Would he have to shove Allen out of the way? "Sandy's my girlfriend."

"Girlfriend, Ryan. Really?" Allen's face twisted into a sneer.

Ryan gulped and hoped Sandy hadn't picked up on the sarcastic remark. "Yes, my girlfriend, and we've got to go. Good-bye." Ryan grasped Sandy's hand and pushed past Allen without looking back.

~*~

The muscular, dark haired man scowled at Sandy, almost as if he hated her. Ryan gave a gentle tug on her elbow, steering her toward the cash register. Why had he acted so strange in front of Allen?

Then she remembered what he'd told her about the night he stole a car with some guy named Allen. This must be him. Seeing his old partner in crime made him ill at ease.

After a short drive, Ryan pulled into a parking place in front of The Falls. He shut off the motor and raced around to open the door for her. "Hope you like this restaurant. I've got reservations."

She accepted his offered hand along with her crutches. His warm touch sent a tingle up her arm. She never dreamed Ryan would bring her here. How could she love anyone more or be any happier?

Ryan moved a strand of her hair over her shoulder when she stepped out. "What are you thinking, Sandy?"

"How glad I am to be here with you. I guess to be anywhere with you."

He put his hand on her back as she limped along. The August weather was lovely. Not too cool, certainly not too hot. Western Washington hadn't betrayed them but brought perfect air and sunshine.

Ryan kissed her cheek as he held the heavy wooden door.

The same college-age hostess smiled.

"Ryan Reid. I called for a table for two by the window." He gave a nervous glance. "Will you be okay going down these stairs?"

"I'll take it slow, but I'm fine."

The hostess led the way to the last table along the window opposite the entrance. "We're crowded this evening. Is this okay?"

"Perfect. We have a view." Ryan held the chair for Sandy and propped her crutches against the wall behind their table. Their shoulders touched when he sat to her right. A candle in the center of the table glowed after the server lit the wick.

She glanced out the window. The Salmon River flowed toward the restaurant, cascaded over an incline creating a twenty-foot waterfall, and curved, pushing past the building. Her gaze moved from the glass panes to Ryan's gorgeous dark eyes.

When the server took their drink orders for iced tea, Ryan picked up her hand and kissed her palm. How could he make her feel so weak and giggly?

He gazed at her. "I want to make you smile every day." He brushed her ear with his lips, his words in a whisper.

Ryan as her husband. Spending the night with him. Her heart blazed. Then she remembered to tell him the good news. "You must have been praying for me. Last night I tried to sleep without my nightlight and guess what? I wasn't afraid. I held on to my bear, pictured Jesus in my mind, and repeated the twenty-third psalm. When we're married, there won't be a light to keep you awake."

His gaze softened. "True, but I don't plan to sleep the whole time either."

~*~

Ryan finished every morsel of his pecan crusted halibut. He and Sandy even succumbed to blueberry cheesecake and coffee. A delicious creamy bite dissolved in his mouth. The color of the waterfall changed from a silver to a soft pink.

Sandy reached for his hand. "I'll be back in a moment. I'm going to the ladies' room." She brushed her fingers across his lips.

"I'll be here waiting for you." His heart beat with pleasure as the woman he now believed God gave him slowly maneuvered her crutches up the steps to the lobby.

He glanced around at the other diners. Tables near the window were full. Next to theirs, a large man sat with his back to Ryan and faced a middle-aged woman. They seemed to be involved in animated conversation.

His gaze moved beyond the man to the next table. To his shock, he saw a familiar person, Maggie facing him and a woman with a blonde ponytail across from her. Dana?

Maggie glared at him then leaned toward her dinner companion, cupped her mouth, and whispered.

Dana revolved around in her seat and stared at him, showing no attempt to disguise her gape.

Ryan scrunched down in the chair. If he could crawl under the table, he would. First Allen, then these women.

Dana stared a few more seconds and turned to Maggie.

When the waiter gathered their empty plates, they picked up their purses and marched up the stairs.

Ryan brushed a hand over his hair with a wet palm and tried to breathe deeply. The front door of the restaurant opened, and they walked out as Sandy emerged from the ladies' room. His lips formed an O as he exhaled a breath. Then a punishing notion struck him. If he'd tell Sandy the truth, he wouldn't have to worry about those two running into her.

~*~

Ryan gazed into Sandy's face as she studied him, a slight smile gracing her lips. Her eyes twinkled in the candlelight as dusk turned the falls a dark purple. Was this a dream?

He felt inside his pocket until his fingers touched the velvet box. "Do you feel like walking down by the water?" He kissed her hand. "It's only a little way."

She gave him a knowing nod. "I do. I mean, yes." She giggled.

Plopping cash on the plastic tray, Ryan held Sandy's chair as she stood. His throat clenched in anticipation. In a few minutes he'd ask her to be his wife.

He slowed so Sandy could shuffle along beside him. They followed the gentle, sloping rock path about twenty-five yards to the bottom of the falls. At the end, a white concrete bench overlooked the tumbling water. He took in the sounds, wanting to memorize every moment. "Wanna sit here?"

"Umm." She eased down on the bench, her gaze once again fixed on him.

He closed his eyes, gathering his thoughts. The bubbling and gushing water created a steady rhythm mimicking the beat of his heart. He fingered the tiny velvet box in his pocket again and remembered the words he'd rehearsed a thousand times. A gentle breeze caressed his face.

He took her hand as he gazed into her eyes. "Sandy, I believe God alone has designed our romance." A couple strolling farther down the path glanced up with a smile.

Sandy lowered her eyelashes. "Those are enchanting words, but I'm not sure I understand." A distant train whistle sounded against the evening air.

"You will one day. I brought you here for a reason." With a wide grin, he slipped down in front of her on one knee. Her gasp reached his ears. "Sandy Arrington, I love you and want to spend my life with you." His chest expanded with his deep breath. "Will you marry me?" He pulled the box out of his pocket and showed her the ring. He'd planned to say more, but somehow the simple words seemed enough.

Tears glistened on her lashes as she gazed at the ring. The movement of her soft pink lips pressed him to kiss her, but he waited.

"Ryan, it's lovely. I want nothing more than to be your wife."

He moved beside her, slipped the ring on her finger, and covered her mouth with his. The kiss took on a new meaning, one proving all he wanted was her.

With his eyes closed, he pulled away a few inches, his forehead on hers, and inhaled a deep breath. When he opened them, her sweet presence sent him reeling. He moved another few inches. "Grandmother's ring looks so good on you." Ryan smiled through happy tears.

Her fingers trembled, but she didn't take her eyes off him. "It's a privilege to wear her ring. I love it and…I love you."

Ryan cradled her palm then pulled her close. "I love you, too." He never got tired of saying it. "I want to marry you as soon as we can."

She ran her finger down his cheek. "I guess I better get out of this air splint first. I don't want to hobble down the aisle on crutches."

He laughed. "Let's plan a Christmas wedding. We can start the new year as a married couple." As if to congratulate them, a new moon arose above the falls.

"It can't come soon enough for me, but we need to talk to my parents."

Ryan sobered. "We'll face them together."

Sandy's smile faded, but then she gave her head a shake. "I know, Ryan. We'll think about it tomorrow." She nestled herself under his chin. "Not tonight."

Though Ryan felt tempted to agree with her and forget the impossible task of getting her parents' approval, he couldn't. The moment turned from joyful to ominous. Somehow, he knew—marriage to Sandy might never happen. Especially if he continued to put off telling her the truth.

Chapter Twenty-eight

The morning sunlight contrasted with Ryan's somber mood as he parked his car in front of the church. Only yesterday he'd proposed. Sleep had evaded him last night. As hard as he tried, he couldn't put aside the notion Sandy's parents would never say yes.

He shook off the dismal doubts and tried to think about why he came. To see the gym's progress with his own eyes. He exited his car and hiked around the church to the construction site. As he neared, he caught his breath.

The inner walls were up. On one side, a worker taped the surface in preparation for painting. On another, two workers used a professional point-spraying rig.

The annex—nearly finished. Finally, a place for kids and teens, like the boy he'd seen in the park the day of the earthquake.

He squared his shoulders. Seeing the construction headway sent a rush of adrenalin through him. He put aside worries about Sandy and considered what the next steps would entail in setting up the outreach program.

With a glance at his watch, he increased his stride to his car. Time to get to work, unless he wanted to be late.

The fifteen-minute drive got him to CF Hardware with ten minutes to spare. He parked and sailed through the employee's lounge. Louise gave him a wave as she chomped on a sandwich.

The board at the information desk directed him to shelve products in electronics. He donned his apron, picked up the hand-held device, and made his way to the warehouse.

A couple of the college-aged employees lined carts up by the wall in the enormous room. He found his and rolled it out toward the electronics aisle.

Maggie stood next to a customer, pointing to wire cutters on the shelf. After last night, he'd rather avoid her, but it seemed doubtful.

"Yes, ma'am. We have several brands," she said, facing the customer.

"Would these work for cutting cables?" The woman tossed her short blond hair as she looked at Maggie and to the shelf.

"No, but let me show—"

"Excuse me." A stocky man with a scraggly beard tapped his toe. "I've been waiting for fifteen minutes to talk to you." He unfolded his arms from his chest. "You're going on and on with this woman and ignoring me. I've had enough." The man marched off in the direction of the information desk.

"Can I help you?" Ryan called after him.

The fortyish man waved him off without turning around.

Ryan lifted his brow and shrugged. The guy was about as grouchy as Ryan some days.

With a glance at Maggie, Ryan pulled his cart closer to the end of the aisle to stay out of customers' way. He whistled under his breath as he stocked fish tape, extension cords, ties, and shrink-wrap tubing.

After shelving for over an hour, Ryan's stomach growled. Break time. He jaunted past the lighting and hardware aisles to the employee lounge.

Long tables ran along the width of the room. Two women sat at the first table eating sandwiches and chatting in lively voices. Maggie slumped over another table with her head in her hands, her shoulders shaking.

He strolled toward her and leaned down. "Maggie. What's wrong?"

Her fingers shifted to reveal a tear-stained face. She moved her head side to side, closed her eyes, and placed her hands over her face again.

She was the last person he wanted to talk to, but if she had a problem, he couldn't let her cry. This probably had something to do with the rude customer. He edged into the chair opposite her. "I overheard what the man said. You were doing the best you could. Did something happen?"

She slowly raised her head and looked up at him with a question on her face. "Why do you care?"

"Come on, Maggie. I don't hold anything against you."

She shook her head and gulped a sob. "Mr. Kinser, you know, Larry's boss, he fired me as I was getting ready to leave."

"Why?"

She put her head in her hands then looked up at him with woeful eyes. "The idiot. He filed a complaint, and Mr. Kinser fired me."

"That's not possible. One little complaint. And it wasn't even your fault." He scratched his head.

"Yeah, but there's more. I've been late a lot trying to get a babysitter for Tommy. I don't have anyone to help me at home during the summer." She hiccupped a sob. "I need this job." She shook her head, her shoulders hunched.

"Maggie, I witnessed the whole thing. Let me talk to him." He rose from the chair. If he had to, he'd spend the rest of his break in George Kinser's office.

~*~

Ryan clicked his scanner after he shelved a box with a ceiling fan and watched Maggie leave for Kinser's office. He hoped he'd helped her chances of being reinstated.

He stocked an entire shelf of degreaser when he saw Maggie edging toward him.

"Ryan, can I talk to you?" She waved her hand and pointed in the direction of the employees' lounge.

He stared at the floor as he marched by her side down the long hall. Was it good news or bad?

She entered the room and faced him. "I...I need to apologize." She shook her head. "I was wrong about you."

Maggie apologizing to him? A different person than the angry mother at school. "Don't worry—"

"No, let me finish. You're an excellent teacher. I allowed my frustrations to dictate my actions the day in Mr. Clark's office. And you saved my job today. Kinser rehired me after you told him what you saw. Since school will be starting soon, I won't have to worry about a babysitter." She studied her shoes. "I'm ashamed of all the things I've said about you."

"It's okay."

A tear rolled down her cheek. "How can you forgive me so quickly?"

Would she laugh at him if he told her of his faith? "The Lord forgave me, and I didn't deserve it. It's the least I can do."

She searched his face as if she'd find an answer there.

"It's forgotten, Maggie."

She wrung her hands. "Ryan, there's something else I need to tell you. Last night after Dana and I saw you with your girlfriend, we had a long talk."

Maggie took a few steps away from him and turned again. "Ryan, can you promise you won't reveal to anyone what I'm going to tell you?"

Chapter Twenty-nine

"Susan, hold my calls, please." Phillip eyed the stocky middle-aged man who reclined in the chair on the other side of the desk.

"Yes, Dr. Arrington." Susan's voice sounded from the speaker on his phone.

Bradley Truelock reached into his black briefcase, pulled out a large manila envelope, and set it on his desk. He gave it a push with his thumb.

Phillip stretched his fingers toward the parcel. Could this be the ammunition he needed?

"I believe you'll be astonished at the facts I uncovered." The balding man smirked.

"Give me an overview." Phillip fingered the envelope then folded his hands on the desk, his eyes on Bradley Truelock.

"Did you know our pal is gay?" Truelock smirked.

"What?" He wasn't quite sure he understood Bradley's words. "You can't mean it."

"I stopped by his place of work to see what I could find. Finally flushed out someone who had info about him, a Dana Feldner. She said Mr. Reid's ex-boyfriend came around asking her if she had information about his new love." Bradley waved his hand in the air.

Phillip shook his head. "I don't believe it." The times he saw Reid with his daughter, he'd treated her with kindness and respect. To listen to Sandy, he'd hauled her all the way down the mountain with no complaints. Phillip had seen stars in the guy's eyes, too, like he'd fallen for her. Well, he could've been wrong.

Truelock raised an eyebrow. "Maybe he's after her money. You're quite a prominent doctor here in Cedar Fork. It's no secret."

Phillip drummed his fingers on his desk. "Okay, go on." Reid was cleverer than he thought.

"It seems Ms. Feldner had the name and phone number of the ex-boyfriend. Allen Canterini. I got in touch with him and offered him a tidy sum for his information. Canterini said he and our boy Ryan were lovers for several years."

"Yeah, but can you take his word for it?" He ran his handkerchief over his brow.

"He gave me quite a story. Most of it was about how in high school he helped Reid steal a car, and then the guy got in trouble when he took off for Seattle. Canterini went on to tell me about Reid's mother and how she abandoned him in high school, but the school district never found out. I was able to locate her whereabouts, drove to Puhoma about fifty miles from here. Offered her a few bucks, and she told me everything I wanted to know. She never knew the name of the kid's father. Charming woman, I must say. If you could ever catch her sober. Everything Canterini told me checked out, including the juvie arrest."

Phillip blew out a breath of air. "Whew. This is much more than I expected. He puts himself out there as an upstanding young man. And he claims to be religious. What a hypocrite."

"This Dana woman has worked with him for six years and said he's never dated a female. Look, it's all in the report." Bradley sat in his chair, his arms folded in front of his chest, a satisfied grin on his face.

"Truelock, you've earned your money." Phillip slid an envelope across his desk.

The detective opened it and counted out the ten one hundred-dollar bills. "All right. The rest of my fee. Anytime I can be of service, doctor, you've got my number. Oh, I need an extra hundred and fifty for the dough I gave Canterini and the mother."

Phillip shrugged and pulled out his wallet to hand the man three fifties. His next step formed in his mind.

~*~

Ryan scratched his head. Maggie was clearly upset. What could she possibly want to tell him? "I can promise you I won't repeat anything to anyone at CF Hardware."

He wouldn't keep anything from Sandy, though. Then a sudden thought brought heat to his face. He did keep something from Sandy—the truth.

"What is it?" Ryan sucked in a breath.

Maggie studied her fingernails then looked up at him. "Dana and I talked last night. We walked down by the Salmon River below The Falls." She bit the nail of her little finger. "She has some friend up in Seattle and is moving in with her." She lifted an eyebrow. "She's getting a job in Seattle at Home Depot." Maggie cleared her throat. "Dana told me last night, Ryan. She's gay."

Ryan's mouth fell open. Gay? She'd made fun of and ridiculed him when she thought he was gay. He didn't like to think unkind thoughts, but she'd behaved like a hypocrite.

He balled his fists. Surprise turned to anger. How dare she make his life miserable?

Forgive even as I've forgiven you. The undeniable thought wrapped around Ryan's heart. He whispered, "Lord, reach this woman for You. I'm no better. I forgive her."

~*~

Ryan enjoyed the airy sensation after finding forgiveness for Dana this afternoon. He brought his attention to his fiancée in the passenger seat next to him. "Do you know when you'll return to work?" The sun set behind them, casting a warm orange glimmer. He pulled up into the circular driveway.

"I'm going on light duty in about ten days, though I'll have the splint on another two weeks after that." Sandy's skin glowed with the golden rays.

He placed the gear shift in park. "The Bible study lesson spoke to me tonight. We are no longer slaves to sin, but have been set free and are slaves to God."

"It blessed me, too. I'm discovering I don't have to be a slave to fear, either. Thank you for introducing me to Jesus."

"Come here, you." He pushed a silky strand of dark brown hair away and nuzzled her cheek. Her skin was warm and soft, and she smelled like fresh flowers. "My life changed when I met you." He ran his finger down her cheek and neck. "I couldn't love you more."

He wanted to tell her how God used her. Yet he knew full well Sandy didn't create the change. It was God alone. God's word and His power brought him freedom, not Sandy. But having the young Christian woman in his life played a part.

Though it felt warm and comfortable to hold her in his arms, he needed to tell her about the past. He and Greg had planned to work on the words at Ryan's scheduled session after work today. But Rosie called to say Greg was sick, something Ryan hadn't anticipated. One more time, he had put it off, until his next session with Greg in a couple of days.

Sandy squeezed his hand. "Come in for some oatmeal cookies and coffee. I think Mom and Dad are out to dinner. I should tell you, I haven't worn my ring at home yet. I'm waiting until we tell my parents." She slipped her ring off and slid it in her purse.

Why were there so many secrets? His secret from her and their secret from her parents? "I haven't allowed myself to fully think about what your father will say." He released a heavy sigh.

She nodded and hiked to the door. "Don't worry. If we have to, we can elope."

Elope? Possibly, but how much better to start married life off with a church wedding. "Hey, you're really scooting along with those crutches. Might win a marathon."

She hobbled through the entry, down the hall, and to the kitchen, leaning her crutches against the broom closet. After she punched the button on the coffeemaker, she peered up toward the cabinet out of her reach. "Could you get the coffee creamer?"

Her long hair hung past her shoulders, gracing her shirt. "Yes, after I finish hugging you." He remembered a time when she slipped her arms around him, and he'd pulled from her. He slid his hands to encircle her waist then kissed her head and whispered, "Sandy, please forgive me for all the times I hurt you. I was such an imbecile. I'm sorry for what you went through because of me."

She turned in his embrace and glided her arms around his neck. His lips found hers again. He could never tire of her next to him.

"Hello, Sandy. Are you home?"

He dropped his arms and took a step back.

Sandy's parents sauntered into the kitchen, Mrs. Arrington wearing a smile. A chill traveled down Ryan's spine. Dr. Arrington pinched his lips and scowled.

~*~

What luck. The jerk came to him. Phillip wouldn't have to seek Reid out. The perfect moment to corner him arrived.

Phillip scratched his head. Was this the right thing to do? When Sandy told him about the annex Reid was building, Phillip couldn't figure out how loyalty to a religion would cause Reid to take on such a large project. Unless the religion held more significance than Phillip thought.

Even Sandy seemed more confident lately after taking up with Reid. Had Phillip perceived his daughter's mindset accurately, or was he imagining things?

He shook his head—couldn't think like this. Reid was no good for Sandy, and he had to do something about it.

The cozy little dessert party didn't last long. They hung around in the kitchen over coffee and cookies. Phillip couldn't stomach a cookie tonight. He trudged into the den and plopped into his easy chair with a newspaper.

He sat up straighter at Reid's voice.

"Guess I'd better get home. I've got some chores to do in the morning."

Phillip was glad he'd always been a patient man.

"I'll walk out with you. Where are my crutches?"

"No, it's okay. I'll see myself out."

Phillip endured several moments of silence before the jerk came out of the kitchen. Was the sissy boy kissing his daughter? Phillip finally found the opportunity he was looking for.

Reid opened the front door and closed it behind him.

Phillip rose from his chair and crept through the entry and out to the porch then stepped down into the circular drive. "Can I talk to you a minute?" He'd finally be rid of the fool.

Reid turned to face him with a look of surprise. "Yes, sir."

"I'm going to make this short. I'm on to your game." His heart pounded with anger. Who did Reid think he was trying to deceive him?

"What?" Ryan's brow formed a frown.

"I'm fully aware you're after Sandy for her money. There's no other explanation."

"I'll assure you my feelings for Sandy have nothing to do with money." Ryan gave him the innocent-eye approach.

"Then how do you explain a person like you is romancing my daughter? It's a ruse. You people don't have an attraction for the opposite sex."

Reid's shoulders fell, and his mouth opened. His face reddened as he looked at the driveway. Truelock's report was correct.

"I…I…it's not true. I'm in love with Sandy. I'm not looking for money."

"I could tell Sandy about your mother and your father, and the trouble you got into in high school."

Reid jerked his gaze to him, standing taller. "Sandy knows all of that."

"But I'll bet she doesn't know you're a homosexual." He paused to wait for a response. When there was none, he continued. "Here's the deal. I'll give you twenty-four hours to break it off with my daughter, or she's going to find out you're gay. Do I make myself clear? Twenty-four hours."

Reid stood next to his car and shook his head.

Phillip started toward the house, congratulating himself on a job well done.

"Dr. Arrington?"

Phillip rotated around. "What do you want?"

"Why'd you let the man who attacked your child walk free? I know you love her. Sandy struggled with fear caused by the deluded person for years. You had to know it would've been less traumatic for her if she knew the man who stalked her, peered in the windows at her, and came into your home after her, was put behind bars or institutionalized."

A knot formed in Phillip's stomach. "I don't have to answer to you."

Reid walked toward him. "No, you don't, but maybe you should try talking to her."

Phillip clenched his teeth and lifted his fists.

Reid's stare went to Phillip's hands then met his eyes. "I love her. I love your daughter with all my heart." He stepped toward him. "And I was confused for a while but I never..." Reid leaned close to him. "I never acted on my wrong desires. By God's grace I am delivered from those thoughts, and I can love Sandy like the husband she needs." He walked to his car. "I haven't told her about my past because I've procrastinated, which I know is wrong, but I am going to do it tomorrow morning and let Sandy decide what she wants." He sat down and stared at his fingers for a long moment, then wiped his eyes before driving away.

Phillip turned and walked into his house, Reid's words taking a bite out of his confidence. Sandy told him about Jimmy. Now the realization struck Phillip like a hammer to his head. His actions were the cause of what he'd always considered an unreasonable and intolerable fear in his daughter.

Though Phillip despised Reid, the man had informed him of something he'd never realized before. But confused about being a homosexual? He wasn't buying it.

~*~

Ryan drove out of the driveway and onto the main road. Time had run out. Sandy had to know the truth, without Greg's help. If Ryan had only told her the rest of the story when Dana and Maggie first taunted her, none of this would matter.

He pulled in at his apartment and stumbled into his room. Prayer was his first action. He quietly closed his door and got on his knees beside his bed. *Dear God, give me direction and the courage to stand up for truth. Forgive me for not being honest with the woman I love. I will accept the consequences, whatever they are.*

Twenty-four hours. Dr. Arrington said twenty-four hours.

He pushed to his feet. Maybe if he put on his jogging shorts and ran to Rainier Park, he could get his head straight.

He pulled on his gray shorts and left the apartment, jogging to release the anger and the pain. When he reached the park, he ran along the path lined with the fir trees and rhododendron bushes. The aroma of the woodsy evening air brought him no relief.

Teenagers on bikes zipped through the park on a late summer evening ride hollering and laughing along the pathways. Would he ever feel carefree?

The sound of the radio from a passing truck boomed, assaulting his ears with rap music. Life went on as usual at the park—but Ryan couldn't outrun Dr. Arrington's words.

Chapter Thirty

The mild August sun reflected off the trees and shrubs, sending shimmers of light into Sandy's world on the deck. A thrill of excitement tickled her spine when she thought about where she'd be living in a few months, with Ryan as his wife. She inhaled a deep breath and absorbed the divine aroma of evergreen trees and rich earth.

Though she missed going to work, time off was okay, too. Plenty of opportunity to dream about wedding plans.

Telling her parents was the biggest obstacle. If Ryan came over later tonight, they could make the announcement together. She stuck her fingers into the pocket of her denim shorts to retrieve her ringing phone.

She glimpsed at the caller ID— Ryan. What an amazing coincidence. "Hello to the most handsome man in the whole world."

"Sandy, can you meet me at Starbucks, the one near Cramer's? I need to talk to you."

She couldn't interpret the shaky, slow tone in his soft voice.

"Sure, Ryan. Is something wrong? You sound strange." She smoothed a strand of hair.

"Can you be there in an hour?"

"Well, yes. I'm pretty sure I can drive with my splint. Just have to be more careful about reaction time."

Her breath caught in her lungs as she heard stony silence.

~*~

Their relationship began at Starbucks—it was as good a place as any for Ryan to tell her the truth he had kept from her. His stomach rolled and pitched. How would she take it? Could she forgive him?

He ordered two lattes and plopped down at a table under the window, grateful the shop was deserted this time of day. The intercom played old show tunes, not his favorite kind of music. He slumped in the chair, crossing his feet under the table.

Movement out the window caught his attention.

Sandy hobbled along in the air splint toward the entrance, her crutches gone. The vision of her in jean shorts and lavender top set his heart pounding, while her anxious face twisted his stomach. Could it be any worse to face a firing squad?

She pulled the door open and walked toward him with a limp. "Ryan, you sounded so serious." Her lips brushed his cheek.

He stood and scooted the chair out for her then she settled down in front of the latte.

"Are you sick? You look terrible. You have dark circles under your eyes. Oh, my sweet guy. What's wrong?" She rubbed his hand.

The theme from *Cats* played now. Somehow the music stirred his emotions. His throat ached, and he prayed he wouldn't resort to tears.

Ryan reached for her hand with his clammy palms. "Sandy, there's something I've procrastinated in doing. I'm ashamed."

Questions gathered in her eyes.

"I've been a coward, too afraid of what might happen if you knew."

Sandy shook her head. "Does this have anything to do with what Dana and Maggie said?" She pulled her hands from his and folded them.

Ryan stared at his latte. "Yes." This was harder than he'd imagined.

"Go ahead. I need to hear it." Her voice was quiet, her words a monotone.

"Everything I've said to you is the truth—almost everything." He blinked at her, no longer able to avoid her stare.

"Most everything. You're saying you lied about something." She narrowed her eyes.

The lump in his stomach turned rock hard, and he nodded. "When I told you that morning on Mt. Rainier, I loved you, I meant it. And I still do. Please remember that when I explain the rest."

Sandy closed her eyes. "I'm afraid I know what you're going to say."

Pain knifed through his heart. "There was a time in my life…dear God, help me…I experienced same-sex attraction. But God has brought me freedom. That part of my life is dead. Please understand."

"So, you deceived me. You lied when you said Dana and Maggie were wrong." She sighed. "Let me ask you a question. What do you feel when you kiss me?" Her gaze shot a dagger into his heart.

"Sandy." Heat crawled up his neck. "I love the feeling of your lips on mine. It's all I can do to restrain myself to wait for more…until we're married." No longer did the old feelings of repulsion plague him. The feelings he associated with intimacy with a woman. Not any woman, but the woman he loved.

Her mouth quivered. "The night after the picnic, did you mislead me?"

Ryan cringed. Had she figured out it was a performance? "That was before...before God brought me freedom."

"I knew it. I knew it then. Something wasn't right." She drew her hand to her throat. "You deceived me. And I asked you for forgiveness."

"I know, but things changed." He reached for her hand, but she drew it away.

She slumped in the chair and lowered her voice. "If you really loved me, you would've trusted me with the truth about your past. I would've understood, in a heartbeat."

"Sandy, I was ashamed." His hand shook, knocking his now lukewarm coffee over. It spilled on her jean shorts. "I'm so sorry." He passed her a napkin.

She stared at him but made no attempt to wipe it up. She placed her thumb and index finger of her right hand on her engagement ring, sliding it off. He stared at it after she placed it on her palm and lifted it to him. With a quivering hand, he forced himself to take it.

Tears streamed down her face. "I can't count the times I asked you to tell me what stood between us. I'm sorry you weren't able to believe in me." She pushed up from her chair and walked toward the door. Her painful glance sliced him in half.

Ryan stumbled out of Starbucks to his car. He tried to pray on the way to his apartment, but the words weren't there. The ring jingled against some loose coins in his pocket. He'd lost Sandy forever—because he'd been a coward.

The heartache turned to anger, then despair. He brought his fist down on the seat. Why did God do this to him? Make him think he could be free from the label "gay"? It haunted him at work—CF Hardware and at school. His past followed him everywhere.

He stopped on the street by Rainier Park and pulled out his cell. The phone slid in his hand as he stared at the keypad. Allen's old number was lodged in his brain. *All right, God. Is that what You want?* He punched the keypad. On the second ring, Allen answered, and Ryan hurled his cell to the floorboard.

He dropped his head into his hands. "Lord, my God. Please forgive me. Whether Sandy is in my life or not, I could never disobey You." He remembered the day he received Jesus as his Savior and all the times the Word nourished him. "You are all I have left, God. But in the end, You are enough."

He picked up his cell and clicked it off. The sun moved lower in the western sky when he finally started the engine and crept to the apartment.

Ryan was numb, yet his life would go on, obedience to the Lord his single goal now. The stairs to his apartment challenged his aching body. "Lord, I'm at the bottom rung on the ladder of life again, and I can't see ever moving up a notch without Sandy." Great, now if any of the neighbors have their windows open, they'd know all about it.

He stuck the key in the lock, but Frank opened the door before he could push it.

"Come on in. I want you to meet Lynn. Then we have news for you." Uncle Frank's eyes glistened.

Lynn? Ryan couldn't meet anyone right now. He only wanted to be alone and begin the long, lonely process of healing after the loss of Sandy's love. The loss of what could've been. Except for his stupid pride…

An attractive middle-aged woman came up next to Frank and held out her hand to him. "Ryan, it is so good to finally meet you. Your uncle and I saw you the other morning with your lovely girlfriend at church. He told me about her accident. Is she doing better?"

Lynn had no way of knowing the pain he bore. He attempted an answer. "Yes, she's…she's off her crutches now. It's so nice to meet you." He couldn't take any more. "Excuse me." He darted toward his room.

"Ryan, we have some news for—"

He had no choice but to close the door.

The tap was soft. "Ryan, may I come in?"

"Later, Uncle Frank, I'm sorry." He lay down on his bed and closed his eyes. Sleep was the only answer now. If it would come.

~*~

Ryan strolled into the cozy kitchen. Sandy stood at the counter cutting lettuce, tomatoes, and cucumbers and placed them in a Blue Willow bowl. He approached her and kissed the side of her face. Then he gazed down at her leg. A toddler held on to her left calf and cooed at her. Ryan extended his arms to the baby, who laughed as Ryan enveloped him in a hug.

He opened his eyes and lifted up out of bed. Outside the window, the sun sat low on the horizon. The soothing memory of the child in his arms swirled around him like a warm blanket. Then reality dawned. Sandy was no longer in his life. The wave of truth blasted him like adding wind and ice to a dreary day of gray skies.

He nudged his door open and lumbered into the living room, not sure what he'd do now. School would start in a couple of weeks. He'd work at CF Hardware, enroll in Cedar Fork State for his master's, serve at the annex, and teach his first graders. If he filled his days, there'd be no time to remember what he'd lost.

Lynn snuggled on the couch next to Uncle Frank, his arm around her and his feet propped up on the coffee table.

Ryan was happy for them, yet a sledgehammer bashed into his stomach. He and Sandy would never sit together the way they did.

Frank craned his neck around to glance at him. "Feeling better now, buddy?"

"Yeah, yeah, sure." He pulled a kitchen chair to the living room and sat in it across from the couch.

Frank tilted his head and stared at him. "Our wedding is next weekend. I'll be moving my stuff during the week. Looks like my last night here will be Thursday."

Ryan nodded then tried to smile. "Great." He closed his eyes and rubbed his forehead.

"Say, Frank. I need to get home now. I'll talk to you later tonight. I love you." Lynn got to her feet. "Ryan, I plan to pray for you." She patted his shoulder. Her tender smile brought momentary comfort.

Frank accompanied her to the door. "I love you, honey." He bolted the lock, wheeled toward Ryan, and put his hand on his shoulder. "Want to talk about it?"

Ryan shook his head.

"Please buddy, speak to me." Frank nudged him. "You look like you've lost your best friend."

He forced the words out. "She was more than a friend."

"Sandy?"

A lump clogged his throat. He nodded.

"What happened?"

Ryan's lips parted. He wanted to tell Frank, but it was painful. Then his cell rang. "I'm sorry. Excuse me."

He glimpsed at the caller ID. Must be something about the annex. "Yes, Greg."

"Ryan, I'm at the church. The fire department's here."

He caught his breath. "What?"

Frank raised his eyebrows.

"Yes. The staff left early today. A neighbor made the 9-1-1 call. It's the annex." Greg's bleak voice jolted him.

"No, dear Lord. No. I'm on my way." A shiver of apprehension burned his skin. He thrust his cell into his pocket. "Frank, come with me. The annex is on fire." Ryan's heart pounded. Could the building really be burning?

"What? How?"

"I'm not sure." Ryan slid on his shoes and grabbed his keys. Frank followed him out into the early evening.

With a shaking hand, Ryan unlocked his door then reached over to open the passenger side. As soon as Frank got in, he revved the motor and shot out onto the main road.

He swerved around a corner onto Olympic Way towards the church. "How could this have happened?"

Frank held on to the dash. "We'll find out soon enough, I'm afraid."

Smoke filled the air as they neared New Day. Two police cars barricaded the road so Ryan had to park a block away.

He threw the car door open and ran toward the church. A fire department van occupied part of the parking lot nearest the annex. One fire engine was in front of the building and another on the construction site about fifty feet from the flames engulfing the entire structure. A steady stream of water shot out toward the blaze.

Greg, Pastor Netherton, and Mr. Clark stood in the church parking lot, staring at the flames. The sanctuary appeared unharmed. Greg's hands covered his face and Pastor Netherton was wide-eyed when Ryan ran up to them.

Mr. Clark turned to him. "We don't know how it started. Vandalism, an electrical short?" Ryan's principal raised his hand to the smoke-filled sky. "Dear Lord, all the work we've put into this project. It's vanished in this inferno."

~*~

Phillip wanted to get home early. He hadn't spoken with Sandy since he'd warned the jerk to break it off with his daughter. He opened the garage door and pulled his Hummer in.

"Victoria. What's for dinner?"

She rushed up to him, untying the frilly apron around her slender waist. The aroma of some kind of soup or stew emanated from the kitchen.

Anxiety drew deep creases in her face. "Phillip, I think you need to talk to Sandy. Something's wrong. She hasn't come out of her room all day." The same look of distress spread across Victoria's face like the times she talked about Sandy's fears. "I've tried to speak to her, and she doesn't say anything, only shrugs. I'm not sure if she's eaten anything."

An excellent indication the loser followed instructions and bowed out of Sandy's life. She'd get over it in a day or two, no problem. He took the stairs two at a time and rounded the corner to her room. "Sandy." He tapped twice at her door.

"Yes."

"May I come in?"

"Yeah."

He turned the knob and pushed the door open.

In her pajamas, she rocked back and forth in her chair holding a pink bear and staring out the window. Was she ready for bed at five in the afternoon?

"Mom said you hadn't come down all day."

"Yeah." Sandy continued to stare out the window.

"Honey, are you sick? Is it your ankle?"

Her answer was a shrug.

"Sandy, look at me. What's troubling you?" Reid obviously met with her, but Phillip hadn't expected her to take it this hard. He thought she'd find solace in Jason, and the whole Reid episode would be behind them.

She didn't move her gaze from the window.

He squatted down beside the rocking chair and covered her hand with his. "Sandy, I can't stand to see you like this. Please talk to me."

But he'd left her suffering for years, if what Reid said was true. He'd never meant to.

She turned her gaze to him with sad eyes. "I found out something about Ryan this morning. Something I'd suspected for a while."

"What, honey?" He knew what she'd say.

"He said he used to be gay. He claims he's changed, but he had plenty of chances to tell me before and didn't. He lied to me. Daddy, he didn't trust me with the truth." Sandy put her head on Phillip's shoulder and sobbed.

Reid had told Sandy the truth—took the chance of losing her forever.

Phillip thought he'd relish this moment. Instead, he swallowed the lump in his throat.

Could Ryan Reid actually be the man my daughter needs?

Chapter Thirty-one

With dry eyes, Ryan peered at the damage the flames had induced. He found no emotions within. The once white interior walls were marred with gray soot. Black streaks ran up the sides of the building. The red tin of the roof was a dingy brown, and the interior rooms they had designated for Bible study and crafts, incinerated. There was nothing left of his dream.

Frank nudged Ryan's elbow. "We can't do any more. We've got to go home."

The fire department's efforts to save the gym had been futile. What did he expect? No one noticed the blaze in time.

"All right, let's go." A curious calm settled on him.

He followed Frank to the sidewalk in front of the main sanctuary then twisted around to the touch on his shoulder.

Greg stood in front of him, his eyes red and face solemn. "We did it once. We can do it again."

"I don't know, Greg. We bought a meager policy with the high deductible. The funds probably won't be there." He headed toward his car. Greg possessed greater enthusiasm than he.

Then the Lord's conviction jarred him. He wheeled to Greg and patted his shoulder. "I'm sorry, brother. I know you're hurting as much as I am." Ryan grasped Greg in a hug.

He gave him a weak smile.

In a few days, the Cedar Fork Fire Department would determine the cause. For some odd reason, he didn't want to know. Yet he feared the very people who could've used it were the ones who burned it down. Ryan's life changed with the first spark. His dreams went up in smoke like his romance with Sandy.

~*~

Ryan sat on the couch with his head in his hands. Frank owned more stuff than he thought. They'd hauled boxes to his truck then to Lynn's apartment at least three times. Hard to believe tonight was his uncle's last night. Tomorrow he'd be a married man.

"Am I wearing you out?" Frank came out of his room with one more box.

"Nah. Actually, I'm glad for the diversion. Keeps me from thinking about…" Which event should Ryan name first?

He begged the Lord to tell him why these things happened—and all at once. Was this the price to be free from his past, Sandy and the annex? Then the small voice of the Holy Spirit calmed him. *Be still and know that I am God.* The words flowed over him as a cool brook gurgles along a creek bed.

"If it wasn't my own wedding, I wouldn't leave you now. You haven't eaten, and all I get out of you are mumbles and shrugs." Frank sat down on the couch beside him.

"I'm sorry. I'm happy for you and Lynn. Please forgive me for not showing more enthusiasm." He'd yielded to the annoying self-pity. "I'm focused inward, I guess."

Frank stretched out his legs. "You never really did tell me about what happened with Sandy."

Ryan ran his hand through his hair. He didn't want to talk about it, but Frank deserved an explanation. "Her father. He threatened me. If I didn't break up the relationship, he was going to tell her about me. About…" Ryan shook his head. He wanted to shove the ugliness away.

"You broke it off with her?"

"No. I tried to tell her the truth." His throat tightened. "The whole thing was my fault. I should've done it way sooner. Her father's threat only nudged me." Ryan wiped a hand over his mouth. "I admitted I lied to her. She called it off because I hadn't trusted her enough to tell her about my past."

Ryan jerked around to face Frank on the couch. "There's something else. The other afternoon before the fire, when Lynn was here, I fell asleep and dreamed I held my son in my arms, mine and Sandy's child. I know it sounds crazy, but I saw our future together. Now we may never have a chance." Ryan shook his head again. He felt an ounce of relief sharing the burden.

"I'm so sorry, buddy. If there is anything I can do—"

"Please tell Lynn I'm sorry I seemed distant. Explain it to her. I'll try to make it up to you guys."

Frank gave him a pat on the shoulder. He picked up the last box and headed toward the door. "Tomorrow evening at seven o'clock at the

Simpsons'. They've opened up their garden and home to us."

~*~

Phillip parked his Hummer in front of the house and came through the front door

Victoria met him in the entry, wringing her hands. "Phillip, we've got to do something. It's been a week now, and Sandy hasn't stopped crying. The hospital's been calling to talk about her startup date for light duty. She won't talk to them or me. She's come down a few times to eat a sandwich or go for a walk."

"All right. I'm going to try again. Where is she?" What more could he do? Sandy needed to get over the jerk.

"On the deck."

Phillip glanced through the window at the wilted young lady scrunched down in the lawn chair. Hard to believe she was his vibrant, fun-loving daughter.

He pushed open the sliding glass door. Sandy sat near the edge of the cedar platform, her feet up on the seat. Her arms hugged her knees, and she held some little black book in her hand. He couldn't make out the title. She put it away when he moved a spare lawn chair from the side of the house and opened it up beside hers. "Sandy, this has gone far enough. You've got to get on with your life."

Dark circles tarnished her brown eyes. "I can't. I've had a lot of time to think. I love Ryan, but I can't live a life with someone who doesn't trust me. And what if his change was temporary? He wanted to marry me, but what if I did, and he lost interest in me?" Sobs burst from her. She dropped her face into her hands. "What if he reverted…"

The sight of his precious daughter, her petite shoulders shaking, ripped his heart out. How could the loser have captured her affections like this? He'd give anything to banish the man's memory from Sandy's life forever. But she wasn't showing any signs of getting over the guy. Surely it couldn't be something about his religion that drew her.

"But baby, look at it this way. He'd never give you what Jason could."

"Dad, you have no idea how I feel. Ryan and I have a connection. I've never loved anyone like I love him. Jason laughed at me. He wouldn't even walk into the house to check it out for me when he knew I was afraid. The day of the earthquake, before he loved me, Ryan went out of his way for me. He made sure I got to the hospital, and he picked me up after he'd worked all evening." She sat up, seeming to gain strength. "And on the mountain when I was nearing hysterics, he listened to me, Daddy. He kept me safe. I know it doesn't seem like a lot to you—my fears—but they were real to me." She took a long quivering breath. "And Ryan never laughed. He asked me the reason, and—and when I told him, the fear lessened."

"He told me you'd talked to him." Phillip looked out over the tree line and to the heights of Mount Rainer. "I always thought you knew, honey."

"Knew what?"

"About Jimmy."

She tilted her head. "Jimmy. Who is he?"

"He wasn't attacking you. He was playing with you—as if you were a rag doll."

"What?" She shook her head. "He was crushing me in his arms. Why would a man do that?"

"A man-child with the mind of a seven-year-old. He wanted to be your friend."

"How—how do you know?"

"Jimmy's father was our gardener, as you know. His mother was a low-income patient of mine. I was working with them to get him into a home. She was dying—congestive heart failure, and Jimmy's father didn't know if he could care for him alone. Since Jimmy used to come with him to work, he must've seen you playing in the yard. He was infatuated with you, but only as a playmate, honey. He was too young mentally to think otherwise. The night when I jerked him off you, I was incensed to see a grown man who needed a shave crushing my daughter in his arms. My little girl was terrified, and I lost my sense of reason. I told your mother to call the police. After they took him in, I went down to the station and explained everything. Jimmy was released into his father's custody. The man never returned."

Sandy blinked her surprise. "He didn't mean to hurt me. He wanted to play?"

"I always thought you knew about him, heard Mom and me talking about his mother. But you were very little. You probably didn't make the connection."

"Where is Jimmy today?"

"Living happily in a home on the other side of the state." Phillip smiled. "He has lots of playmates now. I call and check on him once in a while."

Sandy gazed toward the mountain for several minutes. "I never knew any of this." Her dark eyes lightened a shade. "Jimmy. A man with a child's mind. And to have lost his mother. I'm sorry for him, but I feel better now."

"And you'll continue to feel better about the choice you made where Reid is concerned."

Sandy's face became more vibrant, and she spoke louder through her tears. "I may never see him again, but I'll tell you something no one can take from me." She held up the black book in her hands. "My salvation through Jesus Christ."

Phillip jerked his head. What was she talking about? "Honey, you're confused right now. Maybe what you need is some time away, time to get your head on straight. What about a month in Hawaii to put this behind you?"

Something flashed in her eyes. A flicker of passion he couldn't define. "You don't understand. My love for Ryan isn't something I'm going to get over. Neither is my faith. I'm a Christian, Dad."

His daughter, a believer in fairytales? He'd raised her to have more sense. It was the sissy boy who put theses confounded ideas in her head. Just when he was about to think Reid wasn't so bad after all.

He didn't regret his actions. Despite what she said, she'd forget this religious rubbish and Ryan Reid soon.

Chapter Thirty-two

Ryan scribbled on a CF Hardware order form after the woman showed him the tabs she'd taken from the paint display. "Yes, ma'am. I'll need to combine a couple of base colors. It'll be a few minutes. Three gallons of cinnamon brown and one of cornflower blue." He tried to push the significance of cinnamon brown out of his mind, the color of Sandy's eyes. He shook his head. Sandy was lost to him, like the annex.

He didn't want to think of the reality, but the bad news invaded his mind. It came as no surprise when the officials determined the annex was destroyed by vandals. His heart had sunk once more when the fire department said they'd found graffiti and indecent words sprayed on two walls. The thugs didn't realize they obliterated a place which could've provided restoration for their lives.

The meeting with Greg, the elders, and Pastor Netherton had been difficult. Ryan expected the outcome. Any future plans to rebuild were put on hold. A small amount of pledge money was left, but not enough to start over. They needed a miracle, and God was all out of miracles for him.

The loss of the annex distressed him—every moment he wasn't sleeping. Even then he had nightmares. No more hopes of a future with Sandy. His life came to a standstill with his goals shattered. If it weren't for the Lord—

"Sir, are my cans of paint ready yet?"

The paint mixing machine sloshed. "Not quite, ma'am. A few more minutes." After they were finished, he lugged the cans onto the counter. The lids opened easily with his tool, and she peeked into each.

"Thank you." She lifted them into her cart and smiled. "These came out perfect."

Ryan finished stocking the last of the gallon cans of primer on the shelf behind the counter and peered at his watch. Five o'clock. He didn't relish going home to an empty apartment again. After three nights without Uncle Frank, he should be used to it. At least the teachers' meetings starting in a few days would get his thoughts on something besides Sandy and the annex.

He chided himself. Needed to stop thinking about his own problems. But how could he when Sandy's image infiltrated his mind every second?

The fall quarter at the university couldn't start any too soon either. Working on his master's would keep him busy.

Yesterday he'd found some new-to-him clothes for school at the thrift store—another distraction. Yet nothing had filled the hole the size of Mt. Rainer in his heart. He strolled from the employee's lounge to the parking lot behind the immense building.

He didn't blame Sandy for calling off their engagement. What she said was true. He hadn't trusted her to understand and accept him despite his past. Pride had ruled over truth. Maybe he'd find another relationship one day, but he'd never feel the same about a different woman.

One thing he knew. His faith in God was firm and his freedom genuine. The Lord wouldn't reclaim the work He did inside him merely because Sandy wasn't a part of his life anymore. He found his car and stuck his key in the lock.

"Ryan."

He turned toward the feminine voice behind him.

Becky Whitworth ambled up toward him. "Can I talk to you a minute?"

"Yeah?" He was in no mood to do battle with her.

"Please, Ryan. I need to say something to you." She looked at him then lowered her eyes, her cheeks a rosy pink.

What could she want? To jab the knife in deeper? Though what happened at the picnic was his own fault, the last thing he needed was to relive the afternoon. "I'd like to forget about your conversation with Sandy."

"Listen, please. I've suffered so much since that day. I respect you, and I'm sorry for my part. Will you please forgive me?" She moved her hand up his arm.

He frowned and peered down at her. Could she be sincere, or was she setting him up? "Sure, I forgive you."

"I need to say something else. Maggie and Dana told Sandy you were gay. I opened my big mouth also." She stared at the pavement and lowered her voice. "I've been attracted to you since I first saw you at CF Hardware, but you never noticed me." She cleared her throat. "I told Sandy and it's the truth." Tears trickled down her face.

Ryan swiped a hand over his mouth. Though he didn't want to hurt Becky, he never believed she'd come up to him and tell him.

"So, when Dana started the rumor about you being gay, I figured that's why you never looked my way. It broke my heart because I'd never have a chance with you." She moved closer. "I hope I'm not making you uncomfortable, but I've wanted to tell you this for so long."

He surprised himself as he drank in the comfort of having a woman next to him. All he needed to do was shut his eyes and suddenly she was Sandy. He slid his arms around her waist. The aroma of fresh fruit surrounded her hair and tickled his face as he ran his fingers through the strands. The same as Sandy's.

"I wish you weren't gay." She pulled away from him touching his cheek.

He looked into eyes that were not brown. Her words were a challenge, one he wanted to accept. His lips moved to hers as he wrapped her in his arms, savoring the softness of her body.

When he released her, he stared down into a face which wasn't Sandy's. He'd kissed her, imagining she was the woman he loved. "By the way, I'm not gay."

"I can tell." Becky laughed. "Whew. I'm melting." She pushed her hair off her face and blew her breath out in a stream of air. "I...I'm so attracted to you—and I care more than you know." She blinked her eyes, bright with tears.

Regret washed over him, then guilt. He'd used Becky. His little game went too far. "I guess I have some apologizing to do myself."

"Why?" She wiped her tears with two fingers.

He had to be honest. "Sandy broke up with me. I'm in love with her, and when I kissed you, in my heart it was her."

Becky's eyes widened, and she took a step away. "I...I didn't know you were more than friends. I...I hope what we said didn't—"

"No. It was a small part of the problem."

"I'm so sorry, Ryan."

"Don't be. It was mostly my own stupid fault. I was a coward. And now I'm a phony."

She glanced down at the pavement then at him. "When you come to a place where you can move on from her... you know where to find me"

Ryan couldn't come up with an answer for her. That *when* might not ever come.

~*~

Though Daddy had finally convinced Sandy to return to her old life, she couldn't find the usual enthusiasm. She looked at the passing scenery before turning to Jason. "The dinner was superb. Thanks. I always love the wharf."

Jason turned off I-5 South two exits before the road to her house, but she wouldn't question him.

"How was your first day at work? Weren't you on light duty?" He glanced in the rearview mirror and pushed a strand of blond hair off his forehead.

"Yeah, I took little breaks when I could, tried not to stand for long periods." He should've asked about the condition of her heart, her real problem, instead of her ankle. If she thought too hard, she'd start crying.

"You never did come by to see the pool at my apartment." He winked.

"Well, no time like the present." The sting of leaving Ryan dared her to go.

"I'm glad you found some time for me. I was beginning to wonder if you fell for the schoolteacher." He turned toward his apartment complex on the tree-lined street with the expensive homes.

"No. Things didn't work out with him." Could he stop talking about Ryan? Sandy barely kept the tears from forming in her eyes. She missed him so much. When she heard about the fire at the annex, her heart broke. The pain he must've suffered seeing his worked destroyed. She considered calling him, at least to offer condolences, but she couldn't bear the thought of hearing his voice again.

Jason rubbed her hand. "I'm glad, Sandy. Not for you but for me." He parked to the side of the complex and opened the passenger door for her. Careful of her air splint, she stepped out.

The front of the building was landscaped with St. Augustine grass, winding pebble walkways, and evergreen trees but no pool. "Where's the swimming pool?"

"It's on the other side of the building. Why don't you come up for a drink before we go?"

"Why not? I've never seen the inside of your apartment."

Jason held the door to the front entrance, then they took the elevator to the second floor. A long hallway with an elegant green and black carpet led the way to his apartment.

He put his key in the lock and pushed the door open. "My abode, Miss Sandy." The walls in the huge living room were painted with a muted off-white. Rich hardwood covered the floor. The lengthy couch upholstered in a woven gray fabric sat in front of a white coffee table on an elegant Berber rug. An ornate chandelier hung from the ceiling. Quite a contrast to Ryan's dinky apartment.

"Sit down. I haven't enjoyed the privilege of talking to you lately."

She sank onto the soft couch with its multitude of fabric-covered pillows.

Jason stood over her. "Would you like a glass of wine?"

Her heart rebelled within her. For a crazy moment, she considered saying yes. If she couldn't have Ryan, she might as well set her boundaries free. But then she wasn't sure she wanted to lower her inhibitions. "No, thanks."

"Let me know if you change your mind." He scooted close to her and played with a strand of her hair then kissed her neck. "I've been doing a lot of thinking about us. We're not teenagers anymore. How do feel about me?"

She opened her mouth, but the words froze on her tongue.

His arms folded around her as his lips found hers. The kiss lasted too long, and his arms around her tightened. In Ryan's arms, she melted. With Jason, her heart chilled.

Finally, he released her then gazed into her eyes. "What do you think about us getting married?"

"Let me think about it, Jason. I need some time." His words didn't surprise her. She figured it'd come to this with a little encouragement.

"Maybe I can convince you to say yes." He gripped her arm and pushed her onto the couch pillow in an uncomfortable position.

Jason's body crushed her. One hand moved down her side as his lips smothered her. His muscular body pressed her down against the couch. He suffocated her, not merely with his weight, but with his demands.

He made it plain what he was after. She didn't become a Christian to fall into this sin. Besides, every time she closed her eyes, she only saw Ryan's face. "I can't do this."

"Relax." He kissed her neck then nibbled her ear.

She struggled, but he held her in his embrace. For one moment, panic sent her thoughts whirling. He was bigger than she, much stronger. And he wasn't playing like Jimmy. Was he planning to rape her? "Jason, I said stop."

"Hmm." He murmured in her ear. "You're the most gorgeous, delectable—"

She pushed him back as she bent her elbow then gouged Jason in his chest as hard as she could, a partial *slap and block*.

"Aarrgh." He doubled over on the couch, holding his torso. "Wha...what was that about?"

"When a black belt in Kung Fu tells you to stop, *you stop*." She stood and glared down at him. "I'm taking a cab home."

Chapter Thirty-three

"Daddy, Daddy. I'm scared." The wails sent chills down his spine.

Phillip pushed the sheets back, and his feet landed on the floor all in one quick motion. "Sandy, baby, Daddy's coming." He pulled open his bedroom door and darted out into the dark hallway. Sandy's room. Down the hall and around the corner.

"Dad-dy." She screamed each syllable, drawing him nearer her room. Then her sobs drove him over the edge. He hadn't arrived at her bedside in time.

Phillip sat straight up in bed. Perspiration dripped from his forehead. He ran his hand over the space next to him. Victoria slept undisturbed, facing the opposite wall. The clock on the bedside table ticked in the otherwise silent room.

He pulled the blanket to the side and swung his legs around. The dream shook him to the core. He rested his head in his hands, his elbows on his legs.

Sandy's cries had been so real in his dream. All those years he didn't show compassion. He'd believed she knew the truth. Jimmy was harmless. Instead, fear overwhelmed his daughter because he hadn't figured out she needed to talk about what had happened.

Phillip wanted to lie down but was too rattled to sleep. He lifted his head and gazed at the shadows in the dark bedroom. No moon tonight.

A drink of water would help him escape the effects of the nightmare. He turned the knob on the bedroom door and crept down the hall toward the circular stairs. A noise coming from the second hallway, from Sandy's room, caught his attention. A quiet whimpering. Was he imagining it? He padded with bare feet past the home theater to the end of the corridor and Sandy's closed door.

Now the soft sobbing became louder, and he leaned against the threshold. His heart did a nosedive. He couldn't take it anymore. He knocked softly. "Sandy, it's Dad. Are you okay?"

She hiccupped. "Yeah, I'm sorry if I woke you."

Her soft words wrestled with his heartstrings. Why would his daughter be up in the middle of the night? "Honey, you didn't disturb me, but I heard you crying and got concerned. May I come in?"

"O...okay." She sniffled.

He twisted the brass knob and pushed the door open. Once again Sandy sat in her rocking chair. Her bedside lamp glowed, and a pile of tissues covered the floor near the chair. She dabbed her face with one.

Phillip rubbed his wrist, his throat drier than before. "Honey, what's wrong?" He crept near her and sat on the edge of her bed.

Her body slumped forward. "Oh, Daddy. You'll think I'm crazy." Her words were barely audible.

"No, baby. I need to know. Is it...uh...Ryan?" He didn't want to admit it, but his daughter fell hard for the guy.

She burst into tears. "Daddy, I'll never get over him. I miss him so much. I want to call him, but I can't take the chance of things going wrong later."

Sandy's sobs yanked his heart out. "Honey, what can I do? I can't stand to see you so unhappy." He raked a hand through his already tousled hair. "Are you certain you love him?"

"Yes, Dad. More than before. I don't think I'll ever love anyone else. I always thought he was the man God gave me. But he wasn't honest with me. What would happen if he returned to his old way of thinking and tried to hide it from me?"

"It doesn't make sense. I don't know too much about God, but why would He give you someone you couldn't trust?" Hard to believe he'd ever encourage his daughter in a relationship with the sissy boy—or talk to her about God.

Sandy stopped crying and peered at him. "Maybe...maybe you have a point. Maybe I need more faith in God."

"Honey, what if I could look into things, to discover Ryan's real feelings for you? What would you say?" Did he honestly speak those words? But he'd do anything to alleviate her distress.

She gasped as she blinked at him. "How?"

He never imagined he'd want Sandy to make up with the guy. Maybe if she did, she'd find he hadn't changed at all and dump him for good. "I don't know. But if Ryan is what's going to make you happy, I'll see what I can do."

~*~

Ryan channeled his way through the piles of charred rubble. Heaps of burnt lumber littered the ground. A lone wall stood like a brave soldier who refused to surrender. The acrid odor of scorched remains invaded his nostrils. An unhappy reminder of another occasion when he'd viewed destruction along with Sandy in the aftermath of the earthquake.

So often lately an image of their days together slammed into his heart. He had a choice. Entertain the thoughts and be miserable, or disallow them. He determined to push the memories away, but each time it felt like he lost a little more of her. He didn't want to.

What good did it do to trudge through the debris? Even Greg said as much yesterday when they met for counseling.

A refuse removal company was coming to clear off the site in a few days. Afterward, the annex would only exist in his mind. Ryan tramped around a pile of red ceiling tiles and lifted his eyes to the dogwood and alder trees growing in front of the church, untouched by the fire.

How many times had he asked God why? He endured a crop of disappointments and failures now. His faith in the Lord was all he had left. No man or vandal's fire could take it from him.

The vibration in his jeans pocket alerted him. He dug his cell out from the other items, a collection of coins, a small knife, and two buttons he hadn't sown on his shirt. His mouth fell open. The caller ID displayed Cedar Fork General. *Sandy was calling, ready to forgive him.* Ryan's pulse raced.

"Hello." For the first time since Starbucks, he found a lyrical tone in his voice.

"Uh, Ryan. This is Phillip Arrington. I was...uh, wondering if I could talk to you."

And give the man another chance to humiliate him? "Look, Doctor. I'm out of Sandy's life now. You should be happy. I don't think there's anything for us to talk about." Was this new trouble brewing?

"Yes, I know. But if you don't mind, I'd like to speak with you anyway. Could we meet somewhere?"

What more could the man say? Ryan scratched his head. Strange, but the doctor's voice held a degree of concern rather than his usual haughty tone. He better talk to him. "I'm at New Day Community of Faith Church on Olympic Way."

"I'll meet you in fifteen minutes."

What was the use in torturing himself with the spectacle before him? He'd wait for Dr. Arrington on the front steps of the church. Ryan turned away from the rubble and curved around the corner. He eased down on the top step, his feet on the one below.

Questions drummed in his head. The doctor wasn't driving over here for idle chatter. With a deep breath, Ryan watched cars breezing by on Olympic Way. *Lord, grant me the strength and the wisdom to deal with the man. Keep me from resentment.*

True to his word, after fifteen minutes Dr. Arrington parked the orange Hummer in front of the church.

Ryan lifted himself up with a slow motion.

Dr. Arrington stepped out and raised his head to look at him. Did Ryan have the energy to face his foe prepared for battle?

The doctor closed the door, swiveled around, and peered at the side parking lot, the yard in front, and finally the church building itself. As if Sandy's father knew he wasn't on his own turf, he walked toward Ryan with faltering steps. He looked less official without a suit and tie, wearing only a white dress shirt and black slacks.

"Hello, Dr. Arrington. Would you like to see the burn site?" The fire was in the news. Maybe he was curious about it.

"Sandy told me about it." He glanced around.

Did the man have any interest at all? "This way." Ryan led him to the side of the church.

Dr. Arrington sucked in a breath of air and his eyes grew wide. "Looks like a total loss. How'd it happen?"

"Arson." Saying the words again jabbed Ryan with a searing pain in his belly.

"Do they plan to rebuild?" He scratched his head and looked toward Ryan.

"Not unless we have the funding, which is highly unlikely. Most people gave all they could afford." Ryan stuffed his hands in his pockets. "Now, did you want to talk to me?" They might as well get right to the task ahead.

"Can we...uh, go somewhere with a little privacy?" The doctor looked around him.

"How about the sanctuary?"

The doctor scrunched his eyes and scratched behind an ear. "Well, okay."

Ryan led the other man through the front doorway and pointed to a pew in the back of the large worship area.

Sandy's father shifted on the seat and craned his head as if he surveyed every part of the room. The man wiped his brow then brought his gaze to Ryan.

The church was quiet now, so different than on Sunday morning with the bustle of the crowds, the joyful singing, the prayers, the preaching.

Ryan's foe somehow looked small in Ryan's eyes. This wasn't the monster he'd painted him to be. The man needed Jesus. Compassion replaced resentment.

The doctor remained mute for a long moment. Then he cleared his throat. "I came here to talk to you about…about Sandy. What are your feelings toward her? I need for you to be candid with me."

Ryan let out a rush of air. Of all the topics he anticipated, this wasn't one of them. "You may not believe me, but I love Sandy and would do anything for her. Since she told me to get out of her life, I've felt incomplete, as if a part of my body was missing. Sandy is the woman God gave me, and it's tearing my heart to shreds not to be with her. Is that what you wanted to know—how miserable I am without her?" He spoke each word louder than the one before.

"Odd. Sandy said the same thing about you. You were the man God gave her. She told me she was a Christian." His eyes bore down upon him. "You must be very persuasive."

"Sandy asked to go to church with me. I never invited her, though I was glad when she came. I took no part in the decision she made."

"Let me ask you something else. I've suspected you only pursued her for money."

"Look, doctor. I'm not trying to brag on myself, but when I took the SAT, I scored at the top. My career options were wide open. I did well in math and science and showed an aptitude for engineering. I could've chosen a field where I'd earn a large annual salary. My goal wasn't monetary when I picked the teaching profession. I wanted to serve children. So no, I never pursued Sandy for financial gain." Ryan gazed at the stain glass window over the altar. He told the man nothing but the truth. He wasn't ashamed of his career or his salary.

Dr. Arrington lowered his voice. "What about…uh…you know, your penchant for…"

Say what you mean, doctor. "Same sex attraction. It was an issue I dealt with for many years, but because I'm a Christian, by the grace of God, I refused to live the lifestyle." Why was the doctor asking all these questions? Ryan took a breath. "The thorn in my flesh gave me quite a workout, but God freed me of it. And I love your daughter." He looked down at his boots and cleared the lump in his throat. "Even if Sandy isn't a part of my life, I'm committed to a heterosexual way of life."

"So, you never had…a connection with anyone."

Ryan took a deep breath. "No. I didn't, but even if I had, God forgives." Ryan ran a hand through his hair. "But I want to make it clear. My thoughts weren't pleasing to God. The same as committing the sin."

"I don't see how you could change."

"Because I've received salvation through Jesus, I don't have to be in bondage to sin. He's available to you, too."

The doctor cocked an eyebrow. "What?"

"Everyone carries burdens weighing them down, isolating them from God's love. I'm sure whatever guilt you have on the road you've traveled, He can free you, too."

Dr. Arrington bit his lip. "I'm not sure you're the man my daughter should marry, but Sandy told me how instrumental you were in helping her over fear. Ryan, you asked me about that night. I never knew Sandy didn't understand Jimmy had the mind of a child. He didn't want to harm her. I should never have called the police but should've sent Jimmy on his way. My zeal to protect my daughter prompted me to do the wrong thing. His mother almost died from shock, ending her life earlier than the two years she had left with her son."

Ryan nodded. "I should've realized everything you did you believed was in Sandy's best interest."

Phillip stared at him for a long, uncomfortable moment. "Sandy's in love with you, and I don't think she'll ever be happy unless you're in her life."

How could this man be saying these words when he ordered Ryan to break if off with Sandy? "But she's the one who told me to get lost. I don't blame her. I never told her the truth. I lied about it."

Phillip gave a half smile. "I can't believe I'm getting ready to say this, but Ryan, I also believe everything you've done for Sandy has been for her protection. All I want is for my daughter to be happy, whatever it takes." He picked up a hymnal from the seat and replaced it in the rack in front of him.

Ryan's mouth fell open, and he couldn't believe the words he heard. "I...I don't understand. You've been against me all this time."

"Yes, you're right. But I've witnessed my only child grieve until I can't take it anymore. The guilt..." He wiped his brow. "She's miserable without you, and I can't stand to see her in tears day and night. We've got something in common, Reid. You and I. We both love Sandy with all our hearts."

Dr. Arrington rose and glanced around once again then looked at Ryan. "You know I'm surprised I'm saying this, but I believe everything you've said. And I'll tell my daughter so. Let's hope she trusts my opinion." He turned to walk out the door of the sanctuary.

Ryan blew out a breath, shook his head, and pivoted toward the front altar. Could he believe his ears? Dr. Arrington had given his blessing? The same man who gave him twenty-four hours to get out of his daughter's life told him he believed what he said.

Ryan sat down in the pew, the silence tranquilizing him. Finally, he arose and headed to his car. He wasn't glad Sandy suffered, but the doctor's words brought a scrap of hope to his aching heart.

~*~

Phillip punched the garage door open and pulled in. He cut the ignition and leaned his head on the headrest, taking a deep breath. The talk today with Reid went well. Though the guy would never be able to give Sandy the life Jason could, he made her happy.

What did Sandy see in Reid? He was dedicated to his work and loyal to the things he found important. Reid treated Sandy like the most valuable person in the world. Is that what she needed?

Victoria met him in the hall. She stood on tiptoes and kissed his cheek.

He slid his arm around his wife's waist giving her a real kiss, something he hadn't done in months.

He loved Victoria. Why didn't he pay more attention to her? He was wrapped up in his own life and took her for granted. "Victoria, I'm sorry I've put our relationship on the backburner lately. I've been wrong."

"What's got into you, Phillip?" She placed her hand in his as they strolled toward the kitchen.

Where were these revelations coming from? Couldn't be the result of his talk with Reid. "I…uh, I want to tell you how much I love you." The field of medicine dominated his life far too long.

Phillip pulled out a wrought iron chair from underneath the round glass kitchen table and sat Victoria on his lap.

"You must've had a good day today." She kissed his cheek again and pushed up to stir something on the stove, then poured tea over a glass of ice.

"I stayed pretty busy."

Victoria set the glass of sweet tea on the table, and he took a gulp. *Delicious as usual.* She turned to stir the pot again.

"Oh yeah, I chatted with Ryan today. I'm starting to believe if Sandy really loves him, we shouldn't stand in her way."

Victoria whirled around from the stove. "I'm surprised to hear you say that. But I agree." She pulled out a loaf of bread from the oven and a knife from the drawer. "Phil, you need to tell *her*."

He nodded. "I plan to." A month ago, he wouldn't have spoken those words. He surprised himself at the subtle changes in his attitude.

Sandy slid the glass door open and strolled into the kitchen. She removed her sunglasses, revealing puffy eyes rimmed in red. "Hi, guys."

Phillip wouldn't put it off. "Sandy, sit down. I need to talk with you."

She raised her head in a slow and determined gaze. "And I need to talk to you, too." She hunched in the kitchen chair.

Victoria stirred the contents of the pot on the stove once more and lowered the flame. She settled in the chair next to Sandy.

"Why don't you go first, honey?" He couldn't guess what she wanted to say.

Sandy fingered her sunglasses then set them on the table and lifted her gaze. "I haven't told either of you, but the night after my injury on the hike to Mt. Rainier, I decided to try to sleep with my nightlight off. I prayed then fell asleep. There's been no need for it since." She blinked and wiped away a tear.

The news was incomprehensible. For twenty years of her life she suffered from fear. Could she be totally free of it? But if God could take a man attracted to males and make him into the kind of man his daughter loved, God could do anything. Phillip stared at her as he marveled at her words. "Do you think it's because…does it have something to do with this new faith of yours?"

"I'm sure of it. God's love replaced fear in my life. But I want to let you both know I'm moving out on my own into an apartment. I think it's about time." Her face held a look of determination.

Phillip caught his breath. Sandy's presence in his home pleased him, but she needed to find her own life. "What I tell you may have some bearing on your decision." He grinned. "If you were to marry Ryan, you wouldn't need to get your own apartment."

Sandy's mouth fell open. "You would encourage me to marry Ryan?"

He nodded. "I'm thinking, honey, if Ryan is the man God gave you then you'd better go to him."

Sandy's eyes were filled with wonder. "Dad, I…I never thought—"

"You never thought you'd hear me say it." Phillip couldn't believe it either.

A shadow fell over her eyes. "But you know the issues."

"I'm fully aware of them." He sat up straight in the chair. "I spoke with him at his church."

Sandy sucked in a breath then clamped her hand over her mouth. "You went to the church? I don't believe it."

He didn't think she'd be quite this astonished. "Yes, and I even saw the burn site, though we didn't talk much about the fire. It's a shame someone did it on purpose."

"It is. I'm sure Ryan is distressed over it. But what did you say to him?" Sandy jerked her attention to her mother and to him.

"I asked him some questions, and he responded to everything. I don't believe he held anything back. It's my opinion the man is sincere in telling me he's changed. And I can say one thing. He loves you, and he's miserable without you." Phillip winked at his daughter.

Sandy bit her lip. "But Daddy, what prompted you to call him?"

"Seeing you content is more important to me than anything." Phillip paused, not trusting his voice anymore.

Victoria's lips curved up as she patted Phillip's hand. "Your father is beginning to realize his preconceived notions about what's best for your life may not be the best."

Sandy leaned forward in her chair and folded her hands under her chin. "I'm overwhelmed. But, Dad, I wish you hadn't talked to him. No matter what he says, I can't believe him. He may think he loves me and is unhappy without me, but someday the newness of married life will wear off. What if after ten years of marriage, he found someone else? And I'm not talking about another woman." She stood, wiping away a tear. "I can't take the chance of asking him into my life."

Phillip stiffened and rose to look into Sandy's eyes. "All right, honey. If that's what you want." He'd tried to do what he thought made her happy. But if doubts held on, there was nothing more he could say

Chapter Thirty-Four

The clock on the classroom wall indicated fifteen minutes until lunch. Hard to believe a month had passed since the new school year started. Ryan survived the morning by keeping his mind on the precious group of first graders in his charge… instead of Sandy. If her father had talked to her, and if she was willing to forgive him, she should've called or somehow communicated with him by now.

He gazed out over the classroom. Some of the kids had their noses in a book. A couple pushed a pencil around on their paper. A few used crayons to color a picture.

Without warning, a vision of the dark-haired toddler he'd held in his arms in the dream sprang into his mind. He shook his head hard and eased down at his desk.

"Mr. Reid."

Ryan looked up.

The brown-haired child stood at his desk. "May I get a tissue?"

With Ryan and Sandy's dark hair, would their child look like this boy? "Yes, you may. You don't need to ask next time. They're over on top of the bookshelf, Robert." Yearning swept through him. His little boy slipped from his hands. With a knock on the door, Ryan shook off the regret.

The office-aid poked her head in. "Mr. Reid, Mr. Clark sent me down here to watch your class. You have a telephone call in the office. I'm afraid it's an emergency."

Ryan tensed. Could something have happened to Uncle Frank? The march down the hall seemed an eternity.

Mrs. Cook pointed to the phone on her desk.

With a shaking hand, Ryan lifted the receiver. "Hello."

"Ryan, it's Sandy. I'm so sorry to bother you. I tried your cell but didn't get an answer."

The sound of her voice did funny things to his stomach. Why would she call him at school? "Uh, yeah. I turn it off during school hours."

"Can you come to the emergency room right now? It's your mother." The words echoed like the reverberations of a gong in his mind.

"My mother? She's not in town."

"Yes, Ryan. She is."

"I'll be right there."

Ryan explained to Mr. Clark and raced to his car. The drive to the hospital seemed endless. His mother? Sandy wouldn't call unless it was important.

He pulled up in front of the emergency room and dashed through the front double doors.

"Yes, sir. May I help you?" The same harried woman he always found at the desk looked up at him.

"Miss Arrington called. My mother. She's here."

"Just a minute, sir." She punched a button on her phone and held it to her ear for eons. He tapped his foot and peered at the people in the waiting room. A woman with a frown on her face bounced a baby in her arms. A man paced in front of the television set. "What's your mother's name, sir?"

Ryan opened his mouth.

"Ryan." Sandy's tender voice spoke behind him.

He whirled around to look down at the brown eyes he loved. She was in scrubs, her hair pulled up in a ponytail.

"Come with me."

He gave a final glance at the receptionist. His heart pounded out of his chest as he followed her down a hall and through another corridor. The stark white walls were mostly bare except for the handrails running down the center.

They passed an open double door. He glanced into the expansive room with a variety of medical machines he couldn't identify. The smell of hospitals, disinfectant, ammonia, vitamins, and rubbing alcohol turned his stomach.

Sandy continued her hike down the long passageway. She turned again to her right and stopped at the first room.

Her grip on his arm sent mixed sensations to his heart—comfort, longing, remorse. "Before you go in, I need to prepare you. Your mom is not well. Only the Lord knows our last day on earth, but in my professional opinion, I can't see how she can last much longer." Her caring face heaved his emotions up a notch.

Ryan was a swirling mass of tension. With every word she spoke, he knew how much he loved her and wanted her in his life. Then this same woman told him his mother was dying. "What...what happened?"

"Apparently she was trying to come see you. An ambulance brought her here from the bus station after she collapsed. At first, she was in the central treatment area. After we did tests, we moved her into this room."

Sandy furrowed her brow and placed her hand on his. "Ryan, I'm so sorry, but the doctor thinks she's in the last stages of cirrhosis. He was able to palpitate the lower edge of her liver to find an enlargement. Then we observed small red markings on her chest. The results from the blood test confirmed the disease." Sandy paused. "At first I didn't realize who she was, then I saw her chart—Thelma Reid."

"Sandy." He pulled her to him for a moment, absorbing her strength before he entered the room.

She hesitated then moved into his embrace.

"Would you come with me?"

Her eyes shone as she searched his face. "Yes, of course." Then she frowned. "Are you ready?"

He took her hand. "Yes."

Three beds filled the room, the last two lay empty. Mom lay in the first, her arm attached to an IV from the pole next to her. A heart monitor stood on the other side of the bed.

He gasped when he saw her. Wrinkles and puffy eyes tarnished her face.

Sandy reached for her hand. "Ms. Reid, I have someone here who wants to see you."

He bent over her. "Hi, Mom." His pulse pounded. Brand new emotions stumbled through his heart. He ached from sorrow, yet love filled him.

Mom's eyes fluttered then opened. "Ryan, honey. I was coming to see you." Each word seemed a struggle to enunciate.

"Shh, Mom. Don't try to talk." He gave a desperate glance at Sandy. She rested her hand on his shoulder and gave him a reassuring smile. He returned his gaze to his mother.

"I…want to tell you…" She cleared her throat. "…sorry…for the way I treated you…I was a terrible mother." Mom coughed with deep guttural sounds then wheezed. "I made fun of your religion—what a fine man…you've grown to be…. If your religion is responsible…then I want to know about it…before…"

His mother's words rocketed through his heart. Was she saying she wanted the Lord? "It had nothing to do with me. It's Jesus who died for my sins and offered me forgiveness. He could do the same for you."

"Will you forgive me, son?" Mom moaned and squeezed her eyes shut a moment.

A tear trickled down his cheek. "I forgive you, Mom, as Jesus forgave me."

Sandy patted her hand. "Mrs. Reid, I can vouch for what Ryan is saying. Jesus made all the difference in my life, too. Would you like to pray and ask him to save you?"

Mrs. Reid gasped, moved her head away from them, and closed her eyes.

"Mom, Mom." Ryan stroked her hair. *Lord, don't take her yet.*

Mom turned toward them again. With an effort she opened her eyes. "Will He accept me now? What use am I?"

Ryan closed his eyes and considered God's grace. "Jesus wants you to be His for all eternity. It's not based on what we can do for Him."

"He wants me...like I am?" Her eyelids closed then with a slow motion she opened them again.

"Yes. Would you like me to help you pray to receive Him in your heart?"

Her nod spoke so much to him. "Say these words after me. Jesus, I confess I'm a sinner."

In an unsteady voice, her parched lips moved as she repeated the prayer, her gaze on something unseen. "I confess Jesus died on the cross for my sins. Come live in my heart." Mom's face glowed as she looked toward Sandy and at him with a contented smile.

"Thank you, honey. I'm free now." Her head rolled toward Ryan. "I love you."

He peered at his mother's face. The slight upward turn on her mouth expressed a portrait of peace. This time she didn't move her head.

Sandy leaned over her with a stethoscope. She placed it on her chest in several places then lifted her eyes to Ryan. "I'm sorry." Tears spilled down her cheeks.

He expected bitter tears, but he was mistaken. Instead they were tears of joy.

Sandy stepped toward him. She placed her hands on his shoulders, her gentle touch warmed him.

He wrapped his arms around her knowing she belonged there, always. They remained in each other's embrace until his emotions subsided. His mother was dead, but he'd see her again in eternity.

Sandy pulled away. "I'm sorry, Ryan, I need to notify the doctor in charge."

He nodded and sat in the chair near Mom's bed. "May I stay here a while?"

Sandy laid her hand on his shoulder. "Yes, of course. I'll return in a minute."

Ryan glanced down at his mother's face and pulled the chair closer to her bed. For a while, he sat with closed eyes, reliving the miracle of the last minutes before her death.

Finally, he opened his eyes. For once in his life, he could talk to her. "Mom, I wanted to tell you how joyful I am you asked Jesus into your life. I'm so thankful I'll be seeing you one day. You know the nurse who was with us today? Her name is Sandy. I love her more than life itself. And even if I never see her again in this world, I know I'll see her in heaven someday as well." Then Ryan put his head down on his mother's chest and rested awhile. "Good-bye for now, Mom. I love you."

~*~

Sandy wrenched herself from the room. She located Dr. Davidson on the other side of the building, then updated Mrs. Reid's chart with the day and time of death. She generally didn't become emotionally involved with a patient, but she'd experienced Ryan's pain along with him, almost more than she could endure.

She loved him, yet she'd never feel free to ask him into her life again, though Dad seemed to think she should. Then, this bitter-sweet death. Bitter because Ryan would never see his mother again in this life, but sweet because he'd be with her in the next.

She walked the hall toward Mrs. Reid's room and hung the chart on the outside of the door. The doctor would arrive in another ten minutes or so after he finished with his emergency.

She hesitated to go in as she heard a voice, Ryan's. Who was he talking to? His mother?

"Her name is Sandy. Mom, I love her more than life itself."

She crept into the room. The sight ripped her heart out of her body. He looked like a small boy resting his head on his mother's chest.

After a time, Ryan rose from the chair.

She reached for him. "Ryan, I...I'm sorry about your mom."

He nodded. "Thank you. She's with Jesus now."

"I know. Praise God." Sandy couldn't imagine the depth of what he felt.

~*~

Ryan placed his hand on Sandy's face and opened his mouth to speak, but no words formed. Had she changed her mind about him? She gave no indication. Maybe he needed to walk away before she turned from him. "Excuse me, Sandy. I've got to call Uncle Frank and let him know." He staggered out of the room.

When Sandy held him after his mother's death, he loved her even more. It gave his miserable heart a boost. Yet, he was sure nothing changed. She didn't want him in her life. Where would he go from here?

One thing at a time.

He needed to bury his mother.

Chapter Thirty-Five

Ryan placed the long-stemmed rose on the casket and took four steps away to stand beside Uncle Frank and Lynn.

Pastor Netherton raised his head to look out over the crowd as he stood under the umbrella Greg held for him. "O Death, where is your sting? O Hades, where is your victory? For sin is the sting that results in death, and the law gives sin its power. But thank God. He gives us victory over sin and death through our Lord Jesus Christ." He closed his Bible and bowed his head. "Let us pray. Father, we give You praise for a life which will be Yours for all eternity. Thelma is at peace with you. Guard the hearts of those who remain."

A dozen umbrellas moved from the casket in the direction of the parking lot.

"Ryan, if there's anything we can do..." Orville Simpson patted his arm.

He nodded. "Thanks, sir."

"Brother, we're praying for you." Mr. Aldridge shook Ryan's hand and then Frank's.

Ryan looked around at the departing crowd. Sandy was at his mother's side when she died. He thought she'd be here at the funeral too. Guess he was wrong. Had bitterness toward him trumped all else?

Frank lifted his hand to Ryan's shoulder.

Lynn moved to his other side and slipped her arm around his waist. "Frank and I both want you to know you're welcome to visit our home any time." She squeezed his hand with her warm, soft touch.

Ryan hoisted the umbrella higher to accommodate the three of them. A light October rain had begun to fall when they arrived at the cemetery, and it hadn't let up.

The number of people who showed up pleased Ryan. His church body, his real family, reached out to him when he needed their care. "Thank you for making the arrangements for her funeral, Uncle Frank.

And for your support, Lynn. It's a blessing Pastor Netherton agreed to do the service."

"You know, buddy, this day is a blessing. Your mom is gone now, but we know where she is, and we'll see her again. Your story of how you prayed with her brought me more joy than anything I've ever heard. Praise the Lord." Frank pushed away a tear.

They strolled past granite and marble grave markers dotting the downward slope of the grassy cemetery. The breeze picked up, and Ryan drew his jacket closer around him.

"Remember. Come see us anytime. We're going to have you over for dinner soon," Lynn said.

"Frank, Lynn. Take care." Ryan opened the door of his Toyota and folded up his umbrella. His feelings couldn't be stirred any more than they were. He needed to go.

Frank planted his hand on Ryan's shoulder. "I know the last several months have been tough on you. Sandy, the fire, and now your mom. I don't know how much more the Lord wants you to endure. If there's anything…"

Ryan loved his uncle and hadn't realized how much he depended on him as family until he'd moved out. "Thanks, Uncle Frank. All I can do is bury myself in my work."

Frank and Lynn walked hand in hand to Lynn's SUV and drove away.

Ryan ducked into his car yet couldn't drag himself to the apartment. His papers were graded and his essay for Ethics in Public School Law finished. He had nowhere to go.

He got out of the car again and pulled out the umbrella once more. He'd spend a little more time at the gravesite, maybe pray and ask God for answers. He trudged up the grassy slope to the gravesite.

"Hello, Ryan."

Sandy. He curved toward the voice behind him.

"I came to the funeral, but I don't think you saw me. I stood behind the crowd." She walked closer, no umbrella in her hand. Her hair hung in long wet strands around her shoulders, and her coat was soaked.

She was there after all. The thought soothed a sad place in his emotions. "You're drenched." He held the umbrella out to her and led her under an oak tree to escape the steady downpour. "Thank you for coming to the service."

"I wouldn't have missed this time of celebration." Moisture dampened her face. Raindrops or tears? "I need to talk to you." She gave him a weak smile.

His blood pressure spiked. He couldn't figure out the look on her face. Was she going to remind him again about how he'd lied to her? He breathed deeply, unable to draw his gaze from her.

"You have something of mine." Her hands went to her waist, and a slow smile crossed her lips.

What did I do now? "Yeah?"

"First, you have my heart. But you also have my ring. I don't want my heart back, but I'd like the ring."

Comprehension dawned on him. His stomach did a somersault. "Sandy."

"I'm sorry I didn't trust you. I see what a special, godly man you are."

"What brought about your change of mind?"

"First of all, I realized I couldn't live without you and how much I love you. If I truly believe God gave you to me, then I need to trust Him more." She pushed a strand of wet hair out of her eyes. "But then, my dad gave me a little nudge."

"So, he won't run me out of the house?" Ryan ran a hand through his damp hair.

Sandy laughed. "I don't think so. But there's something else." Her fingers caressed his arm. "In the hospital, I heard you talking to your mom. You told her how much you loved me. I figured you wouldn't say it if it weren't true."

He dropped the umbrella then pulled Sandy to him. His hand slipped down her dripping wet hair as she surrendered her lips to his. When he finally released her, her eyes told him everything he wanted to know. She'd forgiven him.

She blinked a tear from her lash. "I've missed you so much. My arms felt empty without you in them."

Ryan's spirits soared. God answered his prayer even before he asked. He had a future with Sandy.

~*~

The gray sky morphed into a black, starless night by the time Ryan turned in at the mailbox toward the circular drive. Yet his heart told him the sun was shining.

A deluge of memories of the first time he came to this house surged through his mind. He'd been scared to death. In all his wildest dreams, he never imagined proposing to the terrified young lady. Who, he had to remind himself, was no longer fearful, but a peaceful young Christian woman.

Ryan fingered the velvet box in his coat pocket. This time he wouldn't need to put the ring away again. It'd be Sandy's for as many years as God gave them. He shoved the car door closed and bounced up the steps of the well-lit front porch.

He shivered against the cold mist and drew his arms closer to his body in his snug jean jacket.

When Sandy opened the door, her smile thawed his chill. "I've got some hot coffee in a carafe and warm chocolate chip cookies."

"You sure know the way to a guy's affections. Entice him with food." Ryan followed her through the hall past the kitchen to the sunroom.

He marveled at the contrast. Before, guilt had plagued him every time he saw Sandy. Guilt because he couldn't return her love. Guilt because he hadn't told her the truth. Now his emotions were swept clean by God's truth and love.

She sat down in the double wicker chair and patted the seat beside her.

Ryan could barely contain his joy. Sandy would wear his ring soon.

She laced her fingers and clasped them around her knee. "I need to tell you again, I'm sorry I couldn't let go after I discovered you didn't trust me with the truth."

"You had every right to your feelings. I should've told you about my struggle from the start. It's my own fault."

A shadow fell over her face. "I have to be honest. Even though I've given this over to the Lord, and I believe you're sincere now, I have a few nagging doubts." She gripped her hands in her lap. "What if after we've been married a while, you change your mind about me?"

"Sandy." Ryan looked into her brown eyes. If he could do it, he'd take his heart out of his body and show it to her. "I'm sorry for our relationship in the past." He cupped her cheek and kissed the corner of her mouth. "God doesn't perform a work only to undo it again. I could never go back to…" Ryan held her with his gaze then pulled her into his embrace.

Sandy yielded to his touch. Her fingers stroked his hair, and she ran her hand down his neck. He feasted his eyes on the woman who'd be his one day soon.

She brushed her lips over his cheek. Her kiss glided down his neck. He took a deep breath. Why he hadn't been attracted to her at first was beyond him. When she nibbled his ear, desire struck like a firebolt in his stomach.

With a hand on Sandy's waist, he drew her in closer. He loved the way her body felt against his, feminine softness yielding to him. His fingertips itched to explore the curves proclaiming her a woman. She tempted him. "Sandy." His pulse pounded. "I need to stop. It's all I can do to keep my hands off you. We have to wait."

Sandy gazed at her lap then looked up with a seductive smile. "I'm pretty sure I don't need to have any doubts about our wedding night."

Ryan chuckled and reached for a cookie. "I can guarantee you have no worries. When we're first married, on our tenth anniversary or twentieth, or when we're seventy, God willing."

Sandy gazed at him as if drinking in his words.

Sitting here with Sandy was a miracle he thought he'd never see. After all the times he cried out to God with his desperate pleas, the Lord answered his prayers.

Sandy put the red mug under the spout of the carafe and filled the cup with steaming hot coffee. She handed it to him and then studied the tiles in the floor. "I had a hard time sleeping. I was up half the night crying because I missed you so much, not sure I'd ever see you again."

He suffered, yes. But Sandy endured pain as well. Was it possible to redeem the past? "Let's start this all over again." Ryan's heart hammered against his chest as he slid to his knees. He drew the velvet box from his pocket. "I couldn't love you more. Sandy Arrington, I'm asking you again to be my wife."

Sandy gazed at him with a weepy smile. "I want to marry you more than anything. My life is incomplete without you."

For the second time Ryan took the ring and slipped it on her finger. He arose from his knees and eased down beside her. "So...kids? How many do you want?"

Her tender look flamed his yearning for her again.

"Let's try for two or three then we'll see."

The dream he had about their baby boy might become a reality now.

She held her ring finger up to the light then turned to Ryan. "When shall we set a wedding date so I can become Mrs. Sandy Reid, and we can get started on baby RJ?"

"Baby RJ?" He tilted his head.

"Ryan, Jr."

He touched her cheek, brushing her hair away. "You set it. I'll help plan it, and I'll be the first one in the church waiting for you."

Chapter Thirty-Six

Ryan's fingers wouldn't work. For the third time he dropped the pin holding the boutonniere on his black tux jacket. "Uncle Frank. Can you please come over here and help me?" He blew out a breath of air. "Sandy and Mrs. Arrington have worked for two months on our wedding. They want everything perfect. So, I better get this right."

The first time in his life he wore a tux. He'd managed the miniscule buttons on his white shirt, the black paisley vest, and even the bowtie.

His uncle and best man gave him a big grin. "Okay, okay. Relax, Ryan. I realize it's not every day a guy gets married. Think about the beautiful woman who's going to be your wife within the hour."

"I am thinking about her. I can't believe I'm getting married."

Uncle Frank pinned a red rose on Ryan's lapel.

"You're an expert at this. Only a couple of months ago you did the same thing."

"It's something a guy doesn't forget." Frank chuckled.

A playpen sat in the corner of the room. "Don't you think it was a little strange for the groom and his attendants to be dressing in the nursery?"

"Ryan, will you quit complaining?" Greg picked up his coat from the diaper changing table with the sign above: *We may not all sleep, but we will be changed.* "I've never seen you this nervous. You're usually an easygoing guy."

"Watch it, man. I'm going to give you a hard time when you and Suzie do this."

"Okay, I asked for that."

Ryan glanced up at the sound of soft tapping on the door. After Greg opened it and peeked out, he stepped back. "Ryan, someone here to see you."

Ryan pulled at the tight shirt collar, and his palms got sweaty.

Dr. Arrington nodded at Frank and Greg then walked toward Ryan.

"Don't want to take up too much of your time." His almost father-in-law slapped his shoulder. "But I want to tell you how pleased I am to walk my daughter down the aisle and present her to you."

Ryan never remembered blushing in his whole life. Today might be a first if the warmth heating his cheeks meant anything. "Thanks, sir. I can promise you I will protect her and care for her with my own life. I love her that much."

"I know you do." He cleared his throat. "There's something else I want to say. The day I met you at church, something clicked. I'm tossing ideas around about your God and faith." He scratched his neck then held up his palm. "I'm not getting religious or anything, but I wanted to let you know Victoria and I have come to a decision. We want to finance the rebuilding of the annex."

Greg and Frank looked from Dr. Arrington to Ryan, their eyes as round as the wedding cake he'd spied in the fellowship hall.

"I've already spoken with your pastor, and he mentioned a wealthy widow, a Mrs. Mahaney, wanted to contribute money as well. With the two donations, I understand the project will be paid for debt-free." He smiled. "With the proper insurance as well."

Ryan blinked hard. He couldn't possibly let these guys see him teary eyed. Did he dare hug Dr. Arrington? *Oh, why not?* Ryan approached the man and gave him a guy-hug with a slap on his shoulder. "I don't know what to say. I guess…thank you."

"We're family, Ryan. I've always wanted a son. Call me Dad."

Ryan never had an earthly father. Never thought to ask God for one. Never thought it possible.

But the Lord had given him one of his greatest desires.

"You okay, son?" Dr. Arrington asked.

Ryan nodded and cleared his throat. "Yeah, Dad. Better than you could ever know."

Greg shook Dad's hand. "Sir, you don't know how much this means."

Ryan's new father nodded and then walked toward the door.

Ryan hadn't seen Sandy's father quite this constrained. He must've struggled to suppress his emotions.

Frank squeezed Dad's shoulder. "Thank you, doctor."

"Phil, Frank. We're family now, too." He shook Frank's hand and turned to walk out the door. He paused and curved toward them. "I'd better go now. I believe there's a bride waiting for me to walk her down the aisle."

~*~

Sandy waited in the foyer near the entrance to the sanctuary. She glanced up at her handsome father smiling down at her, perhaps a little stiff in his tux. Her gaze fell on her friend Jane Foreman as she strolled down the aisle in her knee length red silk dress. Her maid of honor, Cousin Linda, had loved the pleating at the bust.

Linda glanced toward her and winked, then began down the aisle, holding tight to her flowers—poinsettia and chrysanthemum, adorned with pinecones and fir branches, a white ribbon tied underneath.

"Dad, I'm the happiest woman in the world today." She slipped her hand through her father's arm.

"I can see the joy in your face." A shadow fell over his eyes. "I regret what I tried to do to you and Ryan. I never intended for you to suffer. When I saw how you felt, I fooled myself into thinking you'd get over it. Now I see how wrong I was." He kissed her cheek.

"It's okay. I love you."

"I love you and want your happiness. Thank you for allowing your Mom and me to give you and Ryan a trip to Hawaii. I know how independent young people are."

She squeezed her father's arm.

The wedding coordinator breathed an excited whisper. "Are you ready?"

"I've been ready for a very long time." Sandy smiled.

Two ornate candelabras with seven silver candles in each rested on the walls on either side of the altar. A draping of red roses and baby's breath adorned both. A twenty-foot blue spruce decorated with red and silver bulbs ornamented the bride's side of the church near the altar rail. Red and silver netting with pinecones and baby's breath were strung along each row of aisles.

The strains of Wagner's "Wedding March" brought a lump to her throat. It was time. Dad kissed her cheek as they began their stroll down the aisle. In front of the altar, Pastor Netherton waited. To his left the handsome man who possessed her heart stood next to Uncle Frank and Greg Aldridge.

~*~

Ryan had to return to the moment. His bride glided down the aisle in a floor length white satin gown. The strapless dress hugged her curves and was tied with a silver bow above the waist. For once the tall, dark-eyed man beside her didn't strike fear in his heart. Ryan never thought he'd see the day.

His heart swelled. God was so good to him. Not only had He brought freedom, but He gave him a beautiful Christian wife. Ryan's heartstrings vibrated with joy in his chest.

His new father-in-law took Sandy's hand and placed it on Ryan's arm then kissed her cheek. Ryan and Sandy turned toward the altar to face Pastor Netherton.

"Ryan and Sandy. You're here today before family and friends to be joined together as husband and wife. You have each chosen to write your own vows. Sandy, you may go first." With jangled nerves, Ryan faced Sandy.

"Ryan, I want to thank God for where we are today. He led us on this journey, and now we'll soon be husband and wife. I vow to live my life with you for as many days as God gives me and be the mother of your children, to respect you as the leader in our home. It is my absolute joy to become your wife. I love you."

Ryan fought his emotions as he opened his mouth. "Sandy, you will probably never know the full extent of how God used you in my life. Because of you by my side, God taught me how to love according to His sovereign plan. You're the most patient and caring person I know. You never stopped loving me, even when you should have. I vow to spend the rest of my days with you and to be the father of your children. I couldn't love you more, Sandy. And all of this because of one earthquake." He laughed.

Ryan barely heard the pastor's short message, through the exchange of rings. It was all a blur until they turned to face Pastor Netherton. Good thing the sound man at New Day recorded the entire ceremony.

The older man grinned. "And now, church, it is my great privilege to pronounce this couple husband and wife. Ryan, you may kiss the bride."

Epilogue

Three years later

"'Gin, da, 'gin."

Ryan put his palms over the fat baby hands on the chains which held the swing. He checked the safety buckle around RJ's waist and gave the seat a push. The child giggled as he sailed back and forth through the air.

"'Gin, da."

"Again? Okay, one more time." Ryan pushed, and the dark-headed baby glided through the air. Pride flooded his heart at the sound of his two-year-old son's delighted giggles. His child, a gift from God.

"Okay, buddy. Let's see if we can look for the bird's nest in the tree over there."

He unbelted RJ and pulled him into his arms. On the side of the yard, the twenty-foot poplar soared into the sky. "Look. I think I see it, way up there." Ryan pointed to the nest lodged safely between the forks of a branch near the top of the tree.

"Birdy." RJ laughed

Ryan looked over the fence to the greenbelt behind their house, a wide band of forest comprised of dozens of Douglas firs. His heart ascended in gratitude to the Lord when he thought about their home, his and Sandy's. They were the owners, not the renters. God blessed them.

"Hey, buddy. Want to be Superman?"

RJ nodded.

Ryan held RJ tightly around his waist and ran the length of the yard three times with RJ *flying* by his side. "Whoa. I'm going to have to go on some more runs in the park. I know I'm pushing thirty, but I'm too young to be breathing this hard." He laughed to himself. Sitting at a desk at school and standing at the blackboard didn't give him the exercise he used to get at CF Hardware.

Next year, he'd be assistant principal. Maybe the job would offer him more of a workout. He'd be traipsing up and down the halls of the school, organizing textbooks in the storage rooms, and overseeing building activities.

"You know, RJ, you have a mother who's going to teach you how to relate to women and a father who will show you how to be a man. And parents who will raise you in the instruction of the Lord. Hey, buddy, you've got it made." Ryan chuckled and tapped his baby's little nose. "You have no idea what I'm talking about."

"Where are my two favorite men? Time for lunch." Sandy called from the backdoor.

Ryan had to twirl the wedding ring on his left finger to remind him Sandy was his wife. He glimpsed at the young boy who looked so much like him. "RJ, hear that? Momma's calling us to lunch. Bet we're having ham and cheese sandwiches. You know, the first day I met your mother, she tried to make me a ham and cheese sandwich." He righted RJ in his arms.

Sandy stood in the door waiting for them. At the sight of her, joy swelled in his chest. He strolled up to her, and she held out her arms to their child.

"Come here, you little guy. We're eating a light lunch because we're going to Grandma and Grandpa Arrington's for dinner tonight." The outside door led through the den into the kitchen. Sandy buckled RJ into his high chair.

"Come here, you." Ryan pulled his wife close. "Did I tell you today I couldn't love you more?"

She giggled, a sound very similar to her son's. "What's got into you?"

"I'm praising God for all He's done in my life, my precious family for one thing."

Sandy slipped her arms around him and whispered. "I think it's about time for us to think about baby number two."

He stepped back and captured a mental snapshot of the moment—Sandy, RJ, and perhaps another child one day. *I almost missed it, but by the grace of God I'm whole.*

Note from the Author

I'd like to make my thoughts clear. Ryan's story is fictional. Therefore, he found freedom from homosexuality in a shorter period of time than might seem realistic. Some readers will hold this opinion. I would agree with them.

In real life, freedom and change don't happen overnight. Lifelong behaviors and thought processes take time to be replaced with new ones.

But the ideologies Ryan learned are the same—to allow God's truth to permeate one's life. Ryan had a strong desire to follow the Lord's will and purpose for him. He sought counseling and exercised his faith.

Another point. Ryan embraced Christianity and wanted to live a heterosexual lifestyle. The principles he learned through counseling and studying God's Word would not be effective in a person's life unless they desired change.

Not everyone in Ryan's situation would find marriage and children as he did, but God is in control, directing and guiding His own when they submit to Him. Only the Lord can enrich a person, bringing joy and peace. Yes, Ryan found the family he never had, but his primary joy came from his relationship with God through his Savior Jesus Christ.

I would like to suggest that anyone who wants to begin taking steps toward a new life begin by examining your relationship with Jesus Christ. If He's not Lord and Savior over your life, invite Him in. Attend a Bible believing church. Read Romans 5 and 6. Get into Christian counseling. Then look to God and His Word daily.

There are excellent groups for those seeking to leave the lifestyle. Just as Ryan did, learn who you are in Christ. Don't get discouraged if your progress is slower than you'd hoped. Hold on to your faith and the Word of God. May He richly bless you. June Foster

Writing a review

If you enjoyed Ryan's Father, please leave a review on social media including Amazon. Many readers depend upon the opinions of other readers to determine whether they want to pick up a book or not. The more reviews an author has, the more likely readers will purchase the book for themselves. These days, with the abundance of talented authors, it's difficult for a writer to get his/her books out there. Reviews are the lifeblood of an author's career. They are so appreciated.

Want to read more from this author? Check out the Woodlyn Series.

Flawless

Though Jess Colton gave his life to the Lord, he held onto an old habit. Fueled by alcohol, he spent a night with a girl from his past, defying his Christian principles. When he quit drinking to honor God, he discovered another addiction. Now he can't manage his own life as his weight soars and diabetes threatens to claim him. Jess is baffled when the beautiful Holly Harrison declares her love.

Holly Harrison lived to please herself. But everything caught up with her in one moment of time when a destructive motorcycle accident altered her life forever. Nowhere else to turn, she looked to God for answers. Now, she's convinced no Christian man would be attracted to her. She doesn't plan on falling in love with the handsome Jess Colton seeing past his bulk to the godly, tender man within. When Jess drives a wedge between them, she loses hope of a future together.

Can Holly overcome her handicap? Can Jess find control over his eating and his life? Only God has the answer. Find the book on Amazon.

Out of Control

Tim Garrett saw Jess Colton back to health in *Flawless* but can't control his own life. When Woodlyn Fellowship hires Tim as the new youth pastor, he's still powerless over the uncontrollable anger he learned from his father. If he can't escape the outbursts that hold him captive, he'll lose his job. To further complicate his life, an unlikely church member devises a sinister scheme for his dismissal. Tim has one last chance at Camp Solid Rock. When he discovers a startling secret from a youthful adversary, can he save the boy's life?

Roxanne Ratner's father abandoned her as a young girl, and now she doesn't trust men. They'll only hurt her. Shopping for designer clothes is a poor substitute for the love she craves. The new Christian fights old habits of holding on to a guy. After she tempts Tim to sin, she must seek his forgiveness.

Can God cool Tim's angry heart and teach Roxanne true beauty lies within? Find the book on Amazon.

All Things New

The young fraternity man who coaxed Jillian Coleman upstairs that night is only a blur in her memory. Yet after discovering her pregnancy, she had no other alternative but to get rid of the child. Now she can't escape the guilt that she aborted her baby. God might forgive her, but she can't forgive herself. As Woodlyn's premier gynecologist, she wants to open the Jeremiah House to offer teen girls an abortion alternative, a haven of acceptance and understanding she once longed for. Though the handsome and successful Dr. Jett Camp pursues Jillian with a diamond ring and marriage proposal, he believes the plan is a waste of her skills. More troubling, Jillian's not sure if he holds to her Christian faith.

Riley Mathis fell into the trap of *wanting it all right now*. Booze, women, parties. What more could a young college student ask for? But after getting caught for dealing drugs, he spent ten years in prison. When ministry workers from Prison Fellowship visited him in jail, his life changed. Now as a Christian, he's trying to live according to God's will. Working as a janitor at night, he attends college by day. Finally, he has a chance to earn the degree in accounting which he put on hold all those years before. When he meets Dr. Coleman at the hospital where he works, he recognizes her from the sapphire necklace she wore the night he stole something precious from her. When she confesses the choice she made to abort her baby, Riley can't tell her he's the father of her child. The truth would destroy them. Find the book at Amazon.

About June Foster

June Foster is an award-winning author who began her writing career in an RV roaming around the USA with her husband, Joe. She brags about visiting a location before it becomes the setting in her next contemporary romance or romantic suspense. June's characters find themselves in precarious circumstances where only God can offer redemption and ultimately freedom. To date June has seen publication of 22 novels and 1 devotional.

A reader says of her debut novel *Flawless*: June Foster is a unique author. She has a way of looking at people and seeing what's on the inside and not what's on the outside. She loves to bring characters with unique personalities and problems to the written page.

Find June at junefoster.com.

Sign up for Forget Me Not Romances newsletter and receive a special gift compiled from Forget Me Not Authors!

Join our FB pages to keep up on our most current news!

Forget Me Not Romances Readers and Authors
Take Me Away Books
Winged Publications